TALES OF PANNITHOR

NATURE'S KNIGHT

Written By
JAMES DUNBAR, BEN STODDARD, MARK BARBER, AND BRANDON ROSPOND

*Based on an story originally
conceived by Marc DeSantis*

ZMOK
BOOKS

Tales of Pannithor: Nature's Knight
Edited By Brandon Rospond
Written by Messers James Dunbar, Ben Stoddard, Mark Barber, and Brandon
Rospond.
Based on a story originally conceived by Marc DeSantis.

Cover by
This edition published in 2021

Zmok Books is an imprint of

Winged Hussar Publishing, LLC
1525 Hulse Rd, Unit 1
Point Pleasant, NJ 08742

Tales of Pannithor is published under a license with Mantic Games

Bibliographical References and Index
1. Fantasy. 2. Alternate History. 3. Dystopian

For more information on Winged Hussar Publishing, LLC, visit us at:
https://www.wingedhussarpublishing.com

Acknowledgements

This book is dedicated in loving memory of Jesse "Prophet of the Sacred Pie" Cornwell. A true legend in the Kings of War community who will forever live on in the hearts of those who play the game and were touched by his kindness and guidance. He loved projects that brought the community together like this collaboration did as a culmination of a story that began as a result of the worldwide campaign several years ago. Even now, we can imagine him going through and making remarks on how overpowered some of the monsters or characters in this book are, but in the end, we feel that he would approve of this tale, and the community it was made to entertain.

Chapter I

The sun was high over the forest of Galahir, and not even the weighty boughs of trees as old as the world could shield him from its glow. Between broad trunks coated in moss, everywhere he looked revealed a dizzying green, the spring buds of bracken and spurge swallowing the duff of seasons past. Birdsong danced above, a tuneful contest of melody and rhythm, disjointed constancy that soothed the frayed edges of the young man's mind. He was tired. The hunt had been long, permitting of no sleep the prior night lest their quarry slip beyond grasp. The man paused his stalking steps, removing a gloved hand from his spear to wipe sweat from his brow. Though crouching low to the undergrowth, he was taller than most; though young, his arms were well-wrought. Pale of skin and with long, golden hair bound tightly from his face, eyes of silver-gray scanned the forest from beneath heavy lids and neat eyebrows, laid upon a handsome face of high cheekbones and angled lips. He took a breath. The smell of sun-soaked bark filled his nostrils, humid and earthy. Hand returned to spear, the breath departed.

The hunt resumed.

* * * * *

"Juttah!"

Juttah froze, a clump of mucky straw dangling from her pitchfork. Despite the shade of its thatch roof, the air was hot inside the pen, laden with the smell of livestock. Sweat coated her beneath her tunic, its hem rolled up around her knees as she worked. She listened. After holding her breath for several seconds, her lungs began to ache. Juttah breathed.

The cry had been very faint. Did she imagine it? Hildey certainly seemed to think so, the matronly cow watching her with placid curiosity as she chewed her cuds. Slowly, Juttah set the fork upright against the pen's wattle-and-daub wall. Something about the cry had set her heart pounding. It had sounded

7

panicked. She wiped her brow, pushing back the strands of fair hair which had broken free of her braid.

Can't have been nothing at all, she thought, else—

"JUTTAAAA!"

Scrambling over the divider, Juttah rushed out into the daylight.

"Mannes?!"

Her brother came pelting down the track toward her. Juttah crouched, opening her arms wide. The boy slammed into her, and Juttah had to twist around to prevent them from tumbling. Mannes grabbed on tight, burying his face in her shoulder. He was shaking. Stunned with incomprehension, it took Juttah a moment to speak.

"What's wrong?!"

Mannes shook his head against her shoulder. She pried him off, looking into his face. Fair-haired like herself, both Juttah and her brother shared their father's light-brown eyes, set into the long face of their mother. Those eyes were wide, their whites laid bare to the cloudless noon sky. His bottom lip hung open and was trembling. Juttah had never seen Mannes like this. The six-year old had always been stoical, worryingly so, more likely to make boys twice his age cry than show any sign of weakness. And now he looked up at her, cheeks wet and skin pale, fists gripping her tunic.

"What happened, Mannes? Are you hurtin'? That ol' billy goat nip you?"

Mannes shook his head, letting out a shuddering breath. "I saw'd... I saw'd..." His mouth worked wordlessly.

"What? Tell me."

"...In the house..." His voice was barely above a whisper. " ...'neath... 'neath our cot... it had teeth..."

Relief filled her. Monsters 'neath the cot! If Mannes hadn't looked so afraid, Juttah might have laughed – in fact, she had to bite the inside of her mouth to make sure she didn't anyway. And after he'd teased her so for screaming that time they'd found the snake.

"There, there," she cooed, doing her best to keep amusement from entering her voice. "It were probably just a rat."

Her best wasn't good enough. Mannes's eyes narrowed, and his cheeks reddened. "It weren't a rat! I'm not scared of rats! It were... it were..." Somehow, his fists went even tighter on her clothes.

"Alright, alright! Let's go have a look." She tried to stand, but Mannes held on. He was shaking his head.

"We have to fetch father!"

"No," she said, firmly.

"But—"

"Father's in the fields, and so's mother. I've still got to muck out Hildey's pen, then there's the churnin' and the waterin'." She pried his hands free and straightened her shift. "Did you get the water?"

Mannes nodded, scowling as he wiped his cheeks with the back of his hands.

"Good. Now, c'mon, let's go see about this rat." Juttah set off and was quietly surprised when Mannes slipped his hand into hers, head down as he followed in silence.

He really did catch a fright, she thought.

Their home – a single-room cottar house with irregular stone walls and a low thatch roof – was as handsome as they came out here, far beyond the north-most borders of civilization. That's what their father said anyway, always in a playful tone that didn't quite match the apologetic look on his face. They'd lived somewhere bigger when she was born. Before the Abyssal war. But Juttah could barely remember that. All she'd known was life on the road, years of taking whatever work and bed could be found, both usually alongside animals. That was until they had come here around a year and a half ago. The villagers of nearby Talle, delighted at the prospect of more strong hands to work the fields, had pointed the family to the cottar house. Even in its then dilapidated condition, to Juttah's eyes it had seemed a palace; more than that, it was, finally, a home.

Juttah glanced over toward Talle, squinting through the bright daylight. The village was spread loosely up the hillside, with its sole multistory structure sat proudly atop the crest. Beyond rose the mountains of Nova Ardovikio, the white of their snow-tipped peaks faded by distance to blend with the blue sky. It was one of the rare times she'd seen them without clouds.

The sun beat down on the young siblings as they followed the track's uphill wind. Juttah moved with the confident strides of a first-born, hoping to spur some measure of her brother's usual competitiveness. Their house was the furthest out from the village. As they reached it, Mannes stopped, letting go of her hand.

"Not goin' in."

"No? Don't wanna go in together?"

Mannes shook his head, not looking up from the ground. Though she felt a pang of sympathy for his shame – Juttah was, by her own estimation, an exemplary sister – she nevertheless took some satisfaction at this chance to prove herself braver than he. Yes, she was older, but only by four years.

Hands on hips and with a sigh that sounded exactly like her mother's, Juttah looked round toward the rye fields. Strips of rolling land shaped by ridge and furrow spread out at odd angles, starting at the hill's base. Men and women hunched over the dirt, dressed in faded tunics and shifts, straw hats set against the sun. The only figures standing upright were the half-a-dozen scarecrows. Crows were a much bigger problem out here than rats, as like to pluck the eyes from a calf as the seeds from the earth. The villagers said there had been a big battle near here in the war, and that the birds had grown fat on the corpses. Fat, and bold.

"Alright then," she said, turning to face him. "Not to worry. You wait here while I go take a look, yes?"

Mannes nodded. Although he still didn't meet her eye, Juttah thought he looked grateful all the same. Relieved, certainly.

The door was open. Until hearth was set to flame in the evening, an open door was the only source of light inside the cramped cottar house. It didn't have any windows. Stepping across the threshold, the cool air was welcome against Juttah's skin. She looked about the interior, eyes alert to any movement caused by her entrance. All was still. Above her, a leg of mutton hung drying from the central rafter, not far from a much depleted string of garlic. A simple table was pushed against the opposite wall, host to the dirty wooden bowls from their morning meal. Juttah frowned. Mannes was supposed to have cleaned them by now. But at least he'd filled the water pails. He'd placed them in front of the wood stack, next to the hearth in which a small, black-iron pot hung by its handle.

At the far end of the house from the hearth were the straw-padded cots, one large with a broom set upright at its foot, and one small. There was barely enough room to step between them. Juttah and Mannes shared the small one. She stepped toward it.

With one hand resting on the cot's frame, Juttah began to squat. She stopped almost immediately, torso hunched forward and still. It was dark beneath the cots. What if there's something there after all? whispered a voice in her head. Something with teeth? She glanced back at the house's open door, half-expecting to find Mannes watching her, waiting to see if she was scared. But he wasn't.

Quit being silly, Juttah, she thought, turning her attention back to the cot. But try as she might, she couldn't will herself to bend further. A chill ran down her spine. The coolness of the air seemed to have gone cold.

Juttah stepped back, scooping up the besom broom and holding its brush before her. Then, after a moment's deliberation, she kicked the cot. The wooden frame gave a light thunk as it hit the stone wall. She waited, broom braced to sweep away anything that came running out from the darkness. Nothing. She kicked again, this time at the parents' cot.

"Juttah?" Mannes's voice was muted by the stonework. "Did... did you find it?"

"Hang on!" she called back. Confidence restored by her cot-ward punts, she crouched down on the dirt floor. Though it was too dark to see all the way at the back, it seemed an empty darkness all the same. "I can't see nothin'!"

"It's there! I weren't lyin'!"

"I don't say you were! Only it's not there now!" Juttah allowed herself a chuckle.

"You're laughin' at me!" Mannes had appeared in the doorway.

"Nu-uh!" she protested, looking round from her squat. "I were only-EEEEEEK!"

Something shot out of the darkness toward her. Juttah fell backward, the broom slipping from her grasp. The thing came to within a foot of her before it turned, making straight for Mannes. Unthinking, Juttah swung her arm out to stop it but missed, the base of her palm impacting the ground no more than an inch from her target. Mannes appeared to be frozen in place, face stark-white as it surged toward him.

"MANNES!" Juttah shrieked.

In a lurching motion, Mannes collapsed backward, pinning himself flat against the open door. The dark shape sped past the spot he'd occupied a split second before, making a dash for daylight.

Juttah breathed heavily, barely aware of the ache in her hand. She replayed the scene in her mind. Mannes was clearly doing the same and was the first to voice what they both realized.

"A mouse?"

Juttah couldn't help it. She burst out laughing. It had been a field mouse, small and brown, shivering in fright as it fled from beneath the cots.

"But... I saw'd something bigger!" said Mannes, and Juttah laughed harder. "Stop!" he said, but he was smiling, his relief evident. "You were scared, too! I saw'd it!"

"Were not," she said between giggles. She stood up. "I was just surprised, is all." She rubbed her palm, feeling the beginnings of a bruise.

"Suuuure." Mannes stepped into the house. "That's why you screamed 'Mannes'!" He put on a whiny voice.

Juttah grinned and flung a playful slap with her good hand. Her brother stepped back to dodge.

"Hey, looks like you got it," he said.

"Huh?"

Mannes pointed at the ground. Spots of liquid dotted along the mouse's route from cots to doorway, shining wet even in the limited light. It had been bleeding.

"But... I missed." Juttah held up her dirty, yet bloodless, palm to show him. "And it's there before I even tried," she added, gesturing toward the cots.

Mannes frowned. "Then what–"

He was cut off by a loud clang of metal which burst from the hearth. They spun toward it. The black-iron pot swung gently in the fireless hollow, the sound of whatever had impacted it continuing to ring like an aging bell. Neither Juttah nor Mannes moved a muscle. Eventually the pot stopped its swinging, the sound stopped its ringing. It was another minute before either had the courage to speak.

"Go look," said Mannes in a whisper.

"You go look," she whispered back.

The impasse lasted a further ten seconds.

11

"Together?" suggested Juttah.

Mannes nodded. Taking each other's hand, they counted down, "Three, two, one," and stepped toward the pot.

Empty. Just the lumpy black bottom of the old pot. Juttah began to sigh, but Mannes's hand had gone rigid in hers.

Then she saw it.

It was as if the shadow inside the pot had a face. A face without eyes, or nose, or lips. A face whose only feature was countless rows of black, needle-sharp teeth.

The door slammed shut, the noise sending a jolt through their bodies. Darkness subsumed them, and in that same moment, a shuffling sound began to emerge from within the pot. Hands still clutched tight, the siblings stepped away blindly, horror-struck. There was a dull phwup as something dropped onto the ground, quickly followed by another clang of metal, and another, and then a trio of them, and then–

"RUN!" Juttah cried. They crashed into the door, heaving with all their might. It didn't budge. They pounded their fists against it, bawling incoherent screams. Behind them, the pace of phwups and clangs increased in the hearth, an endless tide of teeth-things plummeting down the chimney. There was a sloshing sound as one of the pails fell over.

"Juttah! The latch!" shouted Mannes. Juttah fumbled for it. She felt something collide into her heels, felt the pain of what seemed like a thousand fangs raking across her flesh.

She found the latch, and the door flung open. Without once looking back, the children ran out into the light. They ran down the hillside track, ran past Hildey's pen. They ran so hard their feet ached. They didn't stop running until they found their mother in the fields, and they clung to her.

Chapter II

The young man unhooked a leather flask from his belt. His movements were slow and deliberate, a practice which owed more to habit than conscious effort. In the forest of Galahir – in any woodland, he supposed – there was no telling what might be disturbed by sudden motion. It was an idea with many implications, all vital. Could be you alert your prey. Could be you are the prey. Reflexively, his left hand moved with restrained purpose to rest upon his spear. It lay within easy reach, parallel to his outstretched legs and with its steel tip hidden in the undergrowth. Life in the forest demanded of a single, simple rule: learn fast, and learn well. The alternative went without saying.

Sitting in merciful shade, he had nestled himself between the buttress roots of an enormous and broad-crowned fig tree. As he lifted his head with the flask, he looked up into the canopy, barely tasting the stale and over-warm water that flowed past his lips. Despite the tear-shaped fruits being still as green as the leaves around them, and small to his sleep-deprived eyes, they seemed plump with promise. Certainly when compared to this hunt, at any rate.

His quarry had been leading him in circles. After more than a year of living in the forest, he should have noticed it sooner, not halfway round the third loop. Worse still, he had lost all sense of his fellow hunters – not a minor problem, when his primary task was to steer the prey toward their arrows. Twisting his torso, he tried to stretch out a knot in his upper back, the dull pain offering a welcome distraction from the itching of his tunic. The greenweed-dyed wool was pinned tight against his chest by a thick leather jerkin, its color the deep, almost black-brown of turned soil. As with everything in his possession, it was well-made but had seen far better days. He smiled, remembering when it had been gifted to him. What a small thing it had seemed, compared to his full suit of knightly armor, earned that same day as he ascended from squireship. He'd learned a lot in the months between then and now. Perhaps the most important lesson was the value of small things.

A jolt shot through his body as he woke. The rustle of disturbed leaves seemed to echo like thunder in his ears. He had drifted off. Only for a second –

at least, he hoped so – but even though his heart was racing, already his eyelids felt as if they bore the weight of mountains. His part in the hunt was over. It was time to get back to the Eastfort.

Trying not to think about what his fellow knights might say – one in particular – he set about fixing the stopper on his flask and hooking it to his belt. Then he laid his arms along the buttress roots, preparing to brace and hoist himself up. There was a flutter of wings above, and he looked up again, head resting against the tree's mossy trunk. The bird was of a kind he'd never seen before, small and blue as the night, its feathers gleaming in the sun. It looked down at him from its branch, head tilted in contemplation.

Slowly, inevitably, his eyes closed.

* * * * *

Cossus and Vandimi Barchet, parents of Juttah and Mannes, weren't the only ones whose offspring met distress that day. It seemed the village had become host to a particularly nasty mischief of rats. Curiously, there was little of the usual evidence: no gnawed holes in the grain sacks, no feces scattered throughout the houses. There was, however, no questioning the bites. Many children had them, and the shallow scoring above Juttah's ankle was about the least of it – one boy had lost a finger. Children being children, it took a long time for them to be convinced that the things they had seen were indeed rats, and not the monsters so easily conjured by young minds in the dark. Eventually, the exhausted and worried parents had persuaded them it was so and coaxed them back inside their homes.

Vandimi's pair still refused to accept it. Hours later, after returning from her back-breaking work in the fields and with no choice but to bring them their meal outside while her husband finished off the children's chores, she was finally able to sweet-talk Juttah and Mannes back indoors. But they would not accept the rats.

"Can't you make it lighter in here, mother?" asked Juttah, rough wool blanket pulled up to her chin. "Please?" Night had fallen, and the only illumination in the cottar house came from within the hearth. Mannes said nothing. He was lying next to his sister, somewhat squashed, the straw stacked thickly under his head so that he could see the room. Though Mannes had recovered a measure of his usual impassiveness, he nevertheless watched his mother closely, alert to her response. They're getting too big to share a cot, thought Vandimi, not for the first time.

"'Fraid not, loves. That wood's gotta last. We can only take so much from the forest." Vandimi withdrew the last bowl from the pail and set it on the table side closest to the hearth. Inside, the fire caused a log to pop, redoubling the woodsmoke smell. "Besides, you'll get too hot," she added, setting the dirty water aside for the morning.

"We won't mind…"

Vandimi felt her heart ache. Those cursed rats had scared her children in a way she wouldn't have credited, and even now the shock of seeing their terrified faces had yet to fully leave her. May gods help any vermin I come across, she thought. She turned to them, smiling kindly. "I know. No more talkin' now, my little Elohi. It's long past the hour for sleep."

"But… the shadows…"

"Nothin' to fear in the shadows. I've checked. The rats have scarpered, and there's no sign of monsters."

Neither child spoke for almost a minute. Sitting down on the stool by the fire, Vandimi began to nurture hope that they were finally drifting off. A glance their way quickly saw it dashed. The children's eyes were restless, and they caught hold of her gaze.

"I heard there's monsters in the forest," said Mannes.

"Forest don't bother nobody that don't bother it," said Vandimi, firmly.

"What if we took too much firewood? What if the Green Lady's angry?" he asked, barely above a whisper.

"Mannes Barchet. Don't tell me you've forgotten all about the Lady's Champion?"

Mannes flushed. "No! I haven't fogot!"

"Well? Do you think the mighty Sir Dillen'd serve a goddess who attacks little children?"

After a momentary scowl, Mannes shook his head. "I'm not little," he muttered.

To the children of Talle village, there was perhaps no greater hero in all of Pannithor than Sir Dillen, knight-champion of the Green Lady of Galahir. The Barchet family had heard Sir Dillen's tale not long after their arrival in Talle, delivered in song by a traveling bard. The gaudily-dressed troubadour, being visibly underwhelmed by the potential patrons to his craft, hadn't even deigned to stay one night; but his final and most thrilling piece had nevertheless left an abiding impression on the locals. It told of Sir Dillen's rise to the role of champion through his exploits against the forces of the Abyss, in a battle that all knew to have taken place a day's journey west of the village, at the tail end of the war little over a year and a half ago.

Juttah had sat up. "Please, mother. Tell us the story again."

"You'd like that too, Mannes?"

"I guess."

Vandimi suppressed a smile. Sir Dillen may be a hero to the other children, but she knew that to her son he was far more than that. He was an idol.

"Alright. Lie down, then. Eyes closed. I catch either of you lookin' and the story ends right there. Clear?"

The children murmured their agreement and shuffled down into the cot. A sigh escaped Vandimi's lips as she got back onto her weary feet, bringing the stool closer to her audience. Although she could hold a tune well enough, Vandimi preferred to tell stories like her grandmother used to: in a low voice, by turns gentle and dramatic. It had seemed to the young Vandimi to be a kind of magic, the way the stories gripped her in their course before sending her soundly to sleep by the end. It had taken practice, but Vandimi now felt herself well-versed in the art.

"You remember the war, when it started near two years past? The Abyss, ancient prison of the Wicked Ones, it were growin', tryin' to swallow the whole world. All Mantica were in a strife, from the kingdoms of the elves to our home in Basilea. Minions of the Abyss, foulest sinners and their demonic masters, were everywhere spreadin' their cruelty across the land.

"We had to leave our home near Samarik, flee south, and we weren't the only folk what did. Weren't none of us had a choice. But while we fled toward safe haven, the Hegemon of Basilea and the Green Lady of Galahir joined together to fight the Wicked Ones' servants. Their armies went north to the very edge of the Abyss itself to hold the demons back.

"The black magic of the Abyss were strong. All could taste it on the wind. The evil armies didn't just appear at the edge – they could go near anywhere they liked. With so many of the Green Lady's loyal warriors sent to fight far from their forest home, a host of abyssals led by the demon-champion Zelgarag attacked Galahir, tryin' to burn their way to the Green Lady herself.

"And so the Hegemon sent an army to protect the Forest, a whole legion of soldiers and an order of mighty paladin knights, the Blades of Onzyan! And among them knights was one who was younger than all the rest, fresh from trainin' and not even a year past boyhood. His name was Sir Dillen, and though he didn't know it, he was destined for great things!"

Juttah gave a sleepy sigh, familiar sign that she was already drifting. But though his eyes were closed, Vandimi sensed that Mannes was still listening intently.

"This was no surprise to those who knew Sir Dillen. Tall and strong, his face were handsome, his hair long and golden, his eyes silver-gray; like he were born of the Elohi, which some say he were and all. None could best him with a blade in hand. When he spoke, only fools paid his words no mind.

"But as fate would have it, a fool was just who the Hegemon sent to lead the army to Galahir. They say that the Dictator Trence Andorset were as simple as he were proud, that he'd bought his title through politics and family, rather than earnin' it in honest service to the people. He had no wish to aid the Forest, and he resented his orders. Ignorin' the advice of better men, he marched the soldiers 'neath his command 'til they couldn't march no more, and they had no choice but to set camp along a narrow trail. The watchful and unblinkin' eyes of the Abyss saw Andorset's folly, and struck!

"The army's vanguard were hit first. Swarms of Abyssals burst out from among the trees, hundreds of foul, red-skinned beings who walk upright on hooves, but hunched and slatherin' like beasts. Balls of hell flame were thrown from among 'em at the brave soldiers, and all around, the forest began to burn!

"As it happened, bein' one of those who'd dared tell Andorset that they should've stopped sooner, Sir Dillen had been banished to the van – the fates, in their fickleness, had put the young paladin exactly where he were needed the most. Rallyin' the men and women of the legion, Sir Dillen repelled the attack, his sword cleavin' through hellspawn to spill their black blood on the forest floor! The base creatures were surprised and fell back – but their numbers were many, and they began to encircle the remainin' soldiery of the van.

"Sir Dillen realized there were no way they could survive another attack. All they could do were choose a lone messenger for their only horse and send him back to the dictator while the rest bought time. That they'd buy it with their lives were certain. Sir Dillen asked who among them were fleetest in the saddle, havin' not the slightest intent to abandon the fight. But the brave soldiers of the realm knew that only a paladin of Dillen's skill would stand a chance – all had heard the tales of the young knight's ridin' talent. Acceptin' their sacrifice with a heavy heart, Sir Dillen rode back down the line as the soldiers charged out at their encirclin' foe.

"His only hope were that he could warn the rest of the army afore it were too late. But the enemy had already attacked the dictator's forces, drivin' into their thin line, spread long by Andorset's arrogance. Not even a paladin as mighty as Sir Dillen could salvage victory – the forest would be their grave. But, as we know, Sir Dillen was also wise. He saw that their last chance – their only chance – would be to find She who they'd come to aid, the Green Lady of Galahir! And so brave Dillen pulled his horse away from the narrow trail, and charged it deep into the darkest heart of the ancient wood.

"Not even half a mile had he ridden when something crashed into the knight, knockin' him clean off his steed. It moved fast, swoopin' down from the treetops, a piercin' cry of bitter rage. Sir Dillen tumbled into the undergrowth as his horse collapsed from 'neath him, dead. Grippin' his sword, the young paladin rose just in time to defend himself. His attacker were a foul and winged succubus, a demon whose form makes even the purest of men weaken in her presence, with long, sharp talons and–"

"How?" asked Mannes. He was looking at her. "What would make them go weak?"

"What did I say about your eyes?"

Mannes shut them quickly. "Sorry…" he mumbled.

"That's better."

Juttah let out a giggle. Clearly her daughter wasn't as close to sleep as Vandimi had thought. She sighed, wondering how or whether to continue. Mannes had opened his eyes, after all. But the truth was she was enjoying telling the tale, even if she now realized it would have been better to skip over this particular part. She recalled how racy the bard had made it when he recounted it to the village, deploying a verse that was leaden with scant-disguised euphemism. It had caused the men and women in the audience to go red, if for different reasons. She was glad at least that young Mannes hadn't picked up on anything untoward. Not that she could tell, at any rate.

"I'm not going to explain why, just trust when I say these demons make men soft in the head. Anyway, Sir Dillen were as much a man in this respect as any other, and for a moment, his blade slowed. The creature struck out with her claws, slashin' across the side of the young man's face. Far from blindin' him, the pain cleared Sir Dillen's sense, and he threw himself into the fight, fendin' off his foe with lightnin' sweeps of his sword. Afeared by his skill, the demoness fled back to her foul kind. For Sir Dillen, whose beauty were ever marred by that fight, it were a lesson he'd not soon forget.

"Unhorsed, the heroic knight had no choice save to dash between the thick and towerin' trunks of the trees, the dire urgency of his task leavin' no time for caution. Night had come, and far from the flames of battle there were not the slightest light in them woods. After near an hour of runnin' in the full plate of his paladin order, with sweat stingin' the cuts on his face, Sir Dillen collapsed to the ground, exhausted, and lost in the darkness.

"None can say for certain how long he were there on the forest floor. But when he awoke, it was with the gentle sway of flowin' water 'neath him. Openin' heavy eyes, the knight found himself in a boat, a slim coracle made from woodland vine, bound more tight and fine than the most skilled weaves of men and elves. It were movin' along a sleepy river, wide enough for Sir Dillen to see the stars above in the sky of early morn'. Afore he could so much as lift his head, a voice greeted him, strange, like the wind itself had took a tongue.

"'The Lady shows you her favor, young one,' said the voice.

"Scramblin' to his knees, the knight drew his sword, lookin' to and fro for any sign of the mysterious speaker. But there were none.

"'Who goes? Show thyself!' he cried.

"The voice laughed, the sound dancin' around the paladin's ears. Then, floatin' over the waters, she appeared. For a moment, Sir Dillen thought she was a ghost, for the woman seemed to be made from barest wisps of fog, lit by starlight – she were, in fact, a sylph, a fey spirit of the Forest.

"'How typical of men you are!' she said, 'Clumsy and tumblin' through our Lady's woods, wavin' yer sword at whatever goes BOO!'

"And Sir Dillen declared, 'Mock me not, irksome fairy! I come on a task of greatest import, for seek I the aid of the Green Lady of Galahir! If thou hast knowledge of where She bides, reveal it!'

"With a 'Humph!' of disdain, the sylph waved its wispy arms, and a fierce gust of wind blew along the river. Thinkin' the woodland spirit were tryin' to knock him from the raft, Sir Dillen ducked down and clung to the sides – but rather than tippin' him into the dark waters, the wind sent him racin' against the current. The coracle skimmed along the surface, bouncin' its way ever deeper into the woods. After several minutes, the wind turned sharpish, sendin' the knight up a narrow tributary and plungin' him toward a ragin' waterfall! Believin' he were about to crash, the knight braced his grip and held his breath – but he passed through without harm, the sylph's mockin' laugh in his ears."

"Serves him right. Dillen shouldn't've been rude," mumbled Juttah sleepily.

"The fairy were the rude one!" protested Mannes.

"I wish I could meet a sylph," Juttah continued in a sigh, ignoring her brother.

"The sylph was the last thing on our young knight's mind," said Vandimi, a hint of warning in her voice. She waited several seconds. The children were silent. Satisfied, Vandimi continued, "Truly, he could think of little at all, so struck were he by the sights before his eyes, lit by first light of dawn. For in the great glade that lay beyond the water's bank stood hundreds of creatures from a dozen or more kinds, noble lords of the Green Lady's realm – there were elves and gnomes, centaurs and sylphs, salamanders and naiads. Livin' trees shambled about the glade's edge, and three humans, two women and a man, stepped forward to meet the knight. They were dressed wild-like, furs and bone strung together with rough-cured leather – they were druids!

"'Well met, paladin!' said they as Sir Dillen stepped onto the shore. 'Your coming was foretold by our Lady!'

"'Then She has expected me?' the young paladin asked.

"'I have indeed,' said a voice in the glade's heart. It were a voice as gentle as a breeze through grass, pitiless as the rumblin' of a landslide, hungry as the crackle of flame, and constant as a flowin' stream. The huddle of creatures in the glade parted, and there in all Her glory stood the Green Lady herself! 'Step forward, Sir Dillen!' said She, 'Let me look upon you!'

"Sir Dillen approached the goddess, his tongue failin' in her presence. Royal in bearin' and taller than an ogre, She were a beauty like none other – her skin white as winter sky, eyes vibrant as greenest spring. From Her head spilled a crown of golden hair, rich like ripened wheat, long and shinin'. Her lips, deep with the bloody red of the hunt, smiled down at him. In Her aspect, the wise young paladin recognized the delicate balance of this world, of blessin' and curse, bounty and ruin, life and death. Not Shinin' nor Wicked One were She, but all of Nature itself.

"'I know wherefore you come, young knight,' said She, 'and verily shall you find that which you seek. But know this! Such things always bear a price, for thusly is the balance preserved. Now, speak!'

"And Sir Dillen spoke, 'O Green Lady of Galahir, within whose noble breast beat the hearts of two Celestians whole! Basilea stands as your ally in these troubled times and sends an army to your cause, though now they are beset by the forces of darkness! I come bearing but one plea – aid us!'

"'Your plea is heard, paladin knight,' responded She. 'I am prepared to grant it, so long as you are prepared to pay the price?'

"'You have but only to name it, Lady!' said Sir Dillen. He spoke without hesitation, concern for his brothers and sisters in arms leavin' no room for considerin' such a pledge.

"The Green lady gave Her command – 'Kneel, sir knight, and hold out your sword!'

"And Sir Dillen knelt, pressin' his fore against the pommel of his blade. Already the wise lad knew what would come next.

"'Do you swear your life and blade to serve my will,' continued She, 'to fight my battles and lead my armies, to bring balance where there is naught, my words where they ought? To be my knight-champion, from this hour to your last?'

"For a moment, the young paladin couldn't speak, for he were awed, not only by the scale of Her demand, but by the honor it bestowed upon him. Then wit returned, and he declared, 'I swear it!'

"No sooner were the pact sealed when a unicorn leapt into the glade, with coat of pure white and a silver horn atop its head. It landed at Sir Dillen's side.

"'Mount your steed, knight-champion!' spoke the Lady. 'Lead my army to war!'

"And so, with a mighty host of centaur warriors at his back and a noble beast between his legs, Sir Dillen rode out of the glade, headin' toward the great smoke plumes that rose in the eastern woods. The unicorn steed were glidin' through the forest, unhindered by the mossy floor and hidden roots. In less than an hour, the knight-champion had returned to the battlefield – and just in time, too. All around our young knight, the golden sunlight of morn' were choked by the smog of burnin' trees, and hunched, foul figures moved freely between their shadows. But there were hope yet, born by the sounds of clashin' blades and the defiant cries of his one-time brothers and sisters. The fool Andorset were dead, and the brave soldiers of Basilea had defended their line throughout the night. But Zelgarag's abyssals were too many, and by morn' the Hegemon's army were surrounded.

"The demon Zelgarag, however, had failed to consider the forest itself. With a cry of battle in his lungs, Sir Dillen led the centaurs' charge – right into the enemy's rear! Panic spread like the abyssals' own wildfire as the base creatures were trampled 'neath hundreds of crashin' hooves, the Lady's warriors cleavin' their way to free the Basileans from their plight. Great eagles joined the centaurs, sharp talons swoopin' from above; naiads burst from a nearby river, tridents in their grip; salamanders marched from the between the burnin' trees, the fire lickin' across their scales without harm. Crushed from all sides, the demons began to flee!

"But Zelgarag wouldn't give in so easily, oh no. The champion of the Wicked Ones let out a roar that were heard for miles – ol' Iam Ackley claims he heard it all the way in the mountains, where the villagers were hidin' from the war. The roar gave courage – or fear – to the abyssals, and many turned back to the fight, their resolve returned. Spyin' the demon-champion from atop his unicorn steed, Sir Dillen readied his grip on his paladin blade. He knew what he had to do…"

Vandimi, whose words had grown steadily softer, stopped. The children's breaths were deep, their faces calm and peaceful. They were sleeping. Taking care not to make a sound, she lifted her stool back to the hearth.

The fire had burned low. She added a log, placing it quietly at the center before turning the embers around it with the poker.

"Vandi?"

It was Cossus. His voice was distant. He was likely halfway up the trail. Grimacing as she got back on her feet, Vandimi slipped out the door, waving at her husband's moonlit form and indicating he be quiet.

"The children have only just nodded off," she explained in a low voice as he drew closer.

"Good," he whispered back. Setting down his pitchfork and pail, Cossus took her by the arms and drew her close, a grin wide across his face. Vandimi stifled a laugh. They were neither of them the pair of naive and passionate youths who had run away to marry in a small temple at the base of the Samarites. Not anymore. The world as much as time had seen them hardened, had left worry lines on their faces and built a levee on their hearts – except when it came to their children, of course. But every time she saw that ridiculously broad grin, it was as if nothing had changed at all, as if they were young fools again. If only for a moment.

"How are they?" he asked.

Vandimi didn't answer right away, instead setting her chin on Cossus's shoulder as she embraced him. "They were shook right up," she said eventually, little more than a breath by his ear. "But I've hope it'll pass by morn'."

"Like a bad dream," Cossus sighed, his body relaxing.

"Yes."

They stayed that way for almost a minute. Though utterly exhausted, for some reason Vandimi couldn't convince her eyes to close for more than a second at a time. A thin mist hung in the air, muting the deep blue of night with its gray. She stared through it aimlessly, sensing the presence of the great forest that lay beyond her view, west across the fields. Something – she couldn't say what – was disturbing her. If the villagers of Talle were right, the battle from the tale of Sir Dillen had occurred just inside the Forest's nearest frontier, nearly two years ago. The Barchet family had worked so hard to escape the war, and now they lived in the shadow of one of its greatest conflicts. Maybe that's it, she thought. No. More likely it was just the rats. The rats, and the fear in her children's faces.

Cossus must have been thinking the same. "I'll have another check over the house tomorrow," he said. They parted, and she met his eye. "I'll look for where anythin' might've got in. Just to be sure."

She nodded gratefully. "C'mon. Let's go to—"

A scream. Husband and wife stood frozen, fear mirrored in the other's eyes as they listened to the piercing wail cut across the night.

"Where…" she began, foundering. Vandimi's first thought had been her children, but the sound was too distant.

"The village!" said Cossus. Vandimi turned toward Talle and realized he was right. The scream kept going, never seeming to stop for breath. Its pitch was high and excessive, pushed by lungs that had yet to acquire restraint. It sounded like…

Vandimi gripped Cossus's arm. "It's a child!" They could hear other voices now, alarmed adults asking what was wrong.

"I better go see what's happenin'," said Cossus, beginning to step away.

"No!" said Vandimi, firmly. Her tiredness had vanished, and she felt an inexplicable clarity.

"Vandi, what—"

"Wait!"

A second scream, another child. A third. Fourth. More. Like a deranged choir, the children of Talle village were crying out in terror. Increasingly, there was panic in the voices of the adults, too, but their shouts were uncomprehending. Not like the screams.

The screams knew.

Vandimi was already moving toward the door of their house when the cries of Juttah and Mannes joined the cacophony.

"I'm here!" she called. "I'm comin'—"

The door was stuck. Heart pounding in her chest, Vandimi lifted door latch and shoved. It wouldn't move. Terror morphed into rage, and she threw herself against it, not even noticing Cossus's own desperate attempt to get at the door as she hammered her shoulder into the wood. The door flung open with a piercing snap, causing the parents to stumble inside.

The fire in the hearth had gone out. Not even an ember glowed in its space. Rushing across the familiar room, they didn't waste time trying to soothe their children in the dark, instead lifting their thrashing forms from the cot and bearing them outside. Crouched and looking into the eyes of her screaming children, Vandimi saw they were still far away, submerged in sleep.

"We have to wake them!" she cried, torn between shaking Juttah and cradling her face. Through the storm of bawls and panic coming from Talle village, Vandimi heard her husband's deep voice attempt to calm Mannes.

"C'mon, son, it's alright, wake up now. Yer havin' a bad dream…"

In Vandimi's arms, Juttah's cries were beginning to abate, her eyes growing clearer. She met her mother's gaze.

"M-m-mother?"

"Shhh, it's alright, I'm here."

Juttah was shaking her head. "They're c-comin'! Comin' from the dark!"

Vandimi's breath caught. She didn't know what to say. Behind her, Mannes had finally woken and was hugging his father. Cossus lifted him as he stood back up.

"I have to go to the village, see if I can't help."

"Don't!" said Vandimi, setting Juttah on her feet as she stood to face him. "Don't you dare leave us!"

"Vandi-" but Cossus was cut off as their son spoke, the emotionless words causing Vandimi's blood to chill.

"It's too late. They're already caught."

It was then they heard the roars. Gargling and cruel, the sound was like nothing they'd heard before, nothing they could possibly conceive. It conjured mouths inside their minds, impossible mouths, black and yawning. And hungry.

Now, finally, the screams were joined by adult voices. The choir welcomed their joining with open arms.

"We have to run!" cried Vandimi. Cossus stared at her blankly. "Cossus!"

Cossus jumped. "R-right!" He looked around, still holding Mannes in his arms. Vandimi saw her son's neutral expression – somehow, it was worse than if he'd shown fear. "No time to grab anythin'," continued Cossus. "We go west. Get as far from here as we can – to the forest if needs be."

Without another word, they set off down the hillside, making to cut across the fields. Cossus continued to carry Mannes. Vandimi and Juttah ran hand-in-hand.

Even as they increased the distance between themselves and Talle, the sounds continued to grow more horrible, with the cries punctuated by pained yells as the roaring things found the villagers. Caught them, as Mannes had put it.

When they reached the fields, Vandimi vomited. They stopped, waiting as she continued to retch long after her evening meal had left her.

"Don't... stop!" she gasped. "I'll... catch..."

"No," said Cossus. He set Mannes down, crouching next to her. "Take a breath. We go together. Always."

Vandimi met her husband's eyes and nodded. As strange a moment as it was for such things, she once again felt gratitude that her children had his eyes.

"Er, father?" asked Juttah.

"Yes?"

"Where're the scarecrows?"

"...What?"

Juttah pointed, her finger moving quickly to a half-dozen directions. Each revealed a thin, wooden cross projecting above the fields. All were empty.

"I... I don't know," said Cossus.

Suddenly, Vandimi recalled the feeling she'd had when looking west. Even before the screams, she'd sensed something was wrong. Though she didn't know what it meant, nor where the scarecrows could've gone, she was now certain that their absence had been the cause of her disquiet. She stood up, taking a moment to steady herself against Cossus. "C'mon, we have to keep–"

Movement flickered at the edge of her vision. She turned to look. Less than ten feet away, something had stood up. Vandimi's mind balked as it moved toward them, its disorganized steps deceptive in their swiftness. Straw hair poked out from beneath a wide-brimmed hat, and its face was empty save for its mouth, contorted by a torn grin. It held a scythe.

"Run!" cried Cossus, moving to meet the thing. Vandimi held to him.

"No! Not without you! We go together!"

They could hear its fodder innards rustling as it moved. It lifted the scythe, and Juttah screamed.

"Take the children, Vandi! I'll hold it back! RUN!"

The scythe came down.

Chapter III

O f all the things that conspired to wake the hunter – the chill in the night air, the shuffling in the dark, the smell – it was the fullness of his bladder which most urgently stirred him to consciousness. Its brimful hold did not last long. Wincing at the stiffness in his neck, he raised his head to look out into the gloom, blinking away sleep. Something stank. The leafy scent of the forest was gone, displaced by a heavy, meaty reek. It seemed to smother the air, coating the back of his throat.

Movement. Alarm shot through him, forcibly rousing his muscles. He'd glimpsed something pass through a patch of moonlight, thick hairs on dark flesh. He could hear its steps, its snorting breaths. Slowly, gaze fixed on the darkness, he reached for his spear.

The boar. Somehow it had failed to notice him sleeping in his fig-tree alcove. Fingers closed around the spear, lifted it silently from the undergrowth. From the sounds of the hog, it was a big one. Far bigger than even Bhadein had suspected. He swallowed and struggled not to retch. Size didn't explain that smell, fouler than any game he'd known. Nothing an hour or two on the spit won't solve, he thought.

This was his chance. The hunt's thrill gripped him, sent a shiver of vitality to every corner of his being. Resting the spear across the buttress roots, he hoisted himself up with care, moving in the barest of increments. Crouched and back on his feet, with one hand he hefted the spear up over his shoulder, holding it ready to throw. The other lay on his dagger, sheathed at his belt. Soundlessly, he began to take stalking steps toward the boar.

In the time it had taken the young hunter to ready himself, the boar had moved further away, its snorts muffled as it sifted through the undergrowth. Unable to see more than an occasional movement in the forest's deep dark, he relied on those sounds as he approached. From what he could tell, the animal had its back to him and was rooting around at the bottom of a shallow furrow. It was a small comfort – the wild boars of the forest were known to be intelligent and unpredictable in equal measure, their tusks more than capable of ripping through leather and flesh – but it was a comfort all the same. As soon as he thought himself to be around twenty feet away, he stopped. He knew he was lucky to get this close, that if he went any further he was sure to be detected. Slowly – painfully slowly – he rose to standing position, bracing to hurl the spear. Skewering it from the back was far from ideal. In the dark especially, he wanted it to turn sideways and present a more promising target. And so he waited. After seconds that felt like epochs, the boar shifted. Its head turned; he glimpsed the dirty white of its tusk. He launched the spear.

Later, when he thought back on that moment, the golden-haired hunter would tell himself that he felt something was amiss long before the weapon left his outstretched arm. The glimpsed tusk had been a great deal larger than he'd expected, and far from him having grown inured to the creature's stink, it had continued to disturb his empty stomach. But the truth of the matter was that when he let the spear fly, he felt nothing save the elation born of a perfect throw. The spearhead cut soundlessly through the air, twinkling once as it caught the narrowest sliver of moonlight. Scarcely had it disappeared into darkness when there came a satisfying thump. It was a sound he knew well – the sound of steel sunk deep. Satisfaction lasted a mere split-second, its memory obliterated by the shriek of pain. Only then did he realize that the beast wasn't obscured by shadow – it was the shadow.

In a lightning movement, the creature charged at him. The hunter leapt desperately aside, landing hard in the undergrowth. Soil pulsed as it stormed past, its nearest tusk a hair's breadth from having disemboweled him. Rolling twice, he looked out at the beast, now turning for another charge. Between the branches of the fig tree, fingers of moonlight pawed the creature's back, confirming to his eyes what his racing heart knew.

Eight feet long from snout to tail, it stood almost as tall as a man, its tough and bristling hide stretched tightly over a mass of muscle. Its face was scarred from a lifetime of battle, and its bulging eyes seethed with rage. It had continued to shriek without pause, agonized and furious, spittle flying from its maw as it gave flagrant violation to the forest's silence. Although the hunter had never seen the like, he'd heard enough stories. It wasn't just any boar – it was a gore. An orc-bred weapon of war.

He tried to stand. Pain gave a warning flare in his hip – it seemed he'd landed against an exposed root. Luckily for him, the gore had paused, head twisting to get a look at its flank. The spear's shaft projected from its shoulder, stuck fast. In a quick motion, the gore closed its mouth on it, the brief lapse in its shrieking filled by a crunch of shattering wood. The hunter managed to get to his feet and saw that the beast was facing him once more.

I have to climb, he thought bluntly. He didn't bother glancing about – according to a memory so thin it could only be considered instinct, he knew that the trees closest to him were smooth and branchless. The fig tree alone offered safety – the problem was that the gore stood squarely in his path to it. For the briefest of moments, he considered drawing his dagger, quickly dismissing the idea as pointless.

The gore came at him. His hip gave a twinge of protest as he leapt again, this time attempting to land on his feet. The charging swine twisted to follow his movement, hooking its snout under the hunter's half-lifted leg and knocking it out from under him. The hunter flipped forward, crashing face-first. Stars danced across the darkness in his left eye. There was a crunch of dead leaves as the gore skidded to a halt, its grunting breath like choked laughter. Not looking back, the hunter scrambled up and made straight for the fig tree, his abused leg and hip restricting him to hobbled lunges. He heard the gore let out a long screech, the sound rapidly coming closer. Pushing off from his good leg, he stretched up to wrap both hands around a scaffold branch, driving a groan through clenched teeth as he lifted his body up to it. He glanced down just in time to see the gore's dark mass slam into the trunk beneath him. His branch shuddered with the blow. His grip failed.

The fall was a confused whirlwind of sensation – abrupt vertigo, fleshy impact, bristles against his nape, a single spin, darkness – and when a second later it was over, the hunter found himself flat on the ground, breathless and with the gore's drooling maw above him, its mad eyes alive with intent.

He reached up and grabbed hold of its tusks, pushing as hard as he could while craning his head back. The gore's jaw closed with a snap, missing him by an inch, but the hunter knew he wouldn't be able to avoid the next one. His lungs refused to take in air, gagging at the stink. His arms felt empty. The beast was too strong.

Moonlight glimmered at the edge of his vision, catching on something in the gore's hair. Something wet. His eyes focused on it. Blood. It was flowing from the gore's shoulder. The spearhead was still in there. Releasing his hold on one of the tusks, he reached up toward the wound, as good as placing his head inside the beast's mouth in the process. Just as he felt the teeth clamp onto his skull, the hunter grabbed hold of the shattered shaft and pushed. The gore released his head, and all at once sound retreated from the world, a screech sending skewers of white-hot pain through deafened ears. The animal began to thrash, attempting to dislodge the source of its agony. Its leg failed, causing its stinking mass to topple and pin the hunter's chest against the forest floor. Remaining breath was expelled in an unheard moan. His vision blurred, a darkness deeper than night encroaching at its borders.

This is it, he thought. This is how I die. Then he thought of nothing save keeping his hold on the spearhead.

In the narrow tunnel of his vision, steel flashed, sweeping down. The hunter felt every muscle in the gore jump and stiffen. Then they went slack. The gore stopped moving.

A weight that seemed to have doubled was rolled off him. Breath rushed back into his lungs, the wheezing faintly audible over the mute whine in his ears. Uncomprehending, he closed his eyes, nursing greedily at the air.

"That's it. You're all right, Farn. Breathe."

The distant voice filled him with warm relief. Blinking away tears, Farn looked up into the face of his fellow knight, a man whom he admired above all others. The man who'd just saved his life.

"Dillen…"

* * * * *

In the low light, Sir Dillen's square and stubbled face displayed a half-smile, slightly contorting the trio of scars across his right temple. He had just finished helping Farn over to the fig tree, and the young knight now sat once more between its buttress roots.

"Your next word better be 'thanks'," said Dillen, still smiling. He stood with one leg planted against the larger root and hands on his hips. Behind him, the massive form of the gore lay in a heap of limp muscle, Dillen's longsword embedded in its skull. "Come, now! I'm not a patient man."

Farn's breathless laugh sent pain arching across his chest. "Keep dreaming! I had…" he gulped a breath, "I had the beast in hand."

"That so? Your breeches tell it different."

Exhausted though he was, Farn made a show of examining the dark stains before shooting a shameless grin at Dillen. "All part of the plan, I assure you!"

Dillen laughed without restraint, throwing back his head. In the minutes since Farn's struggle with the gore, clouds had moved to swallow the moon, reducing his savior to a silhouette of average height and solid build, his head topped with a close crop. Since they'd first met near a year-and-a-half past, Farn had come to know Dillen well, so well in fact that his mind effortlessly filled in the rest. Dark-haired and bronze-skinned, thick-lipped and narrow-nosed, round eyes of hazel set into a square face with a still squarer jaw – Sir Dillen was not the sort that would typically be considered handsome. That said, most would agree that there was an appealing quality to the sum of his aspect, particularly when his large lips drew back in his characteristic half-smile. If his scars played no positive role in that sum, nor at least did they take anything away.

"In all seriousness," said Farn, "I thank you. A second later and I'd have been done for."

Dillen nodded. "Right enough. Though in truth, no thanks are necessary. What kind of a knight would I be if t'were otherwise, eh?"

"A right bastard, to be sure."

Farn sensed Dillen's grin in the dark. "Think you can stand?" Dillen asked.

"Give me another minute."

"Wimp."

Farn shook his head, smiling despite himself. He guessed Dillen to be some twenty years his senior. Not that one would know it from the way he talked. Nor from the way he treated Farn, for that matter, namely as an outright equal. It was a manner of conduct all the more endearing for being, in Farn's view, so obviously without justification.

"Sir Dillen? Is that you?" The voice was deep and sober.

"Over here, Sir Bhadein! The pig is dead!"

Two forms emerged not ten seconds later.

"By the Ones!" exclaimed the shorter, his guttural croak revealing him as Sir Ragneld. "That's some pig! Talk about a stinker!"

"A war gore..." said Bhadein. "It was you who slew this, Dillen?" Farn felt a flicker of irritation. Though many would miss the skepticism that edged Bhadein's typically neutral tone, Farn had spent enough time in the company of his old master to hear it clear as a thunderclap in temperate skies. True, Dillen killed the gore while its struggle with Farn held it in place, but Farn knew for a fact that Dillen could have slain it regardless.

For his part, Dillen answered by setting one foot on the gore's head and reclaiming his sword, freeing it with a wet shunk.

Ragneld laughed, a sound like a rockslide. "What less could we expect from the Great Sir Dillen, hero of Galahir?"

"Enough of that, now," said Dillen, waving a hand in casual dismissal. "I had help. Sir Farn distracted it for me."

Bhadein's towering shadow stiffened in surprise. "Sir Farn?"

"I'm here," said Farn, attempting to push himself to his feet. He faltered, and in a quick movement Bhadein was at his side, bracing him by the arm. Farn began to protest, but the big knight had already hauled him up. "Thanks," he muttered.

Bhadein nodded. "Were you hurt?"

Farn looked up at him, meeting his eye. Tall as Farn had ultimately grown to be, he hadn't come close to matching Bhadein's mountainous stature, over seven feet in all. Darkness hid most of his features – olive skin, large nose, almond-shaped eyes of deepest brown – but Farn could just make out the gray of his shoulder-length hair and trim goatee, not to mention his over-long eyebrows. Being well into his fifth decade, Bhadein was not only the eldest of their group, but he was among the eldest living warriors of the entire Brotherhood people. At least, what was left of it.

"Me?" He shook off Bhadein's hand. "I'm fine! Take a look at the gore! The odd bruise is nothing compared to the wound I dealt it!"

"You aided Dillen's effort?"

"He might've gained the killing blow, but it was I who hobbled the beast!"

"It's true. Farn gave me the perfect opening," confirmed Dillen.

"But you knew Sir Dillen was there? You did not try to fell it alone?"

Farn forced a laugh. "Still worrying for me, Bhadein? I'd hoped our time in battle at the edge of the Abyss would put a stop to that."

"Answer the question."

"Why should I? I'm a knight, same as you."

"Farn."

Farn stepped away, anger building. "So what if I tried to fell it? What does that matter?"

"It matters. To face a gore alone is perilous, even by light of day. In darkness, it is an act of fools."

"Then you say I am a fool?"

"That depends."

Silence followed. Farn's cheeks were hot. He thought he felt the others' eyes on him, but when he glanced around, he saw Dillen was busying himself with cleaning his sword, Ragneld with binding the gore's legs. Only Bhadein was looking his way. He took a deep breath.

"I... I didn't know it was a gore until after I'd speared it. Before that, I only believed it to be a large hog." The words felt true enough, but already Farn was beginning to doubt his recollection of the moments leading up to the throw. What he said next, however, was a truth so certain he'd gladly swear it before each of the Ones in turn. "If I'd known otherwise, I'd have climbed that tree in an instant. That's... that's what I tried to do, when I realized..."

"Good," said Bhadein. "I am relieved to hear that, Farn. I only wished to assure myself that-"

"Well, then!" said Dillen brightly, his words punctuated by a metallic clink as he sheathed his sword. "That's that! The gore's dead, the hunt's a good'un, and Farn's no more a fool than when last we checked!" The moment was dispelled. Dillen cast a half-grin at Farn, who once more felt a surge of gratitude toward the knight. "Come on, let's get this malodorous meat on the move."

"It's going to be tricky," said Ragneld. "Our staves won't bear the weight. We'll have to drag it back."

"Fine," sighed Dillen. Then he put a hand over his mouth and nose, suppressing a cough. "The sooner we set off, the better. If I have to smell this thing any longer than necessary, I fear I'll lose my appetite for good."

"Uh huh. Here, Sir Farn, take this end of the rope and feed it under the beast's neck, Sir Dillen, you lift the head-"

"Have you all learned nothing?"

The voice, sage and feminine, had spoken quietly, yet from so near a distance as to cause the knights to jump in surprise – well, likely not Bhadein, who in any case had been outside Farn's view. As one, they turned to the source. A figure leaned against the fig tree, lithe in form, a bow held loosely at her side.

"Ignoring for a moment that every creature for miles around can hear your harsh, human squawks; would you truly dare to take a bounty from the forest, without first yielding Her due?"

As she was speaking, the moon had emerged from behind its cloud, showering her in a patchwork of silver and shadow. Sharp and symmetrical features were arranged on a slender face, frame for eyes of fathomless, primal green. A headdress of interwoven oak leaves billowed outward and down her back, and her torso was clad in a cuirass of leather plate that was so intricate and form-fitting as to present not the slightest hindrance to mobility. Nor to imagination. Farn's heartbeat sounded in his ears. The wetness on his breeches came to mind, making his cheeks burn hotter.

The elf stepped forward, her movements accompanied by the faintest rustle from the foliage headdress. Only Bhadein stood taller than she, and not by much.

"What say you?"

"We offer our apologies, gladestalker," Bhadein began but got no further as Dillen let out a relieved laugh.

"It's you, Imariel! For a second there, I thought—"

"You believed that I was my mother?" Imariel moved toward Dillen. "Would Elissa's presence give you greater cause for concern than mine?"

"Not at all. You're both equally concerning. My gladness owes only to beauty, in which her daughter is beyond compare."

Imariel said nothing for several seconds, instead tilting her head in contemplation as she peered down at him. Dillen held her gaze. He looked very small next to her. There was something about the sight of them together which made Farn think of a raptorial bird, poised above its prey. "True," she said, finally. "It is… brave of you to say so. I am not sure she will agree."

Imariel gave a slight nod, indicating over Dillen's shoulder. For a moment, all was still, Dillen's nonchalant stance now frozen in place. Then he twisted around quickly, scanning the darkness. Farn looked too. There was no one. Or rather, there was no one that could be seen. As far as the gladestalkers of Galahir were concerned, that was no guarantee of anything.

Ragneld's grinding laugh tumbled briefly across the forest's silence, quickly restrained as he continued to busy himself with the gore. Dillen turned back, his half-smile on display.

"Okay, on 'concern' I'll grant you; but on 'beauty' I shan't waver."

Imariel had already stepped away and was now crouching next to the gore. "The Lady has bestowed a considerable blessing upon your tribe," she said, apparently ignoring Dillen's remark. As with all the forest's elves when they spoke of the Lady, her tone was reverent, but Farn could still sense her condescension. "Such a beast will feed many. Its hide will tan strong."

"We were slow to make prayer in thanks. We will do so now, as your people taught us," said Bhadein.

"It will not be enough." Imariel looked round, catching each knight's eye in turn. "You will have to present a great offering," she finished, her gaze having ended back on Sir Dillen.

Farn felt indignation bite. Not trusting himself, he clenched his teeth, locking back his tongue. Dillen, however, spoke for him anyway.

"Oh please," said Dillen, scoffing. "This isn't some frolicking doe we've felled. It's a gore, a perverse creation of orcs! It doesn't belong to the Lady's realm – if anything," he added, tone slipping into playfulness, "I'd say it's She who should be thanking us!"

"Dillen…" said Bhadein warningly, but Imariel held up her hand. Slowly, she stood up, gaze fixed hard on Dillen. Farn thought many would falter under such a gaze. He knew he would. But not Dillen.

"Such small-mindedness. You say this creature does not belong in Her realm? Have you any idea how many say the same of your kind? Most would, I think, find the gore preferable. But it is not for them to decide; nor for me, and certainly not for you. Only the Green Lady may define Her realm, and only the druids can divine Her will."

"Those same druids gave us this stretch of woodland to hunt in," countered Dillen, "and since then, we've kept them clear of goblins, even driven out a few trolls. But we still say the Lady's prayer. Over every fish hooked and fowl struck, we say it. Yet now, what? She wants more?" Dillen shrugged. "Fine. Like a common baron, She can have her cut. What'll it be? Leg or loin?"

Tension reigned in the silence. While Dillen's unflinching reply had been satisfying to behold, his words had crossed a line. In fact, Farn felt a degree of relief that the Basilean hadn't gone any further.

"I fear my mother may be right," said Imariel quietly. "You will never understand." With that, she turned and stepped out into the forest.

"Gladestalker, please. Wait!" said Bhadein. But Imariel was gone, vanished into the shadows. With a sigh like wind through autumn leaves, he turned to Dillen. "The wisdom of your tongue graces us again, Sir Dillen. Stories hardly do it justice."

"Alright. I get it." Dillen turned away to lean against one of the branchless trees, one hand reaching behind the collar of his jerkin to rub his nape. Ragneld stood up, his work on the gore abandoned. After several seconds of silence, Farn spoke.

"So… what now?"

Chapter IV

The stars were bright. Though dawn was less than an hour distant, not a hint of its approach could be discerned in their astral domain. Across an ocean of black without bounds, their many lights lay bare, undimmed and heady. As if the night would never end. In all her memory – encompassing more than eighty years, in this life – she had never seen a sky quite like it. It was beautiful. It was... troubling. Without knowing why, she foreboded that it would come to haunt her.

Sitting on a bed of moss, legs tucked beneath her and headdress falling about her shoulders, Imariel brought her gaze back down to the world. Ahead, past the treeline of the recently-formed clearing, was a tall and sturdy stakewall, circular stockade to the ancient watchtower at its heart. Torchlight flickered within, escaping through the arrowslits that spiraled up the tower's slender body – at least until the stonework cut short, brought low by time's embrace. The topmost levels were built with wood, an impatient and precarious solution which nevertheless allowed the tower to see over and beyond the tree tops of eastern Galahir. Once, in aeons past, the tower had been known as Thell Enselenor – those who manned it now simply called it the Eastfort.

Movement caught her eye. West of the fort's closed gateway, a cloaked and hooded figure vaulted the stockade, dropping silently to its outer side. Imariel's smile was slight, formed at the farthest corners of her mouth.

That did not take long, she thought. It couldn't have been twenty minutes since she watched the four knights return through the gates, hunting gear slung across their backs, strips of gore hide bundled in their arms. Not a single cut of meat had been taken from the beast – all had been left in offering. After her exchange with the ever-irksome Dillen, and following her apparent departure, Imariel had listened in on the debate that ensued. The men had quickly agreed that, between the hide and the meat, the meat was most needed at the fort – and that, argued Dillen, was why it should be left to the Lady's realm in its entirety. Farn, the youngest – and prettiest – one, backed Dillen to the hilt, and though the gruff one had demurred for a time, the elder had ultimately joined the others to swing it. In darkness the prayer was made, the beast skinned. Imariel had watched from afar and then followed them back to their fort.

The hooded figure moved quickly toward the edge of the clearing, cloak lifting just shy of the ground. Unhurried, Imariel stood, one hand steadying the arrows in her hip-slung quiver, the other clasped lightly on her bow. Not once did her eyes leave the figure. She waited. Reaching the treeline, the figure stopped and looked back briefly at the Eastfort. Then he crossed the frontier, removing himself from her view. But not for long. Closing her eyes, Imariel took a deep and patient breath, feeling the myriad of scents of the forest swirl throughout her mind. Harmony from chaos. A clear eye, surrounded by storm.

She had given him enough of a head start. Her hunt began.

Within moments, the forest became a blur in her peripheries, the deep blues of night blending with untold greens and browns as Imariel bounded between the trees. Only the path ahead was sharp, clarity set down by an instinct whose roots ranged far beyond her own experiences and into the long story of her people. To the ears of her own kind, as well as many others who dwelt in the forest, Imariel's movements across the undergrowth would be as loud as oncoming hail. But not to tonight's prey. In the many times she'd consummated this hunt, and despite his greatest efforts, not once had he heard her draw near. She reveled in the freedom, the chance to cast off restraint, tempt herself ever closer toward the edge – to invite detection.

Reaching a sudden and familiar slope, Imariel leapt, headdress sailing high in her wake. She landed smoothly on an outcropping boulder. Lifting her chin, she took another deep breath, feeling the headdress settle on her shoulders once more. The trail was strong. It always was with humans. But tonight, its smell was truly overpowering. She couldn't have failed to find him if she tried.

He was close. Imariel waited. Too quick. She wanted him to keep going, to make her run. To let her give chase. But the scent did not diminish. Whatever the reason, her prey had stopped.

Hopping down from the boulder, Imariel set off at a walk, giving her bow a single twirl between long fingers. After a short distance, the trail ran through a briar patch, and its thorny branches seemed to strain for her as she passed, eager to catch their barbs on her headdress, to leave marks on exposed skin. She eluded them with ease, and on the other side found herself standing over a small, secluded hollow, its base clogged with thick-stemmed and broad-leafed bracken. Imariel smiled. He had done well. Even to her keen elf eyes, there was no sign of the underbrush having been disturbed. Yet here he most certainly was.

Nothing stirred as she slipped down the hollow's incline, no sound was made as she glided through the bracken. She crouched all the way down, submerging her head beneath the leaves. Through the hidden weald of shoots and stalks, she glimpsed something, spread on the forest floor not five feet away.

A shape that did not belong. Her senses tingled with awareness, the feeling of eyes upon her. He knew she was here. That she was coming closer. And yet…

Her heart pounded with realization. Imariel rose from the bracken, twisting her torso as she set arrow to bow. Undrawn, she tracked high into the silhouette canopy, beyond which the stars continued to burn their disquieting light.

There.

Draw and release were one. The arrow leapt toward the sky, soaring clear of every branch that intervened its mark. There was a dull thunk as it hit the underside of a bough, the sound immediately followed by a yelp. Footing lost, her prey fell. Twigs groaned and snapped as he crashed through their foliage to land midway-up the hollow's incline, rolling the rest of the way before ending face-down among the fern. Imariel dropped her bow and dove forward, pinning her knee against his back and pushing the air from his lungs.

"What's this?" she hissed, reaching out into the bracken. Her hand found rough wool, and she lifted the hooded-cloak from where it had so carefully been placed. The material stank of gore hide. It must have been used to carry it.

Euphoria danced with fury. "Thought to trick me, did you?" With one hand tight at his collar, she bent down next to his ear. "Did you dare hope to make me your prey?" Before he had time to attempt an answer, Imariel removed her knee and, in a lightning motion, flipped him onto his back before pinning him once more. "Well? Speak!"

Dillen's half-smile shone up at her, his hazel eyes flush with starlight. "Fair huntress," he said, somewhat breathless, "I protest! Didn't you yourself say that many would prefer a gore to a man?"

Maddening. But Imariel had already felt her laughter begin to build, surging inevitably from below her still-pounding heart. She put her hands around his face, baring her teeth and pressing tight. Still Dillen continued to grin up at her, and her laughter broke forth, deep and thunderous. She was still laughing a minute later, snatching mirth in the darkness of her oak-leaf headdress, between the press of their lips.

*****

Morning arrived red. Its belated light pushed hard into the eastern sky, expelling the night with stern finality. Spread upon a bed of flattened bracken with arms folded behind her head, Imariel looked on as spears of brilliant crimson forced their way through the canopy, igniting the thin mist of dawn.

"Will I see you tonight?"

Imariel lowered her gaze. Dillen was sitting beyond her feet, watching her as he pulled on his boots. She shook her head.

"I cannot. Besides, you will need to rest." Her eyes returned to the treetops. "I have no interest in spent prey."

Dillen laughed. The sound caused her to smile, being of a different sort to the laughs she heard him give around the other knights. It was an open sound. Less willful. There was a crunching of fern as he crawled over, traveling the length of her naked form until his half-smile came into view. "I think you underestimate the vigor of mortal men!"

She met his eyes. Above him, the burgeoning dawn continued its advance, casting a fiery frame around Dillen's face and exposing the occasional red hair among his raven crop. Freeing a hand from behind her head, Imariel placed it against his cheek. Her fingertips rested lightly on his scars, their harsh lines pale against bronze skin, while her thumb hooked under his square jaw. She could feel the beat of his pulse firm against it. Vigor indeed, she thought.

"Perhaps so." Eyes and thumb moved to his lower lip, tracing its fullness. Imariel enjoyed those lips. "Regardless, I cannot," she said, patting him twice before withdrawing her hand. Dillen paused, the fine, dark hair of his eyebrows drawn together. Then he shrugged, smiling again as he rose from her.

"If you say so." Dillen stood and strode over to the far side of the hollow, gathering up the hooded cloak from where it had been thrown. "S'pose I could use the rest," he added. "We'll be out hunting again today, most likely. There are only so many times a man can eat boiled-root stew."

Imariel sat up slowly, savoring the stretch of her muscles, the touch of air against her skin. Although she kept her hair well short of her shoulders, several of its tawny brown locks spilled forward to cover one eye. "Do you regret your offering to the Lady?" she asked, watching him sideways.

"So you were spying on us."

"Yes."

Dillen laughed again. Her frankness often seemed to amuse him. "I have many regrets," he said. He finished folding the cloak and turned to her, flashing his half-smile. "But that's not one of them."

"A twisted truth."

Dillen's smile faltered. She watched him, sensing his internal conflict, curious to see the outcome. "Bad habit," he said, finally. "Sorry."

Imariel shrugged. "I care not." He laughed.

"I know. And I should also know that you can always tell. The truth – the untwisted one – is that you may have been right when you said that I'll never understand the Lady's ways. But I'll keep trying. For you, if not for Her." Dillen tucked the folded cloak under his arm. Then he bowed low. "Your prey departs, Imariel of Galahir. Bid me fortune, for my own hunt beckons."

"You will not be hunting today."

Dillen straightened, eyebrows lifting in amused surprise. "Oh?"

Imariel nodded. Then she stood, pushing back her hair in an expansive gesture as she rose, fixing the loose locks behind her pointed ear. Dillen's eyes followed hers, his pupils large.

"Come noon, all shall be clear," she said. "Be ready."

Chapter V

The door to the knights' quarters squealed as it opened, waking Farn instantly. He pulled his blanket up over his head, groaning as the sunlight pressed his senses.

"Apologies, good sirs. I must ask that you rouse yourselves."

"Sir Headel?" Bhadein's voice was tinged with drowsiness, but otherwise steady. "What's the hour?"

"Not yet noon."

"Then sod off and let us sleep," grunted Ragneld. "We were out all night, man."

"'Fraid I can't do that. We've been summoned, all the knights. The gladestalker, she... she wants us in our armor."

There was a pause. "Is anyone on patrol?" asked Bhadein.

"Lenel took some retainers out at dawn. Kevmar went to fetch him, we have until they get back." The door squealed shut, restoring the darkness.

Sleep began to draw Farn back into its embrace, shielding him from the sound of Bhadein dismounting his cot, dulling his heavy steps across the floorboards. Then the shutters were opened, and daylight assailed him once more.

"Where is Dillen?"

Farn sat up slowly, squinting through the glare at the shared space. The knights' quarters was a cramped affair. Ten inward-facing cots were arranged along its timber walls, tucked under a roof of water-reed thatch whose beams were low enough that Bhardein had to duck under them. Nothing like his and Farn's previous home, far to the east, between the stone walls of what were now known as 'the Lost Forts'.

"He must already be up," said Farn groggily.

"More likely he wasn't here at all," said Ragneld, his words accompanied by scratching as he reached into the wiry curls of his long, blond beard. "Out on one of his mysterious excursions."

"What of it?" said Farn, more testily than he'd intended. Ragneld gave an indifferent shrug.

"Enough," said Bhardein. "Splash some water on your faces and meet me in the armory." He stepped out, closing the door behind him.

"Bugger to that. I'm getting something to eat." Ragneld slipped into his boots and stretched his arms. "You in?"

Farn dragged his sack from under his cot. "Thanks, but no. I'll grab something for the road." He began to sift through the contents, attempting to fish out a tattered pair of breeches. He'd not had time to deal with his other pair.

"Suit yourself." Ragneld left, and Farn caught a glimpse of horses being saddled before the door closed once more.

Farn paused his search. His hand had come up against something, an object long since stashed at the furthest depths of his sack. And his mind. Slowly, he ran his fingers across the smooth leather, tracing the indents on its spine. When did he last look upon its pages? A month ago? Two? Reading from it had once formed an integral part of his routine, so much so that he remembered much of it by heart. It had been a source of certainty, a touchstone to purpose. Now...

Before the guilt could grow, Farn pushed the book aside to resume his search. Less than a minute later, his breeches were bound in place, followed by boots. Farn stood, wincing as various welts announced themselves. Souvenirs from his brush with the gore. He took a moment to rub sleep from his eyes. Then he crossed the room in two long-legged strides and stepped out.

Few would ever describe the Eastfort as abounding with activity, but this was about as close as it came. Retainers hurried to and fro across its grounds, stirred to action by the knights' imminent departure. Like the knights' quarters themselves, life in the Eastfort was intimate. Excluding its central watchtower, the fort left little more than a hundred square feet of space for its inhabitants – ten knights and some two-dozen retainers in all. In addition to the work going on at the stables, they tended to the varied tasks necessary to sustain their community, since, as had always been the case with the Brotherhood people, it was as much a community as a garrison. With the exception of the very old and the very young, all were soldiers in the Brotherhood. That much at least had not changed with the sundering of their nation. Nor were the knights averse to pitching in where required, even if other lands might have deemed the tasks less than knightly. The Eastfort was itself proof. During the months of its construction more than a year ago, Farn and the other knights had labored as long and hard as any other, felling the lumber to raise a stockade and restore the watchtower.

Eastfort's armory was on the ground floor of the watchtower. As he navigated his way there, Farn cast a greeting toward a trio of fellow knights who stood waiting by the open gates, their suits of full-plate gleaming in the sun. Only Tyred spotted him, nodding acknowledgment before turning back to Edmond and Aldever. They seemed to be having an intense discussion. Attempting to read their faces, Farn was so distracted that he almost crashed headlong into Sir Bhadein.

"Careful now, son." Bhadein set a gauntleted hand on Farn's shoulder.

Bristling at the choice of words, Farn met his old master's eye. "My apologies, Sir Bhadein," said Farn finally. Bhadein's long eyebrows furrowed. He removed his hand.

"Don't take long. We'll assemble out front." Bhadein left him before he could respond, armor clinking heavily with every step. Watching him go, Farn was momentarily held by a familiar and unwelcome stew of emotions. Then he pushed it aside. Crossing the rest of the fort grounds, he drew back the watchtower's simple door, incongruently fitted beneath the ornate carved archway of its original elven builders. When Farn emerged ten minutes later, it was with his set of burnished plate strapped in place, his longsword at his hip, and great helm tucked under his arm. By the time he returned from the outdoor kitchen with a lump of bread in hand, the horses had already been led out the gate. Both Lenel and Kevmar were back from patrol, and all but Ragneld were astride their mount. Farn joined them wordlessly, mounting his charcoal courser with practiced ease. The knights of the Eastfort were assembled. Save for one.

Wondering where Dillen was, Farn tried to catch someone's eye in hopes of asking. He quickly stopped himself. There was an odd atmosphere in the group.

"What's your guess, then, Sir Farn?" asked Tyred, twisting around in his saddle. "Any idea what the gladestalkers want with us this time?" He jerked his thumb toward the treeline, where five elves stood just inside the clearing. They were dressed in the typical form-fitting leathers of the Sylvan Kin and held elegant bows of bright yew firmly at their sides. Though their eyes were hidden beneath the various leaf and frond headdresses, there was no doubt that all were fixed upon the knights. It was common enough to see them so, standing at the border of their realm for anywhere up to an hour at a time, staring unerringly at the Eastfort. Yet, somehow, it was a sight that never became familiar. Perhaps it was simply the alien beauty of the elves themselves that troubled their nerves. More likely, it was the knowledge that they were always watching, and the fact that if ever you could see them, it was only because they wished it so.

"I can't begin to imagine. It's been months since they last called on us, and that was to show us those hidden crossings on the river Omocia. They've never wanted us in armor before. Anyway," Farn continued, biting into his bread. "I saw you all talking. What's the prevailing theory?"

Tyred grunted in response, turning back.

"We haven't got a clue," said Headel. "Although fighting seems a safe bet."

Farn considered this, chewing slowly. It used to be that the knights of the Brotherhood could expect a fight to come at any moment, on any day. Thus far, their new home in Galahir had offered a different pace, with only the occasional

39

goblin warband to test their combat skills. Not to mention the odd giant boar, he added mentally. Farn swallowed his mouthful. "Have the other forts been called on?"

"There's no way to know," said Lenel, fixing him with his one good eye. "This isn't the Isles, we can't just send out a messenger on a forsaken beast."

Mention of the Brotherhood's ancestral homeland was followed by silence. It was often that way now, after the sundering, and the second exile of their people.

There was movement at the treeline. Two more gladestalkers had emerged. Unlike the others, they were continuing to come forward, crossing the clearing in graceful strides. It wasn't until they were halfway across that Farn could confirm who they were, although he'd guessed the moment he saw them. To human eyes, the ageless and defined faces of elves, not to mention their tall and supple forms, could make it difficult to tell their kind apart from one another. This was especially so when those in question were related. Imariel, moving a half-step behind her mother Elissa, was her mirror in every respect, save for the length of her tawny-brown hair; where Imariel's was hidden beneath her oak-leaf headdress, Elissa's flowed far past the limits of her own ash-spun hood.

Farn thought that if he hadn't known better, he would have mistaken them as sisters. That said, there was something in Elissa's face which suggested eldership, a softness of features where Imariel's were sharp. A steadiness in the eyes.

"Hail, gladestalkers," said Bhadein, his hand raised in greeting. The elves stopped. Elissa returned the gesture wordlessly. She cast her gaze across the assembled knights, peering at them in turn from beneath the jawless fox skull that crowned her headdress. "As you can see, we are ready to depart."

"Ten are the knights of your hold, yet only nine do I see." Elissa spoke slowly, the words fringed with the barest of accents. "Where is he?"

"We... don't know. He went out riding before your message arrived. But surely we needn't delay for his sake?"

Farn felt a flash of indignation, but he was assuaged by Elissa's response. "The druid specifically requested he be present."

"Well, there you go, Bhadein," said Kevmar, looking satisfied. "That settles it. We wait for Sir Dillen."

"No need, now," rumbled Ragneld. "Look." He was pointing west along the stockade, where a horse and rider had emerged into view. Spying the assembled group, Dillen heeled his white destrier to a gallop, his gold-trim armor catching the sunlight in glaring bursts. The impressive creature seemed to fly across the distance, powerful legs driving hard against the earth, before skidding to a halt between the knights and the two elves. Then the warhorse reared, forelegs tucked back, and leapt up to perform a flawless capriole.

The cheers of the knights were interspersed with laughter, many shaking their heads in mock disapproval. Farn whooped, clapping his gauntlets together as Dillen bowed from his saddle. Only Bhadein was silent.

Rising from his bow, Dillen looked around, half-smile flashing through the opening in his barbute helm.

"It would seem that I'm a little late!"

Chapter VI

There were no roads between the trees of Galahir, and few open paths of which to speak. Instead, the denizens of the forest made use of a great web of trails, said to extend the entire length of the woodland. It was a fraught practice. Often a trail's presence was so subtle as to defy pursuit; other times it might appear clearly at first, then decide to vanish from beneath the trusting traveler's feet. Sometimes, Farn could swear the ones around the Eastfort had upped and relocated in the night.

For the first half hour as the knights followed the gladestalkers into their domain, Farn did his best to keep track of the twists and turns of their route, at one point noting the small red-berry copse to their east, then the mushroom-laden outcropping to their west not ten minutes later. It was as the elves led them to double back for a third time – or at least, that's how it seemed to him – that Farn gave up, having lost all sense of direction. Drawing his horse off the trail, he heeled it to a canter, moving along the line until he reached Dillen at the front. He drew up beside him.

"Farn," said Dillen, not so much as glancing at him. His head was bare, the barbute helm hanging against his horse's flank, his mail coif down. "Whatever it is had better be important. I'm in no mood for games." Before Farn could begin to think of a response, Dillen flicked his head sideways, half-smile bright. He winked.

Farn laughed. "You? Games? Never would've crossed my mind."

"I should hope not. Can't go risking my reputation as a model of seemliness."

Farn shook his head, helpless not to grin. "It's nothing. Just wanted a change of view."

"Tired of looking at horse-rump? I know the feeling."

They rode on in silence for several minutes. Farn continued to snatch glances at Dillen's Basilean armor. There were no two ways about it; the set was magnificent. Every piece was a work of art, from the pointed pauldrons and their golden-wing ornamentation, to the intricate inlays on the poleyns, which depicted excerpts from the Eloicon written along flowing scrolls. Robes of celestine blue were wrapped around the breastplate, held in place by a gold pin, into which was set a large, red gemstone. In contrast, Farn's suit was almost entirely functional, being smooth-faced and solid plate with nary an auriferous strand in sight. A handsome set to be sure, and robust enough to endure a full campaign season with little upkeep. All the same, Dillen's armor was about as different from the Brotherhood's as plate could be, while still just as effective.

Many of my ex-brothers and sisters will be wearing such armor now, thought Farn, not for the first time. It was a thought that bore many others in tow, all troubling. Basilea presented itself to the world as being the front line against the corruption of the Abyss, when in fact that title had always belonged to the Brotherhood. For centuries while the Basileans flourished in the sun-soaked south, it was Farn's people who had shielded them from hellflame, dedicating their entire society to the Eternal Watch. Only on those occasions when the Abyssal forces gathered with such strength that they could break past the Brotherhood line did the armies of the Hegemon sally forth, halting the already-blunted attack and proclaiming their glory before the Shining Ones. No aid had been offered by Basilea during the long years of the Watch, no supplies or coin. Not without attendant demands, at any rate, all of which the Brotherhood had refused to countenance, preserving both their independence as well as the purity of their cause.

Then it happened. A little over two years ago, the borders of the Abyss had suddenly expanded, swallowing in an instant many of the Brotherhood's strongest bastions and rapidly encroaching upon the others. Recognizing the calamity that faced Pannithor, the Brotherhood sent warning to the south. The Basilean Duma dithered in its response, the Hegemon himself having apparently been stunned by the scale of the crisis. But not the Green Lady. Within days, Her forces arrived to bolster the line, and it was She who had spurred the Golden Horn to finally sound.

When the floodwaters settled, and the Abyss was contained beneath the surface, the surviving members of the Brotherhood were faced with a choice. The first option was that they keep what little remained of their lands, but only as vassals to Basilea; the second, that they leave and pledge themselves to the one whose aid had mattered most. The one who had led them to victory. Most fell in with the former, but the Devoted, mages of the Brotherhood, were undivided in their support of the latter and swung many to their cause. Some rejected the choice altogether, arguing that the Brotherhood should continue to forge its own path in the world, independent of all others. The ensuing debate was fierce. On several occasions it had nearly come to blows between the Exemplars. In the end however, it was clear that unity could not be preserved, and the factions went their separate ways. At the time, Farn had been torn. He felt no desire to leave the Warden Lands behind, but nor could he stomach seeing them become yet another holding of Basilea.

But then something Bhadein had said resonated with Farn, giving him the resolve to choose a path. His old master had been full of sorrow, watching from horseback as the people of the Brotherhood literally pulled apart from one another. Farn had been at his side, both he and Bhadein initially resigned to follow Master Odo of the Order of the Abyssal Hunt into the grip of their old rival to the south, a choice born more from inertia than conviction. He could recall their exhaustion, the ache in their limbs and the ash in their throats. Their hair was still short.

"The Eternal Watch," Bhadein had growled suddenly. "Show me greater hubris than that oath, and I will name it rival to Calisor himself."

Farn had looked round at him, stunned. Even if he had at times been an overly-tasking master, Bhadein was still in many ways an ideal knight of the Brotherhood, his heart just and his honor pristine. More than anything, Bhadein had always been a devout believer in their cause.

"What claim can we humans make to the eternal? None. Yet we swear it anyway. But a god... a god who acts when the world needs it... Her watch is more than eternal. It is boundless."

Then Bhadein had turned in his saddle, gazing past Farn toward the flooded Abyss.

"Let them have it," he'd muttered. "Let them hold their line in the sand, for all the good it does. And let the Hegemon foot the bill. I'd rather be a sword in the Green Lady's hand than a brick in their wall."

And with that, he had gone, spurring his horse toward the column that was marching west. Farn had watched, the clarity of Bhadein's words ringing out in his mind. When he followed a minute later, Farn did not look back.

None of which was to say that he did not miss his previous life. They all did, Bhadein perhaps most of all. But it was another reason why Farn felt so grateful for Sir Dillen; a paladin of Basilea, whose feats of valor were fast seeing him become the most legendary hero of the age, and he had left behind a future of fame and glory in the south to swear himself to the Green Lady. He had chosen to stand with them.

"You should take care, Farn."

"Hm? Why's that?"

Dillen was looking at him, round eyes full of amusement. "If you keep thinking so hard, you'll put lines all over that pretty face."

"That so? I'll have to think on that."

Dillen laughed. "Ahh, what a waste. If I looked like you, I swear, I'd be living far, far from here."

"...I don't believe that."

"No?" Dillen sighed. "You're probably right. At best it was a... twisted truth." He laughed again and met Farn's eyes. "Anyway, out with it. What's on your mind?"

Having no desire to share his reflections, Farn grabbed the next nearest thought. "Just wondering where we're headed, I s'pose."

"Ah."

"...The others think we're going to fight."

"And you?"

"I think it's something else. The elves are secretive, but I can't imagine why they wouldn't tell us if we were facing combat."

Dillen nodded. Then, in a declarative tone that imitated the elven accent, he said "'You will not be hunting today.'"

"...Is that a riddle, Dillen? Here I thought you were in no mood for games."

"I've been known to change moods on occasion. But yes, I believe you're right. There shouldn't be any need for fighting. Not where we're going."

"Ha! So you do know!"

"Shhh! Not so loud!"

Farn glanced back. "What? The others can't hear–"

"Not them!" Dillen gave an upward flick of his head, square jaw indicating toward the gladestalkers. They were far along the trail, spread out among the trees.

"But... surely they can't..."

"Perhaps not," said Dillen, speaking in little more than a whisper, "though I wouldn't stake much on it."

He leant over slightly, lowering his voice further. Farn hunched to listen.

"Yes, I believe I know where we're going. They're trying to throw off our sense of direction, of course. But I've been there before. I can see them doing it."

"Then where–" Farn stopped, a possible answer having leapt to his mind. "The Lady's glade? Where you went for aid in the battle against Zelgarag?!"

Dillen frowned. "What? No! By the Ones, Farn, if you're going to be so ridiculous then I won't tell you anything."

"...Of course. Sorry."

The paladin let out a long breath. "...It's fine." Dillen was still frowning, but he now looked more sheepish than annoyed. Farn cursed himself inwardly. His excitement had got the better of him. All among the knights knew that Dillen didn't like talking about his famed fight against the demon champion. Though he'd never say why, Farn thought he could guess. War was hell, but never was it more so than when faced with servants of the Wicked Ones. If there was even an ounce of truth to the stories – Farn felt certain there was far more than that – then only those who wished to boast would ever return to it. Dillen, for all his swagger, never boasted of battle. It was yet another quality for

Farn to admire, although he did at times find himself wishing that Dillen would renege on that particular virtue. Just once, he'd have liked to hear Dillen's version of events.

"So... where are they taking us?" Farn whispered.

Dillen turned to him, the half-smile creeping back across his lips.

"Why, to their most closely guarded secret! A place where only true servants of the Lady may enter!" He laughed. "I tell you, Farn, it's something to behold."

Farn blinked. "You're not saying..."

"Do not ask me why, I haven't the slightest notion – but yes! We're going to Calenemel – a settlement of the Sylvan elves!"

Chapter VII

Crossing the threshold of Calenemel was like stepping into a dream. One moment the forest was a familiar wild of spruce and pine; majestic, as with all he'd seen of Galahir, yet solid. But the next it was filled with trees the likes of which Farn could never have imagined, broad as houses and taller than the towers of the Lost Forts. Birdsong slid from competitive chirrups into harmonious refrain, and warm, green-hued light floated down to the undergrowth in broad curtains.

Turning to express his astonishment to the others, Farn saw that they were all gazing upward, faces open with childlike wonder. One look was enough to see why. Carved from the heavy boughs of the trees themselves was an organic network of bridges and walkways, connecting the many arched buildings that clung to their trunks, suspended beneath the endless canopy.

"I told you it was something, didn't I?"

"What…" began Farn. He swallowed. So many questions. "How do they get up there?" Far above them, several of the elves had stopped to peer over the intricately patterned parapets. Most continued as if the knights weren't there.

"Beats me. Perhaps they fly."

"Why have you stopped?" called Elissa.

The knights lowered their gaze. All seven of the gladestalkers were standing in a line a short way ahead, looking back. While their expressions were impassive, Farn thought he could feel the displeasure radiate from them.

"We haven't arrived, then?" asked Dillen.

"No." The elves turned and strode off. Dillen gave Farn a shrug, his great pauldrons bouncing. The knights followed.

The forest beyond Calenemel did not return to the sort of familiar groves which surrounded the Eastfort. Rather, it seemed the elven settlement sat on the frontier of an entirely different woodland, by turns extreme and ordered; extreme in its patches of blue-topped toadstools, whose glowing heads were wide as a dwarf's; ordered in the symmetry of its profile, the sense that the contours of each and every tree were made just so. Beams of light fell along their path at regular intervals, and where they were absent, luminous insects danced in languorous figures of eight. Not long after crossing through Calenemel, the knights were surprised to hear their horses' padding steps be replaced with the bright clack of iron on stone. Though mostly hidden by dirt, a quick scan of the trail revealed the lichen-stained remnants of a flagstone floor. The path began to climb, the condition of the stonework gradually improving with every step. As they followed it around what appeared to be an over-broad beech tree, they saw the elves had turned to them once more.

"Dismount here," said Elissa. "You will continue on foot."

"I don't see anywhere to tie the horses," said Kevmar. "Our rope won't get around these trunks. Someone will have to stay with behind with them."

"No. You will leave them. Worry not, they shan't wander, here."

Their armor produced a roll of clinks as the knights stepped down onto the forest floor.

"Do you hear something?" asked Tyred.

"...No?" said Farn. Beyond the dreamlike birdsong and the occasion grunt from the horses, he couldn't detect anything new. "Why? What are you hearing?"

"I'm not sure. Humming?"

The knights stopped moving. Farn realized that there was something. A hum as Tyred said, distant, not the sort of sound produced by one thing, but by many things happening at once.

"You are hearing the assembly," said Elissa.

"Assembly?" asked Dillen. "Assembly of who?"

"Those who've sworn oaths of loyalty to the Lady," answered Imariel.

Elissa met her daughter's eyes and nodded. "All must be represented." She turned her attention back to the knights. "Even men."

The knights were quiet. Each of them had sworn such an oath when they came to Galahir a year and a half ago, their vow made under guidance from the druids who'd met them at the forest's edge. Not one of them was of a type to treat sworn words lightly. Nor to break them.

"No chance you'll want to tell me just what it is we're assembling for?" asked Dillen, his tone breezy. Elissa looked at him steadily.

"Enough questions." Elissa turned to set off, the other gladestalkers turning with her. Except for Imariel.

"It is not far now," she said. "You will see it soon."

"Imariel," said Elissa, stride unbroken. Then she said something in elven tongue, the mellifluous words made stern by her pitch. Curious to see Imariel's reaction, Farn found himself looking into her face. She met his eye for a second, and in the stillness of her features, Farn was once more reminded of a hunting bird, though one which now sat idly on its perch. Imariel turned away, following her mother. The knights set off after them.

By turns, the hum of voices grew louder and clearer as they continued up the incline, while beneath their feet the path of pockmarked flagstones slowly morphed into a deep-stepped stairway. More stonework began to appear at either side, some being no more than the crumbled remains of a wall projecting above the frond, while others were for the most part intact, such as a plateau courtyard framed by trios of tall lancet archways, at the center of which stood an elaborately sculpted plinth. The statue it must once have held aloft was gone; only its bare feet remained.

Farn soon stopped looking at anything beyond his next step. Sweat was thick on him, his hair sticking uncomfortably against the back of his neck. Normally he could go far longer than this in his armor, and in far higher temperatures – depending on the wind that day, the lands surrounding the Abyss could range from merely warm to resembling the inside of a sulfur-choked kiln. The forest was not nearly so hot. Unlike his previous home however, the air here was weighted with a cloying moisture. It felt as though each breath gave him less, and each step cost him more.

"Look there!" said Aldever, pointing up the stairway. Farn looked and saw a line of the same lancet archways running along the top of the incline, curving away on the far sides to circle inward. Only a handful of trees stretched their limbs over the arches, leaving the sky beyond clear for as far as could yet be seen. They were almost there.

"I suggest you put your helmets on," said Imariel, glancing back, "and keep one hand on the pommel of your blades. All must arrive as warriors of the Lady."

Lesser men and women would have grumbled, or at the very least have let slip a sigh. No such sounds emerged from the knights as they drew up their coifs and donned their helms. Wordlessly, they adopted a marching column of two by five, Dillen and Bhadein at the fore. With left hands resting on pommels, they set off in effortless lockstep toward the assembly.

Even with armor now placed over the knights' ears, the hum of abundant voices was transformed as they crested the final step, lifting sharply from deadened lows into an expansive crash of sound. It was noise unlike any crowd Farn had ever heard, a throng of language and vocal chords whose extremes lay far beyond those of men alone. The smells too were distinct, being neither the unwashed odor of lower classes nor of soldiery long on march, but rather an intermix of disparate scents. All were alien.

Whatever his other senses had to report, it was Farn's eyes that were in for the greatest shock. Through the narrow field afforded by his visor, he saw the forest thrown back at least sixty yards in every direction, displaced by rows upon rows of deep stone steps sweeping outward and down into the form of an enormous semi-circular structure, centering around a broad platform of white marble. Each of the rows were lined with beings, sentient denizens of the forest who were grouped according to kind – there were Sylvan elves of Calenemel, famed forest guard arrayed with their tall helms and narrow shields; salamander warriors, mighty lizard folk whose scales seemed to burn with a blood-deep heat; naiad hunters, blue-skinned and red-eyed amphibians whose bronze armor and tridents were hued by cool verdigris; a variety of bestial men, many with hooves and horns not unlike the abyssal enemy, but formed upon creatures of noble bearing and countenance, fauns and satyrs. Farn had seen many of their kinds before, indeed he had fought alongside salamanders when the Lady's armies marched to assist the Brotherhood – but he had never seen them all together like this. He had never seen anything like this.

The knights were directed by the elves to stand along an empty row at the back of the structure, from which Farn could continue to gaze out across the incomprehensible spectacle. A number of individuals turned to look up at the knights as they arranged themselves.

"What sort of a place is this?" Farn asked Dillen, raising his voice over the din. Many of the assembled creatures were talking among themselves, and though none seemed to be shouting, the volume of their voices was inexplicably magnified into a broiling sea of sound. Only the elves were silent.

"An amphitheater."

Farn glanced at him, and despite the great helm hiding all but his eyes, Dillen must have sensed his blank expression.

"Don't tell me the Brotherhood don't have them? Where did the bards entertain in your lands? Where did dramatists display their craft?"

Farn frowned. Southern frivolities, he thought. "We didn't have time for such things."

"Pity. But you had temples, of course. You remember how the priest's voice would carry across the pews? The temples were built with that in mind. It's the same idea here, only bigger. When the druids start to speak from down there, we'll be able to hear them clear as if they were ten feet away!"

Farn looked to where Dillen had pointed and realized he'd missed the most remarkable sight in the amphitheater. Beyond the marble stage at the structure's center were the crumbling remains of what must once have been a grand building, its stonework delicate and its walls punctuated with narrow columns in the style of the lancet archways. A line of centaurs stood before the ruin, facing silently toward the assembly with polearms in hand. But what truly caught Farn's eye was the tree. It wasn't particularly large – not when compared with those they'd passed on the way through Calenemel – but it was striking. It had grown inside the ruined structure and looked to have burst its way free from the confines of the masonry, its thick boughs punching through the walls, its cherry-blossom crown supplanting whatever roof had once enclosed it. At the center of the crown, projecting above the pink and white efflorescence, a single length of trunk formed the uncanny likeness of a maiden, her arms held wide and a pair of antler-shaped branches atop her head. The tree's bark was near black in color, contrasting starkly against the maiden's flowering hair. Except, Farn realized it wasn't a maiden at all. It was a lady.

As soon as Farn thought to point out the curious effigy, he saw movement among the line of centaurs. Their formation was parting at the center, revealing the arched entrance to the ruin around the tree. The assembly hushed as several figures stepped through the gap. At their fore walked a pair of druids, the first of them a human woman, tall and lithe as an elf, dark of skin and hair, draped in well-worn leathers and with a pelt of brown fur slung about her shoulders. Even at this distance, Farn recognized her instantly. The druid Haili leaned on her staff of interwoven vine as she walked, the assortment of inlaid glass and stones glinting in the daylight. She had been among those who heard the knights' oaths those many months ago, and it was she who had then directed them to their track of woodland around the ruined watchtower which would come to be named Eastfort. They had not seen her since.

The druid to Haili's left was also tall, at least eight feet by Farn's estimation. There however, all similarity ended. Living wood had formed in the likeness of noble races, walking straight-backed on timber legs, its body the bone white of exposed hardwood, its face the gnarled gray of aged bark. Clutched in long arms, its winding staff was topped with a single shard of red shale, itself host to a range of colorful mosses and lichens, and atop the creature's head a ruff of grass sprouted green and hale between large, flat antlers. Its heavy steps rang out across the amphitheater. The pair was followed by three others, two men and an elf, who while also bearing the look and attire of the Green Lady's cult, seemed younger and more deferential to the druids. Farn wondered if they were apprentices. The druids stopped, and when the tree figure looked up along the rows, Farn saw its eyes glow blue.

"Loyal soldiers of the Green Lady," began Haili, her voice rich and her accent exotic. Dillen had been right, the druid had only to speak firmly to be heard by all. "The call was given, and you have answered!"

As soon as she finished, the three apprentices began to address the various groups in attendance, each employing a different tongue. Their continuing translation quickly came to resemble a warped echo of Haili's speech.

"Before we commence with the sorry task that lies before us, let us make our prayer to She who leads us in Her purpose, and reaffirm the ties of faith that bind us to the Balance." Haili pointed her staff up to the effigy tree as she spoke, and once the translations were complete, she immediately began to lead the assembly in prayer. Farn repeated the familiar words mindlessly, his thoughts consumed by what might await them in this meeting. Haili had greeted them as soldiers and now spoke of a sorry task ahead. Could it be that they faced a fight after all?

The prayer given, Haili turned to face the assembly once more.

"Sit, friends."

They sat. Farn saw the ranks of elf forest guard removing their helms, and he took that as sign enough to follow suit. Freed from the confines of his visor, the scale of the gathering before him redoubled its impression.

"It warms my spirit to see us together again. Not since the war of two-years past did we last have cause. A time of great conflict has seen its upheaval brought to balance by a time of peace."

Murmurs of agreement rippled through the assembly, heads nodding lightly. Farn cast a sideways glance at his fellow knights. All to his left had removed their helmets, and behind their frowns, Farn thought he could detect the same question that had risen in him. Peace and war in balance? It made no sense. For the Brotherhood, the war against the Abyss was without end. One did not earn a reprieve, not even through victory. Did the followers of the Green Lady see it differently? Farn glanced the other way and saw that even Dillen was looking on with a stiff expression, his lips tight. Bhadein's face was a mystery – he hadn't removed his helm.

"Alas, as with the constant change of the seasons, or the cycles of the moon, so too does peace end. The time comes for us to turn our attention toward the world, and to those who would seek to upset the harmony of our Lady. Our actions must be guided by a single purpose – to protect the forest of Galahir."

Haili let the words hang for several seconds, her gaze slowly passing across the assembly. Farn suppressed a shiver. For a moment, it felt as if the druid and he had locked eyes; worse, that she had somehow reached into his thoughts. Her gaze continued across the rows, and the feeling passed as quickly as it had come.

"Let today's proceedings serve as a reminder of that purpose. There can be no cause in our hearts greater than that of the Lady, and no path save that which She has set before us."

With that, Haili turned toward the line of waiting centaurs and nodded. They parted again, and three more centaurs emerged from inside the ruin. The two on each side were armed with broad-headed axes, while the central one had his hands clasped at his front. No, not clasped, thought Farn. Bound. He was a prisoner.

The guards led their charge across to center stage, the druids having stepped to either side. Then they moved to join the line of others, the rhythmic clack of their hooves sounding loudly across the rows of silent onlookers.

"Inadru Rainborne, Chief of Gray-Crow. You are here before this gathering to face the consequences of your actions, and thereby expunge the ignominy you have brought upon your clan."

"I know why I'm here." The centaur spoke in a flawless Basilean accent, not so much as glancing at the druid. Inadru Rainborne was an impressive example of his kind, his face handsome and his form powerful. The rich auburn of his mane and beard contrasted gently with the pale mahogany coat of his horse half, and his sun-kissed skin suggested a great deal of time spent in lands beyond the forest. Though his voice bore the assuredness of one familiar with command, Farn got the sense that Inadru was young; or rather, younger than he would have expected for a clan chief.

"On the charge of defying our Lady's will," Haili continued, "in a trial by the laws of your clan, your people have made their judgment – you are guilty!"

A hissing sound emanated from the assembly. It reminded Farn of the noise made by the many volcanic fissures that surrounded the Abyss, steam spitting through cracks in the rocks.

"When one of your standing is so found, punishment may only be pronounced before the eyes of the Lady's servants. This assembly is your sentencing."

More hissing. Inadru looked out across the rows, his gaze unflinching.

"Before we commence, have you anything to say?"

The hissing faded slowly. "I remain a loyal servant of the Lady," began Inadru, his voice steady, "and I accept without condition both the judgment of my clan and whatever fate awaits me." He spoke with finality, and Farn looked to Haili for her response. Then, as if on impulse, the centaur added, "I only acted in accordance with my conscience."

Shouts burst forth from the across the amphitheater, none more furious than those of the naiads, who got to their feet and rattled their tridents against their bracers. Even the elves were shaking their heads in open disapproval. For their part, the knights looked on in stunned silence.

Haili raised her hand and the assembly fell quiet once more. "Conscience has no bearing in these matters, Inadru. You of all people should know that."

Inadru said nothing, although he did finally meet the druid's eye. They stayed that way for several seconds. Then Haili turned to the effigy tree and lifted her staff in both hands.

"By the Lady's will, this assembly seeks a path of justice!"

"And only in Balance may we be just!" intoned the assembly. Farn almost missed what was said, so confused was the overlay of different languages.

Haili faced the prisoner. "Inadru Rainborne. For your crime, we strip you of all titles, and we commit you to an exile of no less than ten summers in the darkest corner of our Lady's land, as to the darkest corner of Her hearts. May you find the path of Balance, or else perish in the turmoil of your peregrinations."

At the completion of Haili's pronouncement, the centaur guards stepped forward once again. Taking Inadru by the arms, they began to lead him up the center of the amphitheater. This time the crowd was silent, and there was no sound save the clacking of their march up the steps. Each row stood up as the centaurs passed, turning to put their backs to them. The knights were on the final row and followed suit when their time came. Farn had no name for the feeling in his stomach as he turned away from the ex-chief, but he found it unpleasant all the same. When Inadru was gone, the assembly resumed their seats.

"That concludes this matter," said Haili. "Depart, friends, and…"

All eyes in the amphitheater turned to the tree-druid. It seemed to Farn as if he had heard it speak from across a great distance, only not with his ears, but in his mind, a foreign thought rumbling like far-off thunder. The druid was looking at Haili, and she was looking back. After several seconds of silence, Haili nodded.

"Of course." She turned to face the assembly. "The druid Haranak wishes it be known that the omens foretell of dark times ahead. The sorry cause of our gathering today is only the beginning – we must remain vigilant, and mindful of our duty to the Lady."

With that, the assembly rose as one and then split as the various races departed for their realms. Soon the knights were reunited with their mounts, and Elissa's gladestalkers led them back through the mysterious forest, through Calenemel and along the winding trail of familiar woodland. They did not speak until they had returned to the Eastfort, where a bowl of boiled-root stew awaited each of them. Even then, sitting around their table with stodgy soup in hand, not a word was uttered about what they had witnessed that day. It hung over them in silence.

Chapter VIII

Farn was alone in the knights' quarters. Sitting upright in his cot, he stared down at the patch of daylight that spilled through the window and across his lap, illuminating the faded ink of an open book. He hadn't managed to read much. In fact, he hadn't turned the page in close to an hour. The text swam before his eyes, the assuredness of its words and phrases making awkward bedfellows to his thoughts.

The door swung open noisily. Stirred from his rumination, Farn looked round in surprise.

"There you are." Bhadein's great figure had to hunch to peer through the doorway. He was wearing his riding leathers. "They've spotted something from the tower. Lenel and I are heading out."

"Goblins?" asked Farn, turning to set his legs on the floor. As he did so, Farn flipped the book closed and dragged it behind his back.

Bhadein shook his head. "Lookout doesn't think so. He said it seemed to be a handful of human folk, peasants rather than soldiers. Bandits at worst."

"Right." Farn slipped into his boots and stood. "Let me gather my gear, then."

"No time. Sir Lenel and I are ready now. As I said, it's probably just some poachers. But get ready all the same – just in case."

Bhadein closed the door before Farn could respond. Rankling slightly at being so ordered, he stood motionless for several seconds, listening to the sound of Bhadein and Lenel's horses riding out of the Eastfort. Then he turned and looked down at the closed book, its silver letters bright against the dark leather cover.

Holy Eloicon

Farn returned the book to the sack beneath his cot and went outside.

*****

"I can't remember the last time we had this much excitement."

Farn looked round to see Dillen coming toward him. The Basilean had just emerged from the watchtower and was fiddling with the strap on one of his bracers.

"And just our luck, too. With all the hunting, we haven't slept a full night in… Ones," said Dillen, stifling a yawn, "a couple of days at least." He stepped up next to Farn. "Aren't you tired?"

Farn forced a smile. "I suppose." He was already back in his plate and had been watching the retainers as they re-readied his horse. The other knights, similarly suited-up, were standing by the gates in anticipation of Bhadein and Lenel's return, ready for whatever came of it.

Dillen grunted. "As if I needed another reason to envy your youth." Then he smiled and patted Farn on the back, his gauntlet clinking against plate. Farn was barely listening. His gaze had once more fallen upon Dillen's poleyns and the ornate Eloicon script that was carved into them.

"Dillen…"

"Hm?"

Farn met his eye. "Do you… do you still pray to the Shining Ones?"

Dillen's eyebrows rose. "…Yes."

"Often?"

"…About as often as ever, I'd say."

"As often as you pray to the Green Lady?"

Dillen held Farn's gaze in silence for several seconds. Then he looked away. "Ah. I see."

"Please, don't misunderstand. It's not that I regret my oath…"

"No?"

Farn shook his head. "Far from it." He cast his gaze about, as if something in the Eastfort grounds might help him find the next words. "Only… only before, it all made sense. I never noticed at the time. Life was demanding in the Warden Lands – drills, patrols, the endless fight with the Abyss. But it was also… I don't know. Neater?" He looked at Dillen, feeling more than a little embarrassed for such an inarticulate ramble. I shouldn't have said anything, he thought.

"There's a saying in the western realms," said Dillen, still looking away. "It goes, 'Even though a sword has two edges, it cannot cut two ways at once.'"

"But… doesn't that mean we can't follow both–"

A call sounded from the watchtower. "Movement! East treeline!"

The knights at the gate rushed out, one hand on the blades at their hips. Dillen turned to Farn.

"It means that each swing must choose its edge, not that the two aren't part of the same weapon." Then with a flash of his half-smile, Dillen set off at a steady run toward the gate. Farn followed, his thoughts swirling around Dillen's words. Try as he might, they would not sit well.

* * * * *

The lookout had been right. Arriving at the forest's eastern frontier, Bhadein and Lenel came across a group of peasant folk taking shelter beneath the canopy's shade. The group was small – only nine – and they were about as far from poachers and bandits as either could have imagined. Most were women, and they had children among their number, a girl and her younger brother. Of the two men, the first was barely out of adolescence, and the second was badly wounded, apparently slashed across the chest from shoulder to abdomen. They had no possessions save for the clothes on their backs, and though their faces showed gratitude as the knights led them into the Eastfort, all could see the fear it masked, the residue of horrors witnessed. It was a familiar sight for those acquainted with the consequences of war, which all in the Brotherhood were.

"They're from a village named 'Talle', about a day's journey on foot to the east. They say they were attacked in the night," explained Lenel. He was filling in Farn and the others, save for Tyred, who was examining the wounded man with Bhadein. It appeared to Farn as if the man's family had been the only one to escape intact, his wife and their fair-haired children looking on anxiously as the two knights cut away the blood-soaked tunic. It was uncertain if the family would remain so for long. Sweat coated the man's skin, and he spluttered as Tyred attempted to give him water.

"A day's journey on foot, you say?" confirmed Dillen. "That likely means they didn't stop 'til they reached the forest. Not easy, with a wound like that."

Lenel nodded. "Apparently they had to take turns hauling him the last mile or so."

"Who attacked them?" asked Farn. "Bandits?"

"Abyssals."

They looked round in surprise. "What?!" exclaimed Kevmar.

Lenel's expression was grim. "I know. But there's no other explanation. Not for what they described."

"And what did they describe?" rumbled Ragneld.

"A nightmare."

Several seconds of silence passed before any could think of a response to this.

"No chance it was just a group of bandits? Perhaps they were confused?" asked Headel finally.

"Oh, they were confused all right," said Lenel. "But not so much that they'd mistake a bandit raid for a demonic massacre."

"What about orcs?" asked Aldever. "Many who don't know better would take them for demons, and Ones know they're as disposed to carnage."

Lenel shook his head. "If it was not abyssals, then I am at a loss. Talk to Bhadein if you want. He thinks the same as I. Only, don't ask them," he added, nodding toward the peasants. Retainers had given them bread and broth, and they ate in a huddle, casting nervous glances toward the watchtower's elven architecture. "It was hard enough for them to tell us the once. We should give them some peace, for now."

"Of course," said Edmond. He paused, then added, "Assuming it is abyssals that attacked them, then there is a chance they are not the only survivors."

"Not yet, you mean," said Ragneld.

"Sir Dillen!" Bhadein had stood up from the wounded man and was beckoning Dillen forward. Straight-backed, Dillen strode over to join them.

"Someone lend me a hand, here," said Tyred. He'd helped to sit the man up and was preparing to wrap binding around his torso. "Sir Farn?"

Farn stepped over smartly, but the man's wife had already crouched at Tyred's side.

"Beggin' your pardon, sir knight," she said, bracing her husband's back. "You'll be lettin' me help?" Despite the respectful tone, the determined look in her eyes suggested to Farn that there was little chance she'd take no for an answer.

"Vandi…" said the man, barely managing a whisper.

"Try not to speak," said Tyred firmly. Then he turned to the wife. "That's perfectly fine. You hold him steady while we get this set. Sir Farn?"

Farn crouched down, and together they bound the clean fabric tightly across the man's chest.

"What's his name?" asked Tyred.

"Cossus, sir," said Vandi. "Cossus Barchet."

"And those are your little angels, I take it?" Tyred nodded toward the two children who were holding hands a short distance away. They seemed to be staring wide-eyed at Dillen. Must be the armor, Farn thought.

"Yes, sir," said Vandi, "Juttah's our first, and Mannes the little one…"

Farn stopped listening. Absently passing the roll of fabric around Cossus's torso, he instead focused his attention on Bhadein and Dillen, catching the edge of their conversation.

"…was able to ease his pain a little," Bhadein was saying in a low voice, "but I never did have much talent for healing magic. I'm given to understand that the paladins place greater priority on such skills?"

"Depends on the order in question," said Dillen. "I'm afraid my power in that area is next to none."

"…I see." Neither said anything for several seconds. They didn't need to. Farn knew a dying man when he saw one. There was still a chance that Cossus would pull through, but it was between him and the gods, now. It was out of the knights' hands.

"All that remains then is the matter of the attack itself. Did Sir Lenel fill you in?"

Dillen took a moment to answer. "He did. Said you also think it was... you know."

"I do. We have to send word to the other forts. If the servants of the Wicked Ones are this far west, it means they must have broken through the Warden Lands."

"How can that be? I thought..." Dillen lowered his voice further, and Farn only caught the end of what he said, "...flooded?"

"It was."

"So, what? The waters are gone?"

"Perhaps. Or perhaps they were less effective than we thought. Regardless, we have to alert the forts."

"...All due respect, Bhadein, but that's not the next step."

"What do you mean?"

"You know our orders. Anything we have to report goes straight to the druids. They decide if there's a need to rally the forts."

Farn glanced over. Dillen and Bhadein were squared off, neither shifting their gaze from the other. The difference in their heights meant Bhadein towered over the Basilean, but Dillen stood firm.

"Sir Dillen," Bhadein began, his low voice verging on a growl, "the Brotherhood has been fighting the abyssals for over a thousand years. When an attack occurs on our frontier, we ride out in force to investigate."

"All right. Let's say we do that. The nearest fort is in the Torileth weald, Sir Wilbur and his men. That's, what, two days ride south?"

"...Thereabouts," grumbled Bhadein.

"The druids can get word to them tomorrow, if they choose. Maybe sooner. This isn't the Warden Lands, Bhadein. Things work differently, here. And so must we."

A thought occurred to Farn. Tyred had finished setting Cossus's bind, and with Vandi's help was laying him back down. Standing quickly, Farn stepped over to Dillen and Bhadein.

"We should go to the druids," he said. Bhadein turned to him, his lengthy eyebrows furrowed. Dillen seemed to be restraining a smile.

"There you are, then," said Dillen. "I'll tell the tower to send out the signal." He began to move away but stopped when he saw Farn shaking his head.

"No. We should go to Haili, try to find her at Calenemel."

"Why?" asked Dillen.

"We don't know how quickly she and the elves will come, if even she does at all. And this man needs help." Farn gestured toward Cossus. "They can heal him." Both Sir Tyred and Vandi looked up as he said this. Hope bloomed in the woman's face, and Farn felt the weight of responsibility as it came to rest upon his shoulders.

"That may be so," said Bhadein, "but you are forgetting something, Sir Farn. Without the gladestalkers to guide us, we cannot get to Calenemel." Farn looked to Dillen, who met his gaze with a tight expression. Bhadein followed the look. "Am I wrong?"

Dillen said nothing for several moments. Then he sighed. "Through no fault of your own, Sir Bhadein, I assure you. But yes." He cast a glance across the other knights, all having come forward to listen.

"I know the way."

Chapter IX

It was decided that Bhadein and Lenel would stay behind, where they could ready the fort in case the others should return with marching orders. The rest of the knights would depart on foot. According to Dillen, there was no need for horses. In the end however, two were indeed brought – Bhadein's great charger and Lenel's courser. The first was to bear the wounded Cossus, and the second both of the Barchet children, with their mother leading it by the reins. The family had been adamant – they would not be separated. Any frustrations were quickly diffused when Dillen observed that it might in fact be better for the druid to hear direct testimony of the attack. And so, for the second time that day, the knights of Eastfort set out for Calenemel.

Dillen and Ragneld led the way. They were followed closely by Edmond and Kevmar, then Tyred along with Bhadein's steed carrying a slumped Cossus in the saddle. The children and their mother came next, with Farn a short way behind, both Headel and Aldever taking up the rear. Marching along the narrow trail, the knights' steps took on an instinctual rhythm, the links and joints of their armor sounding together in concord. There was not a hint in their bearing of noon's uncertainty – they were moving with purpose.

The trail curved sharply around a red-berry copse, and Farn noted with mild amusement the way the Barchet children sat up straight and craned their necks, taking their chance to steal a look at the front of the column. They were staring at Dillen.

Acting on impulse, Farn quickened his step, coming up alongside the children.

"That's some suit of armor, isn't it?" he said.

The children spun their heads round to him in a synchronous movement. For a moment, Farn worried he'd frightened them, but no fear showed in their faces. Their expressions were blank, deep shadows under their eyes revealing a sleepless night. Farn supposed he appeared the same, albeit minus their haunted aspect.

"It... er," he tried to continue, smile faltering. "You must be wondering why it looks so different to the rest of ours?"

"It's from Basilea," said the boy. "Paladin plate."

Farn blinked. "That... that's right. Your name's Mannes?"

Mannes nodded.

"Know a lot about armor do you, Mannes?"

The boy shrugged. "I know some stuff."

"What stuff?"

Mannes looked away, apparently trying to catch another glimpse of the gold-trim suit. The girl, however, was still looking at Farn.

"Is that man really Sir Dillen?" she asked.

The question left Farn slightly muddled for a moment. "What do you... how..." Then things clicked into place. "Ah," he said, smiling. "So you've heard Sir Dillen's tale."

"Bard came sung it once. In the village."

"I see. Juttah, wasn't it?"

The girl gave a small smile.

"What did this bard look like? No wait, let me guess. He had... a bright green outfit, bells on his shoes, and a yellow and purple hat?"

"And stripes all up and down his breeches!"

"And he played a lute? And had a bushy beard?"

"Yes!" Juttah was grinning now. "Do you know him?"

"Know him? Not exactly. But I've heard him sing the tale." It had been as the great mass of Brotherhood who'd chosen to ally with the Lady were marching west. The bard had followed them for a spell, regaling the convoy with epic poems around the campfires. Farn tried to remember the troubadour's name but came up empty. "That was how I first heard the story, too. And yes," Farn added, nodding toward the front of the column. "That's Sir Dillen all right. The one and only."

This got Mannes's attention again.

"See, Juttah," said Mannes, "I told you it were him. Got the scars and e'rything."

"Shu' up," mumbled Juttah.

Mannes appeared to either not hear or simply ignore this injunction. "So is it true, then?"

"Is what true?"

"The story!" said Mannes irritably.

"Mannes!" Their mother had been listening, and it seemed had now decided to step in. "You're speakin' to a knight! Behave yourself!"

"Sorry."

"Sorry, sir knight!" Vandi corrected.

"No, no, that's quite all right. The boy has a quick mind and doubtless expects the same of others," said Farn. He felt an inexplicable desire to deliver the lad from his reprimand. Or rather, to move past the moment as quickly as possible.

"Beggin' your pardon, sir knight, that's no excuse–"

"You want to know if the story's true? Any part in particular?"

Mannes squinted his eyes, thinking. "The fightin' at the van?"

"True."

"The sylph?" offered Juttah.

64

"True."

"What about the unicorn?"

"Also true."

"How comes there weren't a unicorn in the stables, then?" asked Mannes. There was no skepticism in his voice that Farn could hear, simply the honest puzzlement of a child. Farn laughed.

"Unicorns are never kept in stables – they're never kept at all, in fact. Too wild."

"What about..." began Juttah, then she lowered her voice, "what about the Green Lady? Did Sir Dillen meet her?"

Farn stepped closer, gesturing that the children lean over. They did, their sleepless eyes wide with expectation.

"How else could She name him Her champion?" Farn whispered.

After a moment, the children straightened up. "So it's all true?" asked Mannes.

Farn nodded. "All of it."

Mannes looked satisfied with this answer. "I knew it." But Juttah's face had taken on a thoughtful expression.

"No," she said, finally. "It's not all true."

Farn looked at her with raised eyebrows. "Why do you say that?" To his complete surprise, the question caused Juttah to suddenly blush bright red. She turned away, hiding her face. Mannes shrugged.

"Is something wrong?" asked Farn. Juttah didn't move a muscle, and Mannes too looked away, his interest lost.

"She means no offense, sir," said Vandi, looking back at him over her shoulder.

"None taken, not at all. Do you... do you have any idea what she was referring to?"

Vandi smiled. It was a small thing amid the ongoing worry that hung across her features, but nevertheless it gave a glimpse of warmth. "I reckon so, sir."

"...Well? If you'd be so kind," said Farn, putting on his most winning smile.

"You said you'd heard the song, sir. Do you recall how the bard described Sir Dillen? What he's s'posed to look like?"

"...I don't," said Farn, honestly. Dillen was Dillen, he couldn't remember imagining him any other way.

"We do, sir, and except for the scars – again I mean no offense, sir knight – except for them scars, the real Sir Dillen don't look anythin' like his story tells it."

"And how does the story tell it?"

Vandi looked at him again, her smile momentarily brighter. "Let's see… 'Tall and strong, Sir Dillen's face were handsome, his hair long and golden, his eyes silver-gray'…" Vandi tapered off, watching for his reaction.

Now it was Farn's turn to blush. Vandi smiled again, amusement briefly touching her eyes. Then the worry resumed, and she turned away. Farn glanced at the children and caught Juttah peeking at him sideways, her face still bright red. Embarrassed, Farn slowed, letting them get some distance ahead before running a gauntleted hand across his long, golden hair.

"Don't worry, Juttah," he heard Mannes say. "It's Sir Dillen. He'll save father. And then he'll kill all the monsters."

Chapter X

Dillen had claimed that the gladestalkers took the knights by a needlessly long path to reach Calenemel. Even so, Farn was unprepared for just how close the Sylvan settlement truly was to the Eastfort. Minutes after his conversation with the Barchets, he began to note the change in atmosphere, the way the surrounding forest seemed to once again hum with harmonious birdsong, and the trees to swell with primordial design. Up ahead, he discerned the shapes of elven homes set high in the distant canopy. It beggared belief that they could have lived in such proximity for over a year without anyone from the Eastfort stumbling onto it. He thought there had to be fey enchantment at work.

Suddenly, the stillness of the surrounding woodland ruptured. Instinct drove Farn's hand to his sword even before he was aware of what was happening. Casting about, he caught the synchronous emergence of tall figures stepping out from behind the great trees. Six elves stood around the knights, arrows nocked in their bows. Thankfully the weapons were neither drawn nor raised, a minor wonder given the expressions on the usually impassive Sylvan kin – who at this moment looked furious.

The knights slowed to a halt, their formation contracting as they turned to face the elves on every side.

"Dillen! How have you come here?!" Elissa's voice seethed with an ire held in barest check. Turning to look at the lead gladestalker, Farn instead spotted Imariel. He was surprised to see her face had gone white and her eyes wide.

"Does that matter?" asked Dillen. "We bring vital news! We must speak with the druid!"

"I have no interest in whatever it is that motivates your idiocy! Tell me how you learned the way to Calenemel!"

"...No."

Dragging his eyes from Imariel, Farn looked over at Elissa. The elf appeared torn between shock and furious indignation.

"No?" she said, a whisper that cut through the air like the edge of a blade. "Do you understand what you have done? What might have followed you?"

Dillen's head twitched, and Farn realized he had made a quick glance at Imariel. "What are you talking-"

"Our purpose is to protect the secret of Calenemel! A secret which you have laid bare!" No sooner had she made her accusation than Elissa raised her bow and drew its string to cheek, the yew-hewn weapon emitting a potent groan. All save Imariel followed suit, and the knights braced before the leveled arrowheads.

"Where in the Lady's name do you think you're pointing that, Elissa?!" yelled Dillen, voice shot through with anger.

"I should put you down!" Elissa seethed.

"Mother, no! They have children!"

Elissa froze, the curl on her lip faltering. Farn saw her eyes flick across the horses, where Vandi Barchet was practically dragging her children from the saddle. She did not lower her bow.

"Those are not of your tribe! You bring strangers from beyond the forest!"

Again Dillen glanced quickly at Imariel, and the look on his face caused something to tighten in Farn's stomach. If he didn't know better, Dillen's expression almost appeared dismayed. At the very least, he seemed uncertain. Then the Basilean raised a placatory hand. "Listen to me, Elissa! These people's village was attacked, and this man has the wounds to show for it! We must see the druid!"

"And see her you shall, Sir Dillen."

All of them, elves included, snapped their gaze toward the source of the voice, its rich and exotic tone unmistakable. A short distance away, atop the mossy remnants of a long-toppled oak tree, the druid Haili sat in a lotus, bear pelt wrapped about her and staff resting across her legs. Farn shivered. The druid had not so much appeared as revealed herself. It was clear she had been sitting there for some time.

Uncrossing her legs, Haili stood up on the forest floor, staff held loosely at her side. "Lower your weapons." The other elves obeyed instantly, but Elissa hesitated. Haili stepped toward her. "You too, Elissa." The gladestalker complied, and Farn let out a breath he hadn't realized he was holding.

"Druid, I protest! No human outwith your order can be allowed to know the location of Calenemel! What's worse, they refuse to say how they came to know it!"

"Oh, I'd have thought that was obvious," said Haili, continuing toward her. "Your attempt to hide the way failed. Sir Dillen may have led them here, but you alone must bear the fault for his knowing."

Movement at the corner of his vision caused Farn to glance at Imariel. She was still now, face lacking all color beneath her oak-leaf headdress. All the same, he felt a strange certainty that she had shaken her head.

"...Perhaps so, Druid. Regardless, the laws of Sylvan kin are clear! Outsiders cannot be permitted—"

"It is the Lady's law that holds here. These men are Her sworn servants."

"But—"

"Enough." Haili turned to Dillen, who bowed his head respectfully as she approached. The other knights quickly followed his example.

"Sir Dillen Genemer. You have come here without invitation, an act of great disrespect to our elf allies, as well as an insult to the trust bestowed upon you." The druid's eyes bored into him, and despite the measure of her words and tone, Farn realized that she too was furious.

"Druid, we meant no—"

Haili held up her hand. "Tell me, why did you not send a signal from the tower, as you were instructed to do when in need of our counsel?"

Dillen began to answer but was immediately cut short by the sound of Cossus groaning. The man had toppled from the saddle, his fall slowed by Tyred catching hold of him. Releasing his grip on his sword, Farn took Cossus and helped lower him to the ground.

"That's why," he heard Dillen say. "These people sought sanctuary, Druid, and this one is dying. We couldn't afford to wait."

There was a second of silence as Haili considered this. "Stand aside and let me see him," she said finally.

The knights parted. Leading Bhadein's horse away from the prone Cossus, Farn glanced at Vandi. She was looking uncertainly at the druid, each hand on one of the children's as she drew them behind her. Her eyes met Farn's, and he gave what he hoped to be a reassuring nod.

As Haili crouched down over Cossus, her movement provoked a rattle from whatever bones or trinkets were hidden beneath her furs. She placed her hand on his forehead and closed her eyes. A minute passed, silent save for the shallow breaths of the wounded man. Despite her stillness, Farn had the unshakable sense that he was watching an act of exertion. This seemed to be confirmed as a layer of sweat formed across the druid's skin, causing its ebony depths to gleam. Exhaling, Haili withdrew her hand and opened her eyes.

"He can be healed." She stood up and looked at Dillen. "I have begun the process, but it will take time." Then Haili turned to Vandi and the children. "As for them... they should not have been brought here. They are soiled with fear." Farn was surprised to see the druid's upper lip rise as she examined the family, her brow drawing together. It was a look of unmistakable dislike.

Indignation flared. "You can't blame them for being afraid!" Farn had spoken in a burst and felt his cheeks grow hot. All eyes turned to him. He met the druid's gaze, his resolve firm. "They were attacked by abyssals!"

Haili's eyebrows rose. She turned to Vandi once more. "Is this true?"

For a few seconds, Vandi could manage no more than to soundlessly open and close her mouth. "It... it is, my lady," she said eventually, "I've never seen an abyssal before, mind, and it were in the dark of night... but they weren't men, I know that. The sounds they made, the way... the way it moved." Vandi swallowed, her eyes taking on a faraway look. A tear fell across her cheek. "They weren't right." The children had pressed their faces into their mother, their hands tight against their ears. Vandi didn't seem to notice. "They weren't right," she repeated.

"You came from a village? What's it called?" Nothing in Haili's tone betrayed any reaction to Vandi's words, and Farn found himself staring at her, taken aback by the impassive expression on her face.

"Talle, my lady. 'Bout a day's—"

"Yes. I know the place." Dismissing the family, Haili turned to Elissa. Since the reprimand, the gladestalker appeared to have more or less recovered her elven composure. "This matter warrants our concern."

"Yes, Druid."

"Ready the wardens and redouble the watch on our borders. That goes for you, as well," Haili added, addressing the knights. "You are responsible for the woods around the Eastfort and must set patrols throughout the night. If you see anyone – anything – then you must sound horns and send out the signal from the tower. I will confer with my order."

"I beg the druid's pardon," said Sir Edmond, stepping forward. "Shouldn't we ride out and investigate the village? Confirm what exactly we are facing?"

"I agree," said Headel. "More than that, there may be survivors. Abyssals like nothing more than to spend days torturing those they've captured. Could be we'd save a few."

Haili tilted her head as she listened to the knights. Then she looked at each of them in turn, a sad smile on her lips. "Spoken like true knights of men. I admire your virtue, just as I admired your people's resolve. But you are not of the Brotherhood any longer, nor you a paladin of Basilea, Sir Dillen. Each of you are sworn to the Green Lady."

"We understand that, Druid," said Edmond slowly.

"Are you sure? Let me tell you what I understand, Sir Edmond of Aramor. Whenever poor souls from beyond our Lady's realm come to you in plight, you will of course grant them sanctuary; whenever the Balance requires our Lady align herself with those who serve the Wicked Ones, you will refuse to join us in that fight. These are things the Lady understood when She accepted your oaths of loyalty. After all, even the best trained gur panther can only curb its nature so far. However, in all other matters, you will serve the forest, whatever the task. You wish to ride out and rescue villagers? They are not of the Lady's realm; for now, they are not your task. Galahir is your task."

None among the knights spoke. Farn glanced about, seeing in the faces of his fellows the same unease that writhed in his guts. And yet, the druid was right. Their duty was different, now. Wasn't it?

"You will guard our border. Any other refugees that come to you are your business. Do not bring them here again." Haili appeared to take their silence for affirmation, giving a satisfied nod. Then she looked down at Cossus. "Speaking of which, these ones will have to stay with us."

"Why?" asked Farn.

"Why do you think, Sir Farn? This man requires more of my attention if he is to heal well, and I'm sure his family will not wish to part with him." The druid glanced over at Vandi. Though the distaste was now absent from her expression, she nevertheless considered the Barchets with an adverse air. "Is that not so?"

Vandi returned a level look, and her words were admirable in their steadiness. "Yes, my lady."

Haili's nostrils twitched. "I'm a druid. There is only one Lady in this forest."

"Of course. Meanin' no disrespect."

Haili had already turned away. "Bring this man," she told the elves. The knights watched as four of the gladestalkers lifted Cossus onto their shoulders and bore him toward Calenemel. "All have our part to play in the Lady's realm," Haili continued. "Cast the rest from your minds, and go forth in Balance." With that, she set off after Cossus and the elves, Elissa following not far behind. Only Imariel remained.

"C'mon, dears. Let's go." Vandi began to lead her children after their father. She murmured her gratitude as she passed the knights, bowing her head, her smile not quite reaching her eyes. Farn opened his mouth to say something, wanting to assure her and the children that everything would be fine. But no words came. As the family passed the knights, Farn noticed that Dillen was the only one whose attention was elsewhere. He and Imariel were staring at one another.

"Sir Dillen!"

Mannes slipped from his mother's grasp and ran headlong into the Basilean, wrapping his arms around Dillen's waist. The knight looked down at him, dumbfounded.

"Mannes, come away!"

"Don't leave us, Sir Dillen!" the boy pleaded. "The... the monsters..."

"Now, now," said Dillen, somewhat scrambling to find the right tone for his words. "It's perfectly safe here. The elves will protect you... look!" he added, pointing to Imariel. "See my friend there? See her bow? She's the finest shot in these entire woods. Nothing can get past her."

Mannes looked at Imariel, taking a moment to consider the gladestalker. Imariel met his gaze coolly.

71

"Listen to Sir Dillen, Mannes! Come on!" Vandi set her hand on her son's shoulder. But the boy was peering up at Dillen again.

"You're goin' to save the village, ain't you? You're goin' to kill the monsters?!"

"I- well, you see…" Dillen floundered.

"You're the Green Lady's champion! You have to!"

"Mannes, come on!" Vandi pulled him back, and the boy let himself be led away, continuing to look over his shoulder with an imploring expression.

"You have to save us!" he cried. "You have to!"

The knights waited until the family had passed out of sight between the great trees of Calenemel. Farn's eyes kept flicking to Dillen, trying to read the expression on his face. It was… dark. Without a word, they turned away and set off for the Eastfort.

Chapter XI

"That was fast!" called Lenel. "What did the druid say?" Both he and Bhadein were standing in the Eastfort's gateway, great helms tucked under their arms as they awaited the knights' return. Light from the afternoon sun shone against their plate, producing a glare that made Farn's eyes water. Crossing to meet them, the knights slowed to a reluctant halt, Farn and Tyred handing the reins of the now unburdened horses back to their owners. Lenel's brow furrowed. Something of the group's mood must have shown in Farn's face. "Well?" he asked.

"The druid heard our message and healed the villager," Headel explained.

"And?"

"She took it seriously, said she'd warn our allies."

"What about us? What are our orders?"

"The same as everyone else's, it seems," said Ragneld. "Redouble our patrols, make sure nothing tries to enter the forest that shouldn't."

The brow above Lenel's good eye rose. "That's it? We aren't to investigate?"

"It seems not."

"But... you explained that the abyssals might have prisoners?"

"We did," said Edmond, quietly.

The silence that followed was heavy. Farn glanced at Dillen. He was looking into the western sky, a far-away expression on his face. A muscle began to twitch along his square jaw, a steady rhythm of clenching and unclenching.

Bhadein broke the silence. "You said the man was healed? Where is he? Where is the family?"

"Haili... the druid said he needed to stay longer, and that Vandi and the children should remain with him," explained Farn.

"I see. Did the druid tell you when-"

"Abyss take them!"

Bhadein's question was cut short as Dillen sprang into motion, striding past the knights and into the Eastfort. He seemed to be moving with purpose.

The knights looked at one another, concern plain upon their faces. Then they heard Dillen call for his horse to be saddled.

"I'm going to Talle." Dillen hadn't even glanced their way as the knights approached. His coif was up, and he was assisting the retainers as they readied his white destrier.

"Our orders are to guard the forest, Sir Dillen." Bhadein's usual monotone was gone, seemingly overwhelmed by incredulity. "We received them directly from the druid, after you sought her out. Now you mean to disregard them?!"

"Not at all, Sir Bhadein. The best way to guard the forest is to investigate. You said so yourself."

"Do not attempt to play such games with me. I would never suggest that so small a group should ride out."

Dillen shrugged. "Then stay."

"I cannot let–"

"What? Let me go?! There could be other survivors, Bhadein!"

"Do you think I don't know that?! Do you think we don't know?!" Bhadein cast an arm across the other knights.

Farn looked on in something of a daze. He felt torn, caught between conflicting impulses. On the one hand, their orders had been clear, and knights of the Brotherhood obeyed their orders. As maxims go, it was as simple as it was fundamental. But Farn now realized that its effortless simplicity resulted from understanding, from an unshakable trust in their cause. Here, far from the land of his birth, understanding continued to escape him.

"Please, Sir Dillen," said Headel, "Your oath was to the forest and the Green Lady. We have to protect her realm."

"And so we are to watch while others suffer on Her doorstep? Talle is not the only village out there. Who will protect the rest?" Dillen drew the last of the bridle straps taut and turned to face the knights. "Yes, Sir Headel, I gave my oath to the Green Lady. It may very well prove to be the last oath I swear. But it was not the first. I've sworn myself to other principles, and I don't recall any part of my vow to Her freeing me from their burden." As he spoke this last, Dillen's gaze met Farn's.

"None of us can serve two masters, Sir Dillen," said Bhadein. "You cannot be both a paladin of Basilea as well as a knight of the Green Lady."

"He doesn't have to be both," said Farn, quietly. He felt all eyes turn to him.

"Sir Farn? Did you say something?"

Farn continued to look at Dillen. The knight's words from earlier that day still swirled in his head, trying to find purchase. *It means that each swing must choose its edge, not that the two aren't part of the same weapon.* Two edges, one weapon. One purpose. The words found their place, and Farn felt the warm embrace of understanding.

The familiar half-smile was on Dillen's lips. Farn nodded.

"I said he doesn't have to be both," he repeated, turning to face Bhadein. His old master looked at him with a questioning expression, and Farn was struck by the wildness of Bhadein's aspect. His armor was as immaculate as ever, of course, but his cheeks were stubbled and his goatee unfettered. His gray hair was long and ill-kempt. And he was not the only one – all among the ex-Brotherhood, whether retainer or knight, had yielded much of their appearance to nature's whims. Only Dillen looked the same as when he'd first arrived, cropped and clean like a paladin of legend.

They had thought that they could leave their home intact, Farn reflected, that they could carry who they were into this foreign realm. But, seemingly without realizing, something had been left behind. Grooming may have seemed a small thing. If Farn had learned anything in his time since coming to the forest, it had been the value of small things.

Farn drew his dagger. The blade gave a bright sigh as it emerged from its scabbard, wrought steel catching the late afternoon glow. Without pause – without further thought – he gathered his long hair into a fist and swept the dagger through it.

"Sir Dillen isn't just a knight of the Green Lady – he's Her chosen champion." Farn held out his shorn hair as he spoke, golden locks hanging lifelessly in his hand. "Chosen to lead Her forces against the enemy. We are Her forces, and I trust his leadership. Anything else would be to doubt the Green Lady's will."

"Farn, you heard the druid…" said Tyred, but already he sounded doubtful. The retainers of the Eastfort had gathered around the knights and were listening intently.

Farn kept his eyes locked on Bhadein's. "We can be a sword in the Green Lady's hand, or just a brick in yet another wall. I know what I choose." He dropped the hair.

Silence followed. Bhadein continued to meet Farn's gaze, his expression giving nothing away.

Then Sir Ragneld grunted. "Farn's right," he said, drawing his own dagger. "I don't mean about this 'chosen champion' stuff – I don't know what to think about all that – but I trust what Dillen says. We didn't come here to watch while abyssals roam unchallenged. I joined the Lady's army to aid others in their time of need, just as She aided us in ours." In a series of quick sweeps, his long beard was cut loose, leaving an irregular patchwork of blond curls against his cheeks. Despite his gratitude to the knight, Farn had to suppress a laugh. If anything, it made Ragneld look more feral. Farn's own cut no doubt did the same.

Ragneld's gravelly words were the stones that set the avalanche tumbling, sweeping away doubt and stirring them to action. Everywhere, daggers were drawn and set to hair. In less than a minute's time, the ground was host to discarded shavings from all the knights. All, save for Bhadein.

Farn looked again to Bhadein but this time could not catch his eye. The old knight's expression showed him to be far away. Then his long eyebrows furrowed, and he mouthed something silently, something Farn was sure he'd understood.

...a sword in the hand...

Bhadein drew his sword and held it out before him. After examining its gleaming length for several seconds, he set it against his opposite shoulder, bunched up his gray mane, and hacked it off. A cheer went up from the assembled men and women. Bhadein turned to face the retainers.

"Make ready our steeds!" he called. The cheers intensified.

Farn laughed. Although he'd not had a proper sleep in days, nor had he felt this awake, felt this vital, in a long time. Longer than he could remember. He looked over at Sir Dillen and returned the Basilean's broad grin.

Just as Farn was turning to head for the stables, Bhadein strode over to the still-grinning Dillen and leaned down to speak directly into his ear. It wasn't until much later that Farn wondered what exactly his old master had said to wipe the smile from Dillen's face.

Chapter XII

For the first time in over a year, Farn crossed outside the boundaries of the forest. Drawing his courser away from the other knights, he paused to look out across the landscape of Nova Ardovikio. It wasn't the sensation he had expected. While the province was different to his eastern homeland in a number of ways, being both greener of grass and lighter of air, it nevertheless bore a far closer resemblance than the Galahir woodlands. And yet, despite the beauty of the distant mountains set against rolling hinterland, lit by the warm hues of the fading day, it felt... strange. As if the sheer openness of it left him naked, the lack of a canopy above or boscage all around. It seemed he'd grown more attached to life in the forest than he'd realized.

Farn glanced over at the knights. They had slowed their pace and were looking back at him questioningly from their saddles. The sight of their haphazard haircuts caused Farn to grin, and he ran a gauntlet across his own truncated mop. The truth was that little to nothing could diminish his spirits. It wasn't the possibility of a fight which elated him – that would be foolish, particularly for one who'd experienced the grim reality of the battlefield. It was something else, a rectitude he couldn't name and had unwittingly lost, now returned to its place.

"Let's pick up the pace!" called Dillen, spurring his destrier to canter. The other knights followed suit. Drawing up his coif, Farn set off after them.

* * * * *

It was deep into twilight by the time they reached the outskirts of Talle. Above, the open sky had finally closed. Its unbroken blanket of cloud was vibrant with a heady fuchsia and promised a night of impenetrable dark. Below, as if in mirror of the heavens, low-hanging fog had settled on the farmland which led up to the village, whose fields were contoured by the dips and swells of ridge-and-furrow earth. Arrayed on a broad hill beyond, Farn could distinguish the shapes of cottages and barns in the dim orange glow. It would almost have been picturesque, he reflected, were it not for the distorted shape of several buildings, their silhouettes suggesting rifts in thatching and breaches in their wattle-and-daub walls. But it was the air that most concerned him. It was tainted with a scent, unchanged through the ages and unmistakable to those who lived by the sword – spilled blood, and fresh corpses. Talle was silent. Finally, the familiar apprehension of battle took its rightful hold on Farn's nerves, displacing all else.

As they stepped into the first of the fields, Dillen signaled them to stop.

"Dismount here. We'll approach on foot."

The knights climbed down from their saddles. Farn put on his helm, supplanting silence with the rhythm of his enclosed breaths.

"Night is imminent. We risk fighting in the dark," said Bhadein.

"Couldn't be avoided," said Dillen curtly. "We've come as soon as possible."

"This quiet doesn't bode well for survivors," Farn observed, his voice low and metallic in his ears.

"No. It does not," agreed Edmond. "The cries of the tortured would have reached us long before now."

Dillen had been about to put on his helm, and he paused mid-motion, staring at the knights. "Whatever chance we have of finding survivors will be gone by morning, and we'd be just as much at risk of fighting in darkness if we wait here for the dawn. I for one will not return to the Eastfort with nothing to show for it." He put on his helm. "At the very least, we can find out what happened."

They began walking toward the hamlet, guiding their steeds by their reins. Tremors bounced in his muscles, and Farn gripped tighter on the handle of his sword as he watched the fields for movement.

About halfway to the village, Bhadein signaled a halt. "We should leave the horses here."

"Someone will have to stay behind with them," said Ragneld. Bhadein nodded but gave no direction. He was looking at Dillen.

"Who do you think should guard the horses, Sir Dillen?"

Dillen glanced round at the mountainous knight. The Basilean's eyes were wide, visible through the narrow t-shaped opening in his barbute helm.

"Pardon?"

"I was asking your opinion on what to do with the horses."

"Ah. Of course." Dillen licked his lips and looked back toward the village. "I trust your judgment, Sir Bhadein."

"And I judge that it is your decision, knight-champion," said Bhadein, lingering a hair too long on Dillen's title. The Basilean swung his gaze back around, brow furrowed. Neither moved. Then the look on Dillen's face vanished, replaced by a half-smile. He gestured at Farn.

"If you would be so good as to watch them, Sir Farn, and only follow if we call. The rest of you should ready yourselves," continued Dillen, slowly drawing his sword as he spoke. "The abyssals may be hiding. We'd best make use of what little daylight remains."

Farn gave an emphatic nod. Although disappointed not to be with them to lend his sword in a fight, it was a job that needed done. As the knights drew blades and prepared to move, Dillen stepped to Farn's side.

"Don't worry, Farn, I'll be sure to leave a few of them for you." Dillen winked, clapping Farn lightly on the pauldron.

Farn shook his head in disbelief, helpless not to smile. "Are all paladins so carefree before battle, Sir Dillen?"

A look passed across Dillen's face with such speed that Farn wondered if he'd imagined it. Then Dillen was laughing softly. "Oh, you know. Only those for whom bards sing praise."

With a final wink, Dillen stepped away. Farn busied himself collecting the other horses. As the rest of the knights continued on toward the village, Farn began binding the reins to a somewhat distraught looking stretch of fence. By the time he'd finished around five minutes later, his companions had climbed the hill and disappeared into the amber fog.

Kevmar's horse was shuffling. Its neigh was anxious. After removing his helmet with a sigh, Farn went to stroke his neck. "Don't you worry now, they'll all be back soon. You want something to eat?" He began searching through his saddlebag. He was sure he had a carrot hidden away.

Something sounded from the direction of the village. Farn swung round, gripping the handle of his sword. It had been short, a quick burst of air from the lungs. Like a yelp. He could make out the distant outlines of thatched roofs rising out of the orange mists, but nothing more.

"I'm sure that was just an animal. Or maybe one of them tripping," he told the horses. "Probably Sir Tyred." Farn wished he could believe his own words. Abandoning the carrot to his saddlebag, he unhooked his kite shield from his mount and strapped it to his arm. It felt like the mist was getting thicker, its fiery hue growing richer even as the sun furthered its departure. Dropping his coif, Farn began twisting to and fro, straining his ears as he looked out across the rows of rye. For the first time, he noticed a pair of wooden poles not far off, erected in the heart of the field to form a lopsided cross.

It wasn't just Kevmar's horse that was nervous. Now all the mounts were whinnying and braying, stamping at the dirt. Turning his gaze from the fields, Farn stared at the animals in stunned incomprehension. He had never seen them act like this. These were experienced warhorses to the last, and yet here they were acting like common mules that had caught the scent of a mawbeast.

More noises seemed to be coming from the village, but it was hard to make out over the panicked horses. Rousing from inaction, Farn stepped forward, moving into their eyeline and doing his best to speak in soothing tones. His efforts were met with mixed success. He checked the reins were tied securely, knowing full-well that if they tried to bolt then the fence would offer little resistance.

From out of the corner of his eye, Farn detected movement in the field. Heart racing, he drew his sword, scanning the rye for any signs of motion. There was no wind, not even the slightest breeze. The crops were still.

They're only waist high, Farn tried to tell himself. Anything that could hide in them can hardly be a threat. But even as this thought occurred, he knew it to be false. He recalled his battles near the Abyss where he had seen swarms of imps stab at men's legs until they dropped, as well as three-headed hellhounds that pounced on soldiers and devoured their flesh–

Something jumped out of the field. The horses screeched, flailing against their restraints. Farn swung round, trying to see where the thing had landed.

It was on one of the horses. The courser bucked desperately, and the creature leapt again. Farn had just enough time to discern a body of impossible black before it reached him and aimed a long-clawed swipe at his chest. Instinct brought up his shield. Wood screeched. The blow bore nearly enough force to send him to the ground. Gritting his teeth at the pain which rang in his arm, Farn stepped back, stabilizing his footing. The creature began to circle him, flattening the rye in its path. In the waning light, his foe was finally visible, and as his mind attempted to understand the sight before him, Farn's blood froze.

Shorter than a gore but just as long, the creature was unlike anything he had ever seen. Superficially it most closely resembled an abyssal hellhound, but the comparison only went so far: rather than blistered red, the creature's skin was deepest black, seemingly impervious to the twilight; while it moved on all fours like a hound, the creature's front legs were more like arms sprung out to its sides, making its posture match that of a man imitating beasts; while it had multiple heads, they were not a canine triad but a pair of eyeless protrusions, recognizable as such only for their enormous, fang-ringed maws. A purple tongue emerged from each. They were swaying. Like snakes.

Those who lived at its border knew that the Abyss housed horrors far beyond the imaginations of most. Indeed, it was not uncommon for men to be driven to madness by the sight of even its lesser denizens. Farn had never forgotten the feeling of his first time. It was a feeling of the mind at war with itself, a battle between acceptance and utter rejection of what his senses were delivering. After all he'd seen since, he had never expected to feel that battle again, nor to witness anything worse.

This was worse. Far worse.

With a twin-headed snarl, the creature struck again, its muscles rippling powerfully beneath ebon skin. Farn managed to divert the attack with his shield before making a quick jab with his blade. Tip caught flesh, sinking several inches through unnatural hide. The creature's cry was piercing and sent shivers up Farn's spine. It jumped back, hissing at him furiously. One of its fore legs clutched the wound in its chest.

Farn glanced at his blade. The tip was slick with blue viscosity, ropes of it hanging tenaciously from the steel. By the time his eyes returned to the creature, it was beginning to circle once more. Its wound was gone.

It heals like a troll, he thought. He'd have to quickly deal a mortal blow.

Slowly, Farn lowered his shield, letting his sword arm go slack. Any seasoned fighter would have seen it for the trap that it was. But the creature charged eagerly, leaping to make a swipe at his exposed face. Farn stepped out wide, bringing his sword up and around in a grand arc. The blade found its target, passing first through the outstretched arm before cleanly removing one of the creature's heads. A keening wail burst from its remaining mouth as it swung around to face him, all caution abandoned as it sprang against his shield.

This time it was enough for Farn to fall, overwhelmed by the creature's ferocity. Collapsing into the rye, he desperately held the creature off him with his shield, taking its entire weight on his left arm. The remaining head was trying to snap at him over the shield.

Not again, he thought. Not this again!

He swung his sword clumsily, hacking at the creature's hind leg, unable to put any strength behind it. His left arm began to ache, then to shudder. Above him, the creature stopped its snapping, instead opening its circular maw wide to reveal...

There was nothing inside it. Not even a tongue.

Nothing.

Farn screamed. Dropping his longsword, he drew his dagger and began to stab desperately at the creature as it writhed against him, his terror driving him into an animalistic frenzy. Finally, the creature stopped struggling and went slack. He pushed the weight from his body. Rolling to his knees, Farn gasped for breath, staring in disbelief at its immobile form.

Even when dead, the creature was horrifying. It wasn't just the unnatural anatomy, alone enough to shred his nerves. It was the way it seemed to exist apart from the world around it, as if only half viewed through eyes, with the rest being projected directly into his mind.

There's no way this was hidden in the field, Farn thought. Yes, it could crouch low, but its body was too broad and long, and the joints in its arms projected outward like spikes. It couldn't have slipped through the crops without disturbing them. And yet, somehow, it had.

The horses had stopped stamping. Several appeared to have bolted, the fence having predictably given out. In absence of the animals' panic, Farn could hear the other knights shouting from the direction of the village, their voices blended with nightmarish roars.

Farn glanced between the horses and the village. His dilemma was short-lived. The others needed him. He recovered his sword and ran toward the hill.

The sound of fighting grew steadily clearer as he followed the path up to the village. Someone was yelling orders, though Farn couldn't tell who. He passed a squat pen, glimpsing the corpse of an eviscerated cow within, then the first of the village homes, a small stone cottar house. He continued without pause, peering through the fog. The light was paler now, distant and washed out. Farn guessed that mere minutes remained until darkness claimed the village.

He passed more of Talle's homes, some stone and thatch, others little more than shacks. Doors were smashed apart, shutters torn from their hinges. Up ahead, Bhadein's thundering voice was calling for the knights to hold their formation. Tightening the grip on his blade, Farn prepared to rush toward the direction of the call when a clash of impacted steel sounded to his right, followed quickly by an unmistakable two-headed snarl. Someone was fighting one of the creatures close by, possibly separated from the group. Without hesitation, Farn charged down the right path.

He quickly found the fight after rounding another of the shacks. A coop of some sort had seen its fence collapsed at various points; inside, Sir Edmond had two of the creatures flanking him and was doing his best to present a defense to both. Charging through one of the breaches, Farn attacked the nearest abomination, driving his blade into its back. He had to grit his teeth as the sound of its perishing scream sent needle-sharp pain into his skull. The remaining creature looked round in surprise, and Edmond brought his sword down in two quick swipes, sundering each of the heads.

"Sir Farn?" gasped Edmond breathlessly. "You have my thanks."

"Where are the others?"

"I don't know. We were checking inside when... when they attacked. These two trapped me here. The others must have managed to regroup somewhere else."

They both looked up as Bhadein's voice once again filled the air. It was cut short by a pained cry. Farn withdrew his blade from the creature's back before using the side of his shield to scrape away the viscid blood. "They're close. We have to get to them."

Edmond nodded. Together they remounted the dirt path, following it up the hillside. What appeared to be the village's only multistory building loomed ahead, lit by the barest remnants of daylight. Legs burning, Farn bounded up in long strides and reached the hill's crest. He was met with a wide and level space, no doubt serving as a village square. A stone well squatted at its north side – at its center, a cluster of figures stood firm, arrayed in a defensive circle against the creatures that stalked them on every side. The creatures were somehow less physical than ever – they were shadows. One of them leapt at the circle of knights, twin-heads snapping, only to be stopped short as a flash of steel swept out from the cluster and cut it down.

"Sir Farn!" called Edmond.

Farn saw it. One of the shadows had noticed them and bounded across the square, its purple tongues flailing. Locking their shields together, Farn and Edmond braced as if to meet it. Just at the moment the shadow-creature's momentum was too great, they lunged apart, dragging their blades along the flanks of their foe. The creature landed poorly, tumbling over and down the hillside before becoming impaled on the jagged ends of a shack's broken wall. One head roared. The other screeched. Across the square, the shadow-creatures paused their stalking movements to look back at the new arrivals.

"CHARGE!" cried Sir Dillen.

Battle cries bellowing in their helms, the knights burst from their formation, pouncing on the creatures. Every swing was a deathblow, cleaving limbs and spraying syrupy gore. Lenel thrust his blade at the joint between one creature's heads, driving it to the hilt; Kevmar and Headel decapitated another in near synchronous hacks. Dillen took on two at once, whirling his paladin blade in a wide, double-handed arc as he made to hew them down. The first creature was too slow, and its heads were horizontally split one after the other. But the second pinned itself low and waited as the blade soared over before leaping at Dillen, driving him to the ground and pinning him beneath its mass. Farn was already halfway there, running as fast as his armor would allow. He crashed shield-first into the creature, sending it sprawling. Not wasting a second, Farn thrust his sword into the exposed underside, a yell surging from his lungs as he dragged the blade up the creature's length.

Satisfied that his foe was dealt with, Farn withdrew his blade and held it ready, casting about for the next threat. The knights stood spread across the square, their breaths heavy as their helmets spun to-and-fro. The shadow-creatures, six in all, lay motionless. The night was silent.

"Told you I'd leave you some," said Dillen between pants. Farn grinned. A sickly elation was spreading out from his stomach, forming an uncomfortable blend with his residual fear. The fight was over. They'd done it.

"I really wish you hadn't," said Farn, voice bouncing as the adrenal aftermath sent shivers through his chest. He helped Dillen to his feet.

"Is anyone hurt?" asked Edmond.

"Bhadein–" Tyred began.

"I'm fine," Bhadein grunted. He was examining his breastplate, probing something with his fingers, although Farn couldn't see what. "One of them got its claws through my plate, but the wound is shallow."

There was a moment of silence in which the knights stared at one another, their slime-slicked blades still held at the ready. Dillen took off his helm.

"My good sirs, I am in awe! You fought like the Elohi themselves!" Around his broad smile, Farn saw that the Basilean's skin was ashen, his scars white. Sweat coated him, glimmering faintly with the bare light of the western sky. Dillen took a breath, eyes darting between the slain forms of their foe. "Has anyone ever seen anything like these... things before?"

Removing his helmet, Ragneld crouched down next to one of the shadow-creature's corpses. "Can't say I've even heard of demons like these," he rumbled, wiping his blade against the ebon skin, darker than the night around it. "They have the look of hounds, only…" Ragneld trailed off as he leaned in closer. Then he stood up sharply, backing away with his sword raised. "What in the–?!"

Farn saw it too. At first he thought the shadow-creature had begun to move, having somehow healed the mortal strike inflicted by Sir Ragneld. Then he realized that it was something still more disturbing. The corpse appeared to be shrinking from the physical world, fading before his eyes even as it lingered in the mind. Casting his gaze across the other bodies, Farn saw the same thing was happening everywhere, that each of the creatures was becoming as intangible as the misty air around them. A groan tried to escape his lungs, lodging itself somewhere at the base of his neck. Farn blinked hard.

The creatures were gone.

"You are correct, Sir Ragneld," said Bhadein softly. "These hounds are unlike anything we have seen before. It would appear the Wicked Ones have a new weapon. Assuming they are of the Abyss at all…"

There was a squeak of metal as Dillen sheathed his blade. "Oh, do banish such dark thoughts, Sir Bhadein, at least for now! Thanks to our actions, these creatures will no longer roam the land and can't attack other settlements. Not to mention we can tell the druids what we've learned." Dillen set his hand on Farn's shoulder. "This is a righteous victory!"

Farn smiled, surrendering as the elation began to return. Dillen was right. This was a victory.

Above Talle village, a slender opening had appeared in the clouds. Through the iron darkness, the stars slipped their light.

Chapter XIII

The knights found no survivors. In truth, after witnessing the feral nature of the shadowhounds, their hopes had not been high. As the mists thinned and the stars broke through, the knights came upon corpses that were savaged beyond reason. Most, it seemed, had attempted to barricade themselves indoors. They had died in their homes.

"Maybe there're more who escaped," Dillen ventured. "We can't be sure." Farn guessed he was attempting to maintain the triumphant feeling in the group. It was a noble effort, given the evident sorrow on the Basilean's face when he looked upon the bodies. But Dillen need not have bothered. The Brotherhood knew well the suffering wrought by abyssal barbarity, something no number of victories could fully prevent. All they could do was help one to bear it. Besides, if there was anything that threatened to undo Farn's mood, it was not so much the sight of Talle's unfortunate souls, but the memory of the shadowhound's maw and the cold void beyond.

It being too dark to do anything about the villagers, they committed to later returning with retainers for the task of burying the dead, then set themselves to recovering the bolted horses. Four had broken free, of which two had already come back by the time the knights left the village. The pair stood a short distance from their bound brethren, alternating between grazing on the rye and looking sheepishly at the approaching knights. Lenel's courser was found dead not twenty minutes later, having bled out from the wound inflicted by the shadow-creature's ambush on Farn, and an hour of searching for Aldever's mount came to naught. With midnight not far off, they finally resigned themselves to a slow journey home. Most of it was passed in silence. The knights' relief at coming through the battle seemed to have left them in state of satisfied torpor, their muscles humming with warmth, their minds blank. Overhead, the thick, continuous cloud cover had gradually come apart. As he gazed at the heavens from his saddle, Farn reflected that the stars too had a sated quality to their light, far and away from their excessive glow of the night prior.

Despite having slowed to accommodate the pair of double-ridden mounts, rotating the horse in question every hour, the forest of Galahir came into view almost as soon as dawn's light began to filter into the eastern sky.

"There she is," said Dillen, twisting in his saddle to flash a half-smile at the others. "Same as we left her!"

Scanning the line of trees that ranged the horizon, their thin spread quickly contracting into a rolling ocean of dark canopy, Farn found himself smiling. He remembered the first time he laid eyes on it, a short distance north of here when the Brotherhood caravan arrived from the east. It had seemed so alien then, almost oppressively so. However, the feeling had faded after taking his oath, and as he now looked out on the forest's verdant depths, he recognized that it truly was beginning to feel like home.

"It's a pity you lot are so averse to drink," Dillen continued. "As far as I'm concerned, no victory is complete without at least one goblet of–"

A bright tone reached them from far away, cutting Dillen short. The knights looked at each other in stunned silence. It was a horn. The note held for some ten seconds before the blower took a breath. Then it sounded again.

"The Eastfort?" said Farn.

Ragneld nodded. "They must have seen us."

"But… they're signaling…" Farn faltered, unable to believe it.

"Attack," finished Bhadein, his tone grim.

"Why would they raise the alarm?" asked Tyred. "If they don't recognize it's us, a group our size still doesn't warrant this response."

"Because they do recognize us, Sir Tyred." Bhadein's eyes were on Dillen as he spoke. "They are sending a message to us."

The rest of the knights looked to Dillen. He was staring out at the indistinct shape of the Eastfort tower. His square jaw hung open, his bronze skin had paled. "It… it can't be…" he stammered.

"Sir Dillen!" growled Bhadein.

Dillen gave a jolt. He looked round at them, and Farn was relieved to see determination firm on his face.

"Right! We ride hard! You four stay behind – the horses won't take it."

"Hold on!" said Lenel, dropping down from the back of Edmond's mount. "Eight are better than six! We'll catch up!"

"Yes!" agreed Aldever. He dismounted from behind Tyred. "Don't worry about us, go!"

Pressing their heels, the eight knights galloped hard for the forest. They reached the boundary in less than ten minutes, slowed briefly to find the correct trail, before charging off again in single file. Hunching forward in his saddle to avoid the grasping branches, visions swirled through Farn's mind: the Eastfort surrounded by shadowy forms, the men and women who lived there fighting desperately to hold them back; the surviving villagers of Talle, beset in the place they had thought a sanctuary; a tree in the uncanny likeness of a maiden, her arms held wide and cherry blossom branches atop her head, looking down with an indifferent expression; but most of all, Farn saw the shadowhound's maw and the dreadful emptiness it had held.

But though the retainers were armed and stood vigilant along the Eastfort's palisade, there was no sign of an attack that Farn could see. As they burst into the clearing, calls announcing the knights' return were met with orders to open the gate, and soon the thick doors were unbarred and swung open. The knights pulled up before it, and the sergeant stepped forward from the fort.

"Master knights! We're glad to see you've–"

"What's going on?" said Dillen, "Why did you sound the horn?"

"There was an attack, sirs! In the night!"

"What? By whom?" Farn saw Dillen cast his gaze across the retainers and knew what he would say next. "You don't look like you were attacked."

"Not here, sirs! The elves! We were woken by the sounds of a battle during the early hours, deeper into the forest!"

"Calenemel?" said Dillen, barely above a whisper.

The sergeant nodded. "One of them gladestalkers arrived not long after it started, looking to summon us to the fight. We told him you were gone, and… and…" The color had drained from the sergeant's face.

"Spit it out, man!" barked Ragneld.

"He said the enemy came through here, through our woods, and attacked their settlement without warning! But we had no idea! Our lookouts couldn't see a thing, sirs, the night was dark as pitch!"

"Where is the elf, now?" asked Bhadein.

"He was badly wounded, sir. We couldn't do anything for him. We'd have gone to help in the fight, sirs, but without the elf weren't none of us knew the way, not to mention it being so dark–"

Dillen turned his destrier sharply and charged back into the forest. Without so much as a moment's thought or hesitation, Farn spurred his horse to follow.

"Farn!" Bhadein called after him. His voice scarcely registered. All of Farn's focus was on Dillen, on the flashes of white horse and celestine blue robes as they sped between the trees. Dillen was riding like a man possessed, driving his steed to leap the dips and turns, crashing it through the undergrowth. Twice Farn lost the Basilean, first for ten seconds, then a full minute. Farn didn't slow; he spurred harder, instinct guiding him to find the trail. It was only after reclaiming sight of Dillen for the second time that he noticed the forest around him, the broken branches and trampled fronds, the arrows embedded in trunks. Some of the arrows appeared to be coated in something – a midnight-blue substance, hanging tenaciously from the shafts.

"Farn! Wait!"

It seemed Bhadein had followed him. Farn had no intention of stopping. Though Dillen had disappeared once more, Farn was almost there.

Just another second, he thought. Another second and I'll see Calenemel, see the elf homes high in their–

The trees grew broad, the birds silent. Slowly, Farn drew his horse to a halt. A cold wave swept through him as he looked upon the elven settlement, bathing him in mute horror.

Calenemel had fallen. No less than half its structures – once set higher than the towers of the Lost Forts – appeared to have been cast to the ground, ripped and hacked from their purchase, their timber strewn wide by the impact. Dozens of elf warriors, forest guards and gladestalkers, lay dead among the shattered homes. Their shields were split, their bodies rent. Most of the elves' foes had vanished, but here and there Farn saw the same semi-corporeal effect the knights had witnessed in Talle, with some of the vague forms appearing to have once been shadowhounds, while others were far larger, and far more distressing in aspect. Close to twenty elf fighters remained and stood with weapons leveled as the nightmarish forms continued to fade.

"By the Ones…"

Farn looked round absently. Bhadein had drawn up next to him and was surveying the scene with a look that seemed caught between shock and fury.

"Stay back! Do not touch me!"

The voice sent a jolt through Farn. It was awash with pain, charged with outrage. He turned to follow it and saw Dillen a short distance away. The Basilean had dismounted his horse and appeared to have backed off from a kneeling figure, his hands held out before him as if desperate to span the gap.

"Imariel… please…"

"Where were you?! WHERE?!" she screamed.

Farn didn't notice himself dismount. As if in a trance, he walked toward the pair, puzzling over the shape in Imariel's lap. The gladestalker appeared to have lost her headdress, and she was caked in a mix of blood and blackened viscosity. Her tears shone in the early light, forging wet gullies through the cruor.

"Our warriors were guarding the outer stretches! We had no warning! You let them through!"

"Imariel, I'm sorry! I'm so sorry!"

Imariel was shaking her head. She looked down at her lap. "We never should have trusted them… we should never…" She stroked a loving hand across long, tawny locks, and Farn's realization dawned.

Cradled in the elf's lap was Elissa. Imariel's mother was dead.

"Please, Imariel! I can explain!"

"Can you?"

Farn turned to the voice, its timber rich and exotic, its tone cold. The druid Haili stepped out from among the elf dead. Dillen looked at her, his expression as helpless as Farn felt.

"I… we…"

"Think carefully, Sir Dillen. Can what you are about to say justify all this? Will it exonerate the dereliction of your duty to the Lady and Her realm?"

Dillen's mouth worked silently.

"No, Druid." Bhadein stepped forward. "It cannot. It will not."

"You are sure, Sir Bhadein? I'd bet it is a thrilling tale: the knights of the Brotherhood, their hair shorn and proper once more, ride to face down the Abyss, all while leaving those who gave them a home, a home they swore to defend, open to attack?" Haili's teeth were bared. "How was my guess, sir knight? Anywhere close?"

"We failed the Lady, Druid. That is all there is to say."

Haili nodded. "Then that is all that need be said. You and your fellows will face the consequences of your act—"

"No!" Dillen stepped forward, barging past Farn before collapsing to kneel before the druid. "It's my fault! All of it! I accept the punishment!"

"Dillen, you can't—!" Farn began.

"You have no right!" barked Bhadein. Farn looked at his old master, eyes wide in astonishment. In all the years he'd known him, he'd never seen Bhadein appear more openly angry, nor heard him speak in such condemnatory tones. "The others followed you willingly! And I am as much to blame, for ignoring what I've always thought of you and your preposterous stor—!"

"The Lady accepts your offer, Sir Dillen." Though Haili spoke without emotion, her words seemed to ride the air like lightning. "Many of those that attacked us have escaped deeper into the forest. Since it was you who you allowed this darkness to breach the boundary of Her realm, you shall be sent into the depths of Galahir after it, not to return until it has been expunged."

As Haili spoke, Dillen had continued to glance over at Imariel. She did not look up from her mother.

"I accept!"

"Druid, please, he has no right!" Bhadein protested. Haili met him with a level stare.

"Any who wish to join Sir Dillen, may."

"I will," said Farn, softly. He looked out across the devastation of Calenemel, allowing it to sear itself upon his mind. "I will go."

He felt Bhadein's eyes on him and waited for his old master to voice opposition. But Bhadein said nothing.

Chapter XIV

F arn was sure that the rain had never fallen so heavily. Gray clouds smothered the light of the sun overhead and cast shadows across the amphitheater where he stood staring down at the procession of creatures that passed by to pay their respects to the gladestalker whose body lay spread on a pedestal at the base of the long steps.

Elissa looked as if she could have been sleeping, but Farn had seen enough corpses in his lifetime already to discern the ashen skin and motionless features of death even from the distance he now stood. The gloom was palpable as he watched a fairly steady stream of mourners and fellow warriors made their way up to the front to pay their respects in whatever manner best suited their individual customs. Most were sylvans, but naiads, salamanders, and even some forest spirits in constructed forms of various types of foliage made their way across the stage.

Farn observed Imariel standing beside her mother's body. He shook his head at the irony of how familiar the scene felt. He had seen many funerals for friends and mentors during his time among the Brotherhood, and he understood what was happening here. The morbid normalcy which this form of grieving took seemed at odds with all of his other experiences he'd had in his time within Galahir. Elissa had lived the drawn out lifespan of her species, and in her lengthened years, she had apparently touched many lives. Farn felt a little ashamed that he hadn't known her well enough to understand these accomplishments and yet was still here to witness the intimacy of those who came to remember her and how she had affected them.

He turned his gaze away from Imariel as she was embraced by a rather large salamander, feeling the heat of embarrassment welling up inside of him. The intimacy of the scene seemed more pronounced than others of the mourners who had come before. He also couldn't help but feel somewhat responsible for Elissa's death, and her daughter's grief by extension. If he had done what had been asked of him rather than riding off foolishly in search of glory, then perhaps...

He cut the thought off before it could fester in his mind. What was done was done. He'd felt similar guilt after surviving the Abyss's expansion that had swallowed most of his Brotherhood. He'd felt similar guilt when leaving the Order to follow Bhadein into the service of the Green Lady. He knew better than to dwell on such thoughts, or else it would overwhelm him and he wouldn't be able to focus on what needed to be done.

What needed to be done. The task at hand was more nebulous and harder to grasp. The creatures they had fought, the ones who had killed Elissa and butchered the villages surrounding Galahir, they hadn't been content with their slaughter; several of the remaining nightmares had pressed further into the depths of the forest. It was as if they were drawn to something. Something that was hidden deep in the shadows of the verdant wood.

Farn suppressed a shiver and allowed his eyes to focus on Dillen, who sat speaking with a naiad with scars on her face a few yards away. Dillen had retreated within himself in the week since they'd returned from their fated rescue expedition. He'd almost completely stopped talking to Farn, and the sudden change in their dynamic had hurt more than Farn had expected it would. Why had the gladestalker's death affected the Basilean hero so deeply? It wasn't as if the sylvans had really gone out of their way to make the newly sworn humans feel at home in these woods. Nor had they really fought alongside each other that much after the fires of the Abyss had settled down some two years ago, beyond a few minor skirmishes here and there.

Dillen was becoming more animated as his conversation with the naiad grew heated. The knight's arms began to gesture more violently even while the naiad remained still. The younger knight watched, trying to imagine what they were speaking about. He remembered that the naiad had been assigned to them as a "guide" as the druid Haili had called her, but Farn knew the title of "jailor" was likely a better fit. Her name was something that made Farn think of the waves rasping along the shore, but he couldn't remember it exactly despite his efforts.

The naiad was a curious addition to their expedition. The knights of Eastfort were to accompany a contingent of naiads deep into the forest, chasing after the creatures who had attacked them. Only a skeleton crew would be left to defend their fort, should trouble arise again. The druid had not been shy in referring to the task as Dillen's penance for his lack of judgment in deserting the post that he had been assigned. Farn had rankled at that. The forsaken forest dwellers had a tendency to talk down to him and the other knights and of refusing to explain their reasoning behind the orders that they were given. How did they expect them to simply abandon those villagers when they had so obviously needed their help? The morality of the situation was a mottled gray mass that swirled in his chest as he thought about it. Haili must have known that the villagers couldn't have been saved, but then why didn't she say something?

A little voice in the back of Farn's mind whispered to him: Would it have mattered? Would it have changed anything? Farn pointedly ignored the answer to that question which he knew sat at the center of the amphitheater. He tried not to think of the utter lack of people who had been saved by their, admittedly, rash actions.

The flow of individuals passing across the stage was beginning to dwindle. It seemed as though the funeral was ending. Farn took another moment to again marvel at the juxtaposition of something so familiar being played out upon a stage so foreign and alien to him before rising and walking down to where Dillen now stood staring after the retreating back of the naiad who had evidently won whatever argument they had been having.

"What did she want?" Farn asked, causing Dillen to turn to face him.

"She was explaining to me what they are going to do with Elissa's body after this," Dillen growled. Farn raised an eyebrow in response but didn't say anything.

"Evidently," Dillen continued, "once this is finished, they will take her body deeper within the forest along with other offerings brought by those who have come to see her off, and they deposit the corpse there to be eaten by the beasts of the wood."

Farn couldn't stop the sharp intake of breath that breached his lips, and his eyes widened in surprise.

"But that's barbaric!" he sputtered. "How does Imariel feel about this? What about the others who fell?"

"Evidently they've all been treated to a similar fate. Something about the natural order of things or some other load of blithering rubbish. Evidently, the natural order involves rejoining the forest as fertilizer from a wolf's droppings!" Dillen sighed and rubbed his temples. "As for Imariel, I have no idea what her thoughts are on the matter, she hasn't spoken to me since all this happened. She might not likely speak to me ever again for all I know…"

There was something in the former paladin's voice that caught Farn's attention. It seemed as though Dillen was saddened more by Imariel's part in all of this than the outrage at how Elissa's remains were being treated.

"Does her indifference bother you that much? It seems as though it is no different than her usual interactions, but at least now you don't have to deal with her hawkish gaze as much." Farn gave a rueful chuckle, but it died in his throat as he found Dillen glaring at him.

"I'm sorry, I didn't mean anything by it," he offered a lame apology. Then, in a bid to distract Dillen from his current displeasure, he pointed in the direction the naiad had fled.

"Did she say when we will be leaving?" There was an awkward pause while Dillen continued to glare at the younger knight and the rain continued its steady patter around them. In the distance, one could hear the echoes of rolling thunder as the storm continued to move away from them.

"We'll go in the morning, before first light if the rain lets up." With that, Dillen turned to walk away. Farn felt a flash of desperation and called out to him.

"Sir Dillen!"

The paladin paused but didn't turn around. Farn didn't wait for him to respond, fearing that his courage might run out before he could say what he felt.

"Have I done something to offend you?" This caused Dillen to stiffen, and he turned to face Farn. The young knight was surprised at what he saw there. He saw Dillen's eyes were red, and what he had assumed were raindrops might well have been tears that threatened to overwhelm his cheeks.

"Why would you ask this?" Dillen's voice was husky and cracked as a harsh whisper.

"It's just that I feel you have been avoiding me these past several days, and even now when I finally get an opportunity to speak with you, you leave seemingly angry at me for some reason that I cannot understand. Good sir, I... I admire the feats that you have accomplished and I value what friendship we have enjoyed in the past, and I would not put such things in jeopardy."

Dillen closed his eyes and raised his face to the sky. The rain streamed over his exposed features. He gave a dry, humorless laugh before lowering his head and fixing Farn with a stare that sent chills through his bones.

"You admire my accomplishments." Another voidless chuckle. "There's the problem, Farn. That's always the problem. I'm not someone you should admire. I only end up killing those who rely on me, so if it's something you need to have faith in, I would fixate somewhere else."

Dillen took a shuddering breath of air and turned once more to walk away. He stopped after a few steps and turned to speak over his shoulder.

"But don't worry. It's not you that I'm angry with."

Chapter XV

D illen couldn't say for how long he wandered, but it was apparent that either he was following the storm or it was following him, as the rain did not let up, nor did it lessen. The branches overhead did nothing to stem the flow of water as it poured down on his head, but still he kept walking. His fingers grew numb from the cold, and his boots were soaked through.

In his mind's eye, he could dimly see the figure of his father, his head shaking sadly from side to side as he looked on his son's melancholic march through the storm-torn wood. A flash of anger shot through Dillen's stomach that shocked him out of his reverie. He gritted his teeth and growled at the sky.

"I know!" he bellowed, "I have another name to add to that list! I'm sorry that I'm such a disappointment to you! I can't even keep up a facade that was practically handed to me…" His voice trailed at the end of his statement, and he stood staring up into the rain as water dripped into his eyes and poured over his face.

The specter of his father still hovered there, in the edge of his imagined vision, still shaking his head in disapproval.

"It's not like you ever did any better! You lost us everything! Our home! Our titles! You couldn't even save Kallas! You couldn't save any of your sons! It's no wonder Mother couldn't stand you!" Dillen's lip was twisted into a snarl, and as he slowly came back to himself, he realized that he had been yelling into the air, the cold patter of rain beating against the mossy soil all around him.

"Maybe that's why she couldn't stand the rest of us, either…" he whispered to the ground, as if averting his eyes from some harsh glare that he couldn't see. He shook his head, sending raindrops flying.

"Why are we always doomed to such failure?" His voice was so low that it was impossible that anyone would have heard him. "And now they want me to chase after these monsters. It seems my penance has finally come back on me. I should've known that I wouldn't be able to keep this up."

Finally the specter spoke, and he heard the husky voice of his father scrape across his mind like a whetstone across a blade.

So what will you do? Will you run? Will you abandon your new brothers? I always knew you were a coward.

"No!" Dillen's outburst sprang to his mouth so quickly that it startled him as it struck aside the quiet stillness of the rain. Though as to which part of the accusation he was protesting, he couldn't say. Yet it had the desired effect, and the figure of his father passed from his mind, vanishing like the wind that began to stir the leaves in the trees all around him.

"I have nowhere else to go. I cannot leave them."

"This is a good thing, Sir Dillen." Dillen spun around in surprise to find Haili standing before him; she seemed taller than usual. Her skin was drenched from the rain, and she showed no signs of discomfort but simply stared at him with her piercing gaze. Her voice was as implacable and calm as it ever was, yet Dillen felt himself suppress a shiver as he stared into her eyes.

"You will not abandon this duty which has befallen you. You have fled from your problems before and taken shelter in circumstances which were not yours to claim. Your windfall has led you to where you are now. You have been as a leaf caught in the current of a stream, driven where you are pushed. But you have reached a point where if you continue to allow events to push you onward, then it will lead to your demise. It is time for you to forge your own path."

"How?! The last time I tried to do this, it got Elissa killed and shattered my connection to Imariel!" Dillen hated the pleading sound that came from his mouth as he spoke, but the tightness in his throat prevented him from changing his tone.

"That wasn't you forging your own path. There is a difference between being obstinate and being resilient. Your choice to disobey your orders before was something that your persona chose for you, and it led to ruin. Perhaps you would have made the same choice, had it been up to you, but you were not strong enough for that. Up until now, you have allowed fate to choose where you go, who you fight, and even who you love. You have been content to simply exist. But now you are a servant of Nature, and Nature devours those things that will not act. As for Imariel, don't worry, she will be accompanying you on your journey."

"What?" Dillen's eyes widened. "Why would you do this? She blames me for her mother's death!"

"There are some things that the Lady does not explain, this is one of them. But I feel that it is important that the link between you and her is repaired rather than discarded. In fact, I think that such is essential to whatever plan she has for you."

"Why me? Why do I have to do this? Why has fate brought me here?"

"If you haven't thought to question that before now, then you haven't earned the right to question it now. If we only think on our fate when it becomes hard, then we will always find ourselves unprepared and unwilling to take hold of its direction."

"That makes no sense, though!"

"Of course it doesn't! You seek only to lighten your own burdens, and such is not how Nature is meant to be. Nature is a cycle. There are dependencies and patterns that must be obeyed if everything is to function as it should. The trees of the forest would not stand if the acorns did not do as they were meant to do."

"So you are saying that I should be willing to sacrifice myself? Am I the acorn that must give way so that your tree is able to grow?"

"If that is what is needed. You seem to think that your individual worth is more valuable than it is. Each living being is not so important that it can be substituted for the value of its place which it should take. Sometimes that place is to die so that other parts may be preserved, sometimes it is to die so that others may take its place and evolve with the new season. Sometimes it is to live so as to protect or give home to others. Everyone is food for something else, from the smallest seed to the greatest predator. Learn your place within this ecosystem and perform it well, or else you will find yourself removed from it to serve another purpose in its perpetuation."

Dillen's reply died on his lips, and he felt a chill run down his spine. Haili stared at him for a moment before speaking once more.

"You thought that this would be a different response? If so, then you have yet to truly understand the way of the forest, and of the Lady whom you claim to follow. Is your service dependent on you receiving elevated status among her other servants?"

"I..." Dillen started but couldn't find any words. He felt a heat rushing to his face and his teeth grinding in frustration.

"You humans have grown up in a society that teaches you that you are special simply because you have such trappings of 'civilization' as language, manners, and government. You don't realize that yours is simply a pale imitation of the grandeur of Nature. You are not special because you were raised to think so, you are simply animals with a higher sense of self-importance. Here in the forest, you have a role to play, and you will either learn that role or you will be replaced. The Balance is far too important to placate the ego of any one individual, no matter his supposed accomplishments." She placed extra emphasis on the last word, and Dillen flinched beneath her flinty gaze.

Haili did not wait for a response, and Dillen sullenly admitted to himself that he was not prepared to give one in any case. Instead she turned and glided away, becoming lost in the shadows of the trees and in the patter of the rain. He watched her go and allowed the melancholy of the storm to envelop him in its cold, wet embrace as the shadow of evening stole across the verdant boughs of Galahir.

Chapter XVI

Dillen shifted uncomfortably in his saddle. Overhead, the branches of the ancient trees of the deeper forest intertwined to form a dark canopy that spread like a dark storm cloud over the columns of soldiers that rode or walked alongside and behind him. Shafts of sunlight pierced down through the gloom like solidified tongues of lightning that lit up motes of dust and pollen disturbed by the passing warriors and gave the eerie sensation of constant twilight. Here in the deep woods, the only way to mark the passing of the day was when the sun sank below the horizon and the murky light of day obscured to pitch black nights.

They had been marching for several days at this point, and it gave Dillen a sense of vertigo whenever he referenced the maps of his childhood in his brain. Cartographers were oftentimes artists by trade, and they were prone to a certain amount of license by that very nature, but the maps that he had seen before coming to Galahir had always painted the forest as a relatively small gathering of trees nestled up against mountains to the south. After the sights he had seen over the past few days, he could not reconcile the amount of time spent marching through the forest with the limited space taken up on any map he had ever seen. It was as if as soon as a tree and its fellows were out of sight, they would hurry around the procession to cut them off and make the forest spread ahead of them in some infinite loop of green. Not even with all of his time in the forest could he imagine the depths and profundity of the forest's reach, nor how long it now stretched out before him in every direction.

Dillen held up a hand, and the column crept to a halt behind him. The forest was still, the only sounds were the uneasy steps of the horses around him and the muttering of his soldiers as they gazed through the shadowed trees.

"What is it?" A voice broke through the gloomy quiet and caused Dillen to flinch. He turned and saw the hulking figure of Bhadein leaning over his saddle, his eyes boring into Dillen's skull. The younger knight swallowed and brought his horse partially around to face the soldiers behind him.

"I need a reference point," Dillen responded, proud at how level his voice came out. "I want to make sure we are still headed in the right direction."

"In other words, you've lost us." Bhadein sighed and shifted back in his saddle. He turned and bellowed a name back into the ranks.

"Farn!"

A figure almost as big as Bhadein pushed his way through the ranks of knights. Farn rode up beside Bhadein, flashing a smile at Dillen before turning toward the tall man beside him.

"Go and fetch the gladestalker and the naiad," Bhadein barked without looking at Farn. The younger man grimaced at his tone but turned obediently and rode back through the now shuffling column of knights behind them.

Dillen felt his insides squirm under Bhadein's intense glare. He tried to contain his desire to shift in his saddle further and instead focused on maintaining the other warrior's fierce gaze.

Go ahead and judge me, old man! Dillen thought defiantly. You don't know what I've had to do in order to survive. You have no right to cast your eyes down that ridiculously long nose of yours. Go burn yourself!

The two sat in silence while they waited for Farn to return, and it took several long, excruciating minutes before their patience was rewarded. Dillen stiffened as he heard the voice of the gladestalker and refused to look directly at her.

"This knight tells me that you have managed to get us lost again, Sir Dillen?" Imariel's voice was sterile with cold dissidence, and Dillen felt something inside him coil itself into knots. His desperation forced itself to the surface and he risked a sidelong glance at her. She stood before him with her arms at her sides and an impassive look on her face; she did not even glance in his direction. Behind her stood a hulking shadow of Lothak, a giant dragon-man whose mouth seemed to glow with an inner fire behind his sharp teeth. He'd been present at Elissa's funeral and had evidently agreed to accompany Imariel on this mission as a way of repaying her mother for some old blood debt. Dillen refused to look at him altogether.

"The fault of this matter is that of the woods and trees, child. Do not be for the putting on his shoulders this blame."

This scratchy whisper came from the figure standing beside Imariel, and Dillen tried desperately to not let his gaze linger on her for too long. Her name was Shesh'ra, and she was a naiad, a type of amphibious humanoid with the figure of a beautiful woman and an alien face made up with thin lips, narrow slits where a nose should be, and great bulbous eyes that resembled those of a fish. Her head was crowned with a halo of crimson fins that flickered and danced depending on her mood. This particular naiad had been burned in some previous engagement some time ago, and the whole of her right side was covered in strange scars that overlapped the shimmering blue scales of her people to create ugly patterns that were hard to avoid staring at. She was the leader of the small contingent of naiads that had been sent with Dillen and his men. Shesh'ra stood now staring up at him on his horse with a small smile on her face. Imariel sniffed at this but otherwise did not respond.

"What do you want us to do about it?" Imariel still pointedly refused to look at Dillen.

"I didn't call for you," he shrugged and pointed at Bhadein, "he did."

Bhadein rolled his eyes and nudged his horse slightly forward.

"I beg your pardon, but we would like to consult with you to best discern how we might get back on track." Imariel shook her head in response.

"The forest has a mind of its own. At this point, we might as well just continue walking down this track and come out wherever the forest wants us to be. I'm not surprised that we are lost, though. The forest knows we are on a punitive quest and accommodates our fate accordingly."

With that, the elf turned and slipped back through the gathered ranks of mounted soldiers behind her, the hulking salamander following closely behind. Dillen sighed audibly as he watched her depart.

"I am glad she can still be cordial." Dillen tried to keep the sorrowful longing out of his voice, and his eyes flickered to the other two standing near him to see if they noticed.

"It is to be a testament of her strength. That one's eyes still weep for her loss," Shesh'ra whispered.

"I was surprised that she came with us," Bhadein muttered, staring after her. "Why would she, if she were given the choice?"

In response, Shesh'ra pulled off her right vambrace and held up her scarred arm. Dillen twisted uncomfortably in an attempt to avert his eyes.

"As I have been told, she was sent with us by the Lady's command."

"But why?" Dillen asked, the revelation causing him to forget his melancholy for a moment. Shesh'ra did not answer but instead focused her gaze on her exposed arm.

"I have seen your eyes shed their attention upon my flesh's carvings." Shesh'ra rotated her burned arm as sporadic scales caught some of the scattered sunlight under the canopy. Dillen, in a desperate attempt to recover his dignity, stammered a frail denial of this fact.

"It is understandable." Shesh'ra smiled up at him and he fell silent. "These memories have been graven upon my scales. At times, this does cause me great pain. But I do endure. This is to remind me of that which I have failed at. This is so that I do not accomplish those failures a second time. The Lady could have taken these things from me. She could have made my scales shimmer once more. But she did want the memory to be ever present and fresh in my eyes. So that I would not forget my folly. I will never again make a gift of my trust to another who does not be worthy of it."

She lowered her arm and stared up at Dillen.

"These are my scars. These belong to me to be for reminding me of my lesson that I must not forget." Shesh'ra turned and pointed back toward where Imariel had departed.

"She is your scar."

* * * * *

The rest of the day wore on at an almost imperceptible speed. Dillen had grumbled, almost as much as Bhadein had, when no other suggestion was offered for their predicament other than to keep marching on and throw their fates to the mercy of the forest. Yet there was no other choice but to keep moving. Dillen had felt a certain amount of vindication when Imarel had implied that the forest was the reason that they were lost, and he held on to that small ember that perhaps it would take the lead in this case. That hope grew dimmer as the day progressed, and they still had no idea where they were or if they were progressing toward their goal.

At long last, the sun began to dip below the horizon, and the onset of the night time gloom forced the column to a halt. A quick scouting group quickly returned with news of a small clearing a small distance ahead of them, and so they pushed forward so that they could pitch their tents with some relief of tree roots and undergrowth.

Exhausted, Dillen flopped down into his cot after the men had finished setting up his small command tent which doubled as his own personal quarters. He didn't even bother trying to secure any food, he was so tired. He very quickly regretted not eating anything, however, as soon his growling stomach refused to let him rest. He sat staring at the canvas roof of his tent, listening to the sounds of the forest on the other side of the thick fabric that surrounded him.

The wind brushed the tree branches together, creating a swishing noise that sounded like whispering voices. Dillen shivered at the thought of the creatures that lay slinking about in that darkness. Even after all of these years, he found himself pining for the home he had known before the trees of Galahir became his permanent residence.

"Father would be so disappointed."

Dillen sat straight up in his cot, his eyes wide open as he looked around the tent for the source of the voice. He spied what he thought was his armor standing in the corner, but as he stared, the pile seemed to shift and move. Dillen swore that he saw a spectral arm reach up to brush a strand of hair out of its eyes.

"Who's there?" Dillen's voice quivered as he spoke. The tent was mostly silent except for the wind outside pushing against the canvas. There was no answer to his question, and the wind toyed with his nerves, building and falling in sudden gusts. Dillen sighed and laid back down on the cot, his stomach still fluttering from the imagined shock.

"But then, it was never difficult to disappoint him, was it?" The voice echoed around Dillen's head and he bolted upright once more. Now a figure sat before him where his armor had lain. In the dim light of the tent, illuminated only by the torchlight leaking in from the camp outside, Dillen could see that the figure had long, blond hair and was sitting on the ground staring up at him. There was something painfully familiar about his visitor, but Dillen quickly reached for the knife he kept under his pillow.

"Wh... who are you?"

The figure did not respond, instead it began to sway back and forth, the blond hair that was lit by the dim light waving in the lazy motion.

"We all tried so hard, didn't we?" The figure's voice came out in a sing-song tone. "We literally gave him everything! Well, except you. You're the only one that escaped his greedy madness, aren't you?"

A solid lump had formed in Dillen's throat. He stared at the rocking form before him and quietly pondered what he would do. How had this person gotten in here? What were they talking about? Why did their words bring such a strong sensation of guilt into his stomach?

"What do you want?" Dillen forced the words out, but the figure still just ignored him.

"We all gave everything, except you. Why did you run away, Dillen? We could all be together now if only you had done what was needed of you!"

The figure stopped rocking and slid soundlessly to its feet. Dillen recoiled and brought his knife up to point at the shadow's chest.

"Stay back!" He barked. The figure paid him no heed and stepped closer. In the failing light of his tent, Dillen could just make out some of the starker features on the face of his accuser. With each word, the figure took another step closer to him.

"Oh, my dear brother! You aren't going to die right now. First you must pass through purgatory! The cleansing fire will bring you home to us! But don't worry. I will be with you every step of the way!"

By now, the figure was close enough that it was able to reach out a hand to touch the side of Dillen's face. He flinched away as he felt something warm and wet press against his cheek, and he stared up into the thing's face. The creature's face was twisted into a strange parody of a smile, but its mouth was too big. Large, shimmering eyes stared down at him with what looked like excitement. The strangest feature of all, though, was the lack of either eyebrows or a nose. Even so, recognition dawned on Dillen, and a name forced itself through his frozen lips.

"Kallas?"

This whisper seemed to break the spell, and the creature reared its head back and hissed, its smile unbroken. It leered back down at the knight sitting before it and lunged forward, its impossibly wide mouth gaping open to reveal rows of mismatched teeth of different sizes. Startled, Dillen reacted instinctively and stabbed his knife upward. As it made contact with the monster's chest, the creature seemed to dissipate into a fog that flowed all around him.

"We will bring you home, brother." The creature's voice echoed in his ears. Dillen shut his eyes, the blood pumping in his temples.

When he opened them, he found himself lying in his cot, staring at the canvas roof of his tent. The simple woolen blanket he had lain down with had been kicked off, and he was shivering in his smallclothes. He glanced over at his pile of armor and was relieved to see that it hadn't moved. Taking a few deep breaths, he sat up and swung his legs over the edge of the cot.

He placed his face in his hands to try and calm his nerves from the nightmare. When his fingers brushed against his cheek, however, he recoiled as they came away wet. Dillen stood up and looked at his hand, it was covered in a liquid that he couldn't make out in the dark. Scrambling over to a chest, Dillen quickly cast about with his other, unsullied hand and discovered a candle and something to light it with.

Finally, after several moments, he was able to get the wick lit and see his hand clearly. What he saw almost stopped his heart.

His hand was covered in blood.

Frantically he clawed at his cheek, feeling for a wound that could be the source. After several long moments, he determined that he was unharmed. The memory of his nightmare came back to him, of the creature pressing its warm, damp hand against his cheek in such a horrible parody of a tender caress. His stomach knotted into a ball of hot coals, and he felt as if he would be sick.

This is impossible! The thought simmered in his mind, throwing off smoke much like the creature in his nightmare had. He couldn't be here! That wasn't real!

He was still pondering this when the screaming began.

Chapter XVII

It started out as a single voice. A high-pitched, wet sound that gargled as it raised in intensity. Dillen quickly pulled on a leather jerkin over his nightclothes and grabbed his sword from the pile of his armor. He quickly scrubbed the side of his face and his hand to try and remove the blood, but he only succeeded in spreading it around. Discouraged, he ran outside to investigate the sound.

The moon was full and it lent its silver light to the orange flares of the torches that were scattered throughout the camp along with the occasional campfire here and there. Dillen cast his eyes about for the source of the screams. It didn't take him long to find it.

Several feet before him, he made out what looked like the back of one of his men, but the man's feet weren't touching the ground, and great spots of darkness were spreading out along his back from the shoulders. The man was screaming in an ever-increasing pitch, and Dillen heard something wet twisting in the dark. Abruptly the man's screaming cut off as something pointed exploded through his lower back. Dillen started at the image as the man's body was quickly tossed to the side, and a nightmare was left standing in his place.

A gaunt figure stood before Dillen now, its legs were bent at unnatural angles, and besides the long claws that made up its hands, two more appendages hovered over each of its shoulders, both ending in sharp points. The most disturbing thing about this apparition, however, was its face, or rather its lack thereof. Two rows of jagged teeth grinned in his direction, but there were no eyes or nose above those awful teeth.

The sight caused Dillen to recoil in disgust, and as he did so, the creature tilted its head as if listening for something. Dillen froze and the creature began chittering its teeth together in a worrying, gnashing sound that caused the knight's spine to tingle. The faceless monster turned its head from side to side, in some strange parody of eyesight. Dillen felt his lungs burn and realized that he had been holding his breath. He slowly released his hold and allowed it to stream slowly from between his teeth. The creature took a step forward, and Dillen's heart leapt into his throat, causing him to almost choke in surprise.

Instantly the creature's head snapped around in Dillen's direction and let out a breathless scream. Dillen had once had to hold one of his friends as he lay dying from a spear through his chest. His friend had struggled and gasped for breath as his lungs had filled with blood and he had choked to death on it. Dillen could still remember the wet gasps as he struggled for air. The creature's scream filled him with the same helpless despair that his friend's terrified, breathless breaths had, and he stepped once more back. A part of him wished desperately to return to the imagined safety of his tent and pretend that this all was just a dream. The creature didn't give him the opportunity to flee, though.

The faceless demon launched itself toward him. Its bladed protrusions scything the air as it ran, its mouth still open with its wheezing cry. Dillen felt himself freeze as he watched the beast close the distance, and only a pure, animalistic instinct pushed him to duck under the monster's first blow. His sword felt slippery in his hands as he straightened from his dodge, and he almost dropped the weapon when he brought it up in a defensive parry against another scything talon that flew at his face.

More from luck than anything else, Dillen held his blade at the wrong angle, and the edge of his sword bit deep into the creature's appendage. The beast screamed another bone rasping cry and attempted to wrench its injured limb back, pulling the weapon from the knight's grasp as it did so. The sword flailed about for a second as the creature shook itself, then fell into the grass at the monster's feet. Dillen's gaze widened as he watched this, but his fighter's instinct took hold.

I don't want to die! Dillen's mind screamed as he pulled his dagger from his belt and stepped in close against his demonic opponent's flailing form. The creature looked around in what Dillen could have sworn was confusion as he pressed up against the grotesquely thin body of the beast and drove his dagger upward into the base of its jaw. The monster's scream cut off as the point of the dagger pierced the base of the faceless skull, and it went limp and tumbled onto the ground.

Dillen stood with his chest heaving and his vision swimming from the dregs of what had just happened. His dagger was still in the creature's skull, and some part of him was screaming at him to retrieve it, or his sword, so that he wasn't defenseless; but it was as if he were watching the entire scene play out from behind a plate of glass. His hands felt numb, and the fire of his terror seemed to be a distant flame that lit up the night sky. Distantly, he became aware of more breathless screams throughout the camp, accompanied by the sounds of fighting as the warriors awoke to the threat all around them. But Dillen could not bring himself to move for several long moments as he stared down at the beast he had just slain.

Finally he found the nerve to move, and he lowered himself to his knees to retrieve his dagger and search for his sword, but his movements were wooden and it took him three tries to pry the dagger away from the twisted corpse.

"That was well done! Father would be proud!" The voice from his tent whispered in his ear, and Dillen twisted so hard to confront it that he ended up toppling onto his side. There was no one there. Dillen breathed a shuddering sigh and pushed himself to his feet so that he could look for his sword. He quickly found it lying a few feet away and retrieved it. He turned toward the sounds of fighting, a thrill of fear running through him at the thought of facing another of these creatures. He hesitated, but the idea of being alone if another creature attacked pushed his feet toward the fight.

He rounded a tent and was quickly met with an awful sight. A small knot of knights had squared up with shields and swords drawn. They had their backs to him, but he could see across the way, about twenty yards in front of the knights was a shuffling mass of bodies that ambled awkwardly forward. At the feet of his soldiers, Dillen could see several corpses, some like that of the strange creatures, others in twisted humanoid forms with knobby limbs and ill-fitting clothing. There were several figures that held shields and swords alongside the grotesque bodies as well. Taking a deep breath, Dillen ran up to stand beside his men.

"Hold strong, brothers!" He knew his lines well, he'd had to speak them on so many occasions, but he felt now was a good time for the solidity of ceremony to bolster their nerves when the very essence of their nightmares was reaching out to kill them. Some of the knights turned toward him as he approached and lifted their swords in a quick battle salute before turning back to face their foe. One figure called out to him and Dillen recognized the familiar tone of Bhadein.

"We are in a bad situation, Sir Dillen! We have this fist of knights here with us who are ready to fight, but we've been cut off from the rest of the camp! If we can fight our way across the glade, we can meet up with the naiads and the rest of our company. But it doesn't look good. We have a host of these bloody scarecrows in our way!"

In spite of himself, Dillen laughed at Bhadein's apt description of the shambling horde before him. His emotions coupled with the stress of the situation to find some morbid humor in the image of scarecrows filled with straw marching toward them. He could almost feel Bhadein's disapproval boring into his skull from the darkness.

"You find this amusing, Sir Dillen?" The older knight growled, and Dillen waved his hand in his direction.

"Not at all, Sir Bhadein! I was just appreciating your appraisal of our situation! It looks as though the scarecrows are revolting from their duties in the fields." He lifted his blade and pointed at the enemy. "But if they stand between us and the rest of our comrades, then it is our harvest time, and we have a bumper crop to pull in, it seems! Come then! Let's take their pumpkins from off their heads so that our horses will have treats in the morning!"

Dillen bellowed his challenge at the scarecrows and took several quick steps toward them, not daring to look behind him to see the reactions of the other knights. This is what heroes are supposed to do, right? Lead the charge? What if they don't follow? The fretful words ricocheted around in his skull for a terrified second before he heard the accompanying battle cries behind him and the boots of his fellow soldiers charging across the glade with him. Dillen swore that he heard Bhadein yelling "You bloody idiot!" behind him.

His feet carried him across the field at an alarming rate, and before he could think about it, he found himself slamming into a figure wearing what looked like a burlap sack over his chest that writhed as if it were filled with snakes under a wide-brimmed hat. Acting on pure impulse and adrenaline at this point, Dillen slashed out with his sword and it passed almost effortlessly through the distorted torso. He sliced again and felt little resistance as another nightmarish figure fell before him. By this time, the other knights had caught up to him and were hacking their way through the shadow-thin bodies before them.

An eerie silence filled the air, and it caused Dillen's sweat to turn cold. The creatures died without a sound. There were no attempts at self-preservation. They really were like the straw men that Bhadein had labeled them. Practice dummies set up on the green for new recruits to practice their thrusts and their parries on. Then the counterattack came.

As if controlled by a single mind, the shuffling creatures lurched forward with arms extended before them. Their suddenly wispy forms becoming more corporeal as the sudden action caused hesitation in the attacking knights. Dillen reflexively raised his blade and sheered two clawed hands from twig-like arms, but the creature did not stop at the loss of its hands as any other living thing might. Instead, the scarecrow pressed forward and wrapped its stumps around Dillen's neck like a lover throwing herself at him in an embrace. In a terrifying parody, the creature drove its face into his shoulder as if it were going for a kiss, but Dillen felt a sharp pain as the thing dug its teeth through the fabric of his undershirt and into the flesh beneath it.

Dillen cried out and pushed the creature away from him. Surprisingly, it fell away with little resistance and toppled to the ground. Dillen stabbed downward through its chest and felt it go still. He held his hand up to the wound and it came away wet. He was bleeding, but he didn't have time to worry about that, as another wave of ghastly walkers threw themselves at him.

The night was no longer silent, as the screams of the knights around him filled the air. Dillen watched as one warrior fell beneath the weight of three scarecrows. His comrades stabbed downward and tried to clear the beasts away from their friend, but when they pulled the beasts away from them, all that was left was a corpse covered in bloody pock marks where gnawing teeth had pulled away chattering mouthfuls of skin and muscle.

Dillen suppressed the urge to vomit as he swung his blade at ever more waves of the wickedly grinning faces of their attackers. He felt the presence of another knight by his side and he glanced over to see Bhadein holding his shield out to cover both his own and Dillen's exposed side.

"We have to fall back!" Bhadein called out as he stabbed his sword out from behind the cover of his shield.

"How?! These things will just follow us and finish us as we run!"

"If we stay, they'll just cut us down where we stand! If we fall back, some of the others might make it!"

Dillen swallowed hard and focused on the monsters in front of him for a few minutes. He hadn't missed Bhadein's intimation that he and Dillen would be the buffer that would give those knights the possibility of escaping.

"Did you hear me?!" Bhadein called out again.

"You order the retreat then! If you're so keen!" Dillen snapped.

"They won't listen to me! They're too busy chasing after the damnable Hero of Galahir! You must do it!"

Dillen did not respond to this, his mind whirling with a thousand possible retorts. Another of the scarecrows pushed itself forward and raked its claws across Dillen's face while he was distracted. A searing pain stretched from above his right eye and extended down across the bridge of his nose. Parallel lines of pain mirrored that on either side but graciously did not strike his eyes. Dillen cried out and staggered back.

"Dillen!" Bhadein cried out and stepped in front of him. Dillen wiped the blood out of his eyes, trying to clear his vision as he watched Bhadein slam his shield into two more scarecrows that tried to claw at his face in the same way that had wounded Dillen. The younger knight listened to the sounds of struggle all around him. Another knight's scream turned into a wet gurgle as he died to Dillen's right. The press of nightmarish bodies weighed in like the feeling of rain before the storm strikes. Dillen tried to look around him, but it was no use. All there was to see were scarecrows before him and knights around him. He forced himself to stand.

"Brothers!" he bellowed. "Prepare to fall back! Form up defense lines!"

In drilled precision, the soldiers snapped together and braced their shields against the warrior to their left to reform their shield wall. They pressed close so that their weapons became useless, but the line was taut and impenetrable. The scarecrows scrabbled their claws against the wooden barrier, but it was no use.

"Advance and step!" Dillen cried out. In one motion, every shield slammed forward and the collective concussive force of the wall crashing into the sickly figures before them pushed the scarecrows back, causing many of them to fall backward onto the ground. Then, with that same unity, the knights took two successive steps backward to open a gap up between them and their attackers.

"Withdraw!" Even as the word left Dillen's mouth, he felt a brush of wind against his cheek as something whizzed past him to strike one of the scarecrows that snarled back at him from beyond the gap. In a moment of shocked realization, Dillen realized that it was an arrow, and it now protruded from the scarecrow's forehead. A greater shock came as he glanced down the line and saw that several more of the creatures bore similar feathered shafts embedded in their foreheads and chests.

Thunder seemed to clap in the clouds overhead, and Dillen shook his head when the noise did not stop after a few seconds but seemed to be growing louder. His head snapped up as he recognized the sound. He saw the pale manes of stark white mares charging toward the flank of the scarecrows they were currently fighting. On the backs of these beautiful creatures were riders with long, silken hair that shimmered in the moonlight. In their hands, they held bows, strung with arrows that seemed to howl as they loosed. The projectiles fell on the remaining enemy before Dillen and his men, and as they struck the creatures, there was a howling explosion as wind rushed up as if from the head of a massive storm. The few remaining scarecrows were thrown to the side as great gusts of air pushed their light frames through the night to land several yards away.

The white horsemen reined in and pivoted away before Dillen could even lift an arm in acknowledgment or thanks; their ghostly images already dancing across the glade to pounce on another target further on down the way. Dillen took several deep breaths and was unable to stop a grin from splitting his face. A voice from behind him caused him to spin suddenly.

"What in all the circles of the Abyss were you thinking?!" A figure clad in animal skins and bearing a long staff topped with what looked like moose antlers stalked toward Dillen, behind him stood a magnificent stag of pure white.

"Who are you?" Dillen managed to stammer before the newcomer was in his face. Up close, Dillen was shocked to see the finely detailed features of an elf staring out at him from behind long silver hair that had been tied together with strips of leather and bits of bone into a type of top knot.

"My name is Velorun. I lead the night hunt in this region of the forest, and you fools made camp on the very edge of the sickness! It was lucky that my trackers found you before it was too late!"

"What do you mean the sickness? What are you talking about?"

Instead of an answer, the elf turned and pointed at the fighting that was still going on across the way.

"No time for answers right now. Just know that I am a servant of the Lady, like you. Right now, let's see if we can save the rest of your friends from being devoured."

Velorun turned and ran back to the stag, swinging himself gracefully up to sit on its back. Without a word, the magnificent beast took off running in the direction of the white horsemen. His shape faded to gray as he galloped through the night, leaving Dillen to stare after with a puzzled look on his face.

Chapter XVIII

The sunrise crept through the morning sky, the shadows of the surrounding trees casting a smoky veil across the clearing. Dillen saw the red light slant through the foliage as he sat on a stone in the middle of the carnage. The bodies of knights, naiads, and elves lay strewn about in the grass, the stink of blood and death lingering in the air like a malignant musk.

Dillen stared down at his hands which lay trembling in his lap. There were no monsters among the slain. No scarecrow corpses or images of those terrible things like the one he had slain by his tent. They were all gone, evaporated like smoke before the morning dew. Or had they even existed at all? Had some madness gripped him and the others through the night and brought them to slaughter each other in their terrified fury?

"You're not going mad." Dillen turned to see the silver-haired elf from the night stepping gingerly through the corpses. He moved gracefully, his staff helping to guide his way through the bodies.

"What?" Dillen's voice surprised him. It was scratchy and husky from disuse.

"The monsters were real. This was not a horrible nightmare, nor did you imagine them." The elf stopped a few feet from where Dillen sat. The knight stared at the elf, and there was a long, uncomfortable silence as he searched for the proper words. Velorun spoke before he could come up with anything.

"Their anchor into this world is nearby, and so before their mortal forms fully perish, they will melt back into whatever void that spawned them so that they will be able to reappear again. That is why you do not see their bodies here."

Dillen was shocked, and his mouth moved for several moments before words actually formed.

"How do you know this?"

"We call these creatures the Nightstalkers, because they find their way into our dreams and so even in our sleep we are filled with the torturous dread of confronting our fears made manifest in the flesh. Whenever we kill one of their number, it joins the ranks of its comrades in our nightmares. As to the idea of the anchor, well, it is, admittedly, just a theory. But there is a jagged demon among them who takes… trophies from its victims. Generally those are taken in the form of ears, or fingers if he is in a hurry. Sometimes he takes bits of jewelry or other shiny things that catch his interest." At this statement, Velorun looked into the still dark part of the forest before them. His eyes were glazed and there was a melancholy to his words which stopped the questions that ached to spill off Dillen's tongue. After a few seconds, the elf spoke again.

"He appears from time to time. A mighty beast with the legs of a giant spider, the arms of a scorpion, and a face of pointed teeth and a multitude of red, glowing eyes. Every time he comes, it means that there will be a heavy toll taken from our ranks. We have named him Ur-chitak, or the Chittering Spider. This beast is big enough to hunt birds in the trees by hurling its webs at them when they come to roost in the branches. We know it is the same creature because of the trophies around his neck.

"I have personally witnessed this brute taken down on three separate occasions. Once, my warriors pierced his chest with no less than three lances. Another time, I saw him cast over the mighty Tre'angun, a mighty waterfall deep within the Sickness. The third time," the elf raised his hand, and small bolts of energy flickered between his fingers, "I saw to his demise myself, and I promise you that there was naught but ash left when I was done. That was last winter. Yet he was spotted about five days back, patrolling along the edge of the Sickness."

"Are you saying that these things can't be killed?" Dillen felt an icicle form in his stomach.

"It would seem so. At least not indefinitely."

"So all of this was for nothing?!" Dillen gestured at the bodies surrounding them. Velorun shook his head, causing the bones and beads in his hair to clack against each other.

"No, this was not for nothing. The more people there are in one place, the more emotions there are for the monsters to feed on. This many anxious minds in one place must have been too tempting and drew them to you. But you fought them back, and even though these creatures don't seem to die, it does seem to require some amount of time and energy to be reborn, so you have bought us some weeks or so of respite. This is a good thing."

"What is the point of all this? What are you doing here?"

"I am a mage of the Green Lady. I guide the Night Hunt which fights to ensure that the Sickness doesn't spread deeper into the forest."

"How can you fight something like that?!"

"We sell our lives to delay the creatures. We can do little else. So far, we have been successful. The Sickness has not gone further than this clearing in the two years since it first appeared and our hunt was formed."

Dillen stood up quickly, his head spinning with this new information. He turned and began walking away, trampling bodies underfoot in his haste to escape the elf's impassive gaze.

"Where are you going?" Velorun called after him, but Dillen did not respond, his breath was already coming in ragged gasps, and he felt the citric taste of vomit welling up beneath his tongue. He staggered through the uneven ground made worse by the dead that lay before him. He moved to where the bodies were less thick, aiming for the treeline. There was shouting behind him, but he ignored it, moving desperately for the cover of the dark forest so that no one would see him be sick.

It was cooler beneath the trees, and Dillen quickly found a large, moss-covered boulder which he leaned against for support while his already empty stomach purged itself of whatever bile it could manage onto the forest floor.

After the retching had stopped, Dillen wiped his mouth and willed his stomach to stop twisting around itself. He glanced upward into the canopy overhead. The tree branches shifted slightly in the morning breeze that felt good on his hot cheeks, and he closed his eyes to better enjoy the sensation.

"Such a predicament, isn't it, my brother?" The voice crackled like boiling water being thrown across ice. Dillen's eyes snapped open and he tried to press himself into the boulder behind him as he spied the twisted face of his nightmare visitor from the previous evening. A wide mouth spread literally from one side of his face to the other, and eyes the size of plates shimmered above its macabre grin.

"What are you?" Dillen choked. He reached for his sword and remembered that he had left it with a retainer to sharpen after the battle. His knife was still at his belt, however, and his fingers scrabbled to pull it from its sheath.

"You know what I am!" The distorted Kallas seemed to purr as it slithered closer. The outline of his figure shivered as if Dillen's eyes refused to focus. He held his dagger out before him, and the creature chuckled; it was something like that of the sound of a dove taking flight over muted thunder in the background.

"I am all that remains of your brother! My corpse has already been eaten through by the worms, or been tossed to the dogs in the house of cruel strangers. You wouldn't know, because you left me unprotected. Alone! I died alone among strangers, and you did nothing to stop it!" Kallas gently pushed the dagger to the side and stepped closer so that his face was inches from Dillen's.

"This is all there is of me! Your memories are all that I have left! That, and your delicious guilt!" Kallas's face let out a deep, contented sigh.

"Get away from me!" Dillen brought his dagger up, but his movements felt leaden, and his brother easily dodged the blow.

"Oh my sweet, sweet brother!" Kallas chuckled. "You don't understand! We are bound together! You sustain me! And I will never leave you, unlike how you left me. I swear to you that you will never be alone." Dillen fought down the urge to scream as Kallas's impossible grin grew wider. He nearly fainted when he felt a hand clamp down on his shoulder.

"What are you doing, you idiot?!" Dillen was relieved when he turned to reveal the fur-clad form of Velorun. "Why would you flee to the Sickness? We must go! Now!" The silver-haired elf hauled on Dillen's arm and pulled him bodily from the forest. As he left the shadow of the trees behind him, he heard a raspy whisper in his ear.

"Ta-ta for now, dear brother!"

*****

"What is going on?!" Bhadein growled. "What were those things last night?"

They were sitting in Dillen's tent. The sun had risen above the treetops now and was glaring down at them through the canvas. They had rolled up the walls of the tent to allow a slight breeze to pass through and cool the air. Imariel, Bhadein, and Shesh'ra all sat on stools around Dillen's table where there was lain out the single, unreliable map that they had been following to bring them here. Standing over them all was Velorun, and off to one side were Farn and Lothak, Imariel's strangely quiet salamander guard, standing at attention away from the camp leaders as they sat in discussion.

Dillen's attention was not with the rest. His mind wandered back to the events of that morning and the strange creature that wore his brother's face like some distended mask. He suppressed a shiver as he thought of the elongated mouth opening wide before him and the dry laugh that had escaped between its sharp teeth. Velorun had dragged him from the forest boughs screaming. Several soldiers had turned to look in their direction, and Velorun had struck him across the face, which had jarred him into a shocked silence. The damage had been done already though. There were worried whispers running through the camp that the horrors of the forest were too much even for the might Hero of Galahir to handle. After last night's battle, morale was at a very dangerous level.

But beyond that, what was that creature that haunted him? Had it been a dream last night? What about this morning? It had known things that he hadn't told anyone... well, not anyone who was still living in any case. What did it all mean?

"Sir Dillen!" Bhadein's bark brought Dillen back with a start, almost causing him to crash to the ground in surprise.

"What?!" He snapped impatiently, recovering his balance.

"What are your thoughts on the matter?" Bhadein's scowl deepened as he saw Dillen's blank stare in response. "Are you even listening?"

"I'm sorry... my mind was elsewhere. What were we discussing?" Dillen gave an embarrassed smile. Bhadein's glare intensified even further. Dillen flicked his gaze at Imariel, but her face was impassive, her eyes devoid of any emotion, and somehow that cut deeper than Bhadein's intense disapproval. Shesh'ra sighed.

"This is of an importance, young knight. Do not be for losing focus now. The mage Velorun was to be giving us the information that we did fear. This Sickness is a work of demons that be not of the Abyss but come from something that is possible to be much older than it. Somewhere that even the stars do not swim. Somewhere the moon holds no sway."

Dillen stared at her.

"What does that mean?"

"It means that we need to make a plan!" Bhadein snorted. "These monsters can't be killed, at least not for good. It seems obvious that they aren't from our world, and if that's the case, then they must have some way of crossing over from wherever they come from somewhere nearby. Velorun says that this 'Sickness' appeared at about the same time that the Abyss began expanding about two years ago, and his troops have been patrolling the edge of this forest almost ever since. So long as they keep killing the creatures, they don't expand past this point. But any attempts to go any deeper always end in disaster."

"The creatures feed on emotion. The more people there are in an area, the more they are drawn to it." Velorun pointed toward the forest where the sun could not dispel the dark gloom that settled upon it like a cloak.

"We feel that there is something there, in the heart of the shadows, that is anchoring these creatures to our world. Perhaps something happened that the echo of it gives the creatures enough strength to manifest here, or guide them back when we've cast them back into whatever void they come from."

"So why not march our army in there and purify it once and for all? With our wits about us, we will certainly fare better than we did last night; and if we can find this 'anchor,' then we should be able to banish them permanently, right?" Dillen looked around at them each in turn. It was when his eyes landed on Imariel's face that he started in surprise.

"Life really has no meaning beyond your own to you, does it?" Her voice was cold. A tightly controlled vortex of frigid emotion. Her face was still the impassible wall that it always was of late, except for a slight downturn of her brows. Without a word more, she stood up and seemed to glide away from the canopy where they stood.

"You really should learn to listen more closely, sir knight." Velorun shook his head. Dillen flashed him a deadly look, but the elf simply shook his head slowly.

"We have tried that route before. I led a column of warriors to try and purify the forest. This was our home, and the Sickness claimed a village not far from here that, to this day, still sits empty, claw marks and shadows etched into the walls of buildings where our children once played. As soon as we entered the darkness, we were attacked by monstrosities like those that assailed you last night, only in greater numbers. The fear in our ranks was ambrosia to them, it seemed, and they surged against us wave after wave. Because our anger and hatred was equally as strong as our fear, we managed to push the shadow back to this clearing, but by then, we were wading in puddles of our own blood. Over one third of our numbers was killed outright by the beasts. I would have pushed us further, but my warriors prevailed upon me to halt, and so I pulled back.

"Since then, we have maintained the border of the Sickness by sending out small patrols. With fewer minds to feed it with emotion, the monsters are less likely to be drawn to us. Without this sustenance, they become lethargic and aimless. Occasionally a handful will wander beyond the borders that we have established in order to find more food, and that is what we guard against. An army invading this area would be a suicidal plan at best. At worst, it would make your most hellish nightmares seem a pleasant dream by comparison." Velorun's face became hard as flint.

"I know. I have seen it. I will never lose those screams or the fear in the eyes of my men as they were assaulted by creatures bred from the bowels of our most cruel imaginations."

Dillen shivered again as the image of his brother's twisted smile flashed before his eyes. By the looks on the faces of the other individuals still listening, their thoughts were turned to similarly bleak images.

"So what are we to do, then?" Dillen muttered bitterly. "We were sent to cleanse the forest, but according to you, that is an impossible feat!"

"The Lady does provide," Shesh'ra protested, but even her voice felt flat and unconvinced.

"There is one thing that we have never been able to do." Velorun spoke in a low tone, and the remaining members of the group turned to look at him. He stared out at the shadowed trees that made up the border of the Sickness.

"There is something in there. Something that binds these creatures to this area. If we could purify that, if we could remove their anchor, then that may purge them from this area. Meaning that if we kill them, they stay dead, or at least banished from our plane of existence."

"That is exactly what I suggested! So why haven't you already done that?" Dillen asked impatiently.

"Because, every time we have ever sent anyone into the Sickness, they have never come out, or if they have, they return as raving lunatics, babbling insanities for the rest of their days, which usually isn't very long as they generally don't eat or drink afterward, either." The elf sighed and turned a pointed gaze on Dillen.

"But perhaps this is your fate then, young knight. Perhaps it is your duty to succeed where my people could not." The elf's eyes narrowed only slightly, but it was enough to let Dillen know that he was not pleased by this sentiment.

"Me?! What am I supposed to do?" Dillen sputtered.

"Surely the great Hero of Galahir, as the songs name you, will be up to the task to save Galahir once more?" Bhadein didn't even bother to keep the mocking tone from his voice. Dillen glared at him.

"His words mark wisdom in a strange tone..." Shesh'ra's voice cut through the tension. Dillen was caught off guard by the sudden interjection that he simply turned to stare at her.

"It does make a strange sense," the naiad shrugged. "I do not take my sight to be that of the Lady's, but she did be the one who did send you here to this place at the edge of the dark. Mayhap she did have a plan in doing this thing."

"One can only imagine," Bhadein grumbled.

"She's right," Velorun broke in. "It does seem rather fortuitous that you would arrive, and that the forest would guide you right to the edge of the Sickness. We knew you were coming and would have stopped you from doing so had we met you, but the forest bypassed us and brought you directly here."

Dillen felt a strange twisting in his gut. Something tugged at the edge of his periphery, and he turned his head to stare at a blank space just over Bhadein's shoulder. He could've sworn he'd seen a gaping face filled with a broken smile hovering just behind the older knight. He shook his head to clear the purple tendrils of fear that were creeping through his chest.

"You want me to go in there alone?!"

"Perhaps not alone, but remember that the more of you that go in there, the more emotions you will generate, and the more of the shadow will be drawn to you," Velorun said. "It is a precarious balance you must strike. Companionship may help bolster your courage and give you strength to carry on, but too many of you, and you will only draw the attention of these stalkers and bring about your demise all the quicker."

Dillen swallowed the knot in his throat and sat down on his stool, rubbing his temples as he did so. He turned when he felt a webbed hand clamp down on his shoulder.

"I do not know of what great fear there is that lies in the shadow. But the Lady did send me to you, and I do trust her sight. I will follow your current, Sir Dillen." Shesh'ra looked down at him. Dillen stared at her, unsure as to the emotions her pledge had stirred up. There was a slight bit of comfort in her stalwart confirmation, but the fear still gnawed at the back of his mind, and he found he couldn't trust his voice to speak.

"I will accompany you as well!" Farn's enthusiasm was only slightly dampened by the prospect of what lay before them. "And I will see if there are any others that will accompany us." Shesh'ra nodded toward the younger knight before turning her gaze back to Dillen.

"If I did offer any counsel, I would be for speaking with the gladestalker, too," she said, "There be bad water between you, but it is a strong current that binds you together. Even one who is blind would have eyes for that."

"Who? Imariel?! I doubt that she would be willing to go anywhere with me." Dillen's voice was touched with a tightness to which he could not place the emotion. Bhadein snorted to his right and he sent him a glare. The older knight simply shook his head and stood up.

"I will see to our defenses here. We lost a lot of good men last night, and I want to make sure that we are prepared for when or if this plan fails."

With that, Bhadein stood up and walked out of the awning toward the still scattered group of tents that made up the ranks of the remaining Brotherhood soldiers. Dillen watched him go and sighed, pushing himself to his feet as he did so. He turned toward Velorun.

"I know it seems an impossible task that has been handed to you," the elf stepped forward and pulled something from his pouch. It looked like a small, emerald stone, polished to a high sheen so that it glistened even in the shadow of the canvas shade over them.

"This is a scale from one of the deep glade wyrms that abide within the eldest parts of the forest. I have kept it with me for some time. It has an enchantment etched into it that should offer some limited protection where you will be going. It is only a trinket, but perhaps it will offer you some small measure of comfort."

Dillen took the scale into his numb hands. He gripped it tightly to help keep from shaking and muttered a thank you.

"I can't tell you what you will be looking for in there. But seek out a place where the Sickness seems most concentrated. The darkest part of the forest. Wherever you fear most to go, that is the surest indication that it is the way you must go. The more terrified you are, the closer you are to your goal. Beyond that, trust that the Lady will guide you." Velorun placed a hand on Dillen's shoulder.

"I do not envy you the task set before you, Sir Dillen." He paused a moment and blinked. "Find the heart of the Sickness. Cut it out and bring it back here. We will be waiting and will sever its connection to this world. Then your penance will be over and you will have helped protect the Lady's forest. Beyond that, you will have saved more lives with this action than you lost due to your inability to obey the Lady's will."

Velorun stood for a few more moments before turning and leaving. Dillen had forgotten that Shesh'ra was still there and so nearly fell over when she started talking.

"I will be for getting us our supplies. You best talk to Imariel and do get us a better tide for this task."

"Imariel wants nothing to do with me, she won't go." Dillen shook his head sadly.

"Sometimes it do nothing to matter if we want it or no. Sometimes it be for us simply to do. Imariel has seen far more moons swim through the sky than you. She knows this thing. She may hate it, but she does know. She will come."

Shesh'ra clapped Dillen on the back, causing him to jump again.

"Best if we depart soon. Cold water is best entered quickly, or else the courage flees and us with it. Let us meet back here before sunset and begin the journey, yes?" Without waiting for a response, Shesh'ra began walking in the same direction as Bhadein.

Dillen stared after her and unsuccessfully tried to stop his hands from shaking as the warm sun beat down on the canvas awning above him.

Chapter XIX

They left in the cold, dark hours of the morning. Before the sun had risen from its bed, they met on the edge of the somehow still darker forest before them, their breath misting the air before them. Dillen looked around at the assorted group that he was supposed to lead into this nightmare, and he swallowed a hot, leaden ball that was threatening to cut off his breathing. He counted them; there were seven of them in total. Shesh'ra stood leaning against her long trident, which she had planted in the dirt beside her. Farn sat conversing with Tyred and Kevmar, the only volunteers who he'd been able to enlist. Tyred was a skinny youth whose ropy frame belied the quick muscles that hid beneath his light armor. Dillen had seen him practicing in the yards and knew that the boy was quick. He had a shaggy mop of brown hair atop his head and his face held a slightly defiant aloofness to it. The other knight, Kevmar, was similar in build to Tyred, but his face was usually more prone to smiling, and his blue eyes generally glinted with some form of good-natured mischief. All three of these young knights had jumped at the chance to follow the mighty Sir Dillen on one of his legendary quests. Dillen grimaced at that thought as he shifted his gaze away from the youth.

The last of their party stood not far off, and Dillen still felt awkward whenever he glanced in their direction. Imariel stood beside her hulking salamander bodyguard, Lothak. The draconian figure rarely spoke, and when he did, one had to listen carefully to his low voice. However, it was Imariel who unsettled him the most. She sat on the ground simply staring at him, her green eyes boring into his own in a way that made the morning chill deepen. The conversation with her yesterday had been an uncomfortable situation, and not for the first time, Dillen wondered if he'd made a mistake inviting her. His mind cast itself back to their cold discussion.

"What is it that you want?" Imariel's voice had held no emotion that Dillen could gauge.

"I have been asked to seek you out," he'd responded, proud that he'd avoided stammering.

"For what cause?"

"I…" Dillen hesitated then cursed silently to himself for pausing, "We are going into the Sickness tomorrow."

"Of course you are. You mean to buy your salvation with the lives of your troops. At least, that's what I gathered from the meeting before I left."

"No! I… I am taking a small band into the forest. We are going to search for the heart of whatever is causing all this and bring it back here." Dillen hated that he couldn't meet her stare, he used to love getting lost in those eyes. Imariel was quiet for a long time before speaking.

"And what, pray tell, brought about this sudden change of heart? I doubt it was someone playing upon your sympathies. Nor do I believe it was the noble spirit that you have tricked others into believing that you have. I don't blame them, I was also deceived. What became of you, then, that you would slip out from behind the guise of your legend and offer yourself up as sacrifice in this?"

Dillen swallowed hard. Even with her usual distant elven features, he could make out the heat in her voice. He risked a glance at her face and saw slightly furrowed brows and a downturned mouth. He could not maintain her gaze for long, though, and quickly turned to look into the shadows of the Sickness, such was an easier sight to behold at present.

"Velorun convinced me that leading the army would only succeed in getting us all killed."

"Obvious wisdom does not keep it from being wisdom nonetheless."

"I'll concede that point." Dillen nodded and closed his eyes, taking a shaky breath as he did so. "I want you to come with us."

Several long, pointed heartbeats passed, and Imariel did not respond. Dillen didn't dare turn to face her, but he opened his eyes and stared into the grim shadows of what lay before him. When she finally did speak, it was only one word.

"Why?"

"Because…" Dillen fumbled to find a reason, his senses whirled about in his head like a summer storm. "Velorun says that maybe there is a reason that you have been sent with us. Shesh'ra agrees and thinks that you should come, too. They both said something about the Green Lady having sent you with us and…" His voice trailed off as he felt movement from Imariel. He turned and saw her clenching her fists, her head bowed and staring at the dirt at his feet.

"Velorun… and Shesh'ra… said I should come?" There was a dangerous edge to her voice that Dillen had never heard before. It was raw, and violent, something that Imariel's detached elven demeanor had never betrayed so obviously. Unwittingly, Dillen took a step back from her.

"Yes, and I agree." He licked his lips. "You know the forest better than all of us, and you are a skilled warrior. Our mission has a greater chance of success if you would come with us."

Imariel stared at the ground with her fists quaking at her sides for only a second before her hands unclenched and she raised her eyes to meet his. The cool stare she leveled at him caused him to take another step back.

"I will go," she said at length, and her voice was back to its composed aloofness. "But know that I go to help save the forest, and for the aid of the others who you take on this errand."

"Of course," Dillen tried to say, but Imariel took two long steps forward to put her face inches from his own, and the words died in his throat.

"I do not do this for you." The cold flame of her voice cut through Dillen, and a wave of deep sadness and fear washed over him. He looked at her fierce features, her hawkish face that was both beautiful and deadly in its countenance. He remembered kissing those lips and touching her hair. The thoughts struck him so suddenly that he blushed in spite of himself, but he did not look away.

"I know," was all he could say. Imariel stared at him for a few more moments, then turned and walked away. Dillen watched her glide gracefully across the clearing, his heart hammering in his ears.

"Sir Dillen?" Farn's voice startled him back to the present, and he realized that the young knight had been talking to him for a few minutes, and he had no idea what he'd said.

"Pardon?" He coughed.

"What is our plan?" Farn questioned again, his voice slightly strained. Dillen could see that the smile on his face was too wide, too tight. The young man was terrified, as he probably should be. He was overcompensating for the fear with a show of bravado. Dillen could understand that. He was distracting himself with memories of sadness to distract him from the terrible present that stood before them.

"We are looking for something, although we do not know what," he said at length. "Velorun said that we should follow our feelings. If you are feeling afraid, do not despair, that means that we are on the right track, at least according to the elven mage. The more scared you feel, the closer we are to our goal."

"So we follow our fear?" Tyred said from behind Farn. Dillen nodded and pointed into the forest.

"Something in there is linked to such a strong emotion that it is calling out to these beasts. They feed on emotions. Our fear is like honey to them, and they yearn for it as bees drawn to sugar. In a way that gives us an advantage."

"How so?" Tyred frowned.

"Their strength is determined by their sustenance, it would seem. Steel yourselves, and by denying them their meal, perhaps we can weaken them." Dillen flashed them a smile, hoping they could not see through his thin veil of bravado. Farn reacted by laughing and clapping Kevmar on his back.

"You give contradictory advice." Imariel's voice cut across Farn's laughter. "You tell us that we must follow our fear, but to shut down our fear also, so that the beasts might not feed. So, which is it?"

123

Dillen grimaced, his smile slipping as he forced himself to look at her.

"It is both, I suppose. Allow yourself enough fear that we might know which direction to tread, but not enough that it gives sustenance to our enemies."

"A wise ruling." Imariel's voice was flatter than usual.

"Perhaps it be best if we are to be embarking upon this journey." Shesh'ra stepped between them and cast a meaningful glance at Dillen.

"Yes. I suppose you are right." He shrugged and turned to face the somehow darker forest before them. He hesitated there, at the edge of the Sickness, with his breath caught in his chest. Images of the monsters he had encountered over the past days flashing before his eyes and the hacking laugh of some crazed beast in the back of his mind.

"Sir Dillen?" A voice brushed his ear and he started, looking behind him, he was surprised to see Imariel's face with her brows furrowed. She did not look angry, which was an additional surprise to him, and her hand was extended out as if she had been moving to touch his shoulder.

"Is everything okay, Sir Dillen?" Farn's voice was back to its former tightness, his smile slipping into a stretched facade over his teeth. Dillen coughed and squared his shoulders.

"Yes! Of course! I was just listening to my gut! It seems we won't have much trouble finding the center of this whole thing after all, if all we need to do is ignore the nagging voice in the back of our heads telling us not to go on." He tried to laugh at this, but all that came out was a hollow choking noise. An awkward pause filled the air, and Dillen turned swiftly back to the forest, forcing himself not to look at the faces of his party as he did so. He lifted one foot and stepped into the shadows.

He didn't dare look behind him to see who followed him into the dark.

* * * * *

It was colder under the trees. The late summer sun could not penetrate the gloom, and everything was cast into a perpetual twilight that never seemed to grow lighter than the evening just after sunset. Red fireflies hovered in the darkness just outside of Dillen's periphery. At least he told himself that they were fireflies. In his braver moments, he would admit to himself that they looked less like the swirls of insects hovering in the air and more like the eyes of some unknowable pack of predators watching them from the undergrowth. He shook himself at this idea, as the thought of whatever kind of beast would stalk its prey in a place like this in such a brazen manner sent shivers down his spine.

They walked for what seemed like hours, but time was impossible to gauge in this place. The sun did not seem to exist as anything other than a memory, and the light never changed as a result. It wasn't until Dillen's stomach rumbled that he realized that they hadn't stopped to eat, yet. He called a halt to their progress, relieved to see that the others were all still with him, and told them to break out their provisions. Strips of dried meat and hardtack were produced and chewed without relish. Each of the party members sent anxious glances about them as they knelt where they were and forced themselves to take another bite of the flavorless rations.

"Here." Shesh'ra handed something to Dillen, who took it hesitantly in his hand and looked down to see a strange, round object that appeared to be wrapped in some kind of dark plant.

"What is it?" Dillen asked cautiously, turning it over in his hand.

"It be called naorm'ei to my people. It is a fish that has been dried with the smoke of a hard wood tree and pressed into these circles that are to be wrapped in water weed. It is quite tasty, at least for those of my kind."

"You eat it?!"

"Yes! I thought it would to be nicer than the food your people have gifted to us." Dillen shot her a sideways glance but popped the disc into his mouth and bit down. The sudden wave of saltiness overwhelmed him and he coughed reflexively, his eyes going wide at the flavor. The algae had the same consistency as some sticky rices he had tasted in the past, and the fish had a subtle smoky flavor that was almost lost amid the intense taste of the ocean that enveloped the entire bite.

"Salty!" He exclaimed, reaching for his waterskin. Shesh'ra tilted her head back and laughed. It was an odd sound amid the intensely dark eaves of the trees overhead, and the rest of the party looked around at them with raised brows of surprise.

"It is a strange taste to those that do not be prepared for it," Shesh'ra chuckled. As Dillen swallowed a great mouthful of water, he found that the strange food left a rather pleasant aftertaste in his mouth; it reminded him of a dish that he had once tasted on the shores of the Infant Sea many years ago when his troop had been returning from a campaign along the coast there. He remembered that they had been flushed with victory, and the locals had been grateful for their assistance in the wars being fought there during that summer. The soldiers had been showered with gifts of food and affection from the villagers. It had been a good day, and Dillen felt his cheeks coloring as he remembered specific details. The images in his mind caused a small grin to spread across his face.

"I think that you did be for giving good advice earlier," Shesh'ra said as she watched his smile grow. "There be a way to be for fighting the scared that grows in our bellies. If we can be for thinking of the good things, the happy things, that did have an effect on us. If we cannot find light in the dark, we borrow it from our past. We fight this gloom with the laughter of our past. There be fear enough to take us to the heart of this darkness that we be able to take the small moments and fill them with the laughter."

"It's good," Dillen said as he took another swig from his waterskin. "The food, I mean. It's a little salty for my taste, but the flavor it leaves in your mouth is actually pretty good!" Shesh'ra nodded.

"In the depths, the fish would not be washed in smoke, but raw instead, with the salt in the water itself to be the flavor behind it. It is delicious."

Their conversation had drawn the other members of their party, except Lothak and Imariel, who sat silently to the side keeping guard. Shesh'ra offered the strange discs of food to each of them and laughed in turn at each of their reactions.

"My sister makes something similar to this," Kevmar declared as he chewed the small disk with relish. "She would steal some of the salt from the smoker's huts and use it to brine some of the fish we would catch in a nearby stream. She'd serve it with warm rice, or boiled carrots, and it was one of my favorite dishes." His smile faded as he spoke, like he'd caught sight of something unpleasant in the distance, but his eyes were unfocused as they stared at the ground.

"What's wrong?" Farn questioned. Kevmar shook himself and looked up.

"Oh, it's nothing. My sister died when the Abyss swallowed so many of our fortresses. We all lost people that we cared about during that time. But this food reminded me of how much I still miss her." The group grew silent once more. Kevmar shrugged.

"Sorry," he said, scrubbing his chin with his hand, "I probably ruined the mood there. We should think about happy things, instead, just to lighten the atmosphere and make this darkness a little more bearable."

"There be nothing that is wrong with your memories that you share," Shesh'ra spoke quietly, and she reached across to grasp Kevmar's arm with her scarred hand. The young knight stifled his reaction to recoil, and he sat staring at her arm. Shesh'ra's eyes stared past him to look at Imariel, who sat behind him.

"There be times when grief be the light that we need. There be no shame to shed water for that which we lose. It be when we refuse to lose the weight of what it is to keep someone alive in our minds that such a thing does become too heavy to hold and does crush the light that such memories hold."

Dillen thought he saw Imariel shift uncomfortably under Shesh'ra's gaze.

"These types of rememberings do cast a light of their own when they be shared. When we do let the people before us into the sadness that we do press into our own hearts. I do be having the knowledge that you were not wanting to share such a burden with one such as I, I be a fish-lady that you do not be having the trust for. But I am of the gladness that you did share it, for we must be as family that have stepped beneath these trees together, cursed as they are, and I am of the happy that you did share this light with us."

"Silence!" Imariel hissed, and Dillen raised an eyebrow in her direction as if to question her intrusion into the conversation. She was bent into a crouch across the way from them, her head swiveling about her as her eyes searched amid the trees.

"If you don't like what we're talking about..." Dillen began, but the elf cut him off once more.

"Don't you hear it?! Listen!"

Chagrined, Dillen tilted his head and tried to cover the heat of his own embarrassment by closing his eyes in an act of trying to focus. At first he heard nothing, then something pulled on the edge of his awareness. He struggled to focus on the sound, trying to identify what it was, but it grew even as he strained, and his face paled as he was finally able to identify it.

It was the sound of a woman crying.

And it was getting closer.

Chapter XX

The sounds of weeping grew closer and closer. Dillen felt his chest tighten as a sense of melancholy and loss swept over him, almost overpowering the terror that gripped his heart as he sat frozen, staring in the direction of the crying. By now, he could tell it was a woman, but what woman would be in this part of the forest? He knew the answer, and that made his mouth go dry in anticipation.

"Hide, you fools!" Imariel hissed, and as if that broke the spell, the entire party scattered away to hide amid the undergrowth. This was done hastily, and in the scurrying to hide, Dillen found himself lying beneath a strange looking plant beside Imariel. In spite of himself, he became increasingly aware of the press of her hip against his, and he shook his head to ward off such distractions.

No sooner had they all settled into their places then the source of the crying appeared. It was a woman, as Dillen had suspected, with her face in her hands, weeping. Her sobs filled him with sadness and remorse. Why had they hidden from such a wretched creature? For wretched was the word he would use to describe her. She wore a dress that was tattered to the point of beggar's rags, her skin was porcelain but smudged with all manner of dirt and what looked like cuts and bruises as well. Her tortured cries made Dillen's stomach knot, and he found his face coloring out of shame that he was hiding instead of helping this poor soul.

Without realizing what he was doing, he found himself rising from the ground. Only Imariel's hand clamping down on his shoulder stopped him.

"What are you doing?!" she whispered. "Can't you tell that this is a trap?"

Dillen shook his head again, and a type of fog fell away in that moment. He knew that it was folly to try and go out to this creature, but the compulsion was still there, singing out to him. He knew that if he let it, that song would lift his body from the ground completely, and he would wander out to see the thing before him. He didn't even need to do anything but stop fighting the compulsion. He was so very tired in any case...

"Margitte?!" Kevmar's voice cut through the weeping song and brought Dillen's eyes into focus. Kevmar stood before the figure, his hands extended before him. The woman, or whatever it was, turned toward the young knight but did not remove her hands from her face.

"I thought you were dead! How did you get here?"

Something screamed in the back of Dillen's mind as he sat staring at Kevmar reaching out to place his hand on the woman's shoulder. He was only vaguely aware of Imariel's hand on his arm or of his struggle to rise from his knees because of it. He needed to go to this poor woman as Kevmar had done. Why was Imariel trying to stop him?

"Margitte! Won't you look at me?" Kevmar's hand moved to the woman's wrist and tried to pry her hands from her face. The woman's cries intensified.

"It's me! Kevmar! Your brother?" The woman twisted violently in his grip, and one of her hands pulled away as Kevmar did not loosen his hold. Immediately, the compulsion that Dillen had been feeling fell away as he stared in open horror at the sight before him.

The woman had no face.

Bile crept up into the back of Dillen's throat as he stared at the smooth skin where the woman's eyes and nose should be. He realized that he was mistaken in one aspect as a wide mouth filled with sharp, pointed teeth split the lower portion of her missing face. But she had no lips, and no tongue rested behind the sharpened teeth.

The woman's cries turned into a hungry snarl, and she lunged at Kevmar, who had stood frozen, staring at the thing he had thought was his sister. The faceless woman wrapped her arms around his neck in a parody of an embrace and clasped her teeth around the meat of his neck. Kevmar screamed and struggled to push her away, but his cries began to diminish as crimson jewels began streaming down from the woman's mouth and onto Kevmar's chest.

The sudden turn of events galvanized Dillen, and he lunged forward out of his hiding spot with his sword drawn. The woman hissed and released Kevmar, who toppled into the undergrowth. Dillen swung at the faceless creature, and she dodged back out of the way of his blade before lunging forward with an inhuman speed and raking her fingers across Dillen's chest. Sparks flew off his cuirass, and he was sent staggering backward from the force of the blow.

Imariel appeared out of the corner of his eye and stabbed forward with a slim blade that struck the faceless woman in the shoulder. The thing didn't even seem to notice her wound and turned to snarl at the gladestalker instead. Her attention diverted from Dillen, the young knight slashed at the horror before him, aiming at the creature's neck. Before his strike could land, the woman lunged forward and tackled Imariel with a speed that left Dillen wide-eyed and staring at nothing where his sword swung harmlessly through thin air.

Imariel yelled in pain, and Dillen turned to see her arm firmly clasped in the faceless woman's mouth, and the creature was biting down hard. Dillen kicked out and landed a blow in the woman's side, throwing her off of Imariel and forcing her to release her bitehold. The faceless creature snarled and fell into a crouch, and she stared at Dillen for a moment, who stood with his sword held in both hands, the tip of the blade pointed directly at the creature in a preparatory stance. Then the woman tilted her head back and howled into the air.

It was a haunting sound, as if several voices were calling out together in shared pain. The sound was pitched high, and it felt as if Dillen's blood had turned to shards of glass in his limbs. His ears screamed out in protest, and his hands felt numb. He had to focus hard just to keep his sword from tumbling from his nerveless fingers.

The sound finally receded, and the faceless woman lowered her head, her mouth still split into a vicious grin exposing rows of sharpened teeth beneath her eyeless gaze. Then she shot forward at Dillen once more. Still recovering from the terrifying scream, Dillen tried to lift his sword, but his arms felt as if they were pushing through water and moved so slowly that he knew he wouldn't do anything to deter his attacker. He braced himself for the impact and the sensation of those sharp teeth to tear into his neck.

But the blow never came. The creature's momentum stopped mid lunge as a shaft of metal sped past Dillen's head and connected with the woman's chest. Dillen's eyes refused to focus for a moment, and he stared down at the corpse before him. A long haft of what looked like a spear stuck out of the still form of the woman, and as he watched, the figure shuddered and seemed to turn into some kind of liquid that bubbled and gasped as clouds of steam escaped its surface.

Dillen watched in horror as the woman's body reshaped itself into something else entirely, something with gangly limbs that ended in sharp, hooked claws, and a cone shaped head that still had the horrible mouth with its wicked teeth. The mouth was still bared in an evil grin. Its skin was a sickly shade of purple. Dillen had seen bodies burned by the fires of the Abyss, blackened skin that had melted away over muscles and sinews. This body resembled those corpses.

"The true form of the darkness." Shesh'ra stepped past him and gripped the haft of her weapon, pulling it free and wiping the trident's three prongs on the greenery at her feet. Even as she did, the clouds of steam from the body began to turn black, and the misshapen corpse began melting away, bits of its skin flaking off and drifting into the air like tiny pieces of ash caught in the hot air of a fire.

Dillen could not tear his eyes away from the sight until he felt a hand on his shoulder. He turned to see Farn's concerned face.

"Kevmar is dead." His voice was pitched low as he spoke. It took Dillen a few moments to register what he was being told.

How delightful was that? Now he is with his sister! Kallas's voice echoed in his head, and he flinched unconsciously.

"What in the Seven Circles was that?" Tyred's voice was a low growl behind him.

"That is what we have come to kill."

Imariel grunted as she pushed herself to her feet, still clutching her wounded arm. The bleeding seemed to have stopped, but by the grimace on her face, she was having a hard time moving the limb without it hurting her.

"It were to be best if we are to be moving along, and quickly." Shesh'ra replaced her trident on her back and looked around anxiously. "That thing did make a hue and cry that would bring the depths to life. We are not unwatched at this time. I fear that more are to be following this one."

Uh-oh, dear brother. Looks like it's time for you to make a decision. How will you uphold your image before these questioning eyes? Will you fulfill your duty as you failed to do with me?

"Shesh'ra is right," Imariel said, a judgmental stare aimed at Dillen. "Every last one of us was shaken by this turn of events, and our emotions are running high. It is likely that the monsters are now aware of us and are honing in on our very position as we speak."

Coward. The voice cackled in the back of his mind, and Dillen's heart beat faster at the accusation. *Best hurry and flee, something is coming.*

Lothak stood protectively to one side of Imariel as she wrapped her wounded arm in what looked like some kind of hemp cloth she had produced from her pack. She finished tying off the makeshift bandage with her teeth and her free hand, then she turned and looked deeper into where the darkness of the Sickness grew morose and purple in its shadows.

"They are coming! I can hear them!" she hissed and reached for her slender blade which had been discarded in her fight with the faceless woman.

"Then we should retreat!" Dillen found his voice at last, but it was sickly and weak. He tried to ignore Farn's furrowed brow as his words balanced on the brink of cracking.

"Trust in the Lady," Shesh'ra spoke without hesitation, although her eyes were fixed in the direction that Imariel was also staring.

"I agree with Sir Dillen. I think we should go back." Tyred's voice also held a slight quiver.

"Then run if you must," Imariel responded without turning. "But we have a mission to accomplish, given to us from the Lady herself. We will not abandon it now."

Dillen felt her words like a shard of ice piercing his gut. Shesh'ra turned her eyes on him with a sadness behind them that pushed the cold sensation deeper. He didn't dare turn to look at Farn's face. Behind him, Tyred shifted uncomfortably.

Father was right. Such a disappointment.

"Sir Dillen, please! We should go! If they will not save themselves, then we need not die in this place!" Tyred's voice cracked.

Dillen's knees felt like they would give at any moment. His mouth felt dry. Yet the ice in his stomach twisted deeper as he desperately tried to avoid Farn's gaze. He weighed his options. They were up against the very essence of fear. There was no shame in fleeing before such an implacable foe. But if that was the case, why then did his innards contract so tightly when he thought of doing it?

May the Shining Ones burn you for this! Dillen was unsure who the curse was intended for, even as he said it in his mind. It's possible it was aimed at any of the party members before him. It could have been aimed at the voice of his dead brother still cackling in his head. It could have been directed at the monsters moving toward them through the shadows even now. But Dillen suspected that his anger was more closely directed at the Lady of the Wood. The one who had forced him to be here.

"We need to split up," he said at last, happy that the quiver in his voice had quieted at least. The rest of the group gave him surprised stares. "Our emotions are marking us like a wounded deer being chased by the wolves. It ekes our strength from us and feeds our enemy. Perhaps if we force them to choose their meal, it will give the other party a chance to find the heart of this Sickness."

"You would have us go deeper into this madness?!" Tyred exclaimed, his voice squeaking in spite of himself.

"His words do have a sense to them," Shesh'ra said, holding up a webbed hand. "We will not be of the ability to fight the monsters that now do come. Our fear will only increase and give them the food that they seek. If we split, we be having the chance of finding something. Better than if we be staying together."

"Then it is decided." Dillen forced a stillness into his voice. "I will take Tyred and Farn, and we will head in what I think is a northeasterly direction. Shesh'ra, you and Imariel and the dragon... man... can head in a more due east fashion. By splitting up, we increase our chances that one of our parties will be successful."

That's right, run away. Like you always do.

Suddenly, there came a crash in the woods, something much larger than what they had heard previously. Dillen stiffened and his hands reached for his sword instinctively. The crashing sound did not cease and only grew louder. Dillen turned to say something to the other party members, but before he could, a large, dark shape broke into view. Crab-like appendages that curved sharply snapped in Dillen's direction, and a thick tail tipped with a scorpion stinger stabbed down in his direction, narrowly missing his head. Dillen backpedaled away from the large creature, and as he did so, something caught his eye.

Around the neck of this new nightmare hung a long, rusty chain. On this chain were strange odds and ends that almost looked like charms worn on the bracelet of some of the more affluent ladies of the court that Dillen remembered from his youth. As he looked closer, though, he realized that the charms were far more gruesome in their nature. They were fingers, ears, tongues, and even the stringy remains of what looked like an eyeball hung from the tarnished metal. A sudden realization hit Dillen as he retreated from the fury of the disgusting fiend.

Ur-chitak, the Chittering Spider, had found them and was looking for new trophies.

Chapter XXI

Dillen dodged to the side as a massive pincer slammed into the ground where he stood moments before. There was the sound of rotten wood crackling as the claw destroyed an old log that lay half-buried in the soil. Dillen continued moving as the monstrosity before him brought its other claw down, aiming to crush his chest with pure blunt force. The wind that followed the pincer's passing as it narrowly missed Dillen's head sent a shiver down his spine.

"Sir Dillen!" Farn cried out over the crashing of the beast as it shifted its attention and stabbed the stinger on its great chitinous tail down. Farn fell backward and managed to avoid the poisoned end of the tail, but the rest of its bulk slapped him away and sent him reeling back to crash against a tree as the monster pulled back and prepared another strike.

"No!" Dillen yelled. He stabbed his sword upward and was surprised when the tip of his weapon bit deep into the chitinous body of the fiend before them. The creature let out a wail and swept one of its claws down. Dillen's vision blurred as he felt himself lifted into the air by the force of the blow.

The wind was forced from his chest as he slammed down onto a moss-covered rock protruding from the ground. His sight was clouded by a purple mist that refused to subside, and he gasped futilely for air. Finally, he was able to suck in a great gulping gasp, and then another. Gradually the mist fell away from his eyes, and he looked back in the direction of his companions.

Tyred was struggling in the grasp of one of the creature's clawed pincers, his left arm clasped tightly in its hold, and crimson blood trickling down his shoulder. The young knight was swinging his sword and yelling, trying desperately to wound his attacker. But he was at an awkward angle, and most of his blows glanced harmlessly off the creature's carapace. Imariel stood over the prone form of Lothak, with Shesh'ra beside her. Both of the women had their weapons readied and were watching intently as the beast thrashed about with Tyred. Dillen couldn't see any sign of Farn.

Dillen staggered to his feet and tried to force his limbs to carry him toward the monster. He saw that the creature had multiple eyes, like a spider, on its head that sat upright like some kind of misshapen centaur whose body resembled that of a scorpion, only much larger. With a violent shake, Tyred's yells turned to screams, and the monster threw him away into the undergrowth, where the screaming stopped suddenly.

The monster's back was momentarily turned to Shesh'ra and Imariel, and they took the opportunity that this presented. Charging forward, Shesh'ra stabbed her trident deep into the side of the beast, who whipped around and swung a vicious claw at her and Imariel. The naiad released her weapon and danced backward out of range of the swing, while Imariel leapt up gracefully to land on the appendage. The monster screamed as it tried to dislodge her with a vicious swipe of its arm. But she leapt up again to land on the monster's shoulder and stabbed downward at its neck with her slender blade. She grunted as the blow hit some of the harder chitin that clung to her target's flesh, causing the strike to go wide and managed only to score a few minor cuts along its chest as the weapon skittered down its front instead.

The fiend reared back and shook ferociously. Imariel tried to cling to its shoulder, but with a violent twist, Ur-chitak was able to fling her away. She tumbled through the air to land softly on the ground, her off-hand extended into the dirt to steady herself.

"Imariel!" Dillen called out, but she waved him away and pointed back at the beast.

Shesh'ra rushed forward to plant a foot just below where her trident was still embedded in the creature's side and grasped the shaft of her weapon. She leaned back, pulling her one foot off the ground and pushing off the beast's bulk as she pulled on her weapon. It came free with a disgusting sucking noise that splashed a black, viscous liquid all around. Shesh'ra wheeled in the air and landed in a roll as she spun away from Ur-chitak, who roared and made several swings to try and crush the naiad with its claws.

"You two! Be for rushing on! I will take this one deeper and then try to return!" Shesh'ra yelled at the two of them as she pushed Imariel out of the way. She turned to make sure the creature was following her. For a moment it stood there, its many eyes turning from Dillen and Imariel to Shesh'ra. As if to help its decision, Shesh'ra rushed back forward and slammed the haft of her weapon against one of its many legs before darting back. The creature was undeterred, staring between two victims that were standing still and one that was trying to run away.

It charged at Imariel. She stood her ground as if frozen in place as the beast bore down on her. At the last possible second, she leapt to the side, but Ur-chitak seemed to anticipate this and swept a pincered claw out to slam against Imariel as she flew through the air. Her body crumpled and she slammed down into the dirt with a cry of pain.

"Imariel!" Dillen called out and ran toward her. Ur-chitak raised both of its claws above its head. Imariel lay stunned with her eyes glazed over in pain as she stared up at the death that was coming for her. Dillen felt like he was in a nightmare, the kind where he was waist deep in water and something was chasing him. He yelled, urging his body to move faster.

Ur-chitak's claws fell toward the earth. Dillen flung himself the remainder of the distance to cover Imariel with his own body. He braced himself for the pain.

It never came. He felt vibrations as the claws slammed down at him, but they didn't seem to touch him. Instead, they slammed into the dirt beside him. Confused, Dillen turned to look over his shoulder. There seemed to be some kind of shimmering green curtain that spread itself over him like a small tent. Ur-chitak seemed to be as confused as Dillen as it brought its claws back up to smash down on Dillen once more. He flinched back as the claws once again glanced off the shimmering green veil.

The monster tried a few more times to slam its way through the strange shield that covered Dillen and Imariel, but each time the claws seemed to simply glance off. The beast paused at this, and in its confusion, Shesh'ra ran and stabbed upward into its side. Ur-chitak roared in pain and turned to face the naiad. Shesh'ra pulled her weapon free and stabbed forward once more for good measure. The beast reared up and swatted her trident to the side before taking a swing at her with its tail. She dodged to the side and danced backward, seeming to taunt the giant fiend.

"Come to me then! I will take you on this journey!" Shesh'ra called out her challenge. The monster hesitated. The green veil flickered and disappeared, and Dillen caught his breath. If the creature turned back to them now, all it would need to do was crush them with a dismissive wave of its limb. Shesh'ra hefted her trident and launched it at the beast. The weapon sailed through the air and lodged itself in the creature's abdomen.

This seemed to decide it for the monster as it tore the trident from its body and tossed it to the side, roaring in pain before finally charging after its attacker. Shesh'ra hesitated only a moment before sprinting back through the underbrush.

The crashing of Shesh'ra's pursuer diminished quickly as they raced deeper into the woods. Dillen released a breath he hadn't realized he'd been holding and looked down at Imariel. Her eyes were wide with uncharacteristic astonishment. Unwittingly, Dillen reached up and brushed her hair out of her eyes. A remnant of their past together caused him to brush his fingers down the side of her cheek. She shivered and closed her eyes at his touch.

"Thank you," she said at length.

"That was a close one, wasn't it?" Dillen tried to smile, but he knew it lacked its usual depth as the sense of dread still sat like a hole in his gut. But sitting this close to her, he found himself breathing deeply. Gods, she smelled so good! Like pine needles and rain.

"Sir Dillen, can you please get off of me now? You're hurting me." Imariel's voice was low, almost a whisper. Immediately Dillen scrambled back to his feet, brushing grass and dirt off his knees as he did so. Imariel lay prone for a few moments longer before rising gracefully to a crouched position. Dillen caught a whiff of something acrid and bitter, something like burned meat.

"How did you do it?" Imariel asked. Dillen shook his head. He placed his hands on his hips, and as he did so, he brushed one of his belt pouches there. The leather disintegrated at his touch, falling to pieces as scorched remains crumpled into dusty pieces of blackened ash. As it did so, something heavy toppled out and landed with a dull thud on the ground. Dillen cocked his head and reached down to retrieve the item. It was small and cold to the touch as he raised it up to look at it.

"Velorun's scale."

He turned the item over in his hand. It no longer glistened like a polished emerald, but rather it was flat and gray. As he held it in his hand, the scale cracked and crumbled away like the ruined remnants of his pouch where it had sat previously.

"That was a dragon scale!" Imariel whispered. "That was some gift he gave you!"

"I hope he doesn't ask for it back." Dillen wiped the remnants of the scale off on his pant leg. As he did so, he heard a groan coming from some bushes.

"Farn!" He called out and ran over to the sound of the pained grunts. Farn lay on his side, he was breathing hard and clutching his ribs. There was blood on his face, but it wasn't a worrying amount. He groaned as he tried to sit up, then he winced as he did so and toppled back.

"I think I broke some ribs." He gasped as he tried to sit up once more. Dillen reached down to help him up.

"What happened?" Farn asked. Dillen shook his head.

"Monster damn near killed us. But Shesh'ra chased it off. Or perhaps the other way around." Dillen gave a hollow chuckle at his attempt at a joke. Farn did not so much as smile.

"Where's Tyred?"

Dillen's smile vanished.

"I..." he began but was interrupted.

"He's over here!" Imariel's voice called out. Dillen helped Farn to his feet and then supported him as they moved over to where the elf sat crouched in the long grass. Tyred lay before her, and Dillen felt bile rising up in his throat as he looked down at him.

His left arm was a bloody mess. It was almost completely detached at the elbow, a broken shard of bone and a bloody tendon was all that kept the limb attached to the rest of his body. Blood was everywhere, and Tyred's face was pale. His chest rose and fell in shallow bursts.

Imariel took a small vial from a pouch at her waist and poured its contents over the shredded remnants of the young knight's arm. Dillen watched in wonder as the bleeding stopped almost instantly and some of the color returned to Tyred's face. His breathing was still shallow but not as irregular.

"It's sacred water, blessed by the Lady herself." Imariel replaced the vial in her pouch. "He seems to have stopped bleeding. He's still in danger, though. He needs a healer."

"What about your scaly friend?"

"I have already checked on him. He has a nasty head wound, and I think his arm is broken from what I could see. But he should live. But he also needs a healer, and soon."

"Farn's not in good shape, either. We may need to fall back and regroup. Try another expedition another day." Dillen watched Imariel carefully, gauging her reaction to his words. She pursed her lips and stared pointedly at Tyred's arm. Dillen wondered how she could do so without getting a little bit queasy. He had seen all amounts of horror on the battlefield, but that was different. There were always other things to focus on rather than the man on the ground and his injuries.

"What about Shesh'ra?" Imariel said quietly.

"I don't know," Dillen admitted, his shoulders sagging as he spoke.

"I agree with you that our allies cannot continue on. But what of the one who is the reason we are even alive right now? Do we abandon her to her fate?"

"What about our mission?" Farn grunted. "All of this would be pointless if we don't at least try to figure out something."

"Farn, you can't keep going. You can barely stand as it is." Farn didn't respond to Dillen for a few minutes.

"I can walk on my own. I will not be the reason we stop." The younger knight pulled away from Dillen and stood defiantly for a few moments while his face turned red from the effort.

"Even if we decided to keep going, you would only slow us down." Imariel stood up and pointed back down at Tyred's unconscious form.

"Your fellow knight will die if we do not get him some form of help. Lothak is also a liability right now. You can walk, and so can Lothak. We need to find some way of transporting this one."

"What about a litter?" Dillen asked. "We can strap two boughs together and lay him on it, and somebody can pull it along. We're really not very far into the forest. About a half day in. We should be able to make it back if we go quickly."

"So you have made your decision about Shesh'ra? We are to leave her, then?"

Her words cut him like a knife. He stopped and his eyes closed as he warded off a wave of shame that pickled his stomach where he stood.

Yes, brother. Are you going to leave her? Can you sacrifice someone else for your own safety? I know you can. You've done it before… His dead brother's voice broke off into a laugh that sounded closer to a sickly cough than any kind of mirth. He winced at how clearly he could hear the voice now. He saw Kallas's twisted face now, behind his eyelids, smiling at him with his inhuman eyes. Another voice interrupted the twisted memory's laughter.

Follow your fear. As it goes stronger, it means that you are getting closer. The voice sounded like Velorun's. He knew which direction he desperately did not want to go. He wavered in his decision for a moment, skitting back and forth between his sense of duty and that of self-preservation like a piece of ash hovering above a fire. He opened his eyes and looked back at Imariel.

"Can Lothak walk? Could he pull the litter with his unbroken hand?" he asked, dragging every word kicking and screaming out of his chest.

"He will move slowly, but yes, I think he can," Imariel responded. Dillen sighed.

"Good, because Farn will not be able to do so, not with his ribs broken."

Dillen turned to face Farn with what he hoped was a determined look on his face.

"You will have to try and make it back to camp on your own, I'm afraid," he said at length. "I will not abandon Shesh'ra. She's the one who's believed in me the most in this endeavor. So Imariel and I will try to find her, and in the process perhaps we will find the other part of what we are looking for in this terrible forest."

Dillen did not hesitate after that. He quickly went over to a couple of nearby saplings that were just taller than he was and hacked them down using his sword, not caring for how it was likely blunting the edge of his weapon. After he had cut down two sufficient lengths of wood from the young trees, he stripped the branches from the sides, took a length of leather cord, and bound them together so that they formed a v shaped litter. He took the branches and piled them between the two lengths to help provide some additional cushioning. He and Imariel gently lifted Tyred and laid him down on the makeshift litter.

By the time they were finished with this, Lothak had roused himself completely and had fashioned himself a makeshift sling for his damaged arm. Farn was dealing with the pain from his ribs as stoically as Dillen could have expected. Imariel explained to Lothak what the plan was. The salamander seemed to become rather agitated at first, and his yellow eyes darted up to stare menacingly at Dillen as Imariel reasoned with him. Eventually, the hulking dragon man agreed to what Imariel was asking him to do, but he was obviously unhappy about it. Dillen turned away and walked a few steps in order to give them further privacy.

"You will need to take care of her, knight." A guttural voice spoke behind him, and Dillen turned in surprise. Lothak stood before him, while Imariel was seeing to the last preparations of the litter and its occupant.

"Are you talking to me?" he asked, and the salamander nodded. Dillen suppressed a chuckle and motioned back towards Imariel.

"I don't know that you've noticed, but she can probably take care of herself better than I can, and besides that, we aren't on the best of terms as it is, much less if I try to impose myself for her safety."

"Disappointment is not the same as anger," Lothak grunted, adjusting his sling, "and grief is a difficult thing to predict. The separation of death is different to a people who live for millenia. It will be many of your human lifespans before she will see her mother again in death, and even then she will be a different person, her beliefs will have changed, her personality. Elves seem immutable and unchanging to those of us who pass through their lives like wind through a forest. Just like the wind, we are here for a time, and then gone by the nightfall of a single day, usually. We do not see the trees of the forest grow, or its streams deepen. Do not think you are consequential enough to merit her eternal scorn, human."

"I appreciate your words of consolation," Dillen's voice was as flat as his gaze while he spoke.

"What I mean is this. She has much more life to live, and at present, her grief has blinded her to that truth. There is much for her to do, still. Yet because her pain is deep and her anger is equal to it, she might be willing to throw it all away for a cause she deems worthy of her life. Only her judgment is not as sound as it usually might be. You failed her mother before, do not fail her in the same way." Lothak did not wait for a response and turned to move back to where Imariel was crouched over the litter.

There was a short silence as the two parties faced each other in the wood. Dillen felt his stomach constrict as his thoughts wandered toward what awaited them in the shadows of the Sickness. He had done everything he could to fight back the urge to run screaming back to camp, to use the wounded soldiers as an excuse to leave this accursed place. No one would blame him for leaving now. It was for the good of his party. They were wounded. It was tempting to give up on Shesh'ra, someone he had only met a few days ago. She was likely dead anyways. What good would come from getting himself and Imariel killed for that?

His resolve began to crumble. He felt the cold grip of fear stealing up his spine. He opened his mouth to speak, to convince the rest that this was folly and that they should all go back. Then he felt a hand on his arm. He looked down and saw Imariel's slender fingers resting gently on his forearm. He glanced over to see her eyes staring at him expectantly. He realized that she'd asked him a question, and he shook his head before responding.

"I'm sorry?" His voice was raspy as he pushed the words out.

"I asked if you were ready," she responded. Dillen swallowed before responding.

"As I'll ever be."

With that, the wounded members of their party melted into the shadows, their forms disappearing into the gloom as they walked away. Dillen watched them leave, the sinking feeling in his stomach intensifying with every step they took.

"Did you know what the dragon scale would do?" Imariel's voice cut through his mental fog, and he stirred.

"What? Oh, uh, no. I thought it was just something pretty, like a good luck charm or something of that nature."

Imariel studied him for a moment, a strange look on her face. Then she blinked and her mouth set itself with a type of grim resolve. She walked over to where Shesh'ra's trident still lay after being discarded by Ur-chitak and picked the weapon up.

"We should go," she said, pointing in the direction that the monster had chased the naiad. "Even a novice tracker would be able to follow that trail. Let us hurry, lest we arrive too late to help her."

With that, Imariel set off at a light jog, and Dillen took a few deep breaths before following after.

Chapter XXII

"What will we do once we find her?" Dillen whispered. His voice seemed impossibly loud in the shadow of the dismal trees overhead.

"Help her to defeat the monster."

"Oh? Is that all? You make it sound so easy."

"What else is there for us to try? We cannot do anything more than that."

Dillen fell into a sullen silence at this, sullen because it was better to be chagrined than to focus on the other emotions that battered on the edges of his frayed nerves. His side ached from when Ur-chitak had thrown him to the ground, and so when the sting of Imariel's gentle rebuke faded away, he focused on that. He allowed the annoyance that came from each step distract him as they went deeper into the shadows of the Sickness.

"We are gaining on them," Imariel whispered, cutting through his thoughts. He felt a flash of irritation at the interruption but smoothed it over in his mind as the fearful reminder of their present situation threatened to charge in and overwhelm him. The shadows seemed to be deepening, the sunlight fading away; and in its absence, the gray, muted tones of twilight stretched their dark tendrils toward him like sickly fingers reaching out of their graves. Suddenly, his mouth was dry, and his fingers began to itch.

"How can you tell?" he croaked.

"The sap on this plant here hasn't dried from where it was broken by someone's passing. I would say we are about an hour's distance from them unless..." Her voice trailed off as they came into a clearing. Dillen looked around but couldn't tell what had caused her sudden distress.

"Unless what?"

"Oh no," was all she replied. She ran around the clearing, testing a stretch of rich brown earth, checking several score marks on various trees, and then finally kneeling down by a patch of long grass to rub something she found there between her fingers.

"This is blood," she muttered.

"What's going on?"

"The creature must have caught up to her here and tried to kill her. She did not have her trident, so there is little hope that she might have fought back. I fear this blood is hers."

Dillen walked over to where she knelt and looked down at a scattering of dark liquid that was splattered. It was thick like honey, but dark. He'd seen it many times before in the healer's tents.

"It's fresh, though. It hasn't had time to dry. She must be somewhere close by."

Imariel looked up at him and gave him the barest ghost of a smile before nodding.

"You are correct, but where could she have gone?"

"If you two were to be my prey, you were to have made it easy to follow your wake." Both Imariel and Dillen spun around to see Shesh'ra. The fins on the right side of her face were ripped, and blood was running freely down her neck. She clutched her shoulder on that same side while the other arm hung limp.

"Shesh'ra!" Imariel cried out and ran to the naiad's side, who slunk down into a dazed kneeling position.

"I shall live, so you can be for saving the shedding of your tears."

"Do not flatter yourself." Imariel's voice was cool, but Dillen could sense the note of worry hidden behind her tone. He hurried over to stand beside them both. His stomach dropped when he saw the amount of blood that was pouring down the side of Shesh'ra's face.

"Shesh'ra, you're..." he started but cut off as he watched a portion of a vicious cut along the edge of her jaw begin to scab over. Imariel had removed another vial of the sacred water she had used on Tyred's wounded arm, but Shesh'ra held out her hand to stop her.

"Those of you that do be living upon the dirt need to drink from the Lady's fountain to be healed by it. I do have it in my veins. Her water is what my people breathe." She smiled weakly, and Dillen gasped in surprise as the cut sealed itself shut on her face, leaving some white skin in its wake. Even as he continued to watch, scales began to form to cover the freshly healed skin. He stared in wide-eyed wonder, and then, inevitably his eyes slid over to the scarred flesh on the rest of Shesh'ra's face.

"Fire is something that we who were born to water are ill prepared to fight. It be the only thing that is to be harming us in such a way as this." She grimaced as she touched her shoulder again. "That and the bones that do complain, and then there are times that they be needing help. Elf, do be for placing your hand here, if you will."

Imariel placed her hand on Shesh'ra's dangling arm, just below the shoulder joint, and pressed hard. Shesh'ra closed her eyes and shifted violently against Imariel's hand. There was a sickening, wet crunch and a quiet cry from the naiad. Dillen felt his stomach roll as he watched. He'd dislocated his shoulder once on the battlefield when his lance had turned at a bad angle in the charge. Putting the joint back in place afterward had left him wary of picking a lance up for months afterward, even when the healer had said he had recovered perfectly from the experience.

"How did you escape?" Imariel asked. Shesh'ra sat for several long moments with her eyes closed before answering.

"I cannot answer for this thing. The beast did catch me here in this place. I was of a good fortune that I were able to make of the good with my running away as I did. It did slash me one good blow with his claws. I do doubt that my fins will match one side of my face with the other." She reached up to touch the still remnants of the fins which splayed out of the right side of her head. It seemed her regeneration abilities could not regrow lost flesh, as the fins were still ragged even after having healed closed from their wound.

"What happened to Ur-chitak? The fiend?" Dillen asked.

"It did run in that way." Shesh'ra opened her eyes and pointed behind her where she had appeared to Dillen and Imariel. Dillen tried to do more than glance in the direction, but he found that when he tried to hold his gaze that way that his stomach instantly tied itself in knots and his fists instantly began to clench. He suddenly realized that Shesh'ra had continued to speak while he had been focused on the darkness where she had pointed.

"I'm sorry, what?" he asked sheepishly. Shesh'ra shot him an irritated glare.

"I did be for saying that the beast did give up its chase of me when I did get not too far into the trees back there. It were a good thing that it did not continue, for I do doubt that I would be for going much further when I was before it then."

"Why did it stop?" Imariel urged her to continue.

"I do not understand why it did stop. It was behind me and then it was not. I know nothing more than that."

They sat in silence for a few minutes longer, mulling over this new information. Eventually, it was Imariel who broke the silence.

"So what do we do now?" No one wanted to respond. Dillen couldn't bring himself to suggest they fall back again, at least not without a good reason to do so.

"Shesh'ra, how do you feel?" he asked instead.

"I am well enough that I will not be left behind, nor will I be for going back myself." She sucked in a sharp breath and pushed herself to her feet. Imariel walked over to hand her the trident she had been carrying. "Thank you for this. I have had this thing for a lengthy time of my life. I was sad to be thinking that it was lost."

"That seems to have settled it, then. We go on." Imariel nodded at Shesh'ra before turning to face Dillen.

"But which way do we go?" she asked. Dillen felt a cold shudder go down his spine as he looked back at the direction Shesh'ra had tried to flee.

Oh, dear brother, where has all this courage come from? His brother's voice crackled across his mind like dry lightning in a summer storm.

Get out of my mind! Dillen growled. You're not real, you're just a figment of my imagination made worse by this terrible place!

Worked that out, did you? The voice chuckled.

"Then why can they see me?"

Dillen whirled around and drew his sword in one fluid motion. Shesh'ra and Imariel gasped and stepped up to stand at either side of him.

Standing before them was the twisted form of Kallas. His too-wide mouth opened to reveal the jagged shards of teeth. His noseless face capped with eyes that were too large and glistened wetly. He was hunched over, and his hands were spread before him like spiderwebs being cast for the spider's dinner.

"Still think that I am only in your head, big brother?"

"Be quiet, monster! You aren't welcome here!" Dillen snarled. Kallas laughed in response.

"I am usually not welcome wherever I go. People tend to go mad, and that is something that generally is frowned upon. Besides, why would I want your welcome? Your regard means so very little, dear brother." His smile widened.

"Why does he keep calling you brother?" Imariel said from Dillen's side. Dillen fought to find the words, but before he could say anything, the beast spoke.

"Ah, yes, forgive me! We haven't met in the flesh before now. In fact, I'm not sure that my brother has mentioned me to you. I am Kallas, this sack of gutless flesh's little brother."

"Dillen has no brothers..." Imariel began, but Kallas's dry chuckle cut her off.

"Yes I imagine he wouldn't want to mention me, wouldn't you, brother? Don't want the embarrassment of the brother you left to die hanging on to your new sterling reputation, eh?"

"Stop it!" Dillen tried to push some steel into his voice, but all that came out was something that sounded pitiful and quiet to his ears.

"Dillen, what is he talking about?" Imariel did not look in his direction, keeping her gaze staring straight ahead.

"Oh my! Guess he isn't the one to kiss and tell, is he?"

"I didn't leave you to die. Father..."

"Father was an oaf and a selfish, small-minded one at that! You know this! We talked about it at great length the last time we spoke before you abandoned me. 'Have faith in you!' That's what you said. Look what that faith bought me."

Dillen felt his shoulders knotting together and his head dropping a little with each pronounced word the warped visage of his fallen brother spat at him.

"You weren't supposed to be fighting. You were supposed to stay with Father." Even to Dillen, his voice sounded tinny and hollow.

"You expected me to stay with him while you went out seeking your fortune?"

"I was called away! It was my duty to fulfill our family's obligation to our Basilean cousins to help them!"

"Your Basilean cousins? Aren't you also Basilean?" Imariel broke into the conversation at this, finally turning away from the dark creature to face Dillen. Her eyes were narrowed and her brows furrowed, a distrustful light in her gaze.

"I..." Dillen tried to speak, but no words would come in response.

"You won't be able to reason your way out of this one, Dillen. You've been caught in your lie!"

"Shut up!" Dillen yelled and charged at the shadowy creature.

"You don't know any of this! You aren't real! You're just something that this darkness has dreamed up from my memories!" Dillen swung his sword with each accusation, and the creature that wore his brother's face nimbly ducked aside each of the blows.

"Ah, but I haven't said anything that isn't true. Which is more than you can say, isn't it, brother? The darkness has no need to twist that which is already so brazenly twisted as you."

The twisted Kallas jumped lithely up and landed beside Dillen before tucking and rolling away from him. When the creature came up, he stared at Imariel intently, who backed away slowly with a twisted expression of horror on her face.

"I am so sorry that he has used you so. You could have been my sister! My sweet sister." Kallas held out a hand as if he meant to caress her cheek. Imariel kicked out and sent him toppling backward. He laughed as he tumbled down and into a crouching position.

"I can see why you like her, brother. She has so much that appeals to your ego. A paladin and his eternal, elven love! The stories they could write of such a tragedy! It fits all the old texts so well. Especially since it, too, is all a bundle of pretty lies."

"You need to stop this," Dillen said through gritted teeth.

"You know that I won't. You know that you don't deserve my silence. I am doing nothing more than giving voice to those terrible whispers that you push into the shadowed recesses of your mind. I am your reckoning. Nothing more." He rose to his feet and stared at Dillen.

"Shut your damn mouth!" Dillen roared as he rushed forward with the point of his blade aimed at his brother's chest. Kallas didn't even bother to move, and the point slammed home at the base of his ribs.

"Burn you!" Dillen cried through gritted teeth, hot tears stung his eyes and dug furrows through the grime on his cheeks. Ripples of glowing embers crackled out along Kallas's body where Dillen's blade had pierced him; wherever they passed, his body turned to ash. In one swift motion, he brought both hands up to cup the sides of Dillen's face.

"Oh I will, dear brother, and so will you. Your torment is delicious and deep. It will supply me for many days to come. I will sup on your tears, and when you are finally left exposed and alone..." Here he paused and pulled Dillen's face close to his own, so that his eyes filled Dillen's vision. "I will devour you, too."

With this last declaration, Kallas tipped his head back and gave a wheezing cackle as the wave of embers washed over his face. The laugh did not cease as his body turned to ash and crumpled into dust, leaving Dillen clinging to his sword which he held suspended before him, and his brother's dry laughter fading away beneath the shadow of the trees.

A deafening silence took hold of the three companions. Dillen's breath came in short, quiet gasps, and nothing else seemed to interrupt the steely silence. Eventually, he sank down to his knees, and the world seemed to sigh as the spell was broken. He scrubbed his face with his left hand, and his palm came away almost black with the mixture of ash and tears that still clung to his cheeks.

"What was that?" Imariel whispered, breaking the silence. Shesh'ra still seemed to be trapped in the well of stillness that had enveloped them before.

"It was something that wore the face of my dead brother and paraded some of my worst memories out for you to see."

"Was any of what he said true?"

"Does it matter?"

"What do you mean?! Of course it matters!"

"Why?" Dillen steeled his voice and pushed himself to his feet so that he could face Imariel. Her eyes were uncharacteristically wide, and a frown cut her features into a frightening aspect. For a moment, Dillen faltered in his bluff of indignation.

"We don't have time for this," he pleaded.

"How do we know that you won't leave us if things get too hard?"

The accusation pushed the air out of his lungs. Part of the sting came from the fact that it was Imariel who had said it, and partly because he felt that it was a fair question. He cast his memory back to before he had decided to follow Shesh'ra. To when he had planned to split the party up and the subsequent choices that followed.

You are the one who let them call you hero.

Dillen wasn't sure if the thought came from himself or was a whisper of Kallas's departed shade. He didn't know if it mattered.

"I'll tell you everything you want to know. But later. Not here." He gestured around him. "Telling that story in a forest that feeds off your emotions would surely draw the monsters to us."

"That is not good enough!" Imariel practically yelled, and Dillen was surprised to see tears glistening in her eyes.

"Why is this so important to you? I thought you didn't trust me anyway, so what's changed?"

The air was still for a moment. Then Imariel tilted her head back and closed her eyes. Dillen waited while she stood there. Her body seemed to shudder momentarily, then her eyes opened and they leveled a cruelly cold glare at Dillen.

"Fine then. Keep your secrets, you fool." Her voice was flat, her face was composed. The conversation was over, and Dillen couldn't tell if he was relieved or wounded that it was.

Imariel sniffed and sheathed her slim blade at her side. She then turned and walked deeper into the woods, toward where Shesh'ra had indicated that Urchitak had stopped chasing her. The naiad moved, finally broken from her spell of silence, and followed quickly after.

Dillen stared after them, the sickening dread twisting in his gut. Everything was going to the Abyss in worse ways that he could imagine. He waited until he almost couldn't see them before hurrying after.

Chapter XXIII

They walked in silence, Dillen with his head down, and the other two staring straight ahead. It was a careful treaty of sorts, some stilled agreement between them that none would speak, and in turn none would have to listen to the other's accusations or insinuations. Dillen could not get his brother's twisted face out of his mind, and he kept hearing his final words echo in his ears.

I will devour you, too.

Imariel's accusing stare also pervaded his waking visions as he skulked like a shadow behind her and Shesh'ra. His past haunted his every step as he walked through the darkening gloom of the sick forest. His chest twisted, and trumpets of alarm kept blaring in his head, warning him of a danger that wasn't there. Waves of minor nausea crept up the sides of his stomach, and the beginnings of a headache threatened to make his vision blur.

It was all unraveling, just as it had before. Where would he go this time? He was so absorbed in these thoughts that he almost ran into Imariel as she came to a halt before him.

"What in the Seven Circles of the Abyss are we…" he began, startled out of his panicked reverie. Before he could finish his sentence, he looked around at what had caused Imariel to pause.

They stood on the edge of a clearing. It was large, spanning easily the size of the large courtyard of Eastfort. There was no sunshine overhead, or any light really. Like all the rest of the wood that was contained within the Sickness, it was gray and dismal, as if storm clouds hung perpetually overhead. But the lighting was not what gave Dillen pause as he stared out over what lay before him.

It was the bodies.

Strewn about the clearing were what appeared to be the corpses of dozens, if not hundreds, of armored figures. This in itself would have been startling, but there was something else that caused Dillen to shudder. Each of the bodies seemed to be arranged in odd and unnatural angles, some with arms held above them, others appeared to be attempting to crawl away from something. There were even some bodies that stood like macabre statues, some clinging painfully to wounds in their bellies or with their heads tilted back in surprise as they clutched at their backs. Several knelt with their hands at their sides. Dillen spied one headless corpse still holding a rusted sword above its prone body, as if trying to ward off an attack. Some of the corpses lay in a state of repose that mimicked sleeping, which Dillen had seen on countless battlefields in his life, yet even those emitted some kind of strange unnatural energy.

"What is this madness?" he whispered. Neither Shesh'ra nor Imariel answered.

A scream rippled around the clearing, causing the three companions to jump and cast their eyes about to try and find its source. The sound reverberated and grew louder and more feverish in its pitch. Dillen found himself dropping his sword that he hadn't remembered drawing and clutching his hands to his ears to try and block out the sound. He felt a pressure building behind his eyes, to the point that tears began to stream down his cheeks.

Then the sound stopped, disappearing as suddenly as it had appeared. Dillen gasped for air, realizing that his lungs were burning from holding in his breath. He glanced to the side and saw both Imariel and Shesh'ra doing the same.

"What was that?" Imariel gasped.

"I do not know," Shesh'ra responded between breaths.

"Something doesn't want us here," Dillen grunted. His headache from before had returned with a new vengeance. "That was a warning."

"A warning for what?" Imariel asked.

"A warning to go away, if I had to hazard a guess."

"This do make a sense of things," Shesh'ra grunted, shaking her head. "If we are to be following our fear, then every part of my heart do be telling me to leave this place and flee."

"It doesn't want us in here," Imariel mused, taking a few steps forward. Dillen scooped up his sword and rushed forward to block her path.

"What are you doing?" he demanded.

"The Sickness does not want us to be here. You and Shesh'ra both say so. If this is the case, then I say that this is exactly where we need to go."

"You mean the thing that has already killed one of my fellow knights, mortally wounded another, and sent the rest of our party back to camp with their tails tucked like beaten dogs in a matter of hours of us entering the forest? Before it was just a general nastiness that just happened to catch us in its path. Now it has focused its attention on us and has given us a specific, focused warning to go away. I don't know about you, but I am tired of having my nightmares trying to kill me. Not only that, but we have no idea what will happen if we disturb those things out there!" he motioned to the clearing filled with oddly arranged corpses.

"Then go! Worry about yourself, it seems that is what you have become accustomed to doing." Imariel's voice was low and filled with venom. Dillen recoiled visibly. Imariel had never spoken to him this way, even after he had sought her out following her mother's death. The elf stepped past him and kept walking. She uttered a single phrase as she walked past.

"Such a disappointing legend."

Dillen stared ahead, his eyes coming in and out of focus as he considered which way his feet should take him. He realized abruptly that Shesh'ra was standing before him. She reached up and laid a hand on his shoulder.

"Remember that we are those who place a meaning upon our scars. Our wounds be natural for us to receive, but it is for us to choose what they are to us. Will yours be those of shame, fear, and regret? Or will they sing songs of how you did overcome those things?"

She stood for a moment, looking at him, before stepping past him to follow Imariel. Dillen hesitated a moment longer, willing the swirling tide of his emotions down in his gut. He focused on the grass beneath his feet, forcing his eyes to sharpen. Then, exhaling slowly, he turned and followed the other two.

Time had become almost immaterial in the darkened realm of the forest, but it felt like it took them hours to traverse the corpse-filled glade. At first approach, something stood out to Dillen that he hadn't realized earlier. The bodies looked fresh. These were not the sunken faces of the long dead, nor the skulls and bones of ancient warriors. Also, Dillen noted that they were all men; there were no elves or beastmen among them. They wore the same armor and bore heraldry that he had seen many of the Brotherhood wear, yet Dillen did not recognize a one of them. Once, when he wasn't watching closely where he put his foot and stepped too close to one of the bodies, he heard a squelching noise and swore as he stepped away quickly. A sticky red substance clung to his boot as he pulled it away from the fallen soldier.

"There is something wrong in all of this," Dillen whispered to himself.

"What did you speak?" Shesh'ra called to him.

"I said something is wrong with all of this. These bodies seem fresh, yet they are Brotherhood, and as far as I know, we are the only troops that have been sent here. At least recently. None of these soldiers are mine."

"I agree, these bodies look as though they have only been here for hours, maybe less, yet I don't see how that is possible," Imariel said over her shoulder. Dillen tried to unceremoniously rub the substance on his boot, that he didn't dare examine too closely, on the grass at his feet. As he did this, he focused on the face of a nearby body. With a shock, he realized that the man's eyes were frozen open, and a pair of striking blue eyes stared far away into the sky above them. His face was a mask of fear that not even death could wash away, and his hands still clasped at his chest where it seemed his fatal blow was dealt.

Something about the man drew Dillen closer. He stopped as he felt the pressure begin to build in his temples, and he feared that another scream like the one that had come earlier was about to intrude once more. He grimaced and closed his eyes against the anticipated sound, but it never came. Abruptly, the pressure disappeared, and Dillen's ears rang as if suffering from the aftermath of a loud noise, like that of a cannon going off near him. He was so shocked that he opened his eyes to look around and see if the others had suffered a similar sensation. What he saw made him backpedal so quickly that he tripped over a body behind him and fell to the ground.

The corpse of the man was no longer staring blankly at the sky, but rather his gaze was fixed on Dillen, and his hand was held out as if to grasp him. His pained expression had turned to one of pleading, his mouth now frozen in an anguished cry that had no sound. Dillen cried out, but the corpse remained still in its unnatural pose.

"Why do you call out?" Shesh'ra's voice pulled his attention to the side. She stood scanning the area with her trident held at the ready in her hands.

"T-That body!" Dillen pointed at the corpse with the outstretched hand.

"I do not understand."

"It tried to take hold of me!" Dillen hated the frenzied note in his voice, but he couldn't push the gorge rising in his throat down far enough to banish it. Shesh'ra studied him for a moment.

"This place of nightmares works its will upon us, it seems."

Dillen stood up, his eyes never leaving the body before him. He shook himself and brushed off his legs.

"I didn't imagine it. He was there, staring into the sky one moment, and the next his arm was outstretched toward me, and he was looking right at me!"

"You did see him move?"

"Well, not exactly. I closed my eyes because I thought... well, that doesn't matter, but when I opened them, he looked like that!"

"As I did say. This place of nightmares, it is for us to see past the fear. Do not give in."

Dillen stared after her for several moments before muttering an oath under his breath and following after. The grasping corpse did not move, even after Dillen looked back at him several times. He was in the process of checking a fourth time when he heard Imariel calling back to them.

"Look! There!"

Dillen glanced up and saw that she was pointing at something. He followed her gesture and saw something beside a tree on the edge of the clearing. It gleamed dully in the murky light. As they got closer, he saw that it was an armored figure. The warrior had been pinned to the tree by something that looked like a giant claw that pierced his chest and was likely embedded in the tree trunk behind him.

The armor that the figure wore was ornate, with bits of jade and topaz worked into the edges of the plate and golden filigree etched into its surface. The helmet was of an ancient style, one that Dillen didn't recognize, the face was exposed through two vertical slits that slanted off opposite each other where the eyes of its wearer would be able to see through. One big, blue crest of horse hair topped the helmet. But the most prominent detail that stood out to Dillen was a strange symbol etched in gold and topaz into the left breast of the armor, just above the heart.

"This man belonged to the Order of Redemption," he couldn't keep the note of shock out of his voice.

"How can you tell?"

"This symbol here," he pointed at the etched image of a triangle with a swooped angle at its crest with an inverted crescent beneath it, stylized to look almost like a drop of water.

"What is it?"

"It's the mark of a specific chapter within the Order. He's wearing what is known as the 'Armor of the Tides,' and all Redeemers have them. It's what makes them Knight Redeemers, and by the plume on his crest, I'd say he was likely an exemplar to boot."

Dillen reached out and tapped the helmet, and as his hand made contact, the same scream as before immediately rippled out through the air, only this time it was louder than before and clearer. Dillen could hear the pain, the terror that laced through the sound even as he fell to the ground and clutched at his ears to block it out. It was ragged, and raw. Dillen's hands did nothing to soften the impact of that sound, and he closed his eyes to try and push back the pressure that once again threatened to hammer its way through his skull.

The sound passed, and he opened his eyes. Imariel knelt before him, shaking her head, and Shesh'ra was also close by, gasping for air. Dillen looked back at the armored figure and gasped. The body was gone, and in its place stood a shimmering individual clad in the corpse's armor. The individual was tinted an ethereal blue color and shimmered like the air on a hot day.

Hold the line lads! Dillen heard the words in his head, but somehow he knew that they belonged to the shimmering apparition before him. With a shock, he realized that the voice wasn't speaking to him, but instead was gesturing to someone that was behind him. Slowly, Dillen turned around, dread settling into his limbs as he did so. His eyes widened as he beheld the clearing which they had just crossed.

All of the corpses now stood, freshly risen, staring with empty eyes at him, not at the armored figure behind him. Each of the dead mean were also tinged blue, but none of them moved. They sat silently, staring at Dillen. Then there came a different movement.

Dark creatures shrouded in purple light began to emerge from the trees. They were all shapes and sizes. Dillen recognized a few of the shapes as creatures he had already fought, with their scythed talons and blades protruding from their backs. Others looked like the scarecrows from the previous night. There were big, ogre-like creatures with three arms and wielding great cleavers smeared with ethereal blood. Some of the figures scurried, some shambled, but they came as the waves of the sea and crashed among the ghostly figures whose gaze still remained fixed on him.

Dillen tried to cry out, to warn them, to do something. Surely they could see the threat that bore down on them? But the corpse warriors did nothing as the nightmares fell on them, and Dillen watched as each one was cut down in turn. Each time a soldier fell, his body crumpled into the positions where their physical counterparts had lain as Dillen, Imariel, and Shesh'ra had walked across the clearing.

As each warrior toppled or died, they clutched their death wound and opened their mouths to scream, and as one, their voices mingled together. At first, the sound was low and quiet, but as the slaughter continued and more voices joined the cacophony, it began to take on a familiar tone.

The voices of the tortured souls mingled together to form a single coherent scream, the pressure of hundreds of voices pressing together rammed itself into Dillen's head, and finally, his voice was freed and he lent his anguished cries to those of the dead before him in the clearing.

The scream from when they had entered the clearing hadn't been a warning. Now that Dillen could hear clearly what the sound really was, it turned the blood in his veins to ice water. He could hear men crying for their mothers, or for lovers they would never see again. Screams of pain, men crying out their protests, their dying wishes, all of these mingled together and became one single, unending scream of horror.

Dread washed over Dillen, and he toppled backward in an effort to pull himself away from the scene. Then something pulled out of the purple miasma that had engulfed the dying soldiers, and Dillen recognized the form of Ur-chitak, lit in its ghastly purple light. The great monstrosity charged toward him, and he screamed even louder, but the beast wasn't aiming for him. The ghostly figure charged through Dillen, who spun to watch his passing. Ur-chitak ran forward and slammed his pincered claw into the phantom armored figure so hard that it pierced him through to the tree. The exemplar raised his head and added his own cries to the gathered screams of his men.

Dillen thought that this would be where the vision would end, but it didn't. From behind the armored figure appeared a new horror. Some demonic beast with a face that seemed to emerge from its chest, and a mouth that split its jaw cleanly in two to reveal jagged bits of sharp teeth. Clawed hands and feet appeared to swim through the purple miasma that surrounded it. The new creature planted its feet next to where the exemplar's corpse lay pinned to the tree. It laid one of its hands across the symbol on the breastplate of the armor and a burst of blue energy spread across the clearing.

As the energy made contact with one of the screaming phantoms in the field, a section of it would break away from the rest and wrap itself around the fallen soldier and cut off his tortured wail. This continued until all of the warriors were enveloped, and the clearing was wrapped in a silence.

Dillen stared out at the view before him. The vision appeared to have ended, as the blue and purple light had ceased pulsating across his vision. He turned slowly back to the tree where the exemplar lay impaled. When he did so, he found himself face to face with the clawed horror which had appeared to curse the dead men.

Dillen gasped as the face on the creature rippled and twisted. It elongated, and a neck appeared to form from the beast's oversized shoulders. The mouth twisted and formed into a more human like jaw, but still wrong. The last things to change were the eyes. They shifted and spun, going from the empty sockets of glowing purple energy until they became a sick parody of human eyes, and then the transformation was complete.

Kallas, the twisted version, stood before him again.

"Hello, dear brother."

Dillen screamed.

Chapter XXIV

The blow knocked Dillen to the ground. He scrambled onto his knees and looked up. Imariel stood over him, rubbing her hand and staring down at him with a furious look on her face.

"Stop your screaming, you fool!" she hissed. "Unless you want to bring the whole forest down on us! What is wrong with you?"

"I..." Dillen stammered. His eyes scanned the area, but he couldn't see any sign of his brother's twisted face.

"What happened?" he asked, rubbing his jaw where Imariel had struck him.

"Something happened when you touched the armor. Your eyes seemed to lose focus and then, suddenly, you just started screaming. We were unable to bring you out of your trance until I struck you."

"It was horrible..." Dillen began, but then stopped and stared at Imariel. "You mean you didn't see it?"

Imariel didn't move. Dillen studied her features for some clue.

"I was for seeing a dream of something terrible. That was, until your screams did cause me to wake." Shesh'ra appeared over Imariel's shoulder; her eyes were rimmed in red, and a haunted expression etched on her features.

"It was a nightmare," Dillen agreed. "I saw all of the men out there in the field slaughtered by the monsters of the forest. Then, the exemplar redeemer back there was killed by the giant fiend that chased us earlier, and my brother Kallas appeared, although he wasn't my brother yet, but then..."

Something caught Dillen's eye, and he stopped. Imariel shifted, and a small frown pressed the corners of her lips. She seemed to realize that he was staring at her and shook her head, but it was too late. Her mask had already slipped.

"You saw it, too, didn't you?"

"I do not know what I saw."

"Bollocks! You recognized the scene I just described!"

"I... I saw the massacre. But I think there was more to it."

"In your dream-vision, did the creature that did become your brother place his hand upon the armor of the man that now lies connected to the tree?" Shesh'ra broke in.

"Yes, he did," Dillen responded. Imariel nodded.

"And at this moment when he did this thing, did there come into being a wave of blue power?"

"Yes! So we saw the same thing!" Dillen exclaimed.

"I saw this, also," Imariel added.

"So why was I the only one to start screaming, then?" Dillen asked, and an uncomfortable silence spread through the trio. Both Shesh'ra and Imariel appeared to be pointedly examining details of the clearing that forced them to look away from Dillen.

"Oh, come now! Didn't the horrible thing that appeared at the end of the dream confront you directly? Didn't my brother not show himself to you at the end?"

"No, the thing turned into my mother at the end. She said that I had failed her." Imariel still refused to meet his gaze.

"For me, it did change into the corpse of one I knew, but whose body is ash in a forgotten forest now," Shesh'ra whispered. "He did not say one thing to me, but did just stare at me as his bones burned before me." She hugged her burned arm to her as she spoke. Dillen's eyes darted between them.

"It was horrible. It was as if I were trapped in a dream from which I could not escape. If it wasn't for your screams, I don't know that I would have been able to tear myself away from her." Imariel shuddered as she spoke.

"Well, I guess I'm glad that my weak heart is good for something at least." Dillen tried unsuccessfully to keep the sulkiness out of his voice.

"I am of a mind that you do not be for understanding her," Shesh'ra said. "You were the one that did shake yourself from the nightmare. I did wish to scream, but it was as if a dam had been placed over my teeth and there was no sound permitted to pass there. You broke your dam, and it was for this that we did wake from our torture visions."

Imariel nodded in agreement.

"This either means that you have some stronger resistance to whatever this thing is, or your visions are more terrifying than what we beheld."

"Or both," Dillen grumbled.

"That is possible, though I doubt it. But what of the vision before that? What are we to make of it?"

"I think that the exemplar's corpse over there is something important."

"Yes, it was his armor that did cause the screams to stop and did push out the blue wave," Shesh'ra mused.

"What was that? You said the screams stopped in your vision when the creature touched the armor?" Imariel turned to face the naiad.

"No, she's right. I remember that. Actually, it was the blue wave of energy that jumped off him when the thing touched him. When that energy touched one of the screaming corpses down below, then that shade would stop screaming, as if the wave absorbed the sound or something." Dillen chewed his lip pensively.

"Does this metal hide of yours that the exemplar wears, does it give you blessings from the Lady as my race does enjoy?" Shesh'ra asked. "It is the blessing of closing our wounds quickly."

"Yes, that is one of the enchantments on any Armor of the Tides. It has the power to heal even grievous wounds dealt to its wearer. Why do you ask?" Dillen looked up at the naiad.

"I do find it to be of interest that the screams did stop when the horror placed its hands upon it. I am envisioning of what purpose it might have been or what this thing might have done, and why the armor was the piece that was important." Shesh'ra frowned as she spoke. Dillen's mind raced as he tried to connect the thoughts that the naiad was spouting, eventually the effort boiled out and the words spilled out of his mouth.

"You think it had something to do with the healing properties of the armor? How would that help them? Especially since they had already defeated the soldiers." Imariel did not respond to him at first but just continued walking back and forth with her eyes scanning the terrible field before them.

"I do not pretend to understand the ways of the Sickness, or of these monsters that dwell here. But we all did see the vision. There must be a reason for this." Even as she said this, Imariel stopped pacing and took in a sharp breath. Both Dillen and Shesh'ra turned to look at her. Imariel shook her head slowly.

"Those poor souls," she whispered. Her eyes suddenly seemed to be staring at something miles away.

"Who?" Dillen asked. Imariel was quiet for several moments until he was forced to repeat his question. Imariel started as if hearing him for the first time. She turned and waved her hand over the arranged corpses of the Brotherhood warriors in the clearing as she spoke.

"Look at them. Doesn't it seem strange how they lay in their death throes?! Some of them are not even lying down!"

"Yes, I believe I mentioned something when we first saw it," Dillen tilted his head as if he didn't understand, but his stomach began to gnaw at his insides. He felt a dread of some unseen revelation that he did not dare admit to himself clawing its way out of his chest.

"Think of it! What does our enemy need in order to survive?! What does it feed upon?" Imariel's face was pinched as she spoke carefully, as if tutoring a young child.

"Strong emotions, in particular fear, as it would appear from this cursed forest," Dillen responded, willing the nauseous feeling in his stomach to calm itself. Suddenly, Shesh'ra gasped beside him.

161

"Oh, by the depths! You believe that this is so?" she exclaimed, Imariel shifted her gaze to her.

"I do not understand how, but yes, I believe that the armor is the key." Imariel took a shuddering breath. Dillen looked between them both with a confused look on his face.

"Can you speak plainly? What is happening here?"

"How many times have you faced death on the battlefield, Dillen?" Imariel said, looking at him sharply.

"More times than I care to remember," Dillen shrugged, "but what does that have to do…"

"What were the feelings that rose in your breast when these events did happen to you?" Shesh'ra interrupted him.

"I've never been more terrified in my life…" Dillen responded, the feeling in his chest dropped down to intensify those that twisted his gut. He barely heard Imariel as she continued Shesh'ra's explanation.

"Not only that, but I imagine several other strong emotions passed through you in those fateful moments. Sadness, regret, anger, anxiety. All of those powerful feelings within the space of a matter of breaths as you awaited your own deathstroke, correct?"

"Yes…" Dillen choked. The image of the blue-eyed corpse from before flashed in his mind. The man's face had seemed as if it had been reaching for him, imploring him for something. The feeling in Dillen's stomach churned, and a low rumbling sound began to sound in his ears.

"What if the monsters found a way to keep you frozen in that one moment, forever? Either just before or just after that final blow was struck? As you felt your life begin to drain away." Imariel's own voice began to dwindle away to a whisper as she spoke.

"This would be quite the feast for the monsters," Shesh'ra finished Imariel's unspoken conclusion. Dillen's vision blurred and he leaned forward, gulping great breaths of air as memories of battles fought in the past washed over him. How many times had he felt a blade score his flesh that he had felt sure of at the time would kill him? How many times had he found himself staring up at a foe with their weapon raised, prepared to drop it down and end his life? How many times had he anticipated the pain of broken bones or a slashed throat? How many times had he coughed and spit blood, not knowing if he was about to choke on it?

Each time had brought with it its own fresh hell in his dreams. He could remember waking in the dead of some nights, clutching his freshest set of scars as the memories had poured over him. He remembered the sweat and tears as he had held the sides of his head and willed the images away, as he forced himself to remember that he wasn't dying, all the while the pressure built behind his temples and threatened to roll out of him in a prolonged scream.

Any soldier who had seen combat had these moments, these memories. Some used bravado, others alcohol, and some tried to pretend as if it didn't happen to them. Everyone found their own way of coping in one form or another. But when those nightmares came, there was no coping strategy in this world that could pause the waves of terror that washed over.

Dillen swallowed hot bile that rose in the back of his throat. Two years. Velorun had said the Sickness had appeared two years ago. Dillen forced his eyes to roam around the glade where the bodies lay. For two years these warriors had experienced the horror of that perpetual moment of their deaths. That unending moment of pain, of watching their friends experiencing that same terror and pain all around them. Their screams had been what Dillen had heard when they entered the clearing. That hadn't been an alarm or a warning. It was a cry of help, to end the suffering. His vision blurred again, and Dillen leaned forward and retched the non-existent contents of his stomach out onto the forest floor.

It was as if he was trying to purge the very memory of those screams, of the blue-eyed corpse as it reached for him out of his very mind. His body pressed violently against his stomach as it tried to clear the emotions out of his stomach and through his mouth.

He didn't know how long he leaned forward gagging, but eventually he became dimly aware of Imariel's hand on his back and her voice speaking in his ear.

"It must have something to do with the regenerative properties of the armor. It must somehow keep them constantly alive and regenerate them just enough to keep them on the cusp of their terror."

Her voice was mechanical, cold, and detached. But when Dillen shot her a sidelong glance, he saw that her lips were pursed into a straight line, and her eyes were haunted as she gazed everywhere but at him.

"The armor is the heart," Dillen croaked, his voice burned by the acid of his stomach. It wasn't a question, but Imariel gave a curt nod in response. Dillen rose shakily to his feet.

"Then we are getting these men out of here. We are ending this." He walked directly over to the pinned body and grabbed hold of the edges of the breastplate. He hauled bodily on the metal, and at first, it groaned in protest and didn't move. Dillen screamed his frustration at the stubborn armor and pulled harder. He felt the edges bite into the flesh of his palms as what he assumed was blood began to slick across his hands. He didn't stop. The metal strained against the clawed pincer that penetrated it. A blue light pulsed around the golden symbol on the left breast, and suddenly the pain in Dillen's hands was gone. He let loose a feral cry as he wrenched one final time, and in a flash of bright, blue light, the armor pulled away from the tree and the pincer fell into the grass where it disintegrated into purple vapor.

Dillen toppled to the ground, his breath coming in ragged gasps. He pulled his hands free to examine the damage there. He heard Imariel gasp behind him as his fingers came away covered in blood, and that it extended up beyond his wrists. But as he looked closer, he couldn't distinguish any wound amid all of the crimson staining his palms. He stared at them incredulously for several long moments.

"Well this won't do at all, dear brother." Kallas's voice caused Dillen to turn. The too-wide grin of his brother's shade knelt beside him, staring down at the recently freed armor.

"I don't give a damn what you say, and may the fires of the Abyss take you for all I care." Dillen spat between shuddering gasps. Kallas laughed, but there was something different this time. The throaty raspiness had been replaced with a simple dryness that held no mirth in it.

"Really? You would say that to your own kin? Especially when it's your fault that I…"

"You are not my brother, so you can stop wearing his face." Dillen interrupted the foul creature. The smile slipped slowly from its mouth, only to be replaced with a sneer.

"You know that I can feed off anger just as easily as fear, don't you?"

In response, Dillen lunged at it and grabbed it by the throat. Pulling his knife out of his belt in the same motion, he pressed the blade into the top of the creature's sternum. Imariel stepped forward, but Shesh'ra held up a hand to stop her.

"The thing about anger is that it can feed me, too!" Dillen snarled. Kallas's twisted face deepened its sneer and it replied in a choked voice.

"What are you going to do? Kill me again? I'll just come straight back."

"I already told you, you are not my brother! Come back all you like, and I will kill you again and again each time!"

"I will haunt you untill you become mad. I will drive you to the brink of your sanity as I drag your sins across the coals of your conscience until the end of your days."

Dillen tightened his grip on the creature's throat.

"I have many things to atone for, it's true," he growled, "but I have seen your sins that litter this glade! What you have done is beyond murder! It goes beyond cruelty! Your judgments hold absolutely no sway over me! I will not be held prisoner to the conscience of a bastard such as you! My brother is dead! He is beyond what you can summon!"

"You will never know how deep and treacherous the mind can be, dear brother." The creature squirmed under Dillen's grip. "I will invent all new ways of torturing you! That's if, of course, you can escape this forest with your lives."

Dillen became aware of a sound coming from the trees. At first, he thought it was thunder, but the sound did not cease. Instead it was getting louder.

"Dillen!" Imariel cried out. The creature choked out something resembling laughter.

"You unfortunately have taken away your one chance for safety. Normally we don't like coming to this glade because this is a doorway, and if we're not careful, we can be sucked back to where we came from. But since you are threatening to remove our anchor, that caution has been thrown to the wind. Soon, every nightmare, every monster will be on you. Your worst imaginations cannot begin to describe the pain that is coming for…"

The creature's voice cut off as Dillen rammed his knife deep into its throat. Instantly, Kallas's body dissipated into a vaporous cloud. Dillen turned around and gathered up the various pieces of the Armor of Tides.

"We need to go, and we need to take as much of this with us as we can." Dillen didn't even look up as he spoke. Without a word, the other two knelt down and began gathering pieces of armor.

In the distance, the sound of growling thunder was growing closer.

Chapter XXV

They ran as fast as they could while carrying the awkward heaps of metal armor in their arms. Shesh'ra had constructed a crude series of straps which Dillen wore around his shoulders that secured certain pieces of the armor to him. He wore the breastplate across his chest, feeling slightly sacrilegious in doing so, but the thing which chased them cared little for the beliefs of those it pursued.

Dillen could hear it now, the cracking of tree limbs and the heavy rustling of undergrowth as the shapeless void crashed behind them. He threw a terrified glance over his shoulder to try and spot their pursuer, but all he saw were shadows and the shaking of trees as whatever it was pushed past them in its rush to claim Dillen and his companions.

The thing was drawing closer to them, that much he knew, but the gloom of the forest made the distance impossible to measure. Already Dillen's chest ached and his legs burned as he pistoned his feet faster and faster against the loamy undergrowth. Lightning arced overhead, followed quickly by a deafening peal of thunder, and he groaned as he felt the pattering of raindrops on his face. Soon, the already treacherous footing of the woodland floor became even more dangerous as it was slicked by the ensuing deluge. Water poured from the skies in buckets.

Dillen cried out as his foot slipped off a log that he had tried to leap over without slowing his pace. He tumbled to the ground, his ankle twisting at an unnatural angle as he slammed into the muddy earth. Fire consumed his foot as he struggled to rise from his ignominious fall, and he glanced down to see his toes pointing in an incongruous angle from his shin. Doggedly, he tried to take a step, but as soon as his weight shifted to the injured foot, he collapsed once more to the floor, a cry of pain ripping through the sheets of rain pouring over him.

"Dillen?!" Imariel's panicked voice shouted over another roll of thunder. Dillen looked up to see the elf's face, her eyes wide and her mouth open, calling his name.

167

"I'm here!" he responded, but she didn't seem to hear him. He called out again, louder this time, but his voice was choked with pain and still she didn't seem to hear. She began wandering in his direction, her movements sharp and frantic. At last she saw him and hurried over to where he was cradling his foot on the ground.

"We have to go!" she yelled over the storm. Dillen nodded in response and pointed at his foot with gritted teeth.

"What's wrong?!"

Dillen was surprised by this question and reached down to pat his injured foot. He was surprised when his foot did not tremble when his hand touched the tender joint.

"It's my ankle! I think I've broken it!"

Imariel gave him a puzzled stare, then reached down and pulled his foot up violently to inspect it. Dillen yelped in surprise and fell onto his back.

"It looks fine to me!" Imariel called out. "Can you walk?"

"I already tried! Leave me!" Dillen struggled into a sitting position.

"Try again!" Imariel wrenched him to his feet and Dillen took in a sharp gasp in anticipation of the pain, but he was surprised when his foot supported his weight with nothing more than a minor complaint. Had he only imagined the pain from earlier? Or had his adrenaline kicked in to help him keep running? He wasn't about to question it, and together with Imariel, they took off running once more through the forest.

A quick glance behind him as they started to run showed the monster was closing on them, and Dillen could make out sharp, scything talons in the gloom now. In fact, it looked like there was more than one monster chasing them. The noise was becoming deafening beside the roaring thunder and the crackling lightning above them.

Monsters began to appear before them, and the trio was forced to run in wide circles to avoid shambling clusters of scarecrows that staggered between the trees. Those that they couldn't avoid, they were forced to cut down as quickly as possible. Each time they were forced to slow as they dispatched another of the twisted creatures caused Dillen's stomach to knot as he glanced behind and saw the rippling shadows hurrying toward them.

He couldn't tell how long they ran. He couldn't remember how long they had been in the forest. He tried to remember the details of their journey. Had they really only been here for a day? That seemed impossible, and yet Dillen hoped that it was true. His addled mind reasoned that if they had only gone so far into the Sickness, then surely they must be approaching the borders of this cursed forest? Perhaps they were near to the clearing where Bhadein and Velorun were waiting?

Directions were meaningless to Dillen in the gray of the forest gloom, so he fixed his eyes on Imariel's back as they sprinted through the woods and dodged the treacherous footings of fallen logs and vines that sought to tangle their feet together as they ran. Twice more he almost twisted his ankle again as the ground seemed to shift under his boots, but each time he righted himself.

"I think I see something up ahead!" Imariel called to him over her shoulder. "I think we are almost out!"

Dillen choked down emotions that immediately threatened to strangle his breathing and instead willed his exhausted legs to move faster. He strained to see ahead, to see what Imariel had promised him was there, but his were normal human eyes and not those of an elf. Then, something seemed to break through the gloom. A flash of fiery orange light that speared its way through the darkness of the Sickness. No such color could exist in this realm of nightmares! Dillen gulped ever bigger gasps of air and forced himself to keep moving.

That was when the Abyss reached out its long, midnight-laden arm and grabbed hold of his hope to thrust it back under. The jet black carapace of Ur-chitak burst through the trees and slammed into Imariel from the side, right in front of Dillen. She screamed as she flew sideways into a nearby tree where she crumpled to the ground and was still.

"No!" Dillen cried out. He saw Shesh'ra turn to look behind her and saw the elf lying on the ground. Dillen dropped the vambraces and pauldrons he was holding and pulled his sword. He pointed at Imariel's still form.

"Get her out of here! I'll hold the monster off!"

Shesh'ra's eyes were wide, but she scurried back and lifted Imariel bodily up off the floor. Dillen was relieved to see her lips move as she muttered something while Shesh'ra placed the elf's arm over her shoulders, and together the two stumbled off toward the shimmering sunset of hope before them. Ur-chitak looked as if he was about to storm toward the two women, but Dillen ran forward and slashed at one of the monster's leg joints. The blade slipped between the joints of the monster's chitin, and he was rewarded with a meaty sound as his weapon connected with nightmarish tissue beneath.

Ur-chitak roared and spun to face him instead, and as it did so, it tore Dillen's sword from his hands, it still being embedded in the monster's flesh. Dillen jumped backward, his eyes swiveling from left to right. He needed to distract the creature until Shesh'ra and Imariel could escape the Sickness. If he turned and ran now, the fiend would simply turn and chase after them, easily catching them before they made it out.

Letting out a yell, Dillen charged Ur-Chitak. He dived for the hilt of his sword still stuck in the creature's leg joint. Ur-chitak turned further, and Dillen fell short of his weapon, instead being forced to tuck and roll in order to avoid a massive scything claw as it struck the ground right where he had landed. He pushed himself into a crouch and glanced back at the pursuing maelstrom of nightmares that he had been trying to escape before. They were almost on top of him. He couldn't stay here, or else they would be upon him; and between them and Ur-chitak, they would make short work of him, anyways.

He looked around, searching for some kind of solution, when something caught his eye. A massive tree trunk, easily big enough that Dillen would have struggled to wrap his arms around, was scored deeply by Ur-chitak's massive claw. It must have been struck when Dillen had dodged to the side just now. Easily a quarter of the trunk was cut through by the fiend's blow, and it was already beginning to creak. A desperate plan formed in his mind, and Dillen took a deep breath and moved around to stand beside the tree.

He yelled at Ur-chitak, waving his arms in the air. The fiend bellowed in response and threw another claw toward where Dillen stood. At the last possible second, he threw himself backward, out of the way of the claw, which struck the tree another massive blow - so much so that it began to groan loudly enough for Dillen to hear it over the sounds of the monsters behind him and the thunder overhead. The massive trunk began to tip, its bark and roots groaning in protest. Dillen felt a moment of hope that was quickly extinguished.

It was falling in the wrong direction. The force of Ur-chitak's blow had caused the trunk to shudder and give way on its opposite side, so now the tree was falling away from the fiend. Dillen acted quickly and began yelling at the fiend even as he stepped into the shadow of the falling pine and began running. He didn't bother to look behind him as he ran, knowing that if the plan didn't work, he wouldn't get far before the tree or the fiend killed him. He clenched his eyes shut as he ran, waiting for the pain to hit him as he listened to the cracking of the tree and the cries of Ur-chitak behind him.

The pain never came, however. There was a loud crash, followed by the strong scent of tree sap, pine needles, and a bellowing cry from Ur-chitak. Dillen stopped and turned back to see what had happened. The monster lay crushed beneath the weight of the massive tree. The upper branches and trunk sat suspended above Dillen's head by mere inches, held aloft by Ur-chitak's bulk, which lay motionless beside the cracked stump. A deep divot held the trunk in place on the creature's back.

Dillen wondered if the nightmare was destroyed at last. It lay motionless, but even as Dillen watched, it began to stir. Another quick glance saw that the swarming hive of monstrosities that had been chasing him were now seconds away from catching him. He scurried over, scooped up the armor he had dropped, and tore off toward where he could just see the outline of Imariel and Shesh'ra stumbling into the light.

The tightness in his chest was overwhelming. He couldn't suck enough air into his lungs, and spots began to appear in his vision. His legs felt like they were pushing through waist deep water as he propelled himself through the forest. The chittering and screaming noises from behind him seemed to be growing louder. On several occasions, he swore he felt a clawed hand touch his shoulder, or some form of talon reach out to grasp his leg. The patch of sunlight didn't seem to be growing any closer.

The spots in his vision began to grow bigger, and soon they were exploding like little swirling galaxies all over. The fuzzy patches of darkness began to consume his vision. He could no longer feel the pain in his chest, and his legs had long since gone numb. He could feel his pace slowing as he ran, but it didn't seem to matter anymore. He just wanted the nightmare to end, and it didn't matter how.

With a last frustrated grunt of exertion, Dillen pushed himself through into the orange patch of light and blinked as he was blinded by the sudden illumination. He heard a gruff voice bellow something that he barely understood.

"Shield line! Advance!"

There was a clatter of metal and the sounds of feet stomping that came from all around Dillen. Something clipped his shoulder and sent him spinning to the ground where he collapsed. The pain in his chest returned, and he found himself sucking in great gasps of air as quickly as he could. So fast, in fact, that he began to hiccup. Feeling slowly began to return to his legs, and he realized that they were trembling.

The fuzzy spots in his vision receded, and his eyes adjusted to the new light. He realized that he was lying in the grass, and that the warm glow of sunset was washing over his body, which was somehow soaked for some reason. Then he remembered the rain, and the forest. He bolted up as he thought of his pursuers and how they should have caught him by now. His body betrayed him and his arms shuddered and suddenly gave out, refusing to support him. He toppled back onto the ground and found himself staring up into dark storm clouds.

Gingerly, he raised his head to glance in the direction that his pursuers must have been following him from. He was surprised to see a sea of soldiers clad in green cloaks, armed with spears and shields, standing between him and the dark gloom of the Sickness beyond.

"It is well," Shesh'ra's voice cut through his confused thoughts. "It does appear that the soldiers of Velorun have been for preparing the way for us. They will fight back the dark now." Her voice was ragged and breathless, much as he imagined his would be if he tried to speak.

"Imariel?" he croaked.

"She did go to the tent of the healer. It appears that she will be for mending. Broken ribs and a heavy blow upon her head."

"How did they know we were here?"

"It would have taken a blind man not to see where you were." Another voice interrupted them, and Dillen turned to see Velorun striding toward them. His eyes were grim, and he pointed at the sky above the forest. Dillen looked up and saw the heavy storm clouds boiling with lightning and recognized the crashing sounds of thunder that he had heard in the forest. Confused, he glanced over to where the sun was hanging low on the horizon. He saw that the storm clouds were advancing on the sunset and threatened to overwhelm it at any minute.

"I have sent for Sir Bhadein to rouse your troops and try and buy us more time, but it seems that all of the legions of the Sickness are roused and on your tail. My soldiers have set up a defensive perimeter, but I do not know how long they can hold against the might of these nightmares when they are in full force as they are now."

Dillen's brain whirled as he tried to process the information that Velorun was sharing with him. He was struggling to even breathe, though, and much of what the elf had told him simply slid through his brain like sand through a sieve.

"Did you find it?" Velorun asked impatiently.

"What?" Dillen stammered.

"The heart! Did you find the heart of the Sickness?!"

"Y…Yes! I…" The words wouldn't come, and Dillen felt foolish as he held up the pauldrons he still clutched in his exhausted hands.

"Is this it?" Velorun snatched the armor out of the knight's hands. Dillen tapped the breastplate he still wore over his other armor.

"This, too."

"How do you know that this is what is giving the monsters their strength?" Velorun rubbed his finger along some of the etching on the pauldron he held. Dillen forced himself to sit up, strength was slowly beginning to return to his limbs. Shesh'ra came forward with a small wineskin that sloshed when she handed it to him. Dillen pitched the wineskin's contents into his parched throat, and the lukewarm water tasted of honey and ambrosia as it spilled across his chapped lips.

After gulping down half the skin, Dillen felt his faculties returning to normal. He noted that the fighting behind them had diminished, and he glanced back to see how the battle line was faring. It seemed as though nothing had changed. The green-clad elves maintained their discipline.

"The nightmarish tide is receding to build up momentum for a second rush. They will attack again shortly." Velorun's voice was tight with impatience. "Now tell me what you have learned!"

Quickly, Shesh'ra and Dillen told their story of how they had found the cursed grove with the strangely preserved bodies, and of the vision that they had when Dillen touched the armor. Velorun listened intently and asked questions where Dillen and Shesh'ra weren't specific enough about the details. He nodded absently as he listened, and when they were done, he was strangely quiet for several long moments. When he spoke, his voice was terse.

"It seems as though the monsters found a way to trap the soldiers in their moments of death, an existence of perpetual pain and fear, anguish and regret. This would make sense how it would feed them and anchor them to our world. I think you are right in that they did something to this armor, perverting its blessing of regeneration somehow in order to keep them in that state. Which means, if I am not mistaken, if we can break the curse on the armor, then that should finally purge the Sickness and allow us to defeat the monsters."

Dillen pushed himself to his feet and began unbuckling the breastplate for the Armor of Tides. Shesh'ra gathered up the rest of the bits of armor they had retrieved, and together the three of them moved back, further away from the Sickness.

A short time later found them sitting beneath the same pavilion that they had sat in the previous day. The pieces of the cursed armor were laid out before them on a small wooden table while Velorun surveyed everything.

"I will implore the Lady to break the curse and act as her conduit for this procedure," Velorun said as he passed his hand over the table. "We should begin as soon as possible. I fear the process will take some time, and the nightmares are gathering their forces for another attack. They must know that we have their anchor, and if they do not take it back, we will destroy their gateway to this world."

Even as he said this, a shadow swept across the clearing as the storm clouds engulfed the setting sun that had already mostly dipped below the horizon. The familiar sound of thunder began rolling in the distance. The sound of dozens of hooves announced the arrival of Bhadein and the rest of the Brotherhood knights. They streamed into the clearing and began taking up formation behind the line of elven infantry that stood presently preparing to repel any nightmarish invaders. It seemed as though the fighting had ground to a halt for the most part, but the ominous flashes of lightning and the sudden darkness brought on by the absence of the sun illuminated a forest of red fireflies that had sprung into existence beneath the eaves of the sickened forest. The red lights rippled and swarmed back and forth throughout the gloom, and a sickening revelation took hold of Dillen as he looked closer. Those weren't fireflies.

The entire forest was filled with monstrosities. Their hungry eyes reflected red in the darkening gloom. Dillen turned to face Velorun even as he saw Bhadein break away from his knights and begin riding toward their pavilion.

"We must hurry."

Chapter XXVI

The rain was falling in heavy sheets while lightning cracked the sky. The thunder drowned out the drums and horns of the battlefield musicians conveying orders across the already muddy battlefield. The darkness the storm brought with it had a distinctly unnatural feel to it, as if it were a palpable entity that was wandering through the ranks of the elves, men, and naiads that stood in staggered ranks across the clearing.

Dillen saw his breath cloud in front of him as he looked across the gathered soldiers and into the glowing sea of glowing red eyes that stared out from the even darker eaves of the sickened forest before them. He was mounted on his destrier, beside at least a dozen other knights beside him. Bhadein had taken command of a similar detachment of knights which had doubled up behind his unit to follow up behind their charges. To their left, further down the line, Shesh'ra stood with two regiments of her heart piercers, who were taking aim at the forest. Velorun's elven rangers took to their right, a small forest of spears and some bowmen beside that, even a few of the living trees that sometimes marched to war beside them.

Behind him, he knew, sat the pavilion where Velorun himself was praying to the Lady and preparing the necessary rites to cleanse the armor of its tainted connection to the otherworldly nightmares even now arraying themselves to attack. Dillen began to wonder why the creatures hadn't yet advanced. Surely they knew what was happening to their precious anchor by now?

As if in response to his thoughts, he felt the wind shift. The eyes began to move forward, and the shadows gave way from darkness to seeing gray shapes form in its depths. The first creatures to appear seemed to hover above the ground in a way that Dillen could not see was possible. They were great tentacled, bulbous entities that had the appearance of skulls cracked open to reveal their brains underneath, which pulsed and throbbed with ethereal energy. Dozens of eyes lined the creatures' various appendages, sprouting from areas placed seemingly at random. The eyes glowed red and rolled in their sockets, fixating on things unseen all around them.

There were three of these floating monstrosities, and Dillen held his breath as they approached the very edge of the forest and stopped. A sea of nightmares rallied behind them, but they too paused as if waiting for something. The rain was still pelting down from a torn sky above them, but as Dillen watched, the air seemed to thrum with an energy, and there came a drawn out hum from somewhere above the enemy line. The hair on Dillen's arms stood on end. It was as if the world held its collective breath. Dillen opened his mouth to call out encouragement to his men, but he never got the chance to speak.

Forked lightning split the air directly in front of him, followed by a deafening clap of thunder that left Dillen staring into a white void. Something was screaming, and it took him several moments of bewilderment before he realized that it was his ears ringing. He felt a wetness running down the side of his neck, but the thought was so detached that it barely registered in his addled mind.

Gradually, his vision cleared, and he found himself on the ground; his whole body ached, and he felt a sharp pain issued from his side. He coughed as he pushed himself up to a kneeling position. He set his hand to steady himself, and it made contact with something fleshy and soft. He jerked his head to the side to see what he was touching and saw that it was what remained of his steed. The creature must have reared up when the lightning struck and thrown him to the ground, but that didn't explain why it now lay in a puddle of mud and viscera while the smell of burnt meat lingered in his nostrils. A muffled voice was saying something, but Dillen couldn't make out the words.

"Sir Dillen!" It was an older knight, Gordram was his name, he thought. Dillen only knew that he was speaking to him because he found himself gazing up as the other man towered over him on his giant warhorse.

"Wha...?" Dillen began but couldn't find the words he wanted to ask.

"The bastards must have wizards with them of some kind! They blasted your unit with this damned lightning. You and a few others took the brunt of it, it looks like. Can you stand?"

Dillen nodded and forced his legs to stand. The screaming in his ears had reduced to a dull roar that made it sound like he had a cloth wrapped around his head, covering the sounds around him.

"I need a horse," he said a little louder than he probably needed to. Gordram nodded and motioned to someone at his left. Dillen turned and saw a younger knight leading a gray mare in his direction.

"Stevens wasn't as lucky as you. The lightning missed both him and his horse, but she threw him before he could recover, and the other horses... well, there was a lot going on, but it was not a heroic death, I'm afraid."

The young knight passed the reins to Dillen, who struggled to lift himself into the saddle. His side ached something terrible, and his head felt like the pressure was going to cause his skull to burst. At last he fumbled his way into the saddle and unsheathed his sword. He'd lost his lance in the explosion, but he didn't have time to find it now.

"How many did we lose?" he shouted to Gordram.

"Stevens, Maiser, Devon, and Surdran. The men are pretty skittish after that barrage, but it seems like the rest of the troops were spared, and so that is giving them a bit of courage."

Dillen nodded and cast his eyes across the field to the enemy line. There were several shambling bodies making their way in front of the floating, tentacled skulls that still sat hovering behind them. They hovered just outside of a comfortable range to charge. They were waiting for something.

"They're going to keep peppering our lines with their lightning bolts," Gordram said beside him. Dillen shook his head in response.

"No, they can't afford that. They know that they need to break through and reclaim the armor before we can remove their attachment to it. What are they…"

Before he could finish his sentence, he heard something that caused him to pause. Above, the clouds still rang with the echoes of thunderclaps, but beneath that sound came something else, something disconcerting. Dillen tilted his head to try and focus on the noise. It seemed like something mundane, but the fact that he could hear it over the thunder and the shouting of his men mad his mouth run dry.

"Do you hear that?" he asked Gordram. The older knight just stared at him. Dillen frowned and shifted in his saddle. He strained to make out what the noise was, motioning for the other knights to be still. The sound was growing louder, and with a shock, Dillen realized what it was.

It was the buzzing noise of insect wings but grown to a horrible cacophony to rival that of the storm that raged around them. All of a sudden, a cloud consisting of thousands of writhing tiny specks burst from out of the forest and sped its way toward their battle line. Dillen watched in horror as it bore down on his men when he began to feel something prickling the back of his calf where his armor didn't cover. He glanced down and yelped, kicking to the side to dislodge a giant spider which was crawling up his leg.

His horse tossed its head and began to shimmy from side to side. Dillen reached a hand out to steady the mare, placing his palm against the side of her neck and making soothing sounds. The horse stilled somewhat, although her eyes were still rolling madly in their sockets. Dillen's gaze happened to focus on the ground as he stroked the mare's neck, and a sickening gorge rose in his throat as he stared at what he beheld.

The ground writhed beneath them. Several other knights began yelling and swatting at their legs much like Dillen had. Spiders began to swarm up the legs of the horses. Great big creatures the size of his forearm with legs that skittered and slid up onto the horses' abdomens and clung to the armor of their riders as they bit and clawed their way through exposed areas. Dillen cried out and swung his sword down to try and cleave as many of the insects from his legs as possible.

He felt several stinging sensations on his feet and the back of his legs. One of the insects leapt up onto his hand as he slashed, and he almost released his sword in shock. A wave of revulsion caused him to shudder as he swept the creature away with the back of his other gauntlet. He found another insect, this one even larger, clinging to the vambrace on that hand as well and cried out, shaking his fist wildly to try and dislodge it. It clung on, however, and scurried up his arm to leap against his helmet. Dillen cried out and smashed his fist against the side of his head. There was a sickening crunch, and the skittering noises of the insect's legs against his metal helm grew still.

Dillen pulled his hand away and for the first time was able to inspect his assailants, albeit briefly, as there were still more which clung to his legs. The creatures weren't like any that he had ever seen before. They had seven legs, which seemed odd, but that was the least startling thing about them. Their bodies were covered in a type of dark purple chitinous armor and a violet steam seemed to be coming from the joints of its legs. The water from the rain didn't seem to touch it, but instead passed straight through. But the most disgusting aspect of the creature was its mouth, easily large enough to fit his hand inside and filled with teeth that were also decidedly human in appearance.

Dillen shivered and tossed the crushed insect from him, realizing now that there were several others that were clawing at his armor. He felt an itchy sensation where he assumed that several of them had managed to find chinks in his armor. He slammed his fist down erratically, attempting to kill as many as possible of the little creatures. They fell rather easily once he dedicated his efforts to swatting them away.

Once the last of the creatures toppled off of him, Dillen glanced up to see rows of scarecrows shambling toward him with their weapons raised in the direction of nature's warriors. A quick glance down their battle line showed Dillen that the rest of the soldiers had all suffered similar attacks to those of his knights. Many were still struggling to throw off the skittering insects. The scarecrows were closing the distance, and many were preparing to charge. Dillen looked to the rest of the knights in his unit, raising his sword above his head and bellowing at them.

"Form up!" he yelled. The other knights quickly shook off the last of the spiders and took up stances in their usual, double-tiered position. Dillen lowered his blade to point at the closest cluster of shambling, withered bodies.

"Charge!" Dillen ordered, and the roar of thunder above was mirrored by the hooves of the knights as they galloped across the short distance between them and the scarecrow horde. Lances were lowered at the last moment before impact, and there came a great crash of splintered wood as desiccated husks were pierced through, some even piercing the other nightmarish beings behind the first line. Dillen hacked away with his sword, severing the head from one set of twisted set of shoulders in one stroke, while cleaving neatly through the skull of another.

The other knights in the regiment cast their broken lances aside and pulled their swords free of their scabbards. As they did so, it created a lull in the violence, and Dillen cast his eyes about the field. Despite the bloody toll their charge had done to the horde of scarecrows before them, the devilish fiends still held their line and were preparing to strike back against their attackers. What's worse was that another gathering of staggering shapes was moving up to the side of them.

A lurch of activity jarred Dillen's attention back to the creatures in front of him. They had shifted sideways and had grabbed ahold of Dillen's legs. Wickedly pointed fingertips took hold of the edges of his plate there and were tugging remorselessly down at him. Dillen slashed downward to try and drive them back, but they were relentless. None of them seemed to notice, or care, when Dillen's blade cut through their twisted limbs or removed a gibbering head from its shoulders. The husks just pushed their incapacitated comrade out of the way and took its place.

Dillen kicked the flanks of his steed and pulled back sharply on the reins, causing the mare to rear up and kick as she had been trained to do. The blows sent several of the scarecrows flying, but when she landed, there were already three more of them waiting for her, each one armed with sharp blades, claws, or teeth. They lunged for the mare's exposed throat even as she landed, and before she could rear back a second time, they were upon her. Crimson jets flew from where they latched on, and the mare lurched from side to side in an effort to dislodge them. Dillen clung onto the saddle for his life as his mount surged underneath him, but it was a useless effort. The mare was unable to push away her attackers; and after several violent lurches, her eyes rolled into the back of her head and she toppled to the ground, sending Dillen flying to land in the mud.

He hit hard, red sparks flashing in his vision, and the breath being forcibly pushed from his lungs. Adrenaline was the only thing that kept him from laying there, waiting for the sparks to recede and his breathing to resume something resembling normal. Instead, he rolled onto his back, coughing and blinking. As his vision returned, he was met with the nightmarish sight of elongated nails and dirty fingers scrabbling at his armor. He thrashed and struck wildly with his free arm, but the bodies of the creatures had already pinned his sword arm to his side. He kicked with his feet, as well, trying desperately to keep himself from being overwhelmed for one moment longer.

Finally, it became impossible. The scarecrows began pressing down on him more. By now, his vision had almost completely returned, but the only thing he could see was a small window of the gray sky overhead that was completely ringed by the dark, writhing shapes of the beasts that were closing in to kill him. He was pinned to the point where it was difficult to breathe. A finger hooked its way around the lip of his eye slot, and with a violent jerk, the helmet came loose. As it left his head, the edge of the helmet caught his lip and slammed his head back into the mud, and he became dimly aware of the taste of blood in his mouth. He closed his eyes and waited for the pain to begin. The monsters must have sensed his terror, and it was driving them into a frenzy.

Then, suddenly, the pressure released, and Dillen found himself able to move. He opened his eyes and was met with the sight of a withered corpse lying across his chest. He looked up and saw Gordram standing above him with his sword swinging, bellowing challenges to the scarecrows who had been forced back by the ferocity of his attack. The knight had also lost his steed, it seemed, but he wasn't about to let that stop him from slaughtering the beasts. He had a long, bloody gash that went from his forehead, crossed his right eye and went all the way down to his jaw from the looks of it, forcing his eye closed.

Dillen pushed out of the mud and came up beside the older knight. He swung his blade, all thoughts of finesse and training abandoned. He swung as if he were chopping firewood, because that was how densely packed the scarecrows were around them. Short, directed overhead chops were the only thing he had room or time to accomplish as the press of bodies threatened to overwhelm him.

The brief spark of relief that had kindled within him slowly began to die once more as the sea of withered monsters slowly began to wash over them again. Gordram had only prolonged their death. Fear was threatening to overwhelm him with the frantic anxiety of impending pain and death, and so he took that energy and pushed it into his arms. He screamed as his sword rose and fell again and again.

Beside him, he heard Gordram cry out in a yell that turned to a gurgle, and Dillen turned to see the older knight clutching at his throat as blood poured through his fingers, a scarecrow standing over him with a bloody, curved dagger in its hand. Dillen didn't have time to allow the shock to register that Gordram was dead, because his foe wouldn't allow him the reprieve. Instead, he was forced to raise his blade to ward off another attack.

As he did so, there came the sound of a trumpet that was echoed with the crack of thunder. Dillen risked a glance over his shoulder and saw the pennants of Bhadein's regiment being carried across the muddy turf directly toward them on lances that were dipping in preparation of making contact with the enemy. Dillen turned back to the sickly things before him and dropped his shoulder. He plowed into the closest two bodies and threw them back to crash against those behind them. With only a moment of breathing space, Dillen turned and threw himself to the side just as the charging knights behind him crashed into the disordered ranks of the scarecrows which Dillen had been fighting.

Dillen landed in the mud and rolled. The sound of battle was raging behind him, and he crawled for a distance through the muck in order to make sure he was clear of the carnage. Nothing stabbed him in the back or took hold of him as he crawled away, so he took that as a good sign.

When he had put a few yards behind him, he rolled onto his back and sat up. Bhadein's regiment had destroyed the remnants of the scarecrow horde that had finished off Dillen's group and was wheeling to face the other grouping of the same creatures.

"Sir Dillen!" he heard a voice calling to him and then saw a lone knight break away from the regiment to ride up alongside him. Dillen's exhaustion mixed with the gloom of the storm overhead prevented him from recognizing the knight until he drew closer.

"Your regiment is gone, get yourself back to the command tent and see if you can be any help there. We don't have any spare horses for you to rejoin the fight. Go on!" Bhadein snapped at him, and Dillen didn't even respond before the older knight turned and rode back to rejoin his men.

Dillen looked around and realized that he was behind the battle line, which was pressing forward toward the forest. He grimaced as the adrenaline began to drain from him, and he began to feel all the minor cuts and bruises that he'd suffered in his fight. He pushed himself to his feet before retrieving his bearings and staggering off toward the pavilion where he knew that Velorun would be praying.

* * * * *

The sight of the tent was something that made Dillen stagger to a halt as he approached. The tent was glowing! Bright green tendrils of energy and wisps of smoke seemed to be pulsating around the pavilion, which had its sides raised. Standing just outside was a lone figure with a bow, launching projectile after projectile into the swarming masses of nightmares that had pushed itself outside of the Sickness.

Dillen took in the lay of the battle and scowled. Several ranks of elven spears had shifted to stand between Velorun and the new monsters that had emerged from the forest, but with a shudder, Dillen recognized the foes that had recently joined the battle. These long-limbed creatures with blades protruding from their backs like spider legs and eyeless faces that chittered and twisted their heads back and forth were the same that had assaulted him outside of his tent only a few nights ago. There were dozens of these monsters that sped across the clearing, and they let loose a keening cry that split the air between claps of thunder. The combination of these sounds caused Dillen's knees to grow weak and the gorge rise in the back of his throat.

He ran toward the lone figure firing off shots from their bow, recognizing Imariel as he drew closer. She was so focused on the enemy before her that when she noticed him, she turned with a start, aiming an arrow at his forehead before blinking and slowly lowering the weapon.

"What happened?" she yelled over the storm, turning to fire her bow back toward the group of eyeless horrors running toward the elven spearmen.

"The left flank is holding, for now, but it seems that we have problems here!" he yelled back. "How close is Velorun?"

"I don't know. But it seems to be working!"

"But is it going to work fast enough?"

Even as Dillen spoke, he felt the air shift and the hairs on his arm stood on edge again. Concussive bolts of lightning slammed down into the middle of the elven warriors preparing for the charge from the bladed spider-like creatures clawing toward them. Several bodies were flung through the air, leaving trails of smoke behind them. When they landed, they didn't get up. Several of the elves looked around in astonishment, many of them clutched the sides of their head as the concussive blast likely reverberated in their skulls.

"They won't hold much longer!" Dillen shouted to Imariel.

"Don't doubt elven courage!"

Imariel grabbed a spear which had been at her feet and ran forward, yelling encouragement to the wavering group of spearmen before her. Dillen realized with a start that it wasn't a spear, but rather a banner pole. The flag that waved from its shaft was soaked in mud, but the fierce wind that whipped around the battlefield still managed to catch its folds and throw it out for its symbol to be seen. A green elm tree on a field of white. One of the signs of the Lady.

At the sight of the banner, the spearmen all seemed to grip their weapons a little tighter and turned back to face the tide of nightmares washing toward them. Dillen ran forward to join Imariel.

"I thought your ribs were broken!" he yelled.

"They are!" Imariel spoke through gritted teeth, and Dillen noticed that one of her arms was pressed against her side to support her as she waved the flag.

"What the hell are you doing, then? You're in no condition to fight!"

"Like I told you! Don't doubt elven courage!"

Dillen shook his head but turned back to face the fight. There was no sense in arguing with her. If those beasts broke through the line, then it wouldn't matter what condition she was in, they would be dead either way.

The chittering madness slammed into the line of elven spearmen. Dillen watched and heard elves scream as razor sharp limbs sliced through simple elven leather gambesons and pierced faces, throats, and stomachs. To their credit, the elven warriors returned their wounds in kind. Their spears slammed into withered chests and cut through skulls where eyes should have been. It was a massively bloody affair, and Dillen cringed as he watched the exchange whittle away at both sides of the fight.

The spearmen fought bravely, but they were outclassed. The ferocity and lack of care for personal well-being on the part of the monsters gave them a definitive edge. Easily two or three elves were cut down for every one of these beasts that they managed to slay. The fight was quickly becoming one-sided as fear and casualties began to take their toll on the spearmen.

Movement registered in the corner of Dillen's eye, and he glanced to the side to see a small cluster of warriors riding what looked like large, red elk riding toward where the spearmen fought for their lives. Velorun must have kept them in reserve to help with the backfield in case anything broke through. They were a small bunch, but they might be enough to turn the fight between the spearmen and the monsters, if the elves could hold out long enough.

The elk riders maneuvered with flawless precision, their mounts leaping with an agile grace no warhorse could ever dream of achieving. They lined up their charge for the far edge of the faceless monsters' dwindling numbers. If the spearmen could only hold out for a few more moments, the effect of the elk riders' charge would be devastating. Dillen turned back to the fight and groaned.

The spearmen, already disheartened by the lightning blasts, and now diminished to less than half their original number by the scything limbs of the creatures they fought, finally broke under the strain. The line buckled as elves gave way before the onslaught. Some turned and fled backward, others simply withdrew into clustered knots of three and four warriors which some of the monsters fell upon and quickly devoured in a fury of red mist and blurred limbs.

The creatures quickly spilled over the last bits of resistance from the spearmen and turned to face the charge of the elk riders. The elven cavalry was already committed to the charge at this point and couldn't have shifted their momentum even if they wanted to. The small cluster of mounted warriors slammed into the swarm of faceless beasts with another clash, their long, elegant spears flashing in the gloom of the storm as they cut deep into the mass of remaining scythed nightmares.

For a moment, Dillen thought that they might still carry the fight, despite the monsters being able to turn and face them head on. But their momentum slowed too quickly, and the few remaining monsters that were left after the impetus of the elven charge was spent quickly began swarming against their attackers.

Before he even realized what he was doing, Dillen found himself charging forward at the skittering things. He didn't know what he hoped to accomplish, but even as he rushed into the back of one of the monsters and his sword pierced its back, he realized he may have made a terrible mistake. The creature writhed and twisted on the point of his blade, its head turning almost completely around with its teeth clacking together as if trying to bite him.

After several long moments of wriggling, the monster grew still, and Dillen reached up with his foot to push the corpse off his weapon. As it tumbled to the ground, he saw that only two of the creatures were left, and they were circling the last two survivors of the elven riders. Dillen ran toward the nearest one, and before it could turn to face him, he swung his blade hard, cleaving clear through the beast's thin neck and sending its head flying through the air.

The other creature seemed startled and turned to look with its eyeless gaze at where Dillen stood. His skin immediately began to squirm, and he felt his mouth go dry; but before the creature could charge him, the two elven riders cut it down where it stood.

Dillen breathed out a sigh of air and felt his knees give way beneath him. Exhaustion clamored over all of his limbs, and he felt as though he could simply lay down in the mud and go to sleep. Far away, he could still hear the sounds of battle raging all around them, but the majority of the dark beasts seemed to have been driven back from the tent where Velorun was purifying the tainted armor.

Dillen looked back at the sylvan elf who knelt before the table where the cursed armor was laid out. Velorun's arms were outstretched imploringly with his head bowed. His mouth moved rapidly as he uttered his supplications. Green energy continued to swirl around him and enveloped the entirety of the tent. Dillen had no idea how much more time he would need, but it seemed as though they could finally breathe for a few moments. Even the rain seemed to be subsiding and the thunder was moving away.

A familiar screech cut through the sky, and it froze Dillen's blood. He forced his numbed limbs to stand, and he stared across the field toward the border of the Sickness. Ur-chitak stood there, its claws extended in a challenge, pointing toward where Dillen stood, although he couldn't be sure if the fiend was pointing at him or at the tent behind him. Either way, it didn't matter as the large scorpion legs were already propelling this new threat directly at them.

Dillen noticed that Ur-chitak seemed to be moving strangely, as if it were limping. He noticed that there was a sizeable dent in its carapace where the tree had struck it from earlier, and something bright green smeared one of its sides that looked remarkably like blood. Dillen brightened at the idea that it was injured, but his hopes were dashed as soon as he realized that the creature was bearing down quickly upon them, and the only thing standing between it and Velorun were the elven riders and himself.

The elves spurred their mounts around to face the creature, but either due to fatigue or injuries, they were moving too slow. Dillen saw what would happen moments before it actually did. Before the elves could turn and charge against the fiend, it was already upon them. It reached out and grabbed the first of the defenders in one of its pincers and squeezed. The elf's face turned bright red, and the scream that escaped his mouth was gurgled and frantic. His hands scrabbled at the chitinous claw that gripped him, but in a sudden spray of blood and viscera, the warrior was cut clean in two and fell to the ground in pieces, his hands still working feebly at a claw that no longer even held him as the life drained from his face.

The other elf fared better, jumping from her saddle as the fiend's massive bulk slammed into her mount, reducing it to a furry red pile before it. The elf flew through the air and rammed her spear home deep in the monster's massive chest. The creature screeched in pain but reacted quickly. Before the elf could even land from her jump, the scorpion tail behind Ur-chitak laced around its body and speared the elf through her back as the tip burst through her chest in a scarlet mist.

Dillen lifted his blade. His feet seemed frozen to the ground as he stared ahead at the monster that had chased them through the dark forest. Ur-chitak seemed to smile as it prepared to charge. Dillen could only stare as the fiend ran at him, its massive insectoid legs churning the mud as it galloped toward him.

Dillen watched everything as if in slow motion. The monster was getting closer, already it was raising its claws to deal the death blow. The fiend was close enough that Dillen could smell the rusty scent of the blood in which it was bathed when two white feathered arrows suddenly seemed to sprout from the side of the beast's face. The creature was thrown off balance as it reared in pain, and Dillen finally jumped to the side, galvanized into action at the last possible second.

Ur-chitak spun around to face him once more, but Dillen was ready this time and leapt forward to plunge his sword, up to the hilt, into the creature's side. Another screech of pain, and the beast reared up much like a horse would.

"Dillen! Move!" Imariel screamed from behind him, but it was too late.

One of the scorpion-like legs kicked out and connected with Dillen's chest. He heard a sickening crunch as bones gave way beneath the force of the blow, and then he was flying backward to land on the ground. He found himself unable to breathe, whether that was because the wind had been knocked out of him or that his ribs had punctured his lungs, he wasn't sure.

His vision dimmed, and he watched as Ur-chitak screeched and once again began to charge where he lay. He thought he saw several more feathered shafts grow from its chest, and then there was a bright flash of green light before Dillen closed his eyes and couldn't open them.

The last thing he remembered before the darkness took him was the sound of someone screaming.

It sounded like his brother's voice.

Chapter XXVII

Sunlight tried to push its way through Dillen's eyelids, filtering in as orange light and a warmth that covered his face. He heard the sounds of a thousand whispering voices as they chattered through the leaves of distant trees. A shadow passed over his face. He felt it more than anything else, and in a start, he opened his eyes and tried to sit up. That was a mistake, as pain instantly exploded in his chest and he fell backward with a groan, screwing his eyes shut to avoid the pain.

"I wouldn't move if I were you," a familiar voice chastised him. He opened his eyes again and saw Imariel's eyes staring down at him. They weren't filled with harshness or judgment, as he might have expected, but rather something sorrowful filled her brilliant irises.

"What happened?" he croaked, his voice was rough and raw. Imariel waited to respond until after she had fetched a waterskin and had knelt to lift his head up so that he could slurp some of the cool liquid down his parched throat. As soon as she released him, his head flopped back onto the cool surface on which he was laying. He guessed it was the ground based on what he could see of his surroundings, though the blanket underneath him suggested that he had not simply been left where he had fallen, but that at least some thought had been given to his wellbeing.

"You nearly died, that is what happened." Again, Imariel's voice was not harsh, like her eyes it seemed as though something was weighing upon her, and she chose her words carefully.

"We must have won, or else I am in the afterlife and it is far different than I would have imagined." He smiled as he said this, and Imariel's mouth quirked into a sad attempt at a smile in return.

"Yes, Velorun was able to purify the armor. While this didn't immediately destroy the rest of the nightmares, it did seem to startle them into retreat. Velorun and his rangers have already left in order to hunt the remainders of their taint from the Sickness. He said that he felt certain that this was a turning point, and that the forest could finally begin to heal from this wound."

"That is wonderful news! Isn't it?" Dillen gave her a sidelong glance, and she nodded.

"Yes, it is. It seems our mission was successful in the end."

"Then what is it? Why the long face?" Imariel paused a moment and sighed before responding.

"I do not know where to begin." Her words were slow and carefully chosen, he could tell. He swallowed and decided to hedge her off before she could get started.

"Imariel, I said I would tell you about my past. About my brother. I said I would talk about it when it was a better time, and it seems as though you have me in a captive situation right now, so what better time is there?"

"I appreciate that, but…"

"But what?" Dillen asked when she didn't finish the sentence. Imariel shocked him then and reached out to cup the side of his face. The movement was so affectionate, and in that moment, he glanced into her eyes and he saw tears brimming there. It was only for a moment, but for her, it was as good as a wracking sob that would have torn itself from her chest. The tears never fell, and in an instant, it passed. She leaned back and the veil covered her face once more, leaving only her placid features in its place.

"You don't need to tell me anything. Not right now anyway. I… I think I have suspicions as to what you would say, and at this time, I do not think that I am ready to hear such things. Not after yesterday, and the night through which we have just passed."

"What if I want to tell you?" Dillen felt a sudden rush of panic. "What if I need to tell you, because if I don't, I won't have the courage to later on?"

"Then you do what you did in that forest. You go where your fear is greatest, and you rip the heart out of it. You do what you must."

They stared at one another for a long moment, and Dillen felt his opportunity slipping by him. He opened his mouth to argue, but she was quicker.

"Let it be." In her voice was a note of finality, and with it, Dillen let his head fall back to rest upon the ground. A cough caused him to turn and see Bhadein standing over the two of them.

"Am I interrupting something?" the older knight asked.

"No, I was just about to leave," Imariel said, rising to her feet. She gave one last melancholy glance at Dillen before turning and walking away. Dillen tried to watch her go, but his head was already aching from the effort to keep it raised, and he eventually found himself lying back and wincing his eyes shut.

"Some rivers were never meant to be crossed more than once," Bhadein said, sinking down to sit beside him.

"What is that supposed to mean?" Dillen grumbled.

"Nothing, don't dwell on it." Bhadein waved a hand in the air dismissively.

"What do you want?" Dillen's voice wasn't angry, but he was so very, very tired. Bhadein didn't respond right away, and when he did, there was a note of hesitation in his voice.

"I wanted to commend you for your actions over these past few days."

Dillen opened his eyes in surprise and looked over at Bhadein, his eyebrows raised in question. The older knight shrugged and stared off into the distance.

"I know I haven't always been the most respectful to you," he harrumphed, "that goes both ways, but that doesn't justify it. I thought I saw in you something of the world that broke my Brotherhood apart, sent us in different directions. All because you were a paladin, and a Basilean at that."

Dillen flinched at this, but Bhadein didn't seem to notice. Instead, he kept talking, and Dillen was content to let him.

"I saw that I was wrong, at least in some regards. You fought your way through that damnable forest and came back with the heart you were sent to retrieve. You put yourself in harm's way again and again, all in the name of accomplishing the order you were given. I spoke with Farn and heard his account of the horrors he saw within the Sickness, and how you kept going even when they were forced to turn back."

Bhadein pointed over to a spot where the grass was especially green and verdant. A strange plant had sprouted up there which Dillen could not remember seeing. It was strange and box-like with huge leafs that sprouted out from thick roots that appeared to be crawling out of the dirt and twining around one another like cords of rope. With a start, Dillen realized that it was the pavilion where Velorun had been purifying the tainted armor, only now it was covered in fresh growth that must have magically appeared overnight.

"I watched from across the battlefield as that great fiend charged you, and you stood your ground. I saw you willing to sacrifice yourself for this cause. I thought the beast had slain you. And beyond all of that, you were able to restore something that is deeply sacred to me."

At this, Bhadein reached into a satchel that he held at his side and produced one of the intricately worked vambraces of the armor that Dillen had carried back from the heart of the Sickness. It was etched with turquoise and gold. Even as he looked at it, Dillen felt a thrill of something stirring within his chest, a sudden tightness that brought his breathing up short.

"This armor belonged to a man I once knew, and who I respected greatly. Sir Dernan of the Order of Redemption. He and I served together, we were initiates together back in the days before the Abyss," here Bhadein coughed, "before the Abyss swallowed our home. There was so much death, so much chaos in those days that I hadn't known what had happened to him and had just assumed the worst. He was like a literal brother to me, and we saved each other on battlefields all across the Abyssal Wastes."

Dillen shifted uncomfortably as Bhadein spoke. He'd never heard the grizzled warrior speak about his past before, or if he had, it was mostly allusions to something, always paired with some moral about which he was lecturing Dillen. This was the first time he'd really heard the old knight speak, and certainly the first that he'd ever heard his voice choked with emotion. He felt like he had stumbled into some affair to which he hadn't been invited.

"I owe you a debt of gratitude." Bhadein said at length, returning the vambrace to his satchel. "To know Dernan's fate, to finally know what became of him, that gives me closure to a grief that I had not known I was bearing. We hadn't been that close since he took the Vows of Redemption and donned his Armor of the Tides. Such is the case with life between two people, though. It can draw you in different directions, and we don't realize it until a gulf separates us. It's a good reminder that petty emotions are not worth the weight of carrying them."

The old knight sniffed and rose to his feet. Dillen reached out and placed a hand on his foot. Bhadein looked down at him, his eyes were agitated, but his face was calm.

"You don't owe me anything," Dillen said, "this was a mission of redemption, remember? I was repaying a debt that I owed when I went looking for that. I am glad that it helped you in some small way, though."

"Even so," Bhadein moved his gaze to look off into the distance. "What is the plan, now?"

"The men have almost finished constructing litters that will be used to carry you and the rest of the wounded back. Then we make for Eastfort as soon as possible. I think the men are ready to be away from this place. Even with the Sickness gone, the memories of this place have saturated it with an air of forlorn anxiety that doesn't allow the body to rest, nor the mind. We should be ready to depart by midday."

Bhadein didn't wait for Dillen to respond and immediately turned and walked away, leaving him alone with the sound of the wind swishing through the trees. He found that in the silence, his chest didn't hurt so much as he thought it had earlier. He struggled to lift his head and look down at his body, but the pain quickly overwhelmed him and he lay back with a grunt. The wound would take some time to heal, a few days before he was able to move again, maybe shorter if the elves shared their healing skills with him. He closed his eyes and tried to drift back into sleep once more.

His mind, however, would not let him. It kept playing an endless loop of the sound of the twisted Kallas's dry, rasping laughter until at last he fell into a fitful world of dreams laced with spider webs and scything talons.

Chapter XXVIII

The soft clumping of hooves from the long lines of riders was interrupted by a few chirps and whistles from the trees to the south, evidence of scores of birds clinging tenaciously to their home in Galahir rather than flying south to warmer climes for autumn. The column was led by a detachment of knights, forty strong, followed by perhaps twice as many foot soldiers and then a lumbering line of sturdy, horse-drawn wagons. The low buzz of conversation could occasionally be heard from the common soldiers, but the knights continued eastward in complete silence.

Leaning forward in his saddle toward the very head of the column, Brother Rowan glanced cautiously into the darkness of the sprawling forest to the south. It was only the second time he had ever laid eyes on the Forest of Galahir – the first had been when their force had traveled westward on this very road two months before on the march to their rather little war, detached from the Brothermark to fight alongside the Hegemon's allies and assist in putting down an undead uprising in the Young Kingdoms. The sheer depth and intricacy of the endless sea of a thousand browns and greens of that tree line had lost none of its impact on Rowan.

The transition from the rolling plains to the north into the forest itself was sudden; almost unnatural in the face of Pannithor's epicenter of nature itself. Fields of green sloped down to suddenly hit a dense wall of thick, ancient trees, their curved branches hanging low and bristling with autumnal leaves of reds, oranges, browns, and every shade of green imaginable. Birds sang, a pair of deer pelted through a small clearing only just visible through the wall of foliage; yet in the presence of all this nature, Rowan found himself chronically uneasy.

"Do you feel it, Brother Rowan?"

Rowan looked up to the one knight who rode ahead of him. Broad-shouldered and powerful, his muscular frame still imposing even as it transitioned from the strength and vigor of youth to middle age, Exemplar Paladin Benedict's green eyes fixed on his as the tall knight twisted in his saddle to regard Rowan. Benedict was the commander of the 5th Company of the Order of the Brothermark, of which only a portion now rode back toward Basilea in the column behind them. His mail coif was lowered, revealing his short, thinning hair and moustache, both of black flecked with silver and gray.

"I… I do not feel anything, Exemplar Paladin," Rowan answered honestly, his eyes flitting between the trees and the imposing stare of his Order superior.

Benedict flashed an encouraging smile as he dropped his horse back to ride alongside Rowan. His warhorse's mail barding was hidden beneath dark blue cloth, simply adorned with a bold, heraldic motif of a tower; the symbol of their Order. That same tower icon was emblazoned on the chest of every one of the hundred Brotherhood knights, illuminating their dark blue surcoats just as the Watchline it represented illuminated hope against the Abyss.

"Do not look so apprehensive, not everything is a test. If you do not sense anything, then you do not sense anything."

Rowan remained silent in contemplation, his curiosity more than aroused by the conversation, but the conditioning of a decade of training and two years as a Brotherhood knight inwardly warned him to pursue that conversation no further.

"But… if I may, Exemplar Paladin, you do sense something?"

Benedict narrowed his eyes and nodded slowly, a hand resting on the plain, circular pommel of the longsword buckled to his waist.

"How old were you when the Brotherhood was severed, Rowan?" he asked, his eyes still fixed on the sprawling forest to the south. "Fifteen? Sixteen? I envy your ignorance, Brother, and I do not mean that to be patronizing or antagonistic in any way. But somewhere in those trees are things that are very precious to us. Things that should not be there. And for those of us who once had the honor of… bearing such things…"

The veteran knight's voice trailed off, but Rowan did not need to hear the end of his statement to understand the pain he spoke of. The Brotherhood had once been whole, a noble and virtuous Order known across all of Mantica, if not to the ends of Pannithor; fighters of evil and guardians of the helpless. Then came the flooding of the Abyss, and the whole word changed. The Brotherhood's lands were lost beneath the waters, a necessary sacrifice to stem the flow of demonic evil spewing forth from the gaping wound of the Abyss. When the war ended, the Brotherhood was torn apart. Contending politics and beliefs replaced the once united morals of the sacred Order, and the Brotherhood was torn in two.

Rowan was, just as Benedict said, merely an adolescent squire when it all happened, but, in the final stages of his training before earning his spurs as a fully-fledged knight, he was still aware of the huge turmoil surrounding the Order at the time. His family had followed Master Odo of Martagnan, who led the contingent accepting Basilea's hand of friendship.

"Different times," Benedict whispered quietly to himself, "how odd that a whole world can become so different so quickly."

Rowan's thoughts were interrupted as the unmistakable sound of the pounding of hooves on the soft earth announced galloping horses approaching from the east. He looked across the open field, along the line of trees, and saw two of horsemen hurtling toward them. The men rode fast horses and wore lighter armor than the knights; coats of mail atop the garb of peasants - villein skirmishers, sent by Benedict to scout around the main force in case of danger. Around him, some of the less experienced knights in the column eagerly pulled up their mail coifs and donned their helmets, whereas the older veterans patiently awaited the arrival of the approaching riders.

The two villein scouts approached the Exemplar Paladin and bowed their heads in salute as they dragged their horses to a halt by his side.

"My lord," Dain greeted, "there's a small village only half a league to the east, just around this shoulder of trees. It has been attacked, recently. There's dead bodies left out in the middle of the village."

Rowan's eyes widened in surprise. Benedict nudged his dark warhorse out from the rank of knights and into the clearer space to the north of the line before turning to bellow out a command.

"Brother Nicolin!"

The named knight, Benedict's most experienced warrior and the company's second-in-command, sped over at a fast canter from the rear of the line of mounted soldiers. A tall man in his mid-thirties with pronounced features and the same cropped short hair as the rest of the knights, Nicolin brought his speckled horse to a halt by the Exemplar Paladin.

"There is potential trouble up ahead," Benedict said calmly. "Dain reports signs of an attack. I sincerely doubt that such a thing has been orchestrated purely to ensnare us on our return to the Brothermark, but one should not discount these things entirely. I will take ten knights up to investigate this further; you keep driving the rest of the group on to catch us up."

"Understood, Exemplar Paladin," Nicolin replied. "Do you want the men formed up in lines of battle?"

Benedict paused for a moment before giving his answer.

"Form them up into units, but no need to march in full battle order."

The Exemplar Paladin turned his horse around and pointed to a knight who was a few paces back from the front of the line.

"Everybody forward from Brother Leigh," he commanded. "Fall out from the line and follow me."

Rowan was one of the riders in the group of ten chosen by Benedict. He nudged his horse out and pulled his mail coif up over his cropped short, ginger hair. He then took his shield from where it hung from his warhorse's side before pulling the shoulder strap over his head and slotting his left arm through the shorter straps on the back. He then fitted his dome-topped great helm over his head and secured its leather strap under his chin. Around him, the other knights of Benedict's group followed his example.

"Dain," Benedict nodded to the villein rider, "lead on."

The ten knights followed the two riders who had recently returned to them, the entire group moving swiftly at a fast canter to follow the thin, dirt road along the northern perimeter of the great forest. A flock of mottled birds took to the air from the trees to their right, disturbed by the calamity of the group of heavily armored riders thundering past their home in the tall, ominous trees.

The road bent to the right, around a natural corner formed by a gentle slope in the fields, heading closer toward southeast. To the north, the fields continued to sprawl out in their uneven blanket of grass toward the Great Plains of the Mammoth Steppe; to the east was the North March, where the peaks of the northern tip of the mountains of Nova Ardovikio would soon be visible, the last barrier between them and their home at the Watchline.

A few ramshackle, wooden buildings appeared to the left of the road up ahead. There were only a few houses and accompanying farm buildings, but within moments, it was clear that they were badly damaged. As the knights drew closer, Rowan made out several houses, a grain store, a tavern, and a few smaller buildings. The closest of the houses had an entire wall bashed in, the broad wooden beams of the wall splintered and snapped as if a great force had punched a fist through them. The next building along had fared similar, with its door torn off its hinges and a hole smashed through an adjacent wall.

Benedict unsheathed his sword as he approached, slowing his horse to a cautious trot. Rowan followed the example of his leader, unsheathing his sword and looking from side to side for any danger. He sensed a darkness of sorts; nothing as overt and tangible as the choking sensation of evil that he had been trained to detect from the forces of the Abyss, but something very real nonetheless. The sensation grew in intensity as the knights reached the edge of the shattered village and rode slowly in among the buildings. In the center of the village, ten peasants lay dead on the ground in various states of dismemberment. Some were missing limbs, two were decapitated, and others had vicious wounds torn into their torsos. The dead men lay where they fell, untidily crumpled at the very scenes of their death rather than dragged to the site and dumped together. The hands of every dead peasant clutched onto wood axes, pitchforks, or other impromptu weapons.

Benedict hauled in his reins to bring his horse to a halt before dismounting and walking over to the dead men, sheathing his sword and removing his helmet as he did. Rowan had long learned to trust Benedict's heightened mastery of divinity magic, but nevertheless remained armed and upright in his saddle, cautiously checking around him as his commander knelt to inspect the corpses.

Dain was the second to dismount, moving over to stand by his commander's side.

"The men of the village amassed here," he speculated, "fighting against whatever did this so that their women and children could escape?"

"Yes," Benedict agreed simply.

Rowan looked more closely at the bodies. Their wounds were not what he would expect from battle, not all of them at least. Some of the dead bore the fatal injuries from bladed weapons, but others were less clean; savaged by claws or bitten. Some even displayed evidence of being partially devoured.

"Undead," Dain whispered the same thought that had entered Rowan's mind.

Benedict shook his head.

"No. Undead would take corpses with them for their own uses."

The aging knight slowly stood up and bowed his head, his eyes closed for a few moments in silent prayer. He then looked up at Rowan.

"Brother Rowan, head back to the main force. Tell Brother Nicolin to find me an experienced tracker among our villeins. The rest of you; search this village for any survivors."

*****

The wind rustled the leaves of the surrounding cedar trees, growing ever so slightly in intensity as a gust briefly flared up and then died away again, leaving Dillen's tiny corner of forest in peace once more. Sat on the trunk of a felled tree, he stared out at the surrounding greenery in all its magnificence as it was illuminated by the autumnal, morning sun.

Thanks to the elves, who had reluctantly shared some of their healing magic with him, Dillen was nearly recovered. He still was sore and had some lingering aches, but he attributed it to scars of his older battles acting up. Velorun had claimed to have purged the taint of the creatures from the Armor of Tides, which Bhadein had helped Dillen bring back to Haili as proof that their task had been a success. And so now, Dillen sat, alone in the forest, reflecting, and enjoying the simple beauty of the world around him.

Nature had, of course, always been there in his childhood but it was never something that had particularly captivated his attention, nor was interest in it encouraged by his various tutors.

He cast his mind back to his childhood, to a very different world of privilege, comforts, the respect that came with his family name. He would be lying to himself if he said that he did not miss it all, in part at least. He knew what was expected of him; that the druids would want him to immediately embrace nature, shun the wickedness of man's abuse of the natural resources of Pannithor, deride all who were so weak to cherish comfort over the worship of nature itself. But the truth was that he was not there, that deep down he still did not see the apparent evil in mining iron ore to provide tools to advance society, or killing animals to feed a family. Nor could he ever bring himself to understand how the Lady's forces could ever think it normal to ally with the darker forces at play in Pannithor, all in the name of balance. What rubbish.

"You look rather deep in thought."

Dillen craned his neck to look over his shoulder and saw Imariel stood a few paces behind him, her slender arms folded across her chest. The motley concoction of stone and wood that formed Eastfort silhouetted the sky behind her, its facing walls darkened in contrast by the low light behind from the rising morning sun. This was the first he had seen her since waking from the battle with Ur-chitak. Dillen threw her a wary smile, still far from at ease after the events with her mother and the battle in the depths of the forest, and held aloft his small prayer book. He looked at the book momentarily, considering how he had just returned to consulting it after the brush with the creature who took his brother's face and the nightmares that plagued him on and off since.

"This new role of mine in life," he explained, "I am very grateful that the former Brotherhood knights have accepted me, just as the Lady did, but as a Brother of the Order it has been pointed out to me... not very subtly either... that my grasp of faith could do with some work."

The golden-haired elf paced over to him, effortlessly displaying the grace of movement that came naturally to all of her kin, and sat on the log next to him.

"I do not think that I have given your changing fortunes enough credit," she spoke, hesitantly. She must have felt the same awkwardness Dillen did. "Your people already live a life of constant change, upheaval, turmoil. I should imagine that is difficult enough without the changes enforced upon you by the war."

Dillen glanced down at the prayer book again, finding it hard to meet her eyes.

"It certainly is a different existence," he conceded. "The disparity of wealth is, perhaps, more uneven in the Kingdoms of Men than anywhere else, and that in itself drives a very different culture from yours. I don't know. I am not particularly well-travelled, or well-read. The gods that humans worship are fickle. Or so I'm told. I'm not really sure."

Imariel narrowed her eyes in confusion.

"But you were a paladin of Basilea. Was faith and prayer not foremost in your duties?"

Dillen turned away and stared ahead. He had let his guard down. His past life was an absolute maze, an intricate web of overlapping threads that was little understood by his new companions, and for good reason. But he had promised her to speak the truth. To fight the fear that was greatest in his heart.

"I... was never much of a paladin," Dillen began, slowly.

Imariel's response was interrupted as a third figure moved across from the direction of Eastfort to join them. The tall, slim figure of Haili drifted through the long grass. She stopped by the log and looked down at Dillen and Imariel, a look of disdain crossing her face for a moment.

"A prayer book. For the worship of the Shining Ones."

Dillen restrained a sigh of despair.

"Surely you do not object to that? They are the deities of all that is good, after all. Granted, I realize that the book is bound in leather, but..."

"The Lady's way is not that of worship for the Shining Ones."

"But it is the way I was raised, and also of my fellow knights," Dillen countered, surprising himself at his vehement defense of a faith he was only lukewarm to in years past, "and while I could never speak on behalf of the Order, I would imagine that the alliance with the Lady came under the assumption that our faith would be accepted and not... quashed."

Imariel stood and stepped over to stand alongside the tall druid, looking down at Dillen from her side. Haili forced a smile as she looked at Dillen.

"The conversation was merely a casual observance that your observance of faith is not shared within our realm. Nothing more."

Dillen leaned forward and rested his chin on one fist. Granted, he would be the first to criticize Basilea's arrogant insistence on omnipotence due to their claimed favor of the Shining Ones, or even the naivety displayed by the dwarfs or the former Brotherhood in sacrificing all to stem the flow of the Abyss for a world that did not support or even thank them for it. But his less than altruistic stance on the ways of the world still did not align with the standoffish nature of the followers of the Lady.

"There is something to be said about the strength drawn from the foundations of faith," Dillen said. "I may be merely human, and nothing more than a rather brutish warrior in addition to that, but I am happy to defend that faith. You know, I wouldn't even call it faith. I would call it my philosophy. It is wider than deities. You refer to the ways of the Lady, yet to many outsiders, this seems to be little more than hiding in a forest as wars rage all around in the vain hope that they will not spread to Galahir."

"Our ways are rather more complicated than that," Imariel replied tersely.

"But you seem to expect this alliance with our part of the Brotherhood to result in instant dismissal of faith and idealistic principles," Dillen countered.

Imariel opened her mouth to reply but was silenced as Haili help up one hand.

"We desire balance," the druid said calmly, "serene, peaceful balance. As we have spoken about at length. And end to violence. An acceptance of other peoples' ways. Balance takes time. You will understand, in due course. You all will."

Dillen stood, closing his book.

"And this balance," he continued, "this balance I have been a part of within this forest for two years now, yet still do not comprehend. Explain to me why my Order has had to issue a decree stating it will not march alongside the forces of the Abyss, ever, under any circumstances. My lords and masters have been forced to state that, because we are allied to you. And you will march with demons."

"If necessary," Haili shrugged.

"If necessary?" Dillen exclaimed.

Haili fixed Dillen with a serious stare. There was not even a hint of annoyance or offense in her features, just a patient willingness to try to explain her ways.

"If an army of the Abyss is set to clash with an army of orcs, who would you side with?" she asked simply.

"Neither!" Dillen snapped. "Let them kill each other!"

"And if one army is considerably larger and more powerful than the other?"

"My answer remains," Dillen said, "let them kill each other."

"Yet, if you sided with the smaller army, you could even the balance, and potentially both sources of evil could be removed, rather than allow one to thrive and cause mayhem and destruction for innocent people."

Dillen paused, his face contorted in confusion. He was raised as a warrior, not a thinker, so he knew full well that he was already on his back foot in a contest of intellect, but the lucidity of her words was completely defective to him.

"That's a flawed logic!" he growled. "That's a completely hypothetical situation, not one grounded in the real world! It is a huge oversimplification!"

"I have started simple with deliberation," Haili replied, her tone still unperturbed, "as my method of tutoring is just so. To start simply and then build from there. Yet with this simple analogy, we can, I hope, agree that while it is not your way, you could see some merit in supporting two armies of evil in destroying each other rather than allow one to prosper? And, as a final addition, it is not hypothetical. I have personally been involved in a scenario almost exactly like the one we are describing. We succeeded. Balance prevailed and innocent lives were spared."

"No," Dillen shook his head, taking a step back, "no. I'll be the first to admit that war causes all manner of decisions to be made that those outside the fighting could never understand. There are times when prisoners cannot be taken, when the so called 'rules' of waging war need to be abandoned to secure victory. But you are describing going to war alongside a demon of the Abyss!"

Haili took her turn to move over and sit down on the log where Dillen had sat. She offered a brief smile before continuing.

"You may not see it, it might be difficult to admit, but they are a culture. That word is important. Culture. The Abyss has its ways, ideas, social behaviors. There is worship of deities, there are societal rungs, there is promotion as a reward for service just as there is punishment for transgressions. It is not just a wild pack of howling demons, tearing each other apart in bloodlust. It is a culture, even if its values are very different to yours."

Dillen looked across at Imariel in exasperation, hoping to find some registration of confusion on her features that might support his own mindset. He found none.

"What possible significance is there in that?" he gasped. "A culture might be truly evil in every way! Just because we band around the word 'culture' does not mean there has to be respect! You cannot, cannot expect the knights of this Order to march alongside demons!"

The tall druid stood, her face still a picture of absolute equanimity.

"I did not come here to lecture on faith or philosophy. I came here because I have a task for you. For both of you. So I will leave you with one, final statement that I wish you to take away. I would never expect anybody to abandon all of their principles overnight, all of the values taught to them in their youth by their society. But people can change. They do change. For the better; in time. So I will end our discussion with this single statement that you will take away and think upon, deeply: Cultures do not need to be violently exterminated. Cultures can be changed."

Dillen's eyes widened in anger at the ridiculousness of what the druid was hinting at. Sitting down with the demons of the Abyss for a polite debate and then agreeing to meet somewhere in the middle? The thought was utterly absurd.

"That is…"

"I said that this conversation was over," Haili cut him off, calmly but assertively. "We can and will debate all day at some point, but not now. I came here because I have a task for you."

Dillen walked a few paces away, inhaling deeply in an attempt to calm the raging waters of his temper. Yes, the ways of the Lady and her subjects were still strange to him after two years, but as a martial man, he knew full well the absolute necessity in obeying orders from the hierarchy; and his current commander was none other than the druid that stood before him.

"Certainly," he exhaled, "what are your orders?"

Haili again gave him a small smile, this one perhaps in appreciation of his acquiescence and the clear turmoil that had to be overcome to achieve it.

"Go and find one of your brethren. The three of you are heading to the northeast boundary of the forest. I fear there has been another disturbance."

* * * * *

Stood with a group of six other knights, Rowan watched in silence as the ten villeins carefully laid the bodies of the dead villagers into their freshly dug graves. Some simple bed sheets and linen had been found in the deserted buildings of the small village, and now each corpse was handled by two men and lowered into their resting places, awkward bundles that seemed almost lifelike again as some bent at the waist during the lowering, their sheets bound tightly enough around them to leave the viewers in no doubt as to what was inside.

Exemplar Paladin Benedict had ordered several knights to move further away from the buildings to form a perimeter to alert the force early in case of danger, while two men from within the ranks of villeins had identified themselves as woodsmen and now busily set about examining the grounds and treelines for further clues as to exactly what happened.

The concept of the villein was fundamental to the Brotherhood's society; very similar in many ways to the societal norms of the Successor Kingdoms to the west but at odds with the Basilean culture that the new Order of the Brothermark now found itself suddenly intertwined with. The villeins rented land or homes from their feudal landlords – titled nobility such as Rowan's father – in exchange for services such as farming. Part of the Brotherhood societal construct was that the payment also required limited military service – for a quarter of each year, villeins were required to be ready to march to war; in times of emergency such as the Abyssal onslaught from two years before, the Brotherhood had demanded every villein in their lands to arm themselves for battle.

Many of the villeins were farmers and laborers who were trained to a decent standard in the use of simple polearms; a very small number who were proficient horse riders were employed as scouts and skirmishers. Others took the more difficult route of training with the bow, which was a skillset that took years to truly master. This was at complete odds to the way the Basileans conducted their military affairs; their legion boasted one of the largest, best-equipped, and most highly trained professional army in Pannithor, while their peasants had no military obligation and no idea how to fight. In contrast, the legion relied on crossbows rather than bows to attack their foes at range, an expensive and complicated weapon to manufacture and maintain, but one that took only a few weeks to become fully conversant with rather than the years demanded of a villein bowman.

The somber group of villeins finished laying the bodies to rest; Benedict must have noticed this and walked over to them. He stood by the front of the graves, opening the pages of his sacred Eloicon, before uttering a few words of prayer to give the deceased at least some element of ceremony and respect before the mounds of earth were shoveled back over them to seal their final resting places. In the absence of a priest or chaplain, an Exemplar Paladin was perhaps the next best thing to conduct the rites. Rowan watched quietly, the silence of his brother knights in contrast to the free conversation from the seventy or so villeins that waited in the open field to the north of the village. It was the Order's way. The idle chitchat of common men had no place in a religious fighting order.

The spectacle of the impromptu memorial service was interrupted as Brother Nicolin walked briskly over from the treeline. The tall knight stopped a few paces from the gathering of seven knights, his mail coif lowered around his neck and his great helm held under one arm.

"Brothers," he greeted, "our woodsmen have some news. All evidence they have located points to a group of villagers fleeing into the forest of Galahir. They believe the size of the group was a little larger than the group of dead we found here, perhaps twice as many."

"Do we know how long ago this occurred?" queried Brother Willem, a youth who had only earned his spurs days before they had marched for the Young Kingdoms.

"Not with any accuracy, no," Nicolin admitted. "Alas, the bard's tales of trackers finding convenient footprints and being able to work out precise details are very much an exaggeration. Our two men here have very little to work with other than some broken branches and disturbed earth."

"What will we do, Brother?" Rowan asked.

"That decision rests with the Exemplar Paladin," Nicolin replied. "My task at the moment is merely to keep the brethren informed of developments. But I believe I have a good idea what the Exemplar Paladin will command of us."

The ruddy-faced knight looked over his shoulder at the ominous, looming forest that sprawled menacingly out for league after league to the south. Willem glanced from side-to-side uncomfortably at his brother knights.

"Surely we will continue?" he stammered. "There are over a hundred of us. We would not risk the dangers of that forest for the sake of a mere twenty?"

"Twenty people who need our help." Nicolin narrowed his eyes.

"But they are not our people, Brother!" Willem countered.

"Every helpless man, woman, and child of the faith are our people, Brother," Rowan said, his voice even as he ensured his tone was passive.

Nicolin glanced across at Rowan. He issued a rare, brief smile and rewarded Rowan's words with the slightest of nods. High praise for Rowan, but nothing more – he said what he believed, to correct his junior, not for acclaim. Nicolin looked across at Benedict – the Exemplar Paladin closed his Eloicon and walked across toward them from the graves as the small group of villeins set about shoveling earth to cover the bodies. Nicolin walked quickly across to intercept him. Rowan watched as the two senior knights held a hushed discussion. He was no expert on people, but judging by their gestures to the trees and the nods they exchanged, Benedict's intentions were immediately clear. They were going into the Forest of Galahir.

*****

Algae clogged the surface of the waters of the small lake as the trio hiked along its shores. Lake Harnii was barely worthy of a name; it was so small, little more than a large pond of a quarter-league's length that did at least provide a welcome break in the ubiquitous canopy of leaves above them. The trudge north toward the forest perimeter would, to an interloper, be an arduous task of several days; but with a seasoned gladestalker leading the way along hidden pathways and through natural roads along the contours, they made rapid progress.

"It still baffles me," Dillen continued as he trudged onward, his face pouring with sweat from the weight of his armor, despite leaving a good proportion of it behind at Eastfort, relying on a coat of mail and a breastplate to see him through, "that your druid would ever think that we would abandon our very principles for an existence of… balance. Of nullifying good as much as evil, so long as nobody with any moral conviction prevails."

"By that argument," Imariel replied, that now familiar hint of annoyance Dillen had a knack for invoking once again present in her tone, "you would be more content allying yourself with the demons of the Abyss than with us here in Galahir."

Dillen stopped dead in his tracks, sweat pouring down his throat to pool at the neck of his mail coat. Marsh birds warbled and chirped from the still, odorous waters to the east of the path.

"Where the blazes did you get that from?" Dillen exclaimed, grabbing his waterskin from his belt. "I just said quite clearly that I won't abandon my principles, and your interpretation of that is that I would ally with the Abyss?!"

Imariel too stopped and turned to face Dillen and Farn – the third member of their little expedition. Not a bead of perspiration spoiled her features, not a hair seemed out of place from a journey that clearly did not tax her.

"You say that the way of the Lady, our way is to ensure that nobody with moral convictions prevails. Your very words. By that line of thought, you insinuate that we who believe in balance, we are pusillanimous sorts who merely seek to avoid confrontation with those who do have principles and beliefs. You further go on to list evil as being a moral conviction. Ergo, you insult all that the Lady stands for while issuing a backhanded compliment to the servants of the Wicked Ones for at least having some form of code that we lack."

"Do you remember those things that we fought?" Dillen gestured generally to the forest around them. "The things that nearly killed all three of us here? The things that did kill a fellow knight?"

"Hard to forget," Farn mumbled, rubbing his chest. "I feel as if I try hard enough, I can still feel where my ribs broke…"

"What is your point, Dillen?" Imariel asked tersely, her eyes narrowing.

"My point is that there is no talking with those creatures. There's no trying to solve things peacefully. They just want death and destruction – and who is to say that the Lady wouldn't ally with them in the name of balance? Would you willingly go to battle, fighting alongside those monstrosities?!"

"If that is what the Lady decrees, yes."

There was no hesitation, no thought. Just loyalty and cold words. Dillen shook his head, and Imariel began to walk once more.

Another hour passed in silence as the lake fell away behind them and the familiar ceiling of greenery resumed to blot out the majority of the autumn sunlight. The trio followed the contours of the ground into a small valley, where a cool stream trickled down along jagged, black rocks to join a broad, ankle deep river that snaked around the forested hills.

"Why would I change?" Dillen ranted. "Why would any of us change?"

"Sir Dillen, why do you vex yourself over this?" Farn raised an eyebrow at him as they walked alongside one another. "Our position is clear on such matters. This will never come to pass."

"Because from I gather, Haili would seem to think that merely awaiting a reasonable passage of time…"

"Patience," Imariel interjected as she ducked beneath a thin branch that sprang out to swipe Farn across the face, "the thing you are trying to describe is called patience. But go on."

"My point is," Dillen growled, "that just waiting for year after year will not make me change my mind! She cannot just blindly assume that because fate has placed me here in the forest, that if she waits long enough, then I will eventually be converted to her way of thought! I have some mental fortitude, you know! I have some courage in my convictions! I won't just abandon them!"

"I have no experience of nautical matters," Imariel shrugged as she hopped gracefully from stone to stone to cross the shallow river, "but there is a saying from my cousins of the Sea Kindred…"

"Yes, your distant relatives from lands afar who have some actual moral principles," Dillen beamed. "Go on – what do they say?"

"The saying goes," Imariel continued regardless, her composure not even dented, "that if a sailor encounters rocks, better to tap the tiller than to force full rudder and capsize the boat."

Dillen stopped, again.

"Oh, enough!" he gasped. "Are you just making this up? I'm not one of the boaty folk! I don't know what a tiller is!"

"What I think the gladewalker is saying," Farn offered, "is that sometimes a subtle reaction is better than a huge over reaction."

"Precisely," Imariel issued a warm and sincere smile to the younger knight, drawing a hiss of contempt from Dillen, "and in this context, a small tap on the tiller to slightly alter course is all that is needed to make you actually start to think. Like Haili did today. It is far more effective than aggressively lecturing you or attempting to indoctrinate you. Look at you! I cannot shut you up, this has provoked so much thought! She is winning, and you do not even realize it! Likewise, in the scenario she described, better to prune and cull the forces of the Abyss rather than smash into them in an all-out, bloody war in that rather typically human way."

"Somebody has to have the spine to do it," Farn said bitterly. "That was the whole point in the Watchline. Digging our heels in to defend the helpless. The Shining Ones gave me the strength to fight evil, and by their holy name, I will fight evil. Head on, overtly, and with full rudder if necessary."

"Yes!" Dillen roared in victory. "You see! He understands! That's what I've been trying to say!"

"Rather unsuccessfully," Imariel sighed bitterly, her composure finally cracking. "Now enough of this, I would hate for you to suffer an injury by thinking of such things too much. If we mean to reach the edge of this forest by midnight, we need to increase our pace."

Chapter XXIX

Beams of afternoon sunshine pierced the lush canopy of foliage above, creating pillars of green-tinged light that illuminated the narrow pathway through the trees. A stream gently babbled to the west of the pathway while birds sang noisily to the east, as if calling the knights and villeins back toward the direction of their enforced home within the borders of Basilea. The overpowering stench of damp moss seemed to synonymously accompany the relentless buzzing and rattling of unseen insects hidden within the vegetation.

Rowan kicked his feet wearily through the ankle deep sea of dead, brown leaves, a sure sign of the changing seasons and the approach of winter. Benedict had ordered half of their force into the forest, some twenty knights and forty villeins, while Brother Nicolin and the others waited at the village with the horses and supplies, and orders to head for the Brothermark if Benedict's party had not emerged from the forest within two days. That would at least ensure some survivors would return to rejoin their eternal duty to defend Mantica against the forces of the Abyss, should something untoward occur within the depths of the ancient forest.

Benedict led the haphazard expedition into the forest from the very front, his shield slung across his back and his sword sheathed. His orders had been very explicit – no outward signs of hostility and never, under any account, was any effort to be made to attack creatures of the forest unless it was in self-defense. Benedict suddenly stopped in place, causing the snaking trail of armed men to stumble to a halt in turn behind him. The broad knight looked from side to side before focusing his eyes on a clump of trees to the south, on the other side of a small, lily-pad encrusted pool that formed the end of the little stream. Rowan walked slowly up to stand by his commander's side.

"Exemplar Paladin?" he whispered cautiously.

The dark-haired knight turned to glance down at him.

"It is there again… that same sensation."

Rowan paused. He concentrated, focusing on his core to summon his scant control over the arcane powers of divinity magic. That same source of magical discipline allowed priests to heal great wounds and cast out demons, or even some Basilean paladins to heal themselves or temporarily bless their weapons against unnatural enemies. Yet, even acknowledging himself as a novice in this arcane discipline, Rowan sensed nothing.

"I cannot sense it, my lord," he admitted quietly.

"The Armor of Tides," Benedict said, his eyes still fixed ahead, "they are here. At least some of them. Perhaps even my own."

Rowan winced at the thought, knowing Benedict's past within the most prestigious of all Orders within the Brotherhood, the Order of Redemption. The Armor of Tides were sacred to the Brotherhood, blessed suits of armor that, perhaps imbued with the spirits of departed members of the Order, called out to those worthy enough to wear them in battle. When the Ranger Swain led part of the severed Brotherhood to side with the Green Lady, the Order of Redemption was one of the first to follow. But there, too, was discord within their ranks. Some knights of the Order of Redemption refused to follow Swain, reluctantly surrendering their sacred armor to side with Master Odo of the Order of the Abyssal Hunt as he led his faction off to accept Basilea's hand of friendship. That, too, was the path taken by Rowan's father, and de-facto, his path also.

"Did you ever consider following Swain?" Rowan tentatively ventured. "If I may ask, my lord?"

The Exemplar Paladin finally turned to look across at Rowan. The intensity of his stare led Rowan to believe that he had, indeed, crossed a line with his questioning, but that assumption was dispersed when the older knight spoke.

"I thought on it for a long time," he said, "as long as I could before I had to give an answer. To go against the direction of my superiors with the very Order of Redemption, the purest and holiest of all orders, seemed to be utter insanity. But then a friend spoke to me. Exemplar Paladin Raymond, if you know him?"

"I know of him, my lord, by reputation. The Exemplar Paladin of our 3rd Company."

"He is worthy of that reputation, and then some," Benedict said, his a wistful smile, "and his words summed up what I knew deep down, better than I could ever articulate. He said that the Green Lady would ally with anything that suited her whims, with forces that good men should never even consider marching alongside."

Rowan nodded. The Abyss. The Green Lady had actually gone to war alongside demons of the Abyss, and while the Order of Redemption in their current form had publicly vowed to never fight at the side of devils and demons, the principle remained.

"I am glad my father made the decision he did," Rowan said, "for all their faults, the Basileans are the very chosen people of the Shining Ones above. Who are we to question the will of the gods?"

The air was beginning to cool a little as the afternoon drew on toward sunset. Up ahead, a pair of rabbits emerged from beneath a thick bush, looked up at the trail of sixty men, and thought better of their actions before scampering away again. Benedict narrowed his eyes and smiled slightly.

"Who are we indeed?" he agreed. "Come on, we should pick up our pace."

* * * * *

In his two years of campaigning, Rowan had encountered many things that folk blessed with a normal life would undoubtedly consider to be terrifying. He had seen the red tide of Abyssal demons as they poured over the horizon from the northeast, threatening to engulf the defenses of the Watchline. He had fought face-to-face against savage, bloodthirsty orcs; the real ones who reveled in killing and relished the fight, not the comical ones from the tales of bards. Most recently he had, for the first time, raised his sword and shield against the very walking death; the stinking, rotting corpses of zombie hordes and the senseless, shambling walls of skeletal warriors bidding the commands of their necromantic generals. But one thing he had never seen was the Forest of Galahir at night.

The merry chirps of birds and the gentle rustle of foliage from passing deer and hares was now replaced with the warning hoots of watchful owls and the chitter of unseen bats in the trees above. Off to the southwest was the periodic and unsettling howl of wolves. Benedict had stopped the group in the largest clearing they had yet encountered, perhaps half an acre at the peak of a shallow plateau, the welcome gap in the sea of trees finally giving glimpses at a black sky punctuated only by the handful of stars visible through the few breaks in the autumn clouds.

Aside from the handful of sentries walking around the edge of the clearing with their lit torches and weapons, the remainder of the group ate some of their meager rations, and they were now settling down for a broken night's sleep, some of them having had the foresight to stuff a blanket in their pack before leaving the village. Rowan had no such luxuries – none of the knights did. All had brought their arms and armor, together with a small pack of food and water, and a prayer book. As both a page and then a squire, many a night had been spent sleeping on the cold floor of a fort or monastery, and so the relative softness of the ground below was more than suitable.

Rowan finished his prayers and carefully tucked his book away into the small pouch hanging from his belt. As was the norm for encampment, the knights and villeins had already segregated themselves, and some men had already managed to nod off asleep. Situated off at the far side of the clearing with four of his brother knights, Rowan reached to his side to commence unbuckling his breastplate but was stopped. His attention was distracted as he heard a slightly raised voice from the northern end of the clearing, and he looked across to see

Benedict angrily reprimanding a trio of villein archers. Even from this distance, he could just about make out the words.

"I do not care if it was a joke!" the Exemplar Paladin scolded in something somewhere between an angry shout and a carefully hushed whisper. "And I do not care how hungry you are! You do not hunt rabbits in this forest! Do not even swat a fly! We are intruders here, and make no mistake, we are being watched! Our presence is permitted, for now, but the moment somebody does something to offend the guardians of this place, we will be fighting for our lives! Do not kill anything, clear?"

Rowan glanced across to where Willem looked up at him from his prayer book, his brow raised. The younger knight closed his eyes again for a few seconds and then closed his prayer book before raising himself from his knee.

"This place," Willem said, "so beautiful to look at yet so…"

"Unwelcoming?" Rowan offered. "I cannot find the words myself. But I know that I am not comfortable here."

Willem's response was cut off when more voices were heard. This time, they were more hushed and coming from the south – from the other side of the trees. Perhaps most noteworthy was that the voice was undoubtedly female. He held up a hand to keep Willem silent as he stared off into the trees.

"You heard that?" Brother Leigh queried, buckling his sword belt back around his waist.

Rowan nodded.

"Spirits?" Willem whispered. "Spirits of the forest?"

"In any other forest, I would scold you as a fool, but not in this place," Leigh replied warily.

The voices were hushed now, but they came from a gap in the perimeter, equidistant between two villein sentries who were both heading away from it. Rowan stood up.

"Brother Leigh, get the Exemplar Paladin, quickly!" he whispered. "Brother Willem, come with me."

Pulling up his mail coif and sliding his arm inside the straps on the back of his shield, Willem walked quickly over toward the wall of foliage, snatching up a torch from the edge of the makeshift encampment as he did so. Other knights watched him warily, rousing their brethren from sleep and recovering their own arms and armor in calm silence. Pushing back a mass of brambles, Rowan walked back into the forest with Willem close behind.

The two knights made their way down a shallow slope, tripping and stumbling on the mass of roots and undulations in the ground at their feet. Within only a few paces, Rowan again held his hand up to silence his younger comrade as the sound of hushed conversation issued from the base of the slope. Straining his eyes to pick anything out in the darkness, Rowan continued forward, inwardly cursing the jingle of his mail armor and clank of his metal plates. Then, up ahead, he saw the unmistakable outline of two figures suddenly dart away from him in the darkness.

"Come on!" he urged Willem as he gave chase.

Branches scratched at his face as he stumbled awkwardly through the darkness, a small sphere of light from his torch making his progress only just possible. He reached the foot of the slope and blundered inelegantly on, crashing through another thorny bush before emerging into a second, much smaller clearing and finding himself surrounded by shadowy figures.

Holding his torch aloft, he saw a sea of faces around him. Terrified mothers clamped hands over the mouths of their trembling children, while two old men bravely stepped out in front of them to stand protectively. All in all, perhaps thirty bedraggled, mud-stained peasants were crammed into the clearing, huddled together in near silence. Rowan took a slow step back, holding his shield and torch out passively to either side. Willem appeared behind him, quickly sheathing his sword and lowering his mail coif.

"Are you from the village?" Rowan asked. "We have been looking for you. We are here to help you."

One of the old men, a thin man with gray stubble half-covering his pale face, limped forward.

"Who are you?" he demanded. "I don't recognize your colors!"

"My name is Brother Rowan, this is Brother Willem. We are knights of the Order of the Brothermark. We were returning to Basilea when we encountered a village. That was your village? Half a day to the north of here at the edge of the forest?"

"Aye," the man nodded, "that was our home. Was."

"What happened?" Willem ventured. "What attacked you?"

Any response from the village elder was interrupted by an authoritative voice that rang out from the far side of the gathered villagers.

"You two. Put your swords on the ground, this instant."

The gathering of villagers parted in the middle and shuffled back to allow a channel through the clearing. Barely visible in the meager light of his torch, Rowan saw two armored figures step out of the trees and pace toward him. Both were encased in plate armor, one of the men a clear head taller than the other. He watched as they approached with purposeful strides until their silhouetted forms reached the edge of his torchlight.

"I shall say it again, once," said the shorter of the two, a knight of perhaps thirty or forty years of age with dark hair and a trio of scars running down one temple, "put your weapons on the ground."

His mind focused but calm, Rowan sensed nothing out of the ordinary from the dark-haired man. The second, taller man emanated the slightest of arcane auras, something tantamount to goodness but certainly not tangible enough for him to register as a user of divinity. Whoever they were, there was certainly far from enough evidence for him to trust them and their weapons in the presence of the helpless villagers. To the cry of alarm from some of the peasants, Rowan threw down his torch and drew his sword.

* * * * *

Raising his own blade, Dillen brought his second hand to the pommel of his sword. Panicked cries rippled through the ranks of villagers to either side of him, and a few made for the cover of the trees, scattering to become swallowed up by the darkness. That was a problem he could remedy shortly; for now, his task was to protect them from the two armed strangers ahead of him.

"Dillen!" Farn warned. "Wait a moment!"

Dillen kept his eyes fixed on the two swordsmen ahead, faintly concerned by the uncharacteristic hesitance from his comrade. At least he knew that Imariel had his back; she waited in the cover of the trees with her bow, only a few paces behind. Dillen lunged forward and brought his heavy blade down in an overhead attack, the sword clanging against the metal, dark blue shield of his adversary. Out of the corner of his eye, he saw Farn rush forward toward the second warrior as the screams from the villagers increased in intensity, and all of the cowering peasants scattered in every direction.

Dillen's opponent lashed out with his own sword, arcing it horizontally around to force Dillen to jump back as the tip sliced through the air only an inch from his midriff. A skillful follow-up attack forced Dillen back another step as he brought his blade up to defend himself, bracing his armored forearm against the back of his sword as a powerful blow clanged against it. A third strike swept down, but Dillen saw faster, sidestepping to avoid the blow and bringing his own sword sweeping up into the gut of his adversary. His lightning fast attack bypassed the warrior's defense, slashing open his blue surcoat, but clanging ineffectively against his thick, plate armor.

A retaliatory blow hacked down against Dillen's shoulder, scraping against his pauldron but likewise failing to penetrate his armor. With a roar, Dillen rushed in to close the small gap between them and planted his other shoulder against the enemy soldier, barging him down and forcing him to stumble back. Quickly taking advantage of the opening, Dillen linked a series of precise attacks that forced the other warrior to frantically defend himself with both his sword and shield, deflecting strikes with a chain of metallic clangs and clashes.

The two continued to trade blows in the sphere of light provided by the discarded torch in the long grass at their feet, Dillen finding himself impressed with his adversary's skill and tenacity but also well aware that he had the edge, the advantage. After only a few moments more, the soldier in dark blue over-extended himself with a high strike, and Dillen saw the mistake he needed. He ducked beneath the savage attack and brought his own sword up, burying it in his opponent's gut to bend the man over double. Drawing his blade rearward, he hacked it down into the man's back and knocked him clattering to the floor.

Sweat dripping down his cheeks, Dillen turned in place to survey the clearing. His eyes opened in surprise as he saw Farn and the second enemy warrior still facing each other in silence, neither of them having drawn their weapon.

"Wh…why aren't you doing anything?" Dillen gasped.

"I tried to tell you!" Farn pleaded. "These men are from the Order of the Brothermark! I will not fight them!"

Dillen looked down at the knight he had just felled and exhaled in relief as he saw the man roll over onto his back, blood staining his wounded abdomen but very much still alive.

"Stay down!" Dillen yelled. "Until I work out exactly what is going on here!"

Before Farn could respond, another torchlight appeared, moving down the same slope as the two Brothermark knights had. Dillen looked across as three more knights forced their way through the foliage and into the clearing. The two warriors on the flanks both carried torches and wore dome-topped great helms, while the central figure wore only a mail coif over his head, accompanying the same plate mail armor and blue surcoat as his comrades. The knight was perhaps in his late thirties, with short, dark hair and a mustache dashed with silver. He looked across at Dillen.

"Step away from my brother so that I may see to his wounds," he commanded, his tone polite but emanating authority.

"Sir Dillen, please. Do as he says!" Farn hissed.

"Wait there!" Dillen growled as the dark-haired knight walked calmly forward toward his wounded comrade.

The man knelt down at Dillen's feet and looked at his brother's wounds. Dillen planted a foot against the knight's shoulder and kicked him away from the wounded man.

"Don't ignore me!" he yelled in indignation. "Just who in the Abyss do you think…"

Dillen's words were cut off as the man's fist blurred out to connect with his cheek, snapping his head back as he cried out in shock and pain. A follow up punch to the stomach bent him over before an armored hand backhanded him in a powerful and undignified attack to cut open his forehead.

With a growl of anger, Dillen lunged forward to swing his sword down toward the mustached knight's head. The older knight calmly stood his ground and reached up to grab Dillen by the wrist, stopping his arm mid-attack before then twisting it painfully behind his back until Dillen yelped out in pain and his fingers sprang open to drop his sword. His opponent grabbed the blade before it hit the ground and tossed it casually away before returning to kneel down and press a hand against the wound of Dillen's previous, defeated adversary.

Pain flaring all along his arm, stars swimming groggily at the edges of his blurring vision, Dillen staggered back around to face the Brothermark knight.

"Sir Dillen! You musn't!" Farn warned.

Yelling out a cry of anger, Dillen rushed forward to attack again with his armored fists. His first swing narrowly missed the jaw of the older knight as he stood to face the attack; a second punch forced the man back. Then a metal-clad fist smashed into Dillen's eye with enough force to half spin him around. By the time he had recovered his senses, he found himself staring along the blade of a sword whose tip was pressed against his throat.

"You wear the colors of a Basilean," the dark-haired knight said, anger leaking into his tone, "but your accent marks you out as an outsider. Your complete and utter lack of magnanimity and basic respect also makes it clear to me that you are not one of the Order I once knew. So as the Shining Ones above are my witness, I tell you in all honesty that if you try to stop me helping my wounded brother one more time, I will kill you."

His eye throbbing from the impact of the latest attack, Dillen lowered his arms. He watched as the knight stepped back and knelt by his wounded brother's side yet again, this time pressing a hand against the wound. Dillen watched as the younger, wounded knight's breathing returned to normality, the injury hidden beneath the bloodied armor no doubt stemmed and stabilized. The wounded knight slowly sat up. The older, dark-haired knight looked up at the two warriors he had arrived with.

"Take their weapons and bind them," he commanded, nodding to Dillen and Farn.

"Wait a moment!" Dillen growled.

The dark-haired knight stood up and fixed his stare impassively on Dillen. Before he could respond, a voice emanated from the darkness behind Dillen.

"You shall do nothing of the sort."

Imariel stepped out into the light cast by the torches, her bow drawn and an arrow notched in place, the deadly tip of the projectile pointed at the lead knight's heart.

"That is an ill-advised move," he said, staring at the elf gladewalker.

"I shall judge my own actions, thank you," she admonished, "but for now, I shall be leaving here with my two companions."

"You appear to be under the misapprehension that you are controlling the situation due to the ability to loose a single arrow," the dark-haired knight warned. "Let me clarify this situation for you. I am Exemplar Paladin Benedict of the Order of the Brothermark. I am in this forest to provide assistance to a group of villagers who, I believe, were attacked by Nightstalkers." Dillen's eyes widened at the name for the creatures that Velorun had used. "Your companion here rushed into a group of women, children, and elderly, drew his weapon, and then tried to kill one of my brother knights. You hold no moral high ground. You also hold no advantage in battle. You will not dictate terms to me."

"Perhaps you refer to those rather maladroit woodsmen moving to outflank me on either side," Imariel said dangerously. "There are but four of them, and from what I have witnessed, they seem to be struggling somewhat in this forest and this level of darkness."

"Yet they can shoot straight," Benedict countered coolly, "and with four of them aiming into a clearing at a stone throw's range at a stationary target backlit by torchlight, both you and I know that they will kill you with ease."

Dillen sighed in disappointment when Imariel failed to counter the Paladin Exemplar's observation.

"Now, I am here to protect innocent people who need help from my soldiers," the Exemplar continued. "I have obeyed all of the rules and conventions of your forest realm. I have ordered my men to respect your forest. We have taken nothing, we have damaged nothing, we are here with noble aims. It appears to me that you are here merely to enforce your territorial boundaries, with the safety of these people clearly being of no concern to you."

"Yet I can still kill you," Imariel whispered, "right now."

"Then do so!" Benedict snapped, pacing forward. "And I shall gladly die knowing that it was for the cause of good and that my men will still prevail in assisting these people without me! And you also can die right where you stand, the difference being that it will only serve to satisfy your typical, tiresome elven arrogance!"

Imariel maintained her position for a few more seconds, her features impassive. Then she eased the tension on her bowstring before slowly lowering the weapon and removing the arrow.

"Brother Willem," Benedict addressed the second of the two knights who had initially encountered Dillen, "get back to the encampment and organize our men into groups. We need to search this forest for those villagers, and quickly."

The young knight nodded and took one of the torches to begin clambering up the slope to the north of the clearing. The Exemplar Paladin turned his gaze to fix on Farn.

"You, what is your name?"

"Brother Farn," Farn replied impassively.

"Brother Farn," Benedict repeated, "clearly you were raised and trained within the ranks of the Brotherhood. While our Order is fractured, I for one do not believe it to be broken. That is why I have faith that if any of my soldiers addressed an Exemplar from your side of the divide, they would still do so using the correct marks of respect!"

"Yes, my lord!" Farn stood up straight. "My apologies, my lord!"

The Exemplar strode over to stare up at the taller knight.

"You can go," he grimaced. "Go back to your own lords and masters. Tell them that Benedict is here, with soldiers in the northeast of the forest. I will be here as long as it takes to assure the safety of these people. If your commander wishes to send help, then it will be gratefully received. If he wishes to oppose me like your brother knight did, then truly your half of this divide has fallen a long way from our tenets. If this is the case, you have proven that Master Odo was right all along about you. Now go."

Farn looked across at Dillen and Imariel, then back at the imposing Exemplar.

"With respect, my lord," he swallowed, "I will not leave without my companions."

"I am not releasing you, Brother Farn, I am giving you an order!" Benedict barked. "And if your two friends conduct themselves with more decorum and less hostility, they will not be far behind you. If they try to oppose my men in doing good again, you can pick up their bodies from this very spot! Go."

Farn looked again at Dillen, who nodded. The younger knight closed his eyes for a moment and hung his head before turning to return to the path they had taken from Eastfort. Benedict turned back to his accompanying knights.

"Confiscate their weapons and take them to our encampment. We have work to do."

*****

"Are you feeling well?" Willem inquired as he lit a second torch from the first that blazed in his right hand.

Around them, the tiny encampment was bursting into activity as knights and villeins were organized into groups; some to remain and guard the camp while others ventured out into the surrounding forest to search for the panicked and scattered peasant survivors. Rowan breathed out, pain still flickering across his wounded abdomen, along a line just beneath the bottom of his breastplate, despite the arcane medical care provided by his Exemplar Paladin. The bleeding had stopped, the flesh knitted together by Benedict's mastery of healing magic, but the irritation of the wound was still well and truly present. As was his antipathy at the attack from an individual who wore the colors of Basilea.

"Well enough," he said to Willem, "much of the impact was taken by the armor, so the wound was not so deep, even before the exemplar Paladin kindly lent his assistance."

"I am glad you are well," Willem smiled briefly, "and I am sorry that I could not lend you any assistance. I… there was a standoff of sorts between me and the other knight."

"Think nothing of it," Rowan said genuinely, wincing in pain as he attempted a careful, tentative stretch. "The whole encounter confused me a great deal. I was not so surprised to see our former brothers now in green, but I certainly did not expect to be attacked by one."

"As the Exemplar Paladin said, I do not think that particular individual was ever one of us before the sundering," Willem said as he took a few paces back. "But anyhow, you shall have to excuse me. I am leading one of these patrols into the forest. The Exemplar Paladin said to report to him as soon as you are able."

"Understood," Rowan nodded, "and thank you, Brother."

Rowan watched as the young knight jogged over to a quartet of awaiting villeins before leading them off into the night. He turned and headed across the field to where Benedict stood with two other soldiers, coordinating the night's activities as the clearing grew quieter around them. Already, the first party of four peasants had been found and safely returned to within the perimeter of the encampment.

"My lord," Rowan bowed his head as he approached the trio of knights, "reporting as commanded."

"Are you well enough? Fit to fight?"

"Yes, my lord," Rowan replied, "my sincere gratitude for your intervention."

"Yes," Benedict smiled grimly, "my intervention."

He turned to address the other two knights.

"Go and ensure the villagers of this first group are uninjured and ascertain whether they know the whereabouts of any of the others."

The two knights quickly departed to carry out their orders while Benedict turned to Rowan.

"I find myself angry, Brother Rowan," he admitted. "Angry at what I saw. We were once the noblest of all Orders, sworn to oppose the Wicked Ones and their servants. A force united in our beliefs and our ideals. I rather naively hoped we were still that, even after events have driven a wedge between us. But what I saw was an arrogant fool, trying to kill one of my knights, while another of our brothers... no, cousins at best, stood idly by and did nothing to stop it."

"They see us as trespassers. They think it is us who are threatening the folk in the surrounding villages."

Benedict turned to stare across at where his two prisoners sat in the center of the clearing, surrounded by four spear-armed villeins. The Exemplar Paladin glowered at the knight and the elf archer, his breath escaping audibly from his nostrils in frustration.

"Come with me," he finally said to Rowan, "let us go and find out."

*****

"Hold still," Imariel repeated, leaning over to dab at the sticky trail of blood around Dillen's rapidly swelling right eye. He gritted his teeth to restrain from an audible sign to betray his discomfort, but he was let down when he felt his shoulders tense up and then shake.

Imariel stepped back and then sank back down on her haunches, ignoring the fascinated stares from the four guards who stood in a loose square around them. Dillen could not blame the men; judging from their attire, they were

215

conscripted peasant soldiers who had probably never seen anything further than a dozen leagues from the spot they were born in; certainly not an elf in an ancient, enchanted forest. Dillen looked around and saw a second group of villagers being carefully ushered into the clearing by the Brotherhood knights, this group being larger than the first. A few fires were being lit in the clearing to provide some warmth – if they were indeed being hunted by the creatures – the Nightstalkers – then, from what little he knew, it would make no difference as those hateful beings did not track their prey visually.

"This marks the second time you have disobeyed Haili's orders in favor of outsiders," Imariel remarked dryly.

Dillen felt his jaw clamp as he turned his face away from her to control an angry retort. The task given to him by Haili was clear enough, but when he stumbled upon a gathering of helpless villagers confronted by armed men, he knew he had to be quick to act, and he did it without apology.

"You took your time in coming to our aide," Dillen said coolly. "How long were you watching us for before you finally deigned to hop down from your perch and lend some assistance?"

"Long enough to listen and comprehend the situation," Imariel replied. "I would heartily recommend you try it at some point."

"I was rather busy fighting off a rather dangerous man!" Dillen scowled. "And with your help we would have…"

"Stop there!" Imariel raised a palm to Dillen, her voice raised enough to cause all four of their guards to turn to regard them. "Enough. Just… enough. There are many reasons I feel compelled to prevent you from delving further into this conversation. First, perhaps foremost and arguably the most simple point for you to comprehend, if I had deigned to join your foolhardy and ill-considered assault, I would have killed a good man. Farn knew this, he tried to stop you, but you would not listen. If I had helped you, we would now be discussing why we had jumped to ludicrous conclusions and then found ourselves as murderers."

"It wouldn't have come to that!" Dillen hissed, leaning forward and pointing with the fingertips of an outstretched hand to emphasize his argument. "You can try to twist this into painting me as the villain, but the simple fact is that you left me out there alone! You left me as good as…well…"

It was too late. He had opened his mouth, and just as well, he might have inserted his foot. Imariel's expression turned dark.

"Like you left my mother when you abandoned us the first time?"

Dillen did not answer. He hung his head. After a moment, Imariel shook her head.

"So that is the crux of your argument. I left you to die. Allow me to enlighten you by re-phrasing your question as a question from my point of view, rather than giving you an unsatisfactory answer. If we faced waves of Abyssals, protecting the innocent from a fate worse than death, would you die by my side for the cause of good?"

"Yes!" Dillen lifted his head and answered, honestly and without hesitation. "Yes! I would!"

"Would you lay down your life for my pride?"

Dillen recoiled, his pained face contorted in confusion.

"What has that got to do with anything?"

"Answer the question. Would you die to satisfy my pride?" Imariel persisted. "Would you abandon everything you have achieved, struggled for, every principle and ideal, your very existence, would you willingly cast it to one side without a moment's thought or regret merely so that I could prove I am correct?"

"Of course not!" Dillen scoffed.

"Then do not expect me to do the same thing for you, you pompous, conceited fool!" Imariel sneered, "I shall not die for you, just because you jumped feet first into a fight without even pausing to consider the consequences of your actions! You actually attempted to prevent a man from administering medical aid to a noble warrior who you had wounded in error! And now you dare to sit there and lecture me as if I had made a mistake by waiting for the correct moment to act!"

Dillen opened his mouth to reply but found no words. After only a few moments more, he realized that he was unable to meet her withering stare, and he turned where he sat to look away from her. Pain raged across his swollen eye; anger and hurt tore at his heart, alongside the humiliation of the ease of his defeat at the hands of the Exemplar Paladin. As if sensing Dillen's thoughts, the Exemplar Paladin himself paced over toward them with the knight Dillen had wounded, only a step behind. As uncomfortable as the situation was, Dillen was almost glad of their intervention, if only to save him from further embarrassing himself with Imariel.

The Exemplar Paladin stopped by Dillen and stared down at him. Resentfully, Dillen raised himself up off his feet, knowing that by accepting a place in the Order of the Brotherhood, it was right and proper for him to show the correct marks of respect to a senior member of the Order of the Brothermark. Nonetheless, Benedict held up a hand to stop him.

"What is your name?" Benedict demanded.

"Dillen."

The older knight's eyes narrowed as his piercing stare bored into Dillen's core. There was an awkward silence for several moments until Benedict spoke again.

"Dillen. Not a very common name. I cannot imagine that there are many knights in this forest named Dillen, and certainly not many who hail from outside of the old Brotherhood lands."

Feeling a nausea claw its way up into his throat, Dillen looked away and remained silent.

"Are you Dillen Genemer, the individual popularized by those rather fanciful songs some years ago?"

Dillen felt his heart thumping. He risked a glance across at Imariel and found that he was, indeed, the focus of her attention. He looked back up at his interrogator.

"Yes. I am Dillen Genemer."

"You are older than the songs describe you."

"Some years have passed," Dillen replied bitterly. "I have aged."

"You know exactly what I mean."

Dillen looked across at the younger knight he had injured and saw nothing in the man's torch-lit features. He returned his attention to the Exemplar Paladin.

"My lord," he whispered. "May we speak of this in private?"

Benedict looked across at Dillen in silence. His head turned slowly to regard Imariel, but still he said nothing. After long moments of silent calculation, he nodded slightly to himself.

"I know all I need to know," he said without emotion, before turning to the four guards. "Back up a little, give these two some space. I feel they may need to talk."

With that, the Exemplar Paladin turned on his heel and paced back across to the northern edge of the clearing as another pair of villagers was safely escorted in from the forest. The younger knight followed him, leaving Dillen to sink back down to a seated position. Imariel turned away from him. He quickly ran through a dozen different scenarios in his mind, a myriad of different options of how he could play through the next few minutes of his life and the effects each option would have on the outcome. This moment, this seemingly trivial moment of sitting on a patch of damp earth under a night sky, surrounded by four peasants and a single elf gladestalker, could dramatically steer his entire existence onto a very new course.

"I feel there is something we need to discuss," Imariel finally said. "Something about your involvement with the expedition led by Trence Andorset."

Dillen paused. The game was up. He had managed to live his lie for some time now. The question was, how much did he reveal and how much of that safety providing lie could he desperately cling to?

"The expedition?" Imariel repeated.

"You knew about that?" Dillen leaned in, his brow furrowed, "I thought you told me that you were on the other side of the forest during the battle?"

"I was," Imariel explained, "but we still heard things. There were songs after the battle, our bards recited them along with the poems. It pays for us to study the cultures of our neighbors. We can become very insular otherwise, very ignorant to what goes on outside our borders. But yes, the songs were different, the few I heard. They offered... different perspectives."

218

"How do you mean?" Dillen asked, his heart racing a little as he swallowed uncomfortably.

"The songs were different," Imariel repeated simply. "Most came from Basilea, naturally, there being some attempt to portray the battle as a great victory for the Hegemon. But then there was one from the Successor Kingdoms, Valentica, I think. It said you were not a paladin. Not even from Basilea."

Dillen turned away, that intensifying feeling of nausea suddenly rising to catch in his throat. Memories of the truth flowed forward, smashing through a dam of lies he had built in an attempt to reinvent himself, to start again.

"What is it?" Imariel asked.

"Nothing."

"It is clearly something. You are upset."

Dillen stood, his arms folded across his gut as the sickness elevated from a simple sensation to a series of short, sharp pains. He looked nervously across to their four guards but reckoned them to be out of earshot. That was something, at least.

"What is it?" Imariel repeated, irritation creeping into her tone.

"I wasn't a paladin," Dillen murmured.

"But... that makes..."

"I wasn't a paladin!" Dillen snapped in agitation, his voice still hushed as he turned to face her. "I'm not even from Basilea! That should be no surprise! I don't even sound Basilean!"

"You know I have spent little time outside the forest, so there is no way I could recognize your accent," Imariel said, her face a picture of confusion. "You told me only this morning that you were a paladin. You said you were never..."

Imariel's features froze for a moment.

"The words you used. You said 'I was never much of a paladin'. So you were equivocating."

Dillen turned away again.

"I didn't lie," he whispered, mainly to himself.

He did not manage to convince himself, so he had no idea how he ever expected to make Imariel believe him.

"You misled me," Imariel said, a note of resentment entering her voice, "deliberately so. If we are to continue along this road together, perhaps it is best that you tell me who you really are."

Dillen looked over his shoulder at her. The eyes that met his were filled with hurt and mistrust. Owls hooted from the trees around them as frightened sobs from the terror-stricken villagers drifted across the clearing. Dillen looked across at them and then back at Imariel. There really was nowhere left to hide.

"Alright," Dillen swallowed. "I promised to tell you the truth, back when we were with Shesh'ra, and my brother's shade haunted us. I suppose there's no time like the present."

Chapter XXX

Two years earlier.
Forest of Galahir
Southeast Boundary

The beating of hooves on the dry path was staggered, uneven, hinting at the horse's problems keeping such a pace. In turn, this was indicative of the horse's poor health, and it reminded Dillen of the fine destrier he once owned, before he was forced to sell him. The thought left a bitter taste in his mouth. Up ahead, the trees were thinning out, allowing rays of evening sunlight to pierce the canopy of foliage above and highlight the dust in the air.

Dillen arrived at the very edge of the forest, wincing as the narrow path suddenly emerged from the last of the trees, and he found himself greeted with the sight of rolling, open pastures undulating southeast toward Basilea. The summer sun hung low in the sky, casting long shadows from the copses of trees punctuating the green fields. The sharp peaks of the mountains of Nova Ardovikio dominated the horizon; the natural barrier that acted as border between the pampered peoples of Basilea and the savages of Galahir.

A solitary rider sat motionless atop a speckled, gray horse a few dozen yards down the path. Dillen spurred his bony, aging steed onward into a trot.

"You're late," the hooded rider grunted as Dillen approached.

"Have you seen what it is like inside that damned forest?" Dillen growled, pointing behind him. "We're trying to move an entire army through that mess! We're barely managing a league per day!"

"Not my problem," the gaunt rider grumbled, leaning over in his saddle to unbuckle a bulging bag attached to the flank of his horse. "My problem is to get this bag of letters to you so that the rich folk in that army can hear all about what is going on back home in their absence. Of course, all the poor folk in the legion can go on, blissful in their ignorance, but fair is fair, is it not?"

"Spare me your petulant insights on class inequality," Dillen spat, leaning over to accept the bag.

He gritted his teeth to suppress an exclamation of pain as his breastplate bit into his midriff. Another reminder of his declining fortunes. His plate armor, presented to him by his father on his eighteenth birthday – over seven years ago now – was once a thing of magnificence. Perfectly fitting him from head to toe, the shining plates were the equal of any other knight on the battlefield or tournament.

Now only the top half remained, as ill providence had forced him to sell half of his armor. The lack of a squire, or even cleaning equipment, had replaced the shine of the remaining plates with a dull, scratched, and dented finish more befitting a struggling mercenary than a knight of a noble house. This was made all the more pathetic by Dillen's growing belly girth, caused by him squandering what little money passed through his hands on ale.

"That's my part done," the rider said, spurring his horse around to face back down the path. "Best of luck to your army and whatever it is you hope to accomplish inside that hellish forest."

Dillen ignored the rider, flipping open the satchel to look inside. Creased parchments and wax-bound letters filled the bag, most with the signet marks of noble families of Solios. One letter caught his eye. A blue wax seal, pressed with the symbol of a bull's head and a seax. His own family crest. Dillen pulled the letter out of the bag and quickly broke the wax seal, rolling the parchment open to cast his eyes over its contents for news from home.

"As I said," the thin delivery rider repeated, "I'm done and I'm heading back south. I... Are you alright?"

Dillen carefully rolled the letter back up, fumbling blindly to push it into his belt as he stared westward toward the Successor Kingdoms and what had once been his family estates.

"Hey! Are you alright? You look pale."

"One of my brothers is dead," Dillen said quietly. "Executed in captivity, so I'm told in this letter. My father couldn't afford the ransom."

"I... I'm so sorry. I..."

Dillen dragged on the reins of his steed to bring the whimpering animal back around to face the rapidly darkening forest again.

"It's the way of the world," he shrugged nonchalantly, "nobody ever said life was fair. And as you say, we have our jobs to do. And I have mine."

Dillen kicked the spurs attached to the heels of his cheap, leather boots into the flanks of his emaciated horse and galloped back into the forest to deliver his satchel of letters.

* * * * *

"Make way! Make way!" Dillen growled, threading his thin horse through the seemingly endless line of soldiers trudging monotonously along the dirt path. The cocoon of greenery had enclosed them again, forcing the line of soldiers to carry lit torches even in daylight as they pushed onward toward the very core of Galahir. Ancient trees, reputedly alive since before the Winter War, pushed straight up toward the heavens above. Dillen had heard it said that there were no straight lines in nature, yet the thick trees stood up as smartly as any guardsman on parade, their trunks almost coal black and their leaves spanning out on branches as broad as any tree trunk he had seen back home. Yet rumor had it that the trees in the heart of Galahir were even older, and even larger.

Birds twittered away in the branches above; their songs somehow sinister and unwelcoming. Insects buzzed and bit; luminous eyes of small creatures watched from beneath the sea of ferns and foliage; the smell of damp moss was overpowering. Snaking through the dense woodland was a line of a thousand soldiers, wearing the blue and white tabards of the 33rd Legion. The shine of their helmets and pauldrons were dulled by the moist environment, and their stout boots were covered in mud. Legion sergeants, distinguishable by the trio of feathers erupting from atop their helmets, shouted orders to their soldiers to keep the line moving as armored men stumbled and tripped in the near darkness, heaving their heavy packs up steep inclines. Calls from up ahead echoed through the trees, and occasionally a man would slip and fall, clattering down a slope to knock over other soldiers in his wake.

Eventually, Dillen reached a large clearing in the forest where evening sunlight had managed to exploit a few gaps in the leaves up above. A hundred horses had been gathered at one end of the clearing – a sure sign that the forest up ahead was even more inhospitable and that riding was no longer an option for anybody. Gently buzzing insects lit up the bleak evening, dancing up above them in showers of orange and yellow light; perhaps beautiful in other circumstances, but here carrying all the hallmarks of a warning to proceed no further.

Finally, at what he believed to be the southern end of the clearing, Dillen saw the dictator. Trence Andorset was every bit the Basilean dictator cut from the traditional cloth; a tall, broad man with a gray moustache falling over his top lip, the wrinkles of his face coming about from decades of fighting experience in the legion. He wore a suit of full plate armor – gray steel lined with gold and adorned with a cloak and sash of vivid blue. A self-made man of sorts, Andorset was born into minor nobility but, due to his military successes, every last branch of his family now enjoyed great luxuries across Basilea. And for Dillen, being the third son of Andorset's second cousin, that family link was what now elevated him out of the utter mess that the Valentican invasion of the Kingdom of Daunticia had wreaked across his homeland.

Andorset looked up and gave Dillen a nod of acknowledgment as the young knight brought his mangy horse to a halt by the dictator to dismount. Stood with Andorset was Lord Paladin Bartolomo Hullus, commander of the 8th Cohort of the Chapter of the Blades of Onzyan, and Lord Paladin Tebald Priscon, the leader of the 3rd Cohort of the Chapter of the Unquenchable

Flame. Both paladins were veterans of many years of campaigning – their combined experience totaling even more than Andorset's, hence their selection to lead the two paladin elements of the Basilean expedition to Galahir.

"We need to press on," Lord Paladin Hullus said grimly, his stocky arms folded around his barrel chest. "This environment is not the natural fighting ground of paladin or legion man-at-arms. If we are caught out here without the support of the natives of this forest, we may find ourselves in a fight that we cannot win."

"Respectfully, Brother, I agree with your sentiment but disagree with your proposal," Priscon countered, standing tall atop the small hillock at the edge of the clearing, his hands clasped at the small of his back as he watched the disheveled procession of legion soldiers file past in silence. "It is our vulnerability in this environment which is the precise reason that we must stop. We are struggling to make headway in broad daylight as it is. If we attempt to hack our way through this forest in the black of night, we will be completely exposed. Stretched out, cut off, unable to provide mutual support. We need a defendable position for the night."

Dillen approached, fishing into the letter satchel for the three scrolls he had found bearing the seals of the Andorset family. His face burned as he thought of the sickening fate of Kallas, his younger brother. Left in captivity at the hands of the bastards of Vallentica for three months, frantically waiting for their father to buy his freedom. He recalled his father's words in the brief letter, a small but rare show of some emotion from the old man: 'I did all I could.'

"Sir Dillen?"

Dillen looked up to see the dictator looking across at him, an outstretched arm awaiting the letters.

"Apologies, my lord," Dillen said, handing across the trio of scrolls.

"These shall have to wait," Andorset said, securing the scrolls inside his belt before turning back to his two paladin advisors. "I agree, gentlemen, that those are our only two viable options. But if the reports which dispatched our force here in the first place are true, this place is teeming with thousands of Abyssal bastards. Now, we've all faced this scum before, and we know darkness means nothing to them. I intend, as always, to shape my battle space as best I can to my advantage, and that does not include fighting Abyssals in the dark. That never ends well."

Dillen took the reins of his horse, intent on taking the wretched animal over to the cavalry dumping ground where some poor fool would be responsible for taking dozens of animals back out of this frightful forest while the paladin knights forged on without them. He stopped and took out the letter from his father again.

Kallas had been a good boy when they were young. A typical youngest brother out of the four in many ways, the other three were always so protective of him. A romantic at heart, he blossomed into the only one of the brothers who could be termed truly handsome. But when Terren, the oldest of the Genemer boys, had been killed in battle fighting the brutish hordes of the orc warlord Makadak, it had hit Kallas hardest. He became a very different man.

"My lord, we are here at the behest of the Lady herself. Her envoys ask for Basilea's help in the darkest of times," Hullus continued. "We cannot afford to waste any more time debating this. We must march on through the night and link our force with that of our host. If we are caught alone in this forest, we are lost."

Dillen thought of that optimistic, foolish boy he had nurtured in their youth, now turned to drink and women. He remembered the last conversation they had, the anger in the words they exchanged, now forever impossible to remedy. Dillen had seen the treatment of prisoners following battle back home in the Successor Kingdoms. He knew full well that there was no respect granted, no mercies given.

"Again, I only agree on a single point!" Priscon said, a hint of anger seeping through in the tall paladin's words. "And that is that there is no more time to discuss this. We need to set up camp, now. We need to see to our defenses."

"Bullshit!" Dillen snapped, turning to face the older warriors. "I've ridden the paths up ahead! Sure, they're not fit for heavy cavalry, but you can get a column of men through there! We can't afford to sit here and be slaughtered like dogs! We need to keep moving!"

The echoing calls of soldiers in the forest and the cawing of birds was all that broke the silence as the three senior soldiers stared across at Dillen. Shaking his head, Dillen swore under his breath and turned away.

"I think you forget your place, young man," Hullus managed a smile. "You just concern yourself with your job, and we will do ours."

"Then march through the night!" Dillen growled. "I may be no grand paladin, but I've fought through seven campaign seasons, and I know war well enough!"

"I've fought through twenty, son," Priscon said without humor. "Now go and…"

"It is alright," Andorset held up a hand to cut off the paladin, "he is my cousin's boy. Give me a moment here."

The broad dictator stepped carefully down the hillock toward Dillen, a slight smile apparent beneath his great moustache.

"Your orders, my lord?" Priscon demanded.

"Set up the defenses," Andorset replied. "The men are exhausted and need to rest. I'm not risking a night march in this. No, Lord Paladin, I have made up my mind. Carry out my orders."

The exchange of words between the two senior paladins was lost within the buzzing of nocturnal insects awaking from their day slumber as Andorset took Dillen by the shoulder and led him away from the hillock.

225

"What was that?" he asked, his voice stern but not without compassion. "You know full well that the three of us have enough soldiering to make these decisions well enough. I know we have only known each other for a couple of weeks now, but I know you well enough to know this is not like you."

Dillen exhaled and looked up at the treetops above him, his fists clenched. Orders were noisily bellowed out from unit to unit as the command to dig in and encamp was relayed around the clearing.

"What has happened?" Andorset repeated. "I saw you but three hours ago, and you were well enough. I always got along with your father, and I would like to think I am doing well by him to take good care of his son."

"Somebody needs to!" Dillen yelled. "Because 'father' certainly doesn't give a damn about his own sons!"

"What?"

"Kallas!" Dillen yelled. "My brother is dead! Drawn and beheaded by those warmongering bastards in Vallentica! All because 'father' wouldn't pay the ransom!"

"Alright, alright," Andorset held his hands out passively in front of him, pushing them slowly down as if that would somehow calm Dillen's raging fury.

Around them, soldiers were already setting about taking axes to the ancient trees of their very allies, beginning the long, laborious process of felling them to provide wood for their defensive walls. Andorset paused for a few moments before speaking again.

"Borders kept your father and I apart for most of our lives," the old dictator said, "but I know him well enough. We were on campaign together for the better part of a year when that idiocy with King Billiam erupted near Tragar. He's a cold bastard at times, I'll give you that, but he would never let down his own blood. He never let me down. I cannot for one moment believe he would abandon his own son."

"He sent me a letter!" Dillen gasped, his words choking in his throat as his shoulders shook. "He told me! He…"

"You don't have all the facts, son," Andorset interjected. "We will find out when we've dealt with this business here. Look, I'm sorry for the news you have received. Truly I am. But right now, we have problems right around every corner we are facing. Let us both put our minds to dealing with this more immediate concern, and then afterward, we will find out what happened with your brother."

"I already know!" Dillen seethed. "The letter tells me all I need to know!"

"And as your family, distant albeit, I will help you," the dictator said sternly, standing bolt upright to look down on the young knight with a less sympathetic glare. "I know loss, boy. My son Alexan fell at the Irasus. You do not own grief alone. But right now, we have a war to fight."

Dillen inhaled slowly, filling his lungs with the damp air of the forest. He exhaled and nodded his head.

"Yes, my lord. My apologies. Sincerely."

"Look, the main force is encamping here. This is not a good position, but it is the best we have. The rear guard will catch up as soon as it can. It is the van that is the problem. You said you've already ridden the pathway up ahead? Good. Take twenty men with you and catch up with the vanguard. Update them on the situation and get them back here, fast. Understood?"

Dillen nodded again, the nausea and anger slowly dissipating.

"Y... yes, my lord."

"Good," Andorset clapped him on the back, "be sharpish about it. Digging in here might be our best option, but it still doesn't mean I am happy about it."

* * * * *

A soldier swore out loud as a branch snapped noisily, the sound stirring a cloud of bats from a nearby tree to screech and flutter up into a black, night sky. At the head of the column, Dillen scowled in frustration and turned to face the Basilean soldier following close at his heels.

"Sergeant Thawne, would you be kind enough to instruct your men to keep the sodding noise down!" he hissed under his breath, his voice reverberating inside his helmet.

"Right you are," the ruddy faced Basilean soldier grinned with a wink before turning to face the column of soldiers picking their way through the winding path in the trees.

"Endreas!" Thawne boomed. "His Lordship up here wants you to keep the noise down!"

"Got it, Sergeant!" another voice yelled in response. "I'll be quiet from now on!"

Smiling wickedly as snickers echoed from the line of legion soldiers, Thawne turned back to face Dillen.

"I've had a chat with the men, my lord," Thawne nodded with sarcastic sincerity. "They say they'll try to keep the noise down."

Dillen stared into the shorter man's eyes, the flickering flames from both men's torches painting the surrounding forest in hues of yellow tinged green. Dillen leaned forward, staring through the narrow vision slits in his helmet.

"Is this a joke to you?" he demanded.

"A joke?" the legion sergeant spat angrily. "We're stuck in this gods-forsaken shithole of a forest, a few hundred of our men are stuck on their own up ahead and possibly dead by now, and you think we see this as a joke? You're here worrying about noise in a place where the majority of what can hunt us can either smell us or can see these torches from leagues away!"

Dillen opened his mouth to speak but was cut off as the sergeant continued.

"If what we've been told is true, and the sodding fairies or whatever is in this forest that we are here to help are actually on our side, then we only need concern ourselves with those bastards from the Abyss. And they can see in the dark anyway; so if they are close, they're already watching us. D'you understand, halfwit?"

Dillen opened and closed his mouth a few times before a verbalized response issued from his lips.

"I'm still a knight! And you're still a commoner! You still need to show me the correct marks of respect!"

"You're not a knight in my army, you're not even Basilean," Thawne sneered. "Look at the state of you. I can recognize a disinherited knight when I see one. I doubt you've got a single coin to your name. So don't pull that lordship crap on me or my men."

The sergeant barged his way past Dillen, holding his torch up to illuminate the darkness of the forest as he picked his way over a maze of tree roots, an owl hooting from a branch somewhere above them. Three or four of the legion men-at-arms had walked on past Dillen before his temper gave way and he decided that the verbal confrontation was not over. Turning on his heel, Dillen took a step in pursuit of Thawne to resume their argument.

Dillen realized too late that his next, ill-thought-out foot step had caught on something in the darkness below when he found himself tumbling over to fall off the path and into the black of the foliage to one side. What little light was being provided by the torches disappeared as he was swallowed up by the forest, vanishing into the dense vegetation and clattering painfully down a steep slope before coming to a stop in a shallow ravine. He let out a cry of frustration as freezing cold water seeped through his armor and clothing, soaking him from head to foot.

Swearing out loud, Dillen shot to his feet and then let out another cry as his head banged painfully against an unseen obstacle above him. His hands frantically clawing at his head, he growled in panic and frustration as he felt only the tight metal loops of his mail coif; his helmet was gone. Scrabbling around in the waters at his feet, he found nothing other than a steadily rising panic. Realizing that the most important piece of his precious armor was lost and gone, Dillen suppressed a cry of rage and set about clambering back up the slope to find the path above him. After a few moments, he emerged into the torchlight again, looking up in embarrassment as the last soldiers of the line of men-at-arms walked past him, looking down at him with utter contempt.

Any response from Dillen was cut off when a glowing sphere of fire whooshed down from the far side of the path, lighting up the forest as it roared through the darkness. The fireball impacted into one of the thick trees by the side of the narrow path, immediately setting the ancient bark alight. A second ball of flames hurtled through the air, slamming into one of the men-at-arms and engulfing him in fire. The doomed man screamed in agony, dropping to the ground and rolling around in a frantic and desperate attempt to extinguish his burning clothing.

"Attackers north!" a voice boomed out from further down the line. "Get in cover!"

Dillen scrambled to his feet and dashed after the closest two soldiers, following them to comparative safety behind a broad tree as more of the deadly, arcane projectiles lit up the night around them. Trees and foliage blazed with the impact of each fireball, casting Dillen's entire world in shades of eerie red as the forest around him burned. He risked a glance around the edge of the tree in the direction of the attack and saw a line of perhaps thirty or forty figures, each the size of a man but hunched over at the shoulders, hurtling through the blazing forest. They wore jagged, brutal looking scraps of armor and carried viciously curved blades. Their dark silhouettes cast against the burning trees behind them highlighted the horns emerging from their heads.

"Abyssals!" Dillen yelled, drawing his sword. "Abyssals! Charging from the north! Form up!"

"Men-at-arms, form up!" Dillen heard Thawne's voice from somewhere further up the line, the second half of his orders cut off as another fireball slammed into one of the Basilean soldiers, and his screams echoed through the burning trees.

Struggling to maneuver in the cramped confines of the forest pathway, the Basilean men-at-arms quickly stood shoulder to shoulder to form up in four ranks, bringing their winged shields up to create a defensive wall. Two more fireballs impacted against them but did little more than burn the paint off their stout shield wall. Dillen looked back up to the gentle slope northward. A ragged line of Abyssal warriors ran through the burning trees, their guttural war cries clearly audible as they drew closer. They hurtled toward them as a barely coherent skirmish line, not bothering to attempt to use anything resembling the battlefield drill and fighting tactics that Sergeant Thawne was attempting to command from his men. Dillen thought the barbaric demons to be the wiser given their environment.

The closest of the Abyssals were only a few paces away now, shrugging off stray fireballs that swept past them, or into them, hurled from their demonic comrades further behind. Isolated, hidden from view, Dillen had the perfect opportunity to escape the ambush. But that had never been his way.

With an angry cry, Dillen leapt out of the cover of the trees and sprinted forward to meet the Abyssals. He met the first red-skinned demon head on, dropping one shoulder to avoid the lower Abyssal's overbalanced strike before hacking the creature's back open bloodily. A second Abyssal was on him in seconds, slamming a heavy hammer against him to impact with his thick armor with a clang. Dillen swung a back fist into the demon's face, splitting open its mouth in a spray of blood before plunging his sword through the creature's gut and twisting the blade inside the wound.

A third demon leapt out of nowhere, wrapping its muscular arms around him and tackling him to the ground. Dillen growled as he slammed an elbow into the creature's nose but let out a grunt as the Abyssal hammered a fist into his own face, splitting open the skin below his eye. Two powerful, taloned hands wrapped around his throat, choking the life out of him as Dillen looked up into the coal-black eyes of the demon knelt on top of him, the fires of the burning forest reflecting in the hate-filled, obsidian orbs. Then, the Abyssal's grip fell limp as the wretched creature slumped over, a Basilean koliskos spear puncturing its torso to emerge through its chest.

The front two ranks of the Basilean men-at-arms advanced slowly forward with their deadly spears pointing ahead, their pace of advance governed by the rhythmic slamming of fists into shields from the rear two ranks. The unit paced steadily forth through the burning undergrowth, straight past Dillen. Thawne broke ranks to dash over and haul Dillen up to his feet.

"Get back to the main encampment!" he shouted over the din of battle as another salvo of fireballs hissed down from the slopes above from an unseen unit of flamebearers. "Alert them to what is going on!"

"I'm not running from this!" Dillen scowled.

"Look around you, man! We're outnumbered! We won't win here!"

Dillen cast his eyes around him. A straggled semi-circle of lower Abyssals, nearly twice the number of the Basilean soldiers, advanced cautiously through the burning trees. Fire was all around, choking the night with noxious fumes and reflecting off the waters of a once tranquil waterfall cascading down into a small pool only a few paces away.

Dillen nodded.

"Give me your rear rank!" he shouted. "One of us will make it through, at least!"

"Rear rank, fall out!" Thawne yelled. "Get back to the main force!"

The four soldiers of the rear rank followed their sergeant's order without question, taking a pace back and then dashing over toward Dillen. Thawne exchanged a final nod with Dillen before sprinting back to take his place at the center of the front rank as his men advanced boldly toward their doom at the hands of the demons.

Dillen turned away, looking around in every direction in a frantic attempt to regain his bearings and calculate which way it was back to the forest clearing and the main force.

"This way!" one of the soldiers shouted, anticipating his dilemma, pointing back to the path.

With no time to query the man's accuracy, Dillen led the retreat back away from the furious melee developing by the waterfall. The five men charged back through the blazing trees, quickly reaching the pathway and then turning to face their escape route. At that moment, a gentle, almost peaceful rush of wind and rustle sounded behind them. Dillen turned back.

Ten figures walked slowly and sleekly out of the shadows. Now illuminated by the fires, the shapely, seductive forms of ten barely clothed women lined up along the slope, their salacious beauty marred by their grotesque wings, horned heads, and demonic tails. The tallest of the demon women took a pace forward, a long blade resting back against one bare shoulder.

"Where are you going, Basilean?" the red-skinned demon woman smiled, the sweet tone of her words at complete odds with the malice in her cold, black eyes. "How about you stay right here with us?"

Dillen felt a moment of utter despair – just a fleeting moment – as he realized there was no escape. Facing creatures that could see in the dark and fly through the flames, there was no hope of a retreat. But then, what was there to retreat to? His country was overrun, his family was ruined, and two of his brothers were dead. Dillen smiled in grim determination. This was as good a way to face his end as any.

"Go!" he screamed to the four Basilean soldiers. "Get back to the encampment!"

Without giving the men-at-arms a chance to argue with him, Dillen charged the succubi. One of the fang-jawed devils flew out to face him, cracking a whip that wrapped around one of his legs. She yanked on the whip in an attempt to fell Dillen, but he powered through her assault and reached her to plunge his sword through her mouth and out of the back of her head. Then the other Abyssal devils reached him.

The succubi surrounded him, clawed hands grabbing at his wrists and pulling his arms to each side as he struggled to overpower them. He managed to get one last sword strike in, hacking at the wing of one of the she-devils before a clawed hand sliced across his face, tearing three great rents down his temple. Shouting out curses and writhing in a frantic attempt to free his sword arm, Dillen looked up as the leader of the succubi walked slowly over to him.

It swung its hips with each step, pausing only momentarily to slit the throat of the succubus Dillen had felled earlier with one razor-sharp toe. The succubus leader leaned in to look at him with interest.

"Are we taking this one back with us?" one of the Abyssal devils hissed.

"No," the leader said, "this one is pathetic. Kill it. We've got a task to fulfill."

Arrows thudded into the demon women, piercing scarlet skin and drawing blood and screams. Four of the succubi collapsed to the ground, dead, the shafts of arrows protruding from their heads and chests. The leader of the Abyssals looked over Dillen's shoulder, its eyes widening in fear.

"Go!"

With one simple command, the surviving succubus fluttered up into the dark sky on hideous, bat-like wings before disappearing into the night. His breathing labored and blood dripping down his face, Dillen turned to look behind him.

At first, he thought he stood face to face with more of the accursed demons. Strange, mutated hybrid forms of part man, part beast, some twenty beings stood before him. Their bare, muscular torsos were matched with four legs not dissimilar to those of large horses, while goat-like horns sprouted up from their faces. Each of the creatures held a bow and stared directly at Dillen, the light of the burning forest flickering across their tattooed chests and fur-covered legs.

Centaurs. Creatures of the Forest. Soldiers of the Green Lady.

"Basilean!" Dillen dropped his sword and held his hands up in a sign of non-aggression. "We came here to help you!"

The largest of the group, a brown-skinned centaur with a long beard, trotted forward to eye Dillen cautiously.

"Can you get a message to the Lady?" Dillen pleaded. "Can you tell her that we are here? We need your help!"

"Yes," the centaur said simply, his strange accent making the solitary word almost unintelligible.

"Can you tell her now? Can you get the message through to her? We need help! We need your army!"

The centaur jabbed his bow up toward the fighting by the waterfall.

"Your friends," he said, "we help them first?"

Dillen looked up at the final ten men-at-arms surrounded by a growing sea of Abyssals. He knew the answer. There was not a moment to spare, and it was but ten men. He knew they were lost. He opened his mouth to speak, but found that common sense failed him when the words came out.

"Yes! Help them! Save them!"

Chapter XXXI

Imariel leaned back, hugging one leg to her chest and looking down at the long grass by her feet. She let out a sigh, staring impassively into the darkness. Dillen stood again to stretch his legs, turning his back on her and breathing out uncomfortably in the silence. More of the missing villagers continued to filter into the clearing, the number of retrieved peasants now most likely nearing the tally of missing. It was some time before Imariel spoke again.

"The stories say you met the Green Lady. That she made you her champion there and then, in payment for her aid."

"No," Dillen shook his head, "I never met her. Not then, not later. There was no bargain struck on that night, just a frantic plea for help. My service to the Lady came some time later."

Imariel's eyes were fixed on him again as he turned and sat once more, his battered armor clanking as he shifted uncomfortably.

"Was there anything else in the songs that was a lie? You are not from Basilea, you were never a paladin. You were not a young warrior, fresh from training, clad in the finest armor provided by the richest of noble families. It was all lies."

"I didn't write the songs," Dillen said defensively, "you cannot hold me to account for what they said."

"The story came from somewhere."

"Not me!" Dillen snapped.

The elf gladestalker leaned forward, yellow flames from the torches of their guards flickering across her green eyes. Her normal impassive, composed exterior had seemingly given way completely to a volatile concoction of bitterness, resentment, betrayal, and confusion.

"None of it?" she insisted.

Dillen let out a sigh and shot to his feet yet again, running his hands through his dark hair in despair. He knew that he was largely innocent, that much of the lies came from a multitude of sources. The worst of it all was

Basilea's painting of Trent Andorset as a misguided fool, an angry tyrant who refused to listen to the sage council of his advisors. That could not be further from the truth. Andorset was a great man, full of wisdom and compassion. But Basilea needed somebody to blame for the disaster, so what better than a dead general? Dillen let out a bitter laugh at the thought. Decades of brave and loyal servitude reduced to nothing, just for the sake of saving face.

"Did you kill an Abyssal Champion?" Imariel asked.

Dillen turned back to face her.

"What?"

"You know the tale. Did you? They say you alone faced an Abyssal Champion and prevailed. I think that's impossible."

The sickness rose up again in Dillen's gut. The greatest lie of all was still to come. His story was not complete.

"Of course I didn't," he collapsed back to sit down by the fire again and finish his story. "Of course I didn't..."

*****

Sprinting past the barricades, Dillen looked around frantically for a figure of authority. Seemingly every tree running along the perimeter of the clearing was now ablaze, lighting up the entire sky above. Sergeants yelled at men-at-arms to form up impromptu units of survivors, while fully armored paladins assembled in ranks before turning to march out to battle. Horses pelted throughout the encampment in panic, and crossbowmen hurriedly set themselves up in positions on the higher ground to give better fields of view for shooting.

A few sharpened wooden stakes had been driven into the ground around the encampment, and barricades had been made out of some of the supply crates carried along with the expedition; but by all appearances, there had been time for little else to set up the defenses. Perhaps five hundred soldiers attempted to organize themselves in the chaos and confusion of the burning forest as commanders ordered them to all edges of the clearing.

The surviving men-at-arms Dillen had returned to the encampment with had already disappeared, subsumed into other units that were quickly turned around and pushed back into the fight echoing from amid the burning trees. Running to the small hillock where he had last seen Andorset, Dillen barged and jinked his way through the bedlam and turmoil of the defense until he finally saw a face he recognized. Lord Paladin Bartolomo Hullus of the Blades of Onzyan stood atop the hillock, hurriedly barking out orders to a group of eight paladins and legion captains.

"Lord Paladin!" Dillen cried as he forced his way over. "Lord Paladin! I must speak to the dictator!"

Hullus glanced briefly across at Dillen as he approached but ignored his pleas, turning back to his task of briefing his commanders on the defense of the clearing.

"Lord Paladin!" Dillen shouted again.

"He's dead!" Hullus snapped. "Andorset was killed in the first wave of the attack!"

Dillen stopped in his tracks. Andorset was dead? What now? That was his lifeline gone, his only link to existing nobility severed, his family reduced to the ranks of common people. But as tragic as that was, it would have to wait. For now, he had his message to deliver.

"The armies of the Lady are mobilizing!" Dillen shouted over the din. "I saw them, northwest of here! They are coming to our aid!"

The collection of paladins and legion officers all turned to stare at him, the surprise clear on every face.

"How many of them?" Hullus demanded.

"Well, I only saw a single group, but they assured me that they would relay..."

"How many of them?!" Hullus boomed.

"About twenty."

A series of groans and sighs issued from the eight leaders, the hope in their eyes transforming to despair just as quickly as it had arrived.

"There isn't time for this nonsense!" Hullus growled, turning back to his subordinates. "You know your orders – assemble your units. North slope, defend and hold position. South slope, counterattack on my command. Go to it."

Dillen watched helplessly as the soldiers quickly dispersed, heading off in each direction toward their awaiting troops. Alone, exhausted, and all but completely unaware what was going on around the encampment, Dillen stared in despair into the flaming trees to the west.

"Who are you?"

The voice addressing Dillen seemed more curious than confrontational. He turned to see one of the legion captains, a thin man of perhaps thirty years with green eyes and a neat beard had stopped to converse with him.

"The dictator's nephew," Dillen shrugged, "I was a messenger."

"But you can fight?"

"Well enough."

"Have you led soldiers in battle?"

"Yes."

"Come with me."

Dillen followed the older soldier in a brisk jog toward the southern end of the encampment.

"I'm Bonn," the man said, "I'm a captain in the 8th. I've got about forty men-at-arms left in good fighting shape, and we're going to take the left flank of the counterattack. There's a line of paladins to the south of here who are holding the Abyssals back. As soon as we are ready, we'll advance past the paladins and push forward while the north slope holds off."

"We're surrounded?" Dillen asked, clamping one hand on his sword scabbard to stop it banging against his leg as he ran.

"Completely," Bonn replied. "They've already broken through once, from the east. We were lucky enough that our rear guard caught us up before they attacked, but the van has disappeared completely."

"I know," Dillen replied, "I was supposed to find them. How many of them are there?"

The legion captain stopped by a collection of upturned crates that had been dumped next to rows of backpacks.

"We have no idea. Quick, look through those crates and get yourself a helmet and shield. You'll need them."

Well aware that every second counted with soldiers fighting and dying to delay the enemy for the counterattack, Dillen rapidly rummaged through the crates and to find a helmet and shield from the pile of replacement equipment. Buckling the helmet to his chin and the shield to his arm, he realized too late that the quality and styling of the armor was not legion. He had taken paladin equipment.

"I don't think they'll care about that," Bonn said, clearly picking up on Dillen's discomfort. "There are more important things to worry about. Follow me."

Bonn and Dillen ran to the southern perimeter of the encampment. A horrifying, animalistic bellow suddenly echoed from their left as lines of scarlet-skinned Abyssal warriors plunged through the camp's eastern defenses. The few legion soldiers holding the line were torn apart as perhaps fifty lower Abyssal warriors rampaged forth, emerging from the blazing trees and hacking down the sparse line of defenders.

A command was shouted from the clearing's hillock, and a rank of twenty legion crossbowmen loosed off their weapons as one. Their bolts whistled through the hot air, smashing into the rampaging lower Abyssals. Demons were upended as they ran, projectiles slamming into their torsos and killing them before their bodies even hit the dirt by their clawed feet. The front rank of crossbowmen lowered their weapons and attached their pulleys to reset their strings while the second rank advanced to kneel in front of them. Another command was shouted out, and a second volley was loosed, felling another dozen of the brutal demons from the Abyss.

"We won't hold against many more of these attacks," Bonn warned. "We need to drive them back!"

The two men reached the southern perimeter, where legion soldiers had been formed up in blocks, ready for the advance. Perhaps one hundred soldiers stood ready, some armed with Basilean daga swords and shields while others held their lethal koliskos spears. Another legion captain was already shouting out to the soldiers of the right flank; a sergeant broke ranks from one of the infantry blocks on the left and ran out to meet Bonn.

"What's the plan, sir?" he asked as he approached. "We moving out to reinforce the line?"

"We're counterattacking, sergeant," Bonn replied, "immediately."

"Counterattacking? In this?"

"The line is holding to the north. The terrain slopes up and doesn't favor a charge, but the ditch at the bottom is delaying the Abyssals. We have ahead of us a slope downward, so in our favor."

"Understood, sir," the sergeant nodded, "the men are ready."

Bonn ran around to the front of the two infantry squares at the end of the attack line and turned to face his men, Dillen following close behind.

"8th Cohort!" Bonn yelled. "Our comrades hold the line to the north! We will push our foes back here! We hold the flank of the counterattack! Stand ready to advance!"

Bonn looked up the line to where the second legion captain stood by the soldiers of the right flank. They exchanged nods.

"March with the men on the left," Bonn told Dillen, "I'll take center. If I fall, you know the plan. Don't let the advance falter. Got it?"

"Yes," Dillen said before turning to sprint over to stand in front of the spearmen at the very end of the line.

"8th Cohort," Bonn shouted, his sword held about his head, "advance!"

Drums struck up from the center of the line, and the legion soldiers marched forward into the blazing trees. Feeling alone and exposed out front, Dillen looked around nervously as he walked steadily forward in pace with Bonn off to his right. The night sky was swallowed up by the burning canopy of leaves above, and the noises of bitter combat echoed up from the slope ahead of them. The sound of the drums faded away as the roaring and cracking of the burning trees grew steadily in volume.

Up ahead, through the haze of the fires, Dillen saw the silhouettes of armored men fighting desperately against grotesque creatures of the Abyss. Corpses appeared by his feet as they continued to advance; some of them red-skinned devils, but most were brutally slain legion soldiers or valiant paladins. Up ahead, a thinly stretched line of paladins held their position, their blue cloaks and surcoats standing out in stark contrast to the licking flames and the waves of scarlet demons they fought. The legion captain on the right flank was the first to call the order; it was then taken up by Bonn and finally repeated by Dillen.

"Charge!"

His sword and shield at the ready, Dillen picked up his pace to a sprint as a hundred soldiers behind him let out a roar. His feet slipping on the slope, struggling to pick his way through burning foliage and ancient tree roots, Dillen ran down toward the melee below. Shouts of warning were issued from paladins toward the rear of the fight, and with disciplined precision, the ranks of Basilea's holy warriors parted as they retreated to allow the fresh troops access to the enemy. Facing a solid line of the snarling, fang-toothed faces of the Abyssal warriors, Dillen let out another cry and threw himself into the fight.

Ramming his way into the enemy line with his shield, he raised his sword to hack down a blow at the closest of the demons but only a moment later felt a colossal thud in his back as the legion men-at-arms caught up with him and charged in. Spears jutted forward to plunge through the first rank of Abyssals, eliciting agonized, unearthly screams from the dying demons. Undeterred, the sea of red bodies washed back into the Basileans, and serrated blades fell down into the front rank, clanging off shields or biting into flesh and bone.

An axe smashed into Dillen's head, failing to penetrate the thick armor of his helmet but leaving him dazed for just a moment. Fighting through the dizziness, Dillen raised his arm to deliver a strike against the snarling, salivating Abyssal attempting to force a muscular arm around his shield to claw at his face. Hemmed in from all sides and barely able to move in the vicious battle, Dillen managed to stab out with the crossguard of his sword, puncturing the quillion through the Abyssal's eye. Swearing profusely, Dillen overpowered the screaming demon and threw the creature back with his shield before stepping forward to lance his sword through its chest.

To Dillen's left, two men-at-arms forced their way aggressively forward into a gap in an attempt to drive a wedge into the Abyssals; to the right, a trio of the scarlet devils smashed their way through the front rank of Basileans as the fight hung in the balance. Struggling to simultaneously defend himself while striking out at any enemy close enough, Dillen found another opening and mercilessly hacked down an Abyssal who had ended up with its back left exposed toward him.

Then, by a miracle, Dillen saw some small amount of hope. He could see trees through the ranks of Abyssals. Their numbers were dwindling. Sweat pouring down his face, Dillen fought with renewed vigor, forcing himself onward to pick out another Abyssal warrior and attack. The fight raged on, the front rank of the confrontation ebbing and flowing like waves as the ancient forest burned down around them. Exhausted, his armor battered and dented from a dozen blows, Dillen fell to one knee as waves of heat from the fire washed over him.

He looked up to see that small kindling of hope growing. Perhaps two dozen paladin swordsmen swept in from the left, carving their way through the ranks of Abyssals. They wore the orange and black surcoats of the Chapter of the Unquenchable Flame; warriors who were tasked with defending the north, not countering attacking to the south. Gasping for breath, Dillen forced himself back to his feet.

"Press the advantage!" he heard Captain Bonn roar over the lull in the fighting. "The armies of the Lady have come to our aid! Advance, and cut them down!"

Looking around, Dillen saw only his own tiny part of the battle where there was little change. There was no great force of nature sweeping in to save them, no unstoppable, fresh wave of Abyssals coming in to join the fight, only fire and smoke punctuated with a few dozen bloodied and battered warriors in every direction. Blinking the sweat out of his eyes, Dillen forced himself onward down the slope after the retreating Abyssals.

Fighting to catch his breath, Dillen slowed and allowed the Basilean soldiers to rush on ahead of him to charge the next line of Abyssals. He looked around again but still saw no sign of any allies from the forest. Within the moments the fighting had resumed, the men-at-arms of Bonn's cohort took the center of the fighting while units of paladins – both the blue clad knights of the Blades of Onzyan and the orange and black of the Unquenchable Flame – closed in from the sides.

A flash of light to Dillen's left caught his attention. In contrast to the endless, raging reds and yellows of the sea of flames around him, the flash was blue. Holding on to the stitch at his side, Dillen accelerated to a quick limp in the direction of the flicker of light, following the slope down away from the fighting as the ground grew steeper beneath his feet. Spluttering as he navigated through the acrid smoke, Dillen continued down the slope until he arrived at the top of a ravine.

The ground dropped sharply below into a small gully, illuminated by the lights of the burning trees around its lip as if it were intentionally done for the benefit of spectators. Below him, two small forces clashed ferociously. Lord Paladin Tebald Priscon of the Chapter of the Unquenchable Flame, together with ten of his paladins, fought against a towering demon, nearly twice the size of a man and festooned in jagged armored plates of midnight black. Five other Abyssals, also wearing thick armor and wielding crude but powerful looking blades, stood toe to toe against the paladins. The ground around them was littered with bodies; over a dozen of the armored Abyssal guards and perhaps half that number of paladins.

With a snarl and a rasp of insults in its unholy language, the towering, winged Abyssal champion extended a clawed hand, and the gully was illuminated as a bolt of arcane lightning shot out from its palm, connecting with one of the paladins and sending the noble warrior crumpling to the ground in a smoking heap. A second paladin leapt up to attack the champion, but his strike was blocked by the demon's blade before the riposte cut the holy soldier in half at the waist.

Looking around frantically for a viable route down into the gully, Dillen saw a mass of twisted vines snaking down one of the steep rock faces. He quickly sheathed his sword and slung his shield across his back before grabbing onto the vines and lowering himself down the ravine wall. Behind him, he heard the curses and clashes of battle continue, the night illuminating with bolts of unholy lightning every few seconds as the Abyssal champion continued its savage assaults.

Urging himself on, Dillen risked a look over one shoulder. The last of the Abyssal guard was vanquished, decapitated by a swift strike from Priscon's sword. The rampaging Abyssal champion, however, continued its ferocious attacks, striking down another paladin with a bolt of lightning before charging into another, barging him down with an armored shoulder and then plunging his sword through the warrior's gut as he lay helpless on the ground.

Desperate to lend his own blade to the Basilean fight against evil, Dillen quickened his descent into the ravine. But he was not cautious enough. One hand slipped on the slick vine, and for a moment, he managed to hold on with the remaining hand, but a painful jolt through his shoulder signaled the full weight of his plate mail armor being forced into that one hand. With a cry of fear, Dillen looked up in desperation as the lip of the gully shot upward away from him as his hands scrambled futilely in the air for a grip that eluded him.

He crashed into the ground with a sickening crunch, crying out as he physically felt the bones of one ankle break on contact. Pain forcing its way through his gritted teeth, Dillen rolled over onto his belly and forced himself up onto his hands and knees. He looked up and saw Priscon with the final two paladins standing against the hulking Abyssal champion, throwing themselves forward into the attack. The demon stood its ground and parried strikes with its blade, but one paladin managed to weave in past the expert defense and slice a grievous wound open across the Abyssal champion's gut. The brave warrior was immediately punished by the roaring devil, hacked brutally down to his knees before the scarlet monstrosity took the man's head off with its blade.

Priscon was next in to attack, fending off the champion's strikes with his shield while forcing home his own determined attacks, slicing open a bloody wound across the Abyssal's knee before a back hand swipe smashed into the Lord Paladin and knocked him through the air and onto his back. By the time he had struggled up to his feet, his final brother paladin had been killed by the champion's blade.

Forcing himself through the pain, Dillen hobbled up onto his good foot. He took one step forward but cried out again as the broken bones of his ankle refused to support his weight, and he collapsed down to one knee. A few yards ahead, Priscon charged the demon again, yelling out in anger as he swung his sword down in a series of precise strikes. The Abyssal champion let fly with another barrage of arcane lightning, the blue bolts slamming against the paladin's shield. A lighter blue light shone ahead of the paladin, something divine and holy that Dillen had never seen as the veteran warrior struggled to move forward with every pace. Priscon forced his way through the lightning, reaching the champion and bringing his shining sword arcing down from above.

The attack cleaved down through the champion's shoulder, splitting apart the dark armor and hacking a colossal rent through the hideous creature's chest. The champion let out a deafening howl of pain but still did not fall. Bleeding from three critical wounds, the demon staggered in place, and for a brief moment, it looked to Dillen that the Lord Paladin would deliver the killing blow.

Then, from nowhere, the Abyssal champion let out a roar and swung its blade down to hack through the paladin's shield and half sever one of his legs. Priscon slumped down, giving the wounded champion the only opening it needed. It leaned in and plunged its blade through the valiant paladin's chest, killing him in one lightning blow.

Dillen let out a howl of rage, raising his sword and forcing himself to take but one step closer to the towering champion ahead of him. Covered in blood, swaying unsteadily on its feet, the champion looked up at him as he approached. With a snarl of rage, the Abyssal devil reached a claw inside the belt wrapped around its waist. It produced a stone – a small gem of purple – and held it aloft. Determined to avenge the deaths of the paladins, Dillen continued his slow hobble forward as the demon growled out words in its dark, forbidden tongue.

A vertical line of shimmering light appeared in the air behind the demon, yawning open to form a shining portal. Dillen saw the fires of the very Abyss itself through the portal, the demon's gateway to its unholy home and escape. He could only cry out in anguish and collapse to his knees as the wounded demon staggered through the portal and disappeared from view as the gateway faded to nothing.

Every time Dillen later tried to recollect the rest of that night, he failed. Dull memories of the fires slowly dying away and the dawn sun leaking light into the ravine were somewhere within his mind. He remembered centaurs galloping past him, following the gully down to join the fight at the bottom of the valley. Perhaps most importantly, he recalled Lord Paladin Hullus arrive by his side with a group of paladins from the Blades of Onzyan, but he could never remember the order in which any of these things happened.

"The Champion?" Hullus demanded as two of his paladins carefully helped Dillen up to stand on his good leg. "Priscon said he was moving in to fight their champion."

"Yes," Dillen said wearily, "he did."

"Where is the champion?"

"He's gone."

"You killed the champion?"

Dillen's eyes shot open. He looked across at Hullus and his paladins, staring at him expectantly. Only yards away, Priscon's corpse lay in a pool of his own blood, the real hero of the hour who forced into retreat possibly the single most dangerous creature the Abyss could muster for the entire battle. But Andorset was dead, and with him, Dillen's last chance at renewing his way of life. He had nothing left; his lands were claimed by a foreign kingdom, his fortune confiscated. He was now nothing more than a poor mercenary, a commoner. But providence had given him an opportunity, and he would be damned if he let it go.

"Yes. I killed their champion."

* * * * *

Dillen felt his shoulders sag and his head hang low as he repeated the words he had told Hullus after the battle. The lies. The truth had never actually evaded him; Dillen had known men who lied so much that they actually began to believe it, but deep down he always knew who he was, and also who he was not. He knew he was not the man described in the tales and the songs, not the hero. Far from it. But even so, given his firm grasp on reality and the truth of that momentous day, it had been two years since Dillen had actually verbalized his actions and words, and doing so now left him feeling sick, drained, and ashamed.

On the other side of the clearing, the Exemplar Paladin was locked in discussion with a small group of his knights. Judging by their gesturing to the north, Dillen guessed that they had rounded up and accounted for every missing villager and would soon be heading off to leave the forest. He looked across as Imariel. The elf regarded him with empty eyes, her face drawn and disappointed, an intense look he had seen not long before.

"We all make mistakes," she said quietly, "but what defines our character is how we react to these things. Some of these mistakes are out of our control, some are not. But I do not believe we should be held accountable for a momentary lapse in judgment or an erroneous decision under pressure. But I do believe we should be fully accountable to cool, measured decisions made without pressure or the burden of time ticking quickly away. Dillen, you had two years to tell the truth. Two years."

Dillen looked away again, failing to meet her disdainful glare. The nausea and shame intensifying within him, he rapidly ran through many options for responses to her and what her likely reaction would be, and he found none of them ended well in his mind. He attempted to turn to face her again, failed, and looked off to the edge of the clearing and into the darkness of the trees. Agonizing seconds turned to minutes in silence as Imariel remained seated behind him, neither of them speaking. Finally, again a welcome interruption from his confrontation with Imariel, Exemplar Paladin Benedict approached his two captives, a sword and a bow held together in one hand. Dillen stood up straight and bowed his head in reverence. Imariel glanced up for a second and then looked away.

"All of the villagers have been found," the dark-haired knight announced as he approached, "so with that, we shall take our leave. My intentions are to return these people to their home where the rest of my soldiers are waiting. I will then wait for a day to see if their attackers return, but that is all I can do. I can delay no longer."

"Of course, my lord," Dillen said quietly.

Benedict handed over Dillen's sword to him and then tossed Imariel's bow back across to her. She caught it with one hand but still said nothing.

"You are both free to go," the Exemplar Paladin said as he turned away. "Let us hope that we do not cross paths again."

Dillen rapidly made a decision and took a pace after the senior knight.

"With your permission, my lord!" he called after him. "I would like to accompany you to the village."

Benedict stopped and turned back.

"Perhaps you think my men need an escort, Brother Dillen?" he inquired wryly. "That we would be better off with, lest we are attacked by an Abyssal Champion, perhaps?"

Imariel let out a derisive breath at the accusation. Dillen looked down at her anxiously and then back up at the scornful stare of Benedict.

"Not at all, my lord," he swallowed as he sheathed his sword with a shaking hand, "but I have made a mistake here tonight. A terrible mistake. I cannot undo my past actions, but I must start somewhere. I am not offering my help to you, my lord. I am pleading for a chance to begin to redeem myself. I know it is not much of a gesture, but at this moment, it is the only opportunity open to me to show some willingness to do something positive. Please, my lord."

Benedict stepped closer, his eyes boring into Dillen's as if assessing his sincerity. His features softened and he nodded slowly.

"Come on, then," he said and then turned to Imariel. "And you? Will you also be accompanying us to the boundary of your forest?"

Imariel stood and slung her bow over her shoulder.

"No," she said coolly before her eyes darted across to Dillen. "I have nothing to apologize for and no requirement for redemption. I shall return to where I belong. Perhaps on completion of this task, Sir Dillen might contemplate doing the same."

With that, the slender elf paced past the two knights and walked over to the edge of the clearing before disappearing into the moonlit undergrowth. Dillen watched her go, feeling more empty and self-loathing than at any point he could ever remember. After a few moments of quiet contemplation, he turned and followed the Brothermark knights and villeins out of the clearing and off toward the north.

Chapter XXXII

I f navigating a path through the thick trees of the dense forest was difficult during the day, it neared impossibility at night. From somewhere up ahead, two of the villein woodsmen led the snaking column of soldiers and villagers back toward the north, Benedict commanding their progress from a few paces behind. For Rowan and Willem, nearer to the center of the column, the pace was staggered and confusing, relying on blind faith in those ahead for not getting lost. The ground seemed almost indecisive, changing its mind every dozen paces as to whether it wished to slope up toward a peak or suddenly plummet down into the depths of a dark valley.

The women, children, and elderly of the group were concentrated close to the middle, stumbling forward through narrow paths that allowed no more than two or three people to stand shoulder to shoulder at any one point. Torchlight flickered off trees that seemed to loom down over the weary travelers, branches extending down in curves like skeletal arms reaching down to grab at the vulnerable peasants below. Children cried and were quickly hushed by their mothers while villeins helped the elderly stumble onward toward the edge of the forest. The branches above rustled and swayed with a gust of wind as a chorus of frogs could be heard from off to the right of the path, their guttural gurglings adding to the disjointed medley of night noises from the forest.

"How much further do you think we have to go?" Willem whispered from next to Rowan.

Rowan glanced up at the sky in a futile attempt to find a clue as to how close they were to dawn.

"I don't know, Brother," he replied honestly, his voice hushed so as to keep any negativity from spreading along the line. "I have completely lost track of time and where we are. Those woodsmen up at the front will get us out of this, you know what they are like. They can tell north from south just by looking at what grows on the sides of trees, all sorts of things like that."

Willem suddenly stopped in his tracks, his shoulders tensing up and his hand shooting to his side to grab his sword. Rowan did not need any other stimulus; he dragged up his mail coif and unslung his shield from his back.

"Left of track, perhaps twenty yards, in the trees by the bend to the right!" Willem whispered quickly as he grabbed for his own shield.

"Mum! What is it?" a child's voice whimpered from behind them.

Rowan peered into the darkness at where Willem had pointed to, but saw nothing out of the ordinary. But then he sensed it. Something dark, unnatural, threatening. Something watching them from the black void of the forest, where the moonlight failed to penetrate.

"Get the villagers to the right of the track!" Rowan ordered loudly. "Spearmen! Form a battle line!"

Metallic rasps rung out along the line as swords were unsheathed and spears were brought up ready. A handful of villeins quickly shoved the vulnerable villagers away from the threat as soldiers stood shoulder to shoulder to form a rank of spears.

Off by the trees at the corner of the path, two clear, almost luminous eyes regarded them from within a row of ragged, thick bushes. Rowan grabbed his great helm from his belt and quickly hauled it onto his head and buckled it under his chin before bringing his sword and shield up, ready to fight. He marched out toward the bushes and the growing sensation of darkness and danger, five brother knights pacing out with him as the panicked message of immanent attack was quickly relayed.

* * * * *

The commotion from the rear rippled along the line, hushed whispers amplifying into the low buzz of conversation. Dillen craned his neck and saw soldiers arming themselves while peasants were unceremoniously shoved off to the east of the path behind a rapidly forming rank of spearmen.

"Do you sense that, Brother?" one of the knights asked an accompanying warrior from up ahead.

Dillen sensed nothing. That part of his training was yet to wield any success, but he did have something the others did not. While it was only two years, he had still spent all of that time in the forest and was beginning to know and understand it better. He stopped in his tracks and focused. There was commotion from behind them, where unseen nocturnal creatures scampered hurriedly away in the darkness, south away from the group. To the north was nothing, silence. Left, he saw a small group of knights moving cautiously out toward a line of hedges. There was silence to the right.

"Get the villagers in the center!" Dillen bellowed as he turned around to call back down the line. "We are surrounded on both sides! Get the villagers in the middle!"

"Follow that command, now!" Benedict yelled, rushing back from the head of the column to appear by Dillen's side. "Spearmen, form ranks on both sides of the path!"

Dillen unsheathed his sword as the commotion from the ranks of villeins grew louder; spearmen stumbling past each other in the darkness in an attempt to form two walls of polearms, keeping the terror-stricken villagers in between them. Growls issued from the west; not the familiar grunts of wolves or bears that Dillen had cautiously grown accustomed to, but something else entirely, something deeply unnatural. Branches and leaves were disturbed to the east as shadowy figures moved in from the right side of the narrow path. To both sides, thin wisps of purple tinged mist crept and crawled along the root-strewn forest floor, sneaking closer to the warriors and terrified villagers caught between the two banks of unnatural fog. Then a black-skinned, shadowy beast the size of a panther leapt out from the bushes and the fighting began.

*****

Rowan jumped back in alarm, pain shooting across his wounded abdomen as the gleaming, black-skinned beast jumped out of the bushes. The creature landed by his feet, a great, guttural roar escaping from the fang-jawed teeth of both of its heads. With a broad, muscular frame and glistening skin, the predatory creature loomed up larger than a wolf, a boney spine jutting down its back with hideous shapes twisting and contorting beneath the thin skin of its flanks. Rowan's eyes widened in horror. The shapes beneath the twin-headed beast's skin looked to be human skulls, their jaws opening and closing as if crying out for help.

Re-centering his concentration after the shock of the beast's appearance, Rowan took a moment to calm his mind. That was the moment the beast leapt forward to attack. Rowan brought up his triangular shield and felt one of the creature's heads smash into it with a colossal thud, knocking him back a step. The second head shot around the rim of his shield on the end of a stubby, muscular neck, its dagger-toothed jaws snapping viciously at his arm. Rowan leaned into his shield and pushed back against the frantic creature, swinging his sword down to cut open a great welt in its back.

To either side of him, his brother knights rushed forward to fight against an entire wave of the hideous, two-headed dogs, at least half a dozen of them leaping out from the undergrowth ahead. He saw one of his brethren, indistinguishable beneath his great helm, knocked to the ground and pinned helplessly beneath the weight of one of the great beasts. A set of huge jaws clamped around his waist, teeth plunging through his armor and drawing blood as the powerless knight was shaken violently from side to side and then torn apart by the two heads. Rowan continued on pushing back against his own monstrous adversary, smashing his shield into one of the two heads while striking out with his sword in an attempt to score a second wound on the other.

Willem suddenly appeared at Rowan's side, his own heavy longsword arcing down to cut deeply into the neck of the creature, gouging open a great tear and half-severing one of the heads. Both heads opened their mouths simultaneously to let out a great roar of pain, and Rowan seized on his moment to thrust the end of his sword through the mouth of the second head, plunging through the creature's cranium. It slumped down dead at the feet of the two knights.

Rowan looked around quickly to assess the situation and saw the force's villeins had formed up two lines of spearmen that now stood to create two sides of a triangle, the villagers comparatively safe within it. More creatures shambled out of the trees to the right, these beings roughly the size and shape of men but with grotesque, oversized jaws packed with sharp teeth and swollen faces without eyes. Armed with rusted axes and long scythes, the creatures limped and staggered out from the trees to throw themselves into an attack against the valiant villeins as the terrified villagers screamed and cried from where they huddled in the dirt only yards away.

* * * * *

Only seconds after the Nightstalker monstrosities jumped out of the bushes to attack the knights, Dillen saw one of the two woodsmen ahead yanked into the foliage and disappear from view. Two other villeins sprinted off ahead, clearly with the intention of dashing to his aid.

"No!" Dillen yelled, grabbing one of them firmly by the elbow. "Get back in line!"

"You heard him! Stay together!" Benedict added before turning to the surviving woodsmen and shouting out. "Get back! Run, man!"

At that moment, the branches and leaves to the east of the path parted and a scraggy line of shuffling figures lurched out to attack them from the other side. Thin, reedy limbs, hideous jaws crammed with needle-sharp teeth, and dressed in the ragged remains of clothes one would expect to see on farm hands and laborers, Dillen recognized these scarecrows from the first village that was attacked.

Two ranks of some fifteen villein spearmen moved to protect the villagers while the remaining villeins, all of them archers, drew their bows and began loosing arrows into the wall of advancing Nightstalkers, felling a handful of the creatures with well-aimed shots.

"Spearmen, hold your ground!" Benedict yelled above the cries of battle. "Brothers! With me!"

The veteran knight charged into the tide of advancing scarecrows, cutting down his first opponent with a heavy strike to the chest before lopping off the head of a second. With a yell, Dillen brought up his sword and charged out to face the advancing nightmares, flanked on either side by knights who once counted themselves as brothers with the very Order he had only recently joined. Reaching the first scarecrow, Dillen ducked beneath a flailing claw and swung his sword around to bite deeply into the ribs of the hellish creature. Drawing back on his blade, he felt an axe clang against his breastplate but without enough force to stop him; his second strike was enough to tear open the guts of the scarecrow and drop it to its knees before it pitched forward into the purple mists swimming over his ankles.

The knights held their ground, a group of ten of them under the command of Benedict forced a wedge into the scarecrows and drove them apart, but some managed to spill past the fight and limp off toward where the villeins held place to defend the villagers. Arrows whistled through the night sky and thunked into their targets with sickening thuds and squelches, the few scarecrows that managed to hobble past the knights and arrows were then cut down by a wall of spears. On the east side of the path, the fight was going well. But then Dillen risked a glance over his shoulder and saw the far side of the fight and realized that the night was far from won.

*****

Despair clawed at Rowan's heart as he saw another of his brother knights killed as salivating jaws clamped around the warrior's head and crushed the great helm into a pulp. Hacking down with his blade, Rowan felled a second of the twin-headed shadowhounds before his brother knight's killer was on him, forcing him back again. He looked around frantically as powerful claws battered against his dented shield and saw that only Willem and Riley remained alive and by his side, surrounded by twice their number of the oily-skinned hounds. A salvo of arrows thudded into one of the beasts, two striking its flank in quick succession before a third plunged through the side of one head and it toppled to the mossy ground below.

"Fall back!" Rowan shouted out, "back to the spear line!"

Locking in against each other and raising their shields to overlap, the three knights stumbled through the darkness toward the line of spears and torches behind them, lancing and thrusting with their heavy swords as the five shadowhounds kept up their relentless and terrifying attack. Another of the beasts was punctured by arrows and collapsed into the purple mists; Willem found an opening to slice open the head of another, but a second later, a roaring snout forced its way in between their shields and clamped its jaws around Riley's sword arm, severing it at the elbow. Rowan turned in place to strike at the hound but succeeded only in wounding it; the black beast leapt upon the screaming body of his mutilated brother and dragged him to the ground before devouring him. Rowan and Willem raised their swords and shields once more, now only paces away from the relative safety of the spear line.

Then, from the north of the line, another trio of knights sprinted in to join their fight. Rowan watched in relief as Dillen, the very knight who had wounded him only hours before, led two of his brothers into the fray and slew one of the shadowhounds with a flurry of powerful blows. The final two monstrosities were quickly overcome, now outnumbered and surrounded by the heavily armored knights. Removing his blade from the final, felled beast, Rowan looked around and saw that his brothers on the far side of the fight had cut down the last of the scarecrows, and the only sound in their corner of the forest was the crying and wailing of terror-stricken children behind the spear line.

"My lord!" Dillen shouted across to Benedict. "We have to leave! These things do not suffer from the darkness, they do not see as we see! Every moment we spend here is a moment they have an advantage!"

"Agreed," Benedict replied, "we carry on north, and quickly!"

"But our fallen, my lord?" Willem urged.

"They will be recovered, respectfully," Dillen promised, "but not now! We must go!"

"Do you know this part of the forest?" Benedict asked, his eyes darting from side to side as he moved in place to check all around them.

"No, my lord," Dillen replied, "but after two years here, I am confident that I can find my way through the dark. With your permission, I shall lead us to the boundary."

"Good. I agree, it is our best chance. Soldiers! Protect the villagers at all costs! Move fast; call out if you cannot keep up! Carry the children! Let us go, quickly!"

✶✶✶✶✶

Color slowly leaked into the world as pastel shades of orange crept over the horizon ahead of the dawn. His legs weary, his body drenched in a cold sweat, Dillen stumbled through the last line of brambles and into the open field beyond. He allowed himself the briefest of pauses, accompanied by a faint smile, before he staggered on to allow the warriors behind him to continue to follow on. The sweeping fields cascading out ahead of him reminded him of his father's estate, and another life that now seemed so far in the past. A life he had resented at times, hated at others, but now missed dearly. A life he would have given anything to begin again with the knowledge he had now, so that he could have told people dear to him things he wished to the gods above he had been given the chance to tell them.

Dragging his mail hood off his head to sit across the back of his neck, Dillen hauled off his armored gauntlets and ran his fingers through his sweat soaked hair. A few exchanged whispers of relief were issued behind him as knights and villeins emerged from the dark depths of the forest and into the dimly lit field as long shadows began to form from the slowly rising sun. On the far side of the field to the north, a series of faint squeals and crunches issued as, just visible over a thick hedgerow, a cart trundled along the road east toward the Basilean border. The cart driver, a solitary farmer, looked across the field in bewilderment and disbelief as the famed forest continued to disgorge lines of battered soldiers. Dillen watched the cart slowly carry on its way behind its thin horse, the normality of seeing a farmer going about his normal business seeming completely at odds with the nightmare journey that had taken them through the entire night.

Dillen carried on across the field, wincing as the glare of the sun intensified in the cloudless, cold sky. He reached a solitary, broad oak tree growing through the hedgerow and leaned against it, turning back to see the peasants they had protected stumble out of the forest. He counted them all as they came. They had lost none. The night had been a success. Some fifty or sixty warriors and half as many again of their charges filtered out into the field, some collapsing to sit in the tall grass while others formed small groups and exchanged relieved, exhausted smiles. The knight Dillen had wounded at the beginning of the night looked across at him. Dillen contemplated offering an apologetic smile but decided it might be misinterpreted, so instead issued a brief nod of respect before looking away again.

The Exemplar Paladin paced over to where Dillen leaned against the tree, his stature and gait betraying not a shred of fatigue from the events of the night. Dillen stood upright smartly and bowed his head in respect as the older knight approached.

"My lord," he greeted formally.

"Brother," Benedict replied, "you have done well. You have led us out of the forest intact. Your actions have saved lives."

Dillen formulated a few options for answers in his mind, but while still debating which was best, the Exemplar continued talking.

"Some of noble birth would look at these people and question whether they were worth saving. Simple farm folk, no land or titles, no riches. If you had led us out of there with thirty Basilean nobles, the Duma would shower you with riches and glory. But for what it is worth, to me at least, a life is a life, and these people are as worthy of living as any others. Thank you for playing your part in keeping them alive."

"Thank you for allowing me to," Dillen said sincerely, "especially after…"

"We do not need to mention that again," Benedict smiled. "Your actions have redeemed that earlier misunderstanding. Perhaps it is worth contemplating how far that path to redemption is worth following."

Dillen paused pensively. There was no way that Benedict could have overheard his long revelation to Imariel. Then again, perhaps his name was enough. Just knowing the ridiculous songs and making some simple, and correct, assumptions would possibly lead the Exemplar to the truth.

"Where will you go now, my lord?" Dillen asked.

"East for another hour or so," Benedict replied. "The village elders recognize where we are. Their village is not far away, and that is where the other half of my men are waiting."

Dillen quickly suppressed an unwarranted feeling of pride, knowing that him leading them so close to the village was far more luck than judgment.

"And then home, my lord? Back to the Brothermark?" he asked.

"I think not," Benedict shook his head, "these people fled their village because of what attacked us last night. I do not believe for a second that we eliminated that entire threat. To simply drag these poor people back to their village and then leave them with this threat still present would be tantamount to murdering them ourselves. No, I believe we should do the right thing and see this through to the end before we can return to the Brothermark."

"And the forces of the Lady? I have very little experience of this place, and while I would never dare be so impertinent as to speak ill of the forest when it has become my home, I am enough of a pragmatist to realize you might meet more opposition if you return. The forest is not welcoming of outsiders. Her forces may think they can expunge the darkness on their own without intruders."

"That is a risk I must take," Benedict said. "You seem to be a good man, at heart. But while your new masters are surely not evil, they are not good either. My soldiers and I must therefore be a force for good in eradicating these stalkers, even if it does incur your Lady's wrath. Even if it does mean battle. We will not step down from our duty to protect those who need it."

Dillen nodded slowly, thinking deeply on those words and his moral conviction in supporting the Lady and her people. He took a step toward Benedict and offered his hand.

"The very best of fortunes with your task, my lord," he said sincerely. "Stay safe."

The Exemplar Paladin accepted his hand and shook it tightly.

"Thank you again for your help, Brother Dillen."

Dillen bowed his head again and turned to trudge back toward the forest boundary. Knights and villeins watched him pass with a mixture of suspicion and unease, while a few of the peasants smiled nervously or whispered their thanks to him under their breath as he passed. Dillen reached the edge of the trees and turned to watch for a few moments as the knights, villeins, and peasants formed a group on the road and moved off toward the east. He headed back into the forest, greeted by the now familiar smells of the foliage around him and the coolness of the close air. Willing his aching legs to negotiate the gentle, uphill slope, he let out a long sigh as he commenced the next part of his journey. It was a long way back to Eastfort.

Chapter XXXIII

Dillen never thought he'd feel comforted by the smell of Eastfort – the aromas of human sweat, horse odor, burning fire, and cooking food. In his time as a member of the Green Lady's forces, he had learned to appreciate just how much it paled in comparison to the wondrous scents of nature, but after the past few hours, he just desperately wanted a place to lay his head; a moment to just relax and embrace his thoughts.

Imariel knew the truth. Shesh'ra probably had an idea of it too, thanks to that nightmarish manifestation of his brother. Farn? Haili? Bhadein? Benedict and his brothers? Who else could have seen through the ever-expanding cracks in his mask?

With every step that brought him closer to Eastfort, his heart pounded more intensely, and a thunderstorm raged within his brain. The secret he had been living with, the lie that had started out as a way of clinging to what was left of his crumbling life, what had only grown as the years went on that deified him into some hero of legend, was now exposed as false.

Should he feel relieved? Should he feel guilty? Did he need to run and start his life anew somewhere else? It all ran through his head. Despite those worries, it felt like a great weight had been lifted; the release of the truth, admitting he wasn't the hero that everyone thought he was, just letting the facade slip with Imariel, it was all liberating.

But at the same time...

That pounding in his stomach twisted into a knot, and he felt his face redden. He had been lying for so long – pretending he was someone that he wasn't, living his life on accomplishments that weren't his, garnishing compliments and respect from deeds and actions he had never had a hand in. Lord Paladin Tebald Priscon had fallen fighting the horrible Abyssal champion, and yet Dillen claimed it was he who had unleashed a finishing blow against it. That moment kept replaying itself in Dillen's head – when Lord Paladin Hullus asked him if he killed the champion.

All he wanted to do was redeem himself, his family. He didn't want to lose everything, and yet... Here he was. In the middle of the Lady's forest. What difference would it have made if he had just told the truth? Would he have just ended up here anyway?

Then there was the look on Imariel's face when he had told her...

"Stupid, stupid, stupid," Dillen found himself muttering out loud and quickly silenced himself. He had mucked it all up – everything was a mess now.

He had barely noticed the guards at the entrance; he forced a smile, but they barely met his eyes with odd looks and half-smiles. The former Brotherhood knights were all out and waiting for him; Farn was in the front, looking like he was having a hard time keeping his eyes on Dillen.

Perhaps he hadn't mucked it all up yet.

"Right," Dillen said as he approached, hands on hips. "I'm sure word has spread, but there is a force of Brothermark soldiers in the area. I don't know why they came here in the first place – maybe returning from patrol – but they're here now to do what we set out to at the start of this whole mess. To help the surrounding villages. There's been another attack by those nightmarish creatures, and the Brothermark forces have managed to find survivors."

"Sir Dillen," Bhadein sighed and stepped forward. "Is it true that you fought our former brothers?"

Dillen looked into the older man's eyes, and he found none of the usual resentment. Ever since he had found the Armor of Tides, there had been a change in Bhadein, and even here, when Dillen expected him to be furious, there was only a longing for the truth.

"Yes. I did. I didn't know who they were, and they were pursuing fleeing villagers that Farn, Imariel, and I came across. From everything we've seen the past few weeks – the first village and the horrors deep in the forest – I was hesitant to trust anything I was unfamiliar with. Especially humans I was unfamiliar with in the Lady's woods. Rest assured," Dillen looked at all of the men, focusing on Farn, who had shown Dillen more respect than he ever deserved, "there were no casualties. We came to a mutual conclusion to help the people, and they let us go."

There was an audible sigh of relief. Dillen could understand; even if a difference in ideals led to the split of the Brotherhood, the last thing he was sure that any of them wanted was to face their former brothers-in-arms.

"Where are they now?" Ragneld asked from the back of the group.

"They're going to try and completely eradicate the rest of the... as their leader called them, Nightstalkers."

"They can't be serious," Farn gasped. "We barely fended them off with the help of the elves!"

"That may be true," Bhadein countered, "but we have purified the source of their strength. With that hold gone, they are surely weakened."

Dillen frowned, looking deep into the forest. "Even so, I'm not sure they can stand alone against the remaining atrocities."

"We need to prepare – surely with those abominations still around, the druids will give us the order to move," Bhadein said, and Dillen saw the conviction in his eyes. He was convinced, that this time, they'd be ordered to action. Dillen wasn't so sure, but he nodded back to the man. They wouldn't make the same mistake as last time.

The men dispersed, a bit more heartened. Farn made his way to Dillen, the wary look replaced with the more jovial smile he was used to seeing on his face.

"When I arrived, I wasn't sure what exactly to say. I didn't tell them much, but needless to say, I was worried about you returning. Glad to see that everything worked out all right."

"Agreed. Had I only listened to you sooner, we might have avoided any conflict at all. I'm sorry, Farn."

"Nonsense!" Farn laughed. "I had faith in the Hero of Galahir all along, I-..."

"No." Dillen shook his head and then placed both hands on Farn's shoulders, looking into his eyes. "No, Farn. Listen to me. You must forget everything you have heard about me – the stories the bards sing, the persona that you've come to know, all the tales of my heroics – you must forget it all."

Farn frowned with a look of confusion contorting his features. His mouth hung slightly open, as if to ask more.

"Dillen!"

Dillen dropped his arms, and both men turned. Imariel stood at the path leading deeper into the forest, beside her were Shesh'ra and the salamander... What was his name – Lothak?

"I-Imariel..." Dillen failed to find words right away. "You have company?"

"The Druid Haili did say for us to accompany Imariel," Shesh'ra spoke and bowed her head slightly. "She is knowing of the humans who are to be marching through her woods and of the creatures of the night still prowling. She is to be wanting us to be with Imariel in case of danger."

Lothak did not speak, but he did exhale smoke from his nostrils as if to emphasize Shesh'ra's point.

"All right, that's understandable, but why are you three here?"

"Druid Haili wishes to see you at once," Imariel spoke, her tone neutral. Her eyes swept across to Farn. "I also come with an order. All of your knights and rangers are to patrol the woods close to Eastfort and expunge any traces of the twisted creatures that you find."

Dillen stared at her and hoped for once the elf would give some sort of emotion, but when her stony gaze did not melt, he turned to Farn.

"Right, there's our cue then. Take care of yourself. And please," Dillen gripped Farn's shoulder with one hand and forced as true of a smile as he could. "Remember what I said."

Farn stared open-mouth at Dillen as he turned to leave for Calenemel.

* * * * *

Upon reaching the elf city, Dillen was shocked when Imariel led them to a big building in the back. He had never been to Haili's temple before. On the few occasions when she needed to address him or the other humans personally, she would meet them in the city and send them on their way, probably not finding them worthy enough to stay in Calenemel any longer than necessary. Beyond their summoning to the amphitheater, having an invitation within the elf city was not common for an outsider. Shesh'ra must have noticed his expression, and she smiled as she spoke low.

"I, too, have not been within the druid's temple. I have to be thanking you for that."

"Me?" Dillen cocked an eyebrow at her. "What did I do?"

"After we have been the parted ways the last time, the druid has asked of me to do some tasks for her. I am not knowing where this path will be taking me, but for now, I am happy to be doing her a service."

They slowed their pace, allowing Imariel and Lothak to take the lead.

"I am very happy to hear that." Dillen felt a smile force its way through the anxiety. "You are a very talented warrior, and a genuinely kind soul. I don't think I ever got the chance to thank you... both for your aid in the forest and... for believing in me. I don't think I would have survived that ordeal without you and Imariel."

Shesh'ra looked at the elf ahead of them, and the scales on her head contorted into what Dillen thought was a frown. "She is not to be speaking with you again?"

"No," Dillen said and felt his heart sink. "It's... complicated."

Dillen had to wonder if she would still not be talking with him even had he not told her the truth. She still had to blame him for her mother's death. It was his call to action, that he kept reminding himself, that led to the attack on the elves. Even though Imariel and Elissa did not have a "typical" relationship, as most humans would see it, he knew just how much she cared for her mother from the alone time he spent with Imariel.

Reminding him of that decision he had made were the ruins of the once glorious city. While not completely destroyed, it was a shell of what it used to be. The elves had busily begun reconstruction, bringing in wood and rope to try and repair the damaged structures; but it would be a while for Calanemel to regain its glory, which was made clear from the scorched and empty plots where trees once stood. With the help of the Lady's wonders, they would surely be able to re-nurture the land back to green.

As he scanned through the remnants of the once-proud sanctuary, he caught the eyes of an elf that glared with a burning intensity. Then he began to notice the others – everywhere he turned, he saw or felt the intensity in which they were trying to tell him that this was his fault. And Dillen knew it was true. He was responsible for this destruction, and for Elissa's death.

He deserved their ire.

Dillen forced the anxiety and the guilt aside as they approached a wooden building, elevated several feet high by planked landings, that seemed to be built into one of the oldest and largest remaining trees. Even with the simplicity of natural beauty, there was an essence of grandness and importance, of elven craftsmanship that went into the walls that blended into the bark of the trees and accented with bits of gold. The two gladestalkers that stood guard saluted Imariel as she led the group through – but not before giving Dillen a lingering stare.

The room they walked into was wide, and flowers grew and spread across the dark-wood walls in a multitude of colors. Sun beamed in from windows that barely interrupted the floras' trail. There were stairs on the right side that curved around the interior up to a second floor, shielded by a banister of twisted roots and vines that led to a curtain of green moss. The lithe form of Haili stood tall before it, despite the gnarled vine cane in her hand, looking down at her guests with a slight smile.

"Thank you, Imariel." Haili slowly approached the stairs and descended elegantly with long strides. "And I trust you gave the order to the rest of the Eastfort?"

"Yes, Druid Haili, I did exactly as you ordered. The knight named Farn relayed your wishes to the others. They have begun assembling men for battle. We did not encounter any signs of the Nightstalkers on the way here."

She smiled warmly at Imariel and took her hands for a moment. Dillen could see Imariel fighting internal emotions; as if in that moment, she and Haili had an unspoken thought about Elissa. The druid turned to the others and nodded.

"Thank you, as well, Shesh'ra and Lothak. I have another task I would ask of both you, but first I'd like to speak with Sir Dillen. Please, take this time to rest until I call for you, all three of you."

"Thank you, Druid Haili." It was Lothak who spoke, guttural and rumbling, and he bowed his head slightly. "I will be awaiting your word."

Shesh'ra bowed and followed Lothak out the door; Imariel left a moment after them both.

"The brute certainly has a way with words." Dillen turned to look at Haili once the trio had left and jerked a thumb toward the door. "That Lothak, I mean."

"Not all people incessantly wag their tongues as freely as you, Dillen Genemer." Haili's smile was thin and her eyes narrowed slightly – but her tone suggested that she wasn't aggravated with Dillen.

"My apologies, Druid." Dillen bowed his head. "You called for me?"

"Yes, I did. Come with me."

Haili pointed with her cane to the hall underneath the branched balcony. Dillen tentatively followed, the sounds of chirping birds echoing every thumping footstep on the wood floor. They passed several moss-curtained doors before Haili chose one. Dillen followed her through, up the stairs, and surprisingly, out to a balcony. They overlooked the entirety of Calenemel, and they stood in silence for a moment as Haili seemed to be watching the rest of the elves working, both on the ground below and eye-level in the trees.

Dillen stood in uncomfortable silence beside her, wondering several times if he should speak. What stopped him was a feeling as if something was calling out to him, reaching into the depths of his mind. He worried for a moment it was the abominations from before, working their strange magic on him again, like the hallucinations of his brother.

But this was different. This was more like...

"You sense it, do you not?"

Dillen was startled and braced himself on the dark oak balcony as he turned to Haili. She stared at him, impassively, for a few moments. Dillen couldn't find the right words to respond to her, and so Haili turned to stare back at her people below.

"I have heard what happened to you during your quest for penance. Those who have transgressed the Lady and her word do not often return. You will recall the centaur, Inadru Rainborne. He was exiled for allowing a mother and her child, who stole from the forest, to leave. That woman, terrified by the sight of Inadru and his scouts, claimed that the centaurs had threatened her, and so her people came back in an attempt to burn down our forest. The Lady, clearly, did not allow that to happen, but those people killed several innocent centaurs in retaliation – including some of Inadru's kin."

Dillen thought back to the centaur who stood trial with his head held high, believing in his convictions. If he was put in the same situation, would Dillen not do the same? What if the villagers he saved were the ones that attacked Calenemel? Would there have even been a chance for penance like the centaur had been offered?

"Inadru did not survive his exile, if that is what you are wondering."

Dillen locked eyes with Haili. He felt a heaviness in his stomach and a strange sadness. "That could have been my fate."

"Yes, it could have." Haili nodded. "But it was not. We are always sad to lose such strong, noble warriors such as Inadru, but such is the path of balance. You, Dillen Genemer, are the other part of that balance. You had allies that believed in you, and warriors that were willing to walk beside you into darkness. We lost a strong warrior, but in you, our forces have gained something extraordinary."

"You're talking about," Dillen paused as that calling reached out strongly to his mind. "You're talking about the Armor of Tides?"

Haili nodded.

"A relic of the former Brotherhood's true power. While the Green Lady has recovered several of them, every one we add to her forces is a great boon to her cause. The power of the armor, the natural affinity with water — it coalesces very well with the forces of nature, does it not?"

Dillen nodded, but he honestly wasn't sure. He didn't know much about magic, and less even about the Armor of Tides or the Brotherhood's history. He did know it meant a lot to Bhadein...

"Forgive me, Druid. What exactly does this armor do?"

Haili tapped the base of her cane on the deck a few times, as if thinking pensively. "Magic works in wondrous ways. All magic or forms of magic don't work the same way. I can sense the power within the armor that you collected, I can feel the touch of the Lady's waters through the very essence of the material. When the pieces were first collected, individually, they did not exude magical energy. But now, water flows from the center of the breastplate, down through the fingertips and toes."

Dillen felt his own hand twitch unconsciously, as if something was running down his elbow to his fingertips. Haili must have noticed this and stared at his hand before she turned to head back inside. He took one last look at the elves and their allies at work below. The tragedy that occurred there would never happen again, if he could help it.

Dillen followed her back down the stairs and through another curtain. The room they entered was small and dark, lit by only a few candles that illuminated a table in the center. There was no mistaking the Armor of Tides that was spread out on it. The light blue pulsing breath of water coursed silently through the connecting joints of the pieces.

Dillen brought a hand up, barely realizing as it moved toward the table. He stopped himself and looked at Haili. She was watching him, her lips pursed into a slight smile and her eyes shining with curiosity.

"I-I'm sorry, I don't..." Dillen stammered but then trailed off.

"Dillen Genemer, you have much to atone for. The destruction of Calenemel is your fault. You led the knights of the Eastfort away from their posts under the banner of 'protecting innocents'. Beyond that, whatever secrets and shadows you hold within your heart are yours to deal with." Haili stared at Dillen when she said this, and Dillen couldn't help but look away, feeling his face flush. "But, it is clear that you have a connection with this armor. It is as if this armor has cho-..."

Haili stopped and looked toward the curtain. Dillen drew himself away from the armor to turn around. At first, he thought there was nothing there; but then he heard it, the sound of someone screaming. They were calling for Haili.

The druid hurried back toward the entrance, Dillen quick at her heels, despite the voice in his head telling him to stay. A young gladestalker, fair of hair and skin tone, nearly threw himself on the planks at the base of Haili's domain. The guards walked down to help him stand. Behind the elf, Imariel, Lothak, Shesh'ra, and many of the inhabitants stopped what they were doing to watch.

"Speak, young gladestalker. What has brought you here to call my name with such urgency?"

"M-My apologies Druid Haili," the elf gasped between deep breaths. "I hurried here as fast as I could. The knights from the Eastfort have been ambushed by the nightmare creatures!"

Dillen looked instinctively at Imariel. She looked away, but he saw her face flash with concern. They might not have been the people of the woods, but she knew how much they meant to Dillen. He turned to Haili, and she regarded him coolly.

"You see the state of Calenemel. We cannot afford to dispatch reinforcements. We need every able warrior here to defend our people. This should not be a new situation for your knights; they wear heavy armor and are trained to fight in wars."

"Yes, against other human foes – but not against these devilish beasts!" Dillen tried putting as much pleading into his voice as he could.

"These Brotherhood men stood against the forces of the Abyss, did they not?"

Dillen felt his heart sink and stumbled to find any words. It was just different; how could she not see that?

"Then... then if you cannot permit any of your people, allow me to go and help turn the tide!"

"If that is what you wish," Haili nodded and turned to leave, "then I allow you to go to their aid."

"Druid," Imariel stepped forward and respectfully kneeled. Haili turned to regard her with slight surprise. "Please allow me to accompany Sir Dillen. I still must avenge my mother, and I would see personally these creatures gone from our land."

Haili nodded. "Do any others wish to aid our human brethren?"

Lothak stepped forward. "I ask that you allow me to go and protect the gladestalker, Druid."

Shesh'ra came after the salamander. "I am to be doing better fighting these foes than I am to be building. My spear yearns to be whetted."

Haili regarded the four warriors for a moment. "Very well. May the Lady be with you all. Dillen Genemer, you have failed Calenemel before. I pray you do not do so again."

Dillen looked at Haili with as much conviction as he could muster. "With these allies, I promise you that I shall not. But before I go, I ask of you to allow me to take the Armor of Tides with me."

Haili pursed her lips in amusement. "To wear into battle?"

"No," Dillen shook his head. "The armor is not mine to wear. I have never been a member of the Brotherhood. But with it restored, I think I know someone who can make use of its powers."

A look flashed across the druid's face – was it disappointment, Dillen wondered? – but she pointed inside with her cane. "Then let us make haste if you wish to aid your allies."

Chapter XXXIV

Dillen leaned into the horse and pressed it as fast as it could go. The Armor of Tides, bundled up and hanging from the saddle beside him, was weighing his otherwise nimble steed down. They managed to avoid any hanging branches, and the horses luckily hadn't tripped over any roots or stumps – as if Nature itself had known their intent and cleared the way for them.

"We are to be drawing close to where the gladestalker did say!" Shesh'ra called out from Dillen's left.

"I can hear the sounds of battle just ahead!" Imariel called from Dillen's right.

Dillen felt his hands trembling as he held onto the reins, and he knew it wasn't just from the speed he was traveling. He exhaled deeply and kept his eyes straight ahead.

"I want to let you know that I appreciate all the help you lot have given me! Even you there, my stoic friend!" Dillen looked past Imariel on the other side where Lothak rode, and he gave the salamander a wink. Lothak sneered and sent smoke pluming from his nostrils.

Dillen started to hear what Imariel had – the sound of blades colliding, of orders being barked, and inhuman things screaming their terror. The latter only grew in intensity as they came closer. Once through the last clearing, Dillen could see the knights and a scattering of elves, their shield wall fending off the creatures as best as they could, but they were being forced closer together. Scarecrows hacked mercilessly with their scythed arms – but interspersed in them were one kind of the other grotesque things that Dillen had seen before. They stood on two disjointed legs and had long pointed appendages that came out of their shoulder blades.

Spurring his horse into one last burst of speed, he tore his blade from its sheath and bore down on one of the creatures with a yell. He cleaved across the back of a scarecrow, sending its head twirling through the air. He turned around to the other side and brought his sword down to sever the incoming talons of one of the other creatures. It screamed at him, and he saw a face full of teeth and no eyes. Wanting to expel the devilish sight from his mind, Dillen thrust his blade through the open maw. Once the creature quivered and became still, he flicked it off the end of his blade.

He swung back over to deflect another attack and watched as an arrow pierced the side of his foe's skull – and then another made sure it was put down only moments after. Before he could continue his momentum, Shesh'ra's armored steed crashed through the lines of scarecrows. The horse's hooves rose into the air and slammed down to trample the nightmarish creatures. The naiad reached down with her spear to swing and impale any that came close.

There was no sign of Lothak's horse as the salamander appeared and charged into the line of horrors. He swung his axe brutally in both hands, cutting swathes through the foes. Dillen pushed through the line, making sure Imariel was still beside him.

"It's Sir Dillen!" someone called as he approached and dismounted.

He handed the reins hurriedly to Imariel. "Find Bhadein – get him the armor! You can unleash your vengeance once I know the armor is safe!"

She hesitated, as if to argue, but she turned and brought the horse with her. Dillen spared her one last glance before he rushed to the front of the shieldwall.

"Knights of the Green Lady! On me!" Dillen raised his sword high before bringing it back into position with both hands. "We push them back as one! Press the attack! Do not let them turn your fear against you!"

One by one, the former Brotherhood knights formed on either side of him. Dillen exchanged determined looks with Lenel on his right and Ragneld on his left, and then the knights moved forward to meet the surge of creatures. He ran forward and tore into the first scarecrow with savage ferocity, plowing through it and into the next one. He ripped the blade up to his left to deflect a claw that just barely missed his face. The scarecrow came on him quickly, grasping onto his sword with both of its clawed hands. Even though the blade cut into whatever 'flesh' the creature had, it remained undaunted as it tried to pull the weapon away. He was saved by a knight who impaled the scarecrow in the head; but it was not defeated. It turned its head, the blade still in it, at the attacker. Dillen used that opportunity to break free and cut the creature down – piercing it on the ground to make sure it was defeated.

He didn't have time to thank the knight or even see who it was. He saw the next vicious foe, with its shoulder-talon appendages, looming at him before he could raise his sword. Dillen was not ready for the embrace of darkness – and just as he cursed his luck, the talons drooped and the creature split in half vertically. Lothak tore the two halves in opposite directions, pushed Dillen behind him with one hand, and cleaved down through another faceless horror poised to kill.

"If you continue to dive headfirst into combat, your carelessness will be your end!" the salamander boomed as he slammed a thick shoulder into a scarecrow that was poised to stab a knight in the back.

"It's not carelessness!" Dillen spat back, sweeping the legs from a scarecrow and then impaling it. "I have to set things right! They can't regroup!"

"Then we must be for taking the leader!" Shesh'ra jumped in from Dillen's other side, pinning a scarecrow down with the tip of her spear. She stabbed again and again until it stopped moving.

Dillen grunted as he parried a scarecrow's scythe-hand. It brought the other one in and tried to pry the blade from Dillen's grasp, but he forcefully kicked it off. Knocked back with its arms sprawled, Dillen ran the creature through. He heard a horrible sound in his right ear that caused him to recoil with his sword brought up. One of the faceless horrors managed to scrape its spike appendage across his Basilean pauldron, but it failed to find an opening. Dillen shook the chills from his body, but before he could fight back against it, two of the knights charged and ran it through with spears. The creature flailed, its shoulder appendages swirling deadly in the air. Lothak hurried to the creature, taking a swiping blow from the talons against his scales, and lopped its head off with a vicious swing.

Dillen spun around; Shesh'ra was right – he had to find the leader and put a stop to their assault. His eyes opened wide as he heard a high-pitched wail. He turned to the sound and felt himself rolling along the ground until he was flat on his back. Dillen looked up at the creature on top of him, and under the hood of the spectral being was a mouth of sharp teeth and a tongue that slowly crawled out and caressed the side of Dillen's face. He screamed and tried to fight his way off, but the creature held his arms fast under the weight of its knees. Dillen felt the urge to fight being drained from him, as if his soul was being sucked from his body.

He saw long nails rise, poised to strike, and Dillen inhaled. With one swift roll, he forced his body off the ground and into a kneeling position. The nails came down, but it jolted the phantom's aim enough that Dillen was able to bring his arm up. It saved him a killing blow, but he felt the talons pierce through his gauntlet and sent a burning pain through his body. He yelped, and the hooded creature forced its nails in deeper. Dillen screamed, and he felt stars blur his vision.

Dillen just barely heard Shesh'ra's own scream as she rushed toward him. The translucent creature pulled its nails out of Dillen, extended them to the length of swords, and it used them to bat away the spear thrust. Dillen clutched his injured forearm and watched the naiad fight as she swung both ends of the spear to beat back the phantom. The creature seemed to be completely made up of a spectral, purple cloak that floated above the ground, with haunting, twisted skulls at the bottom of it that made Dillen wish he could flee. It took all he had in him to stay his ground.

Lothak roared past Dillen and added his brutal axe swing to the onslaught of Shesh'ra's spear. The phantom moved like smoke with every attack; its claws parried one blade while it would twist unnaturally away from the other. Dillen watched and tried to find a pattern in its movements, despite the searing pain. It undulated away from one attack while it would parry the other, swaying almost rhythmically... If Dillen could exploit that...

He stood and grabbed his sword in both hands, fighting his injury as much as his body allowed, and circled around the back of the creature, away from that hideous face. He waited for it to swerve away in one direction, and then he rushed in to attack. With a grunt of exertion, he thrust his sword into the body of the cloak, and he was elated for it to find purchase. It was a sickening noise that didn't sound human, but it was wet.

Dillen stared up in horror as the head whipped around, and its tongue lashed out and wrapped itself around the embedded blade. Tightly it squeezed, until the blade was soaked in strange, purple blood; and then it reared back and whipped the weapon out of his body. Dillen held onto the handle, just barely, as he flew back and rolled against the ground.

He grunted with effort as he got back to his feet, but he smiled. His attack had provided the opening he had hoped for. He heard a howl from the creature as Shesh'ra's spear dug through its body and out the other side.

"To the Abyss with you!" Lothak roared as he raised his axe over his head. The phantom managed to step out of the way to avoid a killing blow, but one of its long arms disintegrated in spectral smoke.

Dillen's smile vanished. Enraged, the creature lashed out with its remaining clawed hand and knocked the naiad and salamander away from it. Its shriek was harsh, like nails being dragged down glass, and its tongue warbled in the air; but Dillen found his courage and charged the nightmare once more. As he went to swing down, the tongue whipped out and struck Dillen on the shoulder, causing him to stagger. Knocked off balance, Dillen couldn't do anything to stop the claws that descended on his chest.

Pain wracked his body and took him to his knees once more. The claws, nightmarish razor-sharp spikes, tore through his Basilean armor in three large incisions. He felt the blood trickle down, warm on his skin, and he fought the urge to vomit. He stared up at the creature, eyes wide, and he felt as helpless as the giant gore that he and Farn had killed all those weeks ago in their hunting expedition. Gods, but that felt like an eternity ago now!

Thwap!

An arrow hit the phantom in the top of the hood. It barely had time to turn before another found purchase. It shook its head vigorously, trying to discard the projectiles, when a third knocked the creature's head back. The Nightstalker drunkenly turned and cried out. Dillen turned and saw Imariel, striding out toward them, loosing arrows as quickly as her arms would allow.

Two more feathered shouts sprouted from the phantom's chest before Dillen heard Imariel cursing his name and barking orders at him.

"Kill it!"

Dillen raised his sword and aimed at the hood. The creature turned, slower, and the tongue hung limp as the sword pierced the dark veil. He pulled the blade out and dropped it from the pain in his arm, and the phantom finally touched the ground. It fell onto its remaining arm with one final groan, and then it gave way to purple clouds of vapor. Dillen dragged his sword up and into its scabbard with his good hand.

Imariel started to walk to him, but she froze. Something like a cross between anger and concern flashed across her face.

"I'm fine," Dillen managed through gasping breaths. "The armor?"

"I... I left it with Farn. Are the others safe?"

"I will be all right," Shesh'ra said as she stepped forward. She held one arm and had small cuts that nearly blended in with the vicious swirls of her burn scars to the point where it was hard to tell where the fresh wounds ended and the old wounds began. Her spear dragged heavily at her feet. Lothak appeared behind her, no more battered than the naiad as he stood tall, back to his usual stoicism.

Like smoke in the wind, the remaining Nightstalkers vanished. The last scarecrows seemed to stop where they were, being run down with ease; and the last of the shoulder-talon creatures were suicidal in their vicious assault, but they lacked the tenacity seen earlier. Silence flooded the clearing.

"That takes care of that." Dillen touched his chest and instantly cringed. Seven Circles of the Abyss, did it hurt. "Right, let's see-..."

"Sir Dillen!"

His name echoed clearly through the otherwise stillness. Dillen's brow furrowed when he saw Farn running to him, panic on his face. He nearly collapsed as he reached Dillen; his body was shaking, and the color was gone from his face.

"Farn? Farn, what is it?"

"Bha... Bhadein, he..." Farn took a deep breath and looked Dillen in the eyes. "He's wounded. Mortally."

Dillen worked his jaw open and shut a few times, but he couldn't find words.

"Go," Imariel said. He turned to look at her; her features had softened. There was almost pity there. He wasn't sure if it was the wound across his chest or the news Farn brought, but Dillen nodded his head and painfully turned to follow him.

He hadn't taken more than ten steps when he knew where Bhadein was; he saw the crowd of knights huddled around the base of a gnarled tree. He pushed past them, Farn in tow, to find Bhadein nestled in the overgrown roots.

His chest had a gaping wound in it, his armor ripped open, and the shoulder-talon of one of the faceless creatures lay mangled at his side; the cleaver was bloody and dark. Bhadein had a slight smirk on his face as Dillen approached, blood dribbling out the corner of his mouth.

"The armor," Dillen said as he turned to face Farn. "Where is the armor?"

"He won't wear it." The blond-haired knight shook his head and pointed to where the bundled pieces were propped up against the tree. "I've implored him, but he refuses to put it on."

"It's... not mine to wear," Bhadein said weakly as Dillen knelt down beside him. "It has not chosen me, and besides... It's too late... for me. I'm an... old man. I've seen my share... of adventures. I've had a... good life. Defended what I loved. To the very end."

"Dammit, Bhadein! Don't be foolish! This armor can heal your wounds, it can save you!" Dillen's hands trembled as he pointed to the nearby Armor of Tides. "You must wear it!"

Bhadein laughed as best as he could, spitting up blood in the process. "As much as you've tried to change... You're still the same... Sir Dillen. Who says I must? I... I cannot. The armor is not... mine."

"To the Abyss with rites and traditions! You'd forego your life because you're not a Knight of Redemption?! I won't hear it!" Dillen moved toward the armor, intent on putting the pieces on Bhadein himself, and he turned to Farn. "Come on, help me with it!"

"No." Bhadein's voice was deep, like a growl. "It will not work... I have not been... chosen. All that would happen... would be that you'd put a suit of armor on a dying man. The magic, it..."

Bhadein's voice trailed off. Dillen's head spun. Magic. He didn't know anything about magic, but this had to work!

"Sir Dillen." The knight was snapped back to the moment as he looked down at Bhadein. "Come close. Please."

Against his better judgment, Dillen abandoned the Armor of Tides and kneeled down next to the barely conscious Bhadein.

"You must wear it. You... have to wear the Armor of Tides."

Dillen's eyes widened and his mouth fell agape. "What?! You refuse to, and in your final moments, you insist that I have to? I... I can't. I..."

"You must!" Bhadein pointed at Dillen's chest. "It has chosen you. Haili had come to me and said... It has chosen, and... Your wound... You must... heal."

"Bhadein, I'm sorry, I..."

"Dillen." Bhadein grew serious, holding Dillen's hand with a great amount of strength. "If not for yourself, do it for the people of this forest. The knights. You must... You must..."

Bhadein's head lolled backward against the tree, and his grip fell slack and slipped silently out of Dillen's hands. Dillen stood and turned to look at the other assembled knights. They were staring at him, and Dillen had a hard time reading their expressions. Was it hate that Bhadein had told an outsider to take their most sacred armor with his final breath and not them? Was it respect for the older knight's last words that Dillen had been chosen by the armor? Was that why Haili had been watching him so intensely?

Farn cleared his throat and Dillen turned to him. His eyes were watery, and he had a hard time maintaining eye contact. "We'll... prepare to bring his body back to the Eastfort."

Dillen could only manage a nod. As Farn and the others tended to Bhadein's corpse, Dillen grabbed the armor and went around to the other side of the tree. He watched and waited a few moments, making sure nothing else was lurking in the forest. He untied the bundle and laid the pieces out carefully. He felt that calling in his mind stronger than ever.

"Why, Bhadein...?" Dillen muttered as he stared at the pieces, his hands trembling from rage. Could it have saved Bhadein's life, if he just put the damn armor on? Dillen didn't know the first thing about magic, but here he was, trying to fight fate once more, only to become a slave to it again. The armor had chosen him. Haili had known it. Bhadein had known it. Seven Circles of the Abyss, even Dillen had known it, deep down. But what did he want for himself? He wasn't even a member of the Brotherhood!

He stared angrily at the armor, ready to cast it all into the forest and scream at the top of his lungs at the Green Lady and her will, but then Bhadein's words kept echoing in his mind. Do it for the people of the forest.

The people of the forest. The same people he had hurt by disobeying orders to try and help outsiders. Everything he did, every choice he made, had been followed by someone getting hurt. His choice to be a mercenary, his choice to claim he had slain an Abyssal beast, his choice to take the knights out of the forest and away from Eastfort, his choice to attack the Brothermark knight.

He stared at the armor. His choices.

He wanted to be redeemed. He wanted to live and fight for the cause of good. He wanted to make something of himself and this wretched life that he had left instead of living in the shadow of a legacy that was not truly his own. And with every thought like that he had, the Armor of Tides pulled at him stronger. Maybe that was why the wearers were called Knights of Redemption.

Maybe, he too, could be redeemed still.

"To the Abyss with fate. I have done so much wrong, I need to start making amends... And this armor. Maybe this can be a tool to help me do so..."

Before he knew what he was doing, Dillen was equipping the armor; the sabatons, the greaves, the gauntlets, and then the cuirass – everything except for the helmet, which was strangely missing. Well, he attempted to put it all on. He cursed under his breath as he fumbled with the buckles.

"I suppose this is what squires are for," he muttered out loud.

"Indeed," Farn said as he came from around the tree and looked at Dillen with a raised eyebrow. "Normally I'd say this is a bit below my station, but in this case, it would be an honor to buckle the Armor of Tides."

Dillen bowed his head, feeling embarrassment color his cheeks. "Thank you, Farn, truly."

With each piece he put on and Farn helped strap, Dillen heard the calming sound of a running stream in his ears, of the flow of water overtaking his every sense and bringing him peace of mind.

"I have to tell you." Dillen could just barely hear Farn over the rush of water. "Whatever reason you had to say what you did back at the fort... One thing I know is true. You are haunted by the past, the stories that they tell, but you are a good person, Dillen. You inspire people. You inspire me. And I'm glad that the armor chose you."

When Farn clinked the last latch of the cuirass in place, Dillen reached down and felt for the triangular crest. He placed his palm against it, and Dillen felt as if a tide of water washed past him.

He looked up, and Bhadein, in a spectral form, stood before him. Dillen was shocked, but he could not move or speak. He almost didn't recognize him – this Bhadein looked younger, more well-groomed, and bore the proud armor of the Brotherhood. The knight beamed as he walked toward Dillen, his arms folded behind his back.

"I am proud to see you wearing the armor of our people. To have the Armor of Redemption carry on its legacy." Bhadein's words flowed into Dillen's ears as if drifting along through a stream of water. He could hear the laugh of a brook flowing over stones underneath the familiar tones of the former knight. "You will do us proud. Watch over them for me. Especially Farn. He's a good lad."

Bhadein put his hand on Dillen's shoulder, and then he was gone. And so was the pain in Dillen's chest. He didn't need to look to know that he was healed. There was a slight coolness underneath the cuirass as the armor's magic must have been working.

Dillen turned to look at Farn, but the other knight said nothing; as if he had not seen Bhadein just standing before them. Instead, Farn stepped back a few feet to get a better look at Dillen fully armored. Imariel, Shesh'ra, and Lothak must have seen this and joined them. Farn let out an audible gasp, and Dillen thought he saw tears – whether they were from before or not, he wasn't sure.

"Your wound?" Imariel asked, anxiety just barely present, hidden in her voice.

"It's healed." Dillen placed his forearm on his chest, over the symbol on the gilded Armor of Tides. "It really has chosen me. I can feel the magic within

270

having activated."

Shesh'ra nodded respectfully. "It is as much one with you now as you are one with it."

Dillen smiled, about to retort, when a horn sounded above the trees and made his heart sink once more. The others shared the same expression as they listened to the call.

"They have begun their final attack in earnest," Lothak snarled into the shadows of the woods.

"We must return to Druid Haili!" Imariel protested.

"At once." Dillen nodded. He looked at the Basilean cuirass at his feet, torn asunder, but still recognizable as what it was. He picked it up and turned to Farn. "You are with us?"

"Of course. I was going to send two rangers and a knight to bring Bhadein back, but the rest of us are ready to claim vengeance on these bastards."

"Can you make sure this gets back to my belongings at the Eastfort?"

Farn awkwardly, almost hesitantly, accepted the piece of armor. He frowned as he looked at it, but he nodded to Dillen. "Yes. Of course."

Chapter XXXV

Dillen led the Green Lady's forces on foot as they charged into a group of Nightstalkers. He felt a peace of mind and determination as he swung his sword at a pumpkin-headed scarecrow. Sure, he was terrified and knew that every breath he took might be his last, but the pull of magic within the armor seemed to soothe the thoughts that would make his sword arm tremble. He knew he stood out in his new golden armor, and he knew the knights were all watching him – both not willing to be outdone by him and determined to follow his lead.

A scythe came in to hook his wrist, and Dillen tussled with the creature. He slammed the pommel of his sword into the pumpkin head; instead of spilling orange strings and seeds, foul purple liquid oozed out of the rent. Dillen was temporarily stunned, and the scarecrow slammed its head forward. Dillen was able to ram his sword through the chest of his foe, but not before the purple fluid dripped onto his cheek. It burned, and no matter how hard Dillen fought to wipe, it would not come off. He dropped his sword and shield, and he fell to the grass to try and clean his face, but it only burned the leaves to cinders. He forced himself to come back to the moment despite the pain, as a scythe swiped down right by his head. He could feel the malevolence of the wielder, and he turned to look as the Nightstalker raised its blade once more.

And again, Dillen was saved by a brutal axe that cleaved the foe asunder. Lothak pushed through and stood before Dillen, blocking the attacks of two more scarecrows. He used his massive tail to bat away a few of the smaller fanged creatures that voraciously dove toward Dillen. Shesh'ra leapt in with her spear, impaling a barking shadowhound that a few elves had pinned, and Imariel's arm flailed back rapidly to keep pulling arrows from her quiver to support the charging knights.

He knew that Velorun's encampment was being attacked – that the Nightstalkers were making their final desperate push; but the question was how? With the anchor purified, their source of power should have been all but gone.

Unless they found a new anchor that was giving them the strength for this show of force...

A shadowhound knocked Lothak aside as if he were a doll and charged straight through to Dillen, howling from both of its heads. The knight managed to find his shield and brought it up to block, but the hound dove and tackled him. They rolled on the ground, Dillen keeping the shield between the gnashing heads; but when they stopped, Dillen could not move his limbs. He was pinned. The beast snapped with both of its maws, but the shield held fierce.

That was, until one of the heads forced its way underneath and knocked the shield up and out of Dillen's grasp. It raised one paw and walloped Dillen, tearing its long nails down the side of his face.

The knight cried out in agony, feeling sick to his stomach from the sound of his skin tearing. The pain was so intense, he nearly didn't hear the scream from behind his foe. He just barely saw as Farn impaled his sword in the creature's side, and it yelped and turned its maws toward him. As it lunged, Lothak intervened and caught one of the heads in his hands, holding the jaw shut. It thrashed and clawed at the salamander with the other one, and Dillen could see wounds forming on his scaly ally. Dillen forced himself up, fumbled on the ground for his sword, and he and Farn as one drove their blades through the hound. That still was not enough. It roared and wheeled on them, knocking Lothak to the ground. But then an elf impaled it with a long spear – and then a knight hacked a wound deep in its side – followed by two more elves joined the fight with spears. The mouths drooped, and the creature's movements became slow. The hulking salamander got to his feet and roared as it cracked down with his axe overhead. The shadowhound seized with a final shudder.

"Lothak!" Dillen croaked as the salamander fell to one knee. "Are you all right?!"

The salamander seemed dazed, but he shook himself upright.

"I will be fine. And it seems you will be as well."

Dillen had felt the cool breeze brush across his cheek, but when he put his hand to it, the burning from the pumpkin head and the mark the claws had left on him seemed to be healing – and after a moment, he felt nothing at all there. Despite the wounds healing, he still felt winded and very shaky. Perhaps the armor could heal injuries, but Dillen knew that the physical body could only take so much.

There was an inhuman wail from the depths of the forest, and it sent a chill down Dillen's spine. That was no creature that served the Lady that he knew of.

"We need to hurry," Imariel said to Dillen as the warriors regrouped around them. "We don't know how many more of these creatures wait between us and Velorun."

Dillen nodded. "You take the lead with me. Everyone else, stay close to us! Leave no man behind!"

Dillen ran as quickly as he could, but between his new armor and still trying to catch his breath, he felt it a daunting task. Imariel started gaining speed, leading them through the darkness of the boughs. Dillen had no idea where he was. Despite knowing the paths reasonably well, every tree looked the same; every trail seemed identical. His breath was coming in ragged as he forced himself through the exhaustion.

All the while, the cackle and screams of the nightmares followed all around.

Panic clawed at the corner of Dillen's thoughts, threatening to become all-encompassing; only the strength provided by the Armor of Tides, channeling his better qualities, kept him sane. Waves of calm ebbed across his mind, keeping his mind on the mission.

"Can you feel that?!" Lenel shouted. "I've spent enough time fighting by the Abyss to know fire!"

"He's right!" Farn said, close by. "Sir Dillen, tread carefully!"

There was a loud pop, and a grand oak tree before them exploded in flames, crashing down in front of Imariel. She brought her arms up to shield herself and stepped back, nearly falling. Lothak ran up to her and pulled her back as another tree came down around them. Lothak brought the elf back, and Dillen's heart sunk as he saw scorch marks on her arms, her eyes wide and confused.

"Is she all right?"

"She is stunned and scorched. She will need time to come to her senses."

Another loud pop and crack, and there was more commotion behind them. The knights pushed forward as their retreat was blocked by another flaming tree. Dillen cursed under his breath.

"We need to be moving away from this smoke!" Shesh'ra barked through a cough.

"We're trapped!" One of the rangers screamed, panic corroding his words. "We'll be cooked!"

"Calm yourself, brother!" Farn shouted back. "We need to pull together and find a way out!"

Despite the increasing chance of death by smoke inhalation, Dillen looked down to his hand. Something felt as if it were reaching out to touch him. That strange, invisible presence that called out to him, that swirled all around him, seemed to be manifesting in his hand. Like the raging ocean, a whirlpool circled around his fist – magic.

He raised the other fist, and it too had a magical current. Without giving it another moment's thought, Dillen thrust both of his fists forward, toward the fallen tree before them, and the water exploded forth. The torrent raged forward, surging across the obstacle, and blanketing the flames. There was a cry, muted by coughs, that went up behind him as the men ran forward, leaping up, over, and around the tree.

Dillen followed them, shock propelling him forward. He had known about artifacts that granted magical power, but to actually cast water! He hadn't actually done it though; he had no control over what just happened. It had come to him. He looked down at his fists; whatever magical energy had been there was gone. The armor must have needed time to reattune its strength.

The other knights around him slowed until they stopped, and Dillen looked around.

"Why," Dillen panted, "why are we stopping? We're not safe yet!" As if to echo Dillen's statement, a deep scream echoed through the darkness.

"S-Sir Dillen, we don't know the way!" Ragneld choked out.

"I can stand," Imariel said weakly, pushing herself out of Lothak's arms. She swayed drunkenly to her feet and walked forward until her balance stabilized.

She looked at Dillen, but there was no time for words. Dillen followed Imariel as they tore through the woods, the rest of their group following close behind. The cries and the now constant heat of the flames were starting to finally pierce his resolve. Dark patches in between trees held faces that shouldn't have been there; every branch that reached out to touch him felt like an icy claw down his spine. They were afraid – all of them he led, and this was exactly what the Nightstalkers fed on. The darkness of the forest that he had once been afraid of was now amplified. Nothing was safe here. Every step, every path, led to death. And Dillen was terrified.

He was trusting Imariel's sense of direction, blindly, and even she was beginning to look confused.

"Imariel, please tell me we're still going the right way." She didn't respond. He glanced briefly back at the knights, rangers, and elves following and could see the mix of determination, fury, and worry on their faces. He turned back to her again. "Imariel? Do you sti-..."

"Yes," she cut in bitingly. "I just need..."

"Need what?" Dillen tried to implore as calmly as he could, but every moment they spent cut off, he felt that the Nightstalkers could pounce and tear them to shreds.

"I just... need..." Imariel swayed uneasily on her feet. Dillen ran forward to support her and turned back.

"Lothak!"

The salamander barreled forward and scooped the elf into his arms. "She needs rest!"

"I know," Dillen barked, looking around them. "We've got to be close!"

Dillen's heart caught in his throat as he saw the shambling shapes coming through the eastern trees. They didn't have much more time.

"Move! Forward, everyone!"

"Lead them, Dillen!" Shesh'ra took her spear out and stood before him. "I will be stalling them."

"Don't stall any longer than you have to!"

Dillen gave her a final confident nod before he rushed past the knights, waving them forward. Everything was a blur. He thought that things began to look familiar; he thought he recognized a familiar rock pattern or dip in the road, but he also thought his mind was playing tricks on him. Everything in the darkness of the woods looked alike, and more than once, he saw shadows of creatures waiting in the depths beyond sight. Stars dotted his vision from the strain on his body.

In his mind, he said every prayer he could think of, begging the armor to give his trembling legs the courage he needed to persevere. He could feel it, niggling in the back of his mind, trying to penetrate through the fear, but it felt like some dark fog was blocking it. He held onto that tiny shred of hope and forced himself to use it to believe they would survive.

Then the sounds of the nightmares began to quiet. The chittering and the moans began to fall off. Panting to the point of wheezing, Dylan turned around to see the monsters had stopped, almost as if they had hit an invisible line. Shesh'ra had rejoined them at some point – they all seemed to be accounted for, thank the Shining Ones.

A barrage of arrows flew overhead, overshadowing the dark around them, and slammed into the Nightstalkers, destroying all of their pursuers. Dillen turned to see the walls of Velorun's encampment, with the elf himself striding out to meet them.

We made it! Dillen couldn't help but think, his legs quivering despite his best efforts to still them, his chest burning with pain. He gave the elf a very weary smile.

"Velorun... I cannot tell you how good it is to see you," Dillen said, his breath catching between words.

"The same is felt for you and your forces, Sir Dillen." There was no mirth in his words, his expression tense. "I fear the situation is grave here."

Dillen held a hand up. "Before we continue, perhaps you could allow us a moment's rest?"

Velorun stared darkly at him. "I understand. But a moment is all we can allow."

Chapter XXXVI

D illen had managed to sit for a brief moment and down a waterskin before he returned to the task at hand. The thought of rest, even just sitting there for as long as he could, was oh so tempting, but the Nightstalkers would not wait for his respite. He forced himself up and headed toward Velorun's command table, but not before Farn, Lothak, and Shesh'ra insisted on coming with him, despite their own exhaustion and wounds. Imariel surely would have come as well, but they had left her in the care of some of Velorun's sages to let her rest and treat the burns.

Dillen took slow, deep breaths as he led the trio toward the elf that stood over a spread out map, staring pensively down at it.

"What's going on? Why have the Nightstalkers returned?" Dillen stopped in front of the table, looking down at the map and then back up at Velorun.

"They had never left in the first place," Velorun exhaled without looking up.

"How can that be the happening?" Shesh'ra crossed her arms as she too stared at the elf. "We did took the armor, and you did perform the cleansing, yes? Did your magic not be working?"

Velorun raised his head and glared at Shesh'ra. "I hope you are not questioning the powers of a druid."

Lothak snorted. "No one here disrespects our Lady's most sacred champions. But even magic has its limits, Druid."

Velorun shook his head and looked back down to the map. "It is true. Balance in all things. Even in magic, I must remind myself."

Dillen looked down at the map. There were markers in different locations across the deep forest that he had recovered the Armor of Tides from.

"If they never left, does that mean...?"

"Something is still anchoring them to the Lady's domain. There must be a piece of armor that we did not purify." The elf looked up from the map to look at Dillen – moreso the Armor of Tides. "It is amazing to see the armor put together, and just as I thought originally, it doesn't look like there's anything missing..."

"Could they anchor to a single piece of the armor? Could there be enough magic to sustain them?"

"Yes, it's entirely possible," Velorun mused and then gave Dillen a sideways look. "That would explain why they're being so aggressive. They're aware we took the base of their power to exist here. They want to push us back as much as possible until they can grasp something else to anchor to. But the question is what is missing?"

"The helmet." Dillen closed his eyes and exhaled deeply. When he opened them, Velorun's expression was a mix of rage and confusion. "I had the helmet when we were fleeing the forest... It must have... I must have..."

When Velorun spoke, his voice started low, almost like a growl. "You knew that a piece of the armor was missing and did not speak of it?"

"Honestly, no!" Dillen threw his arms out to the sides. "In case you forgot, there was a lot going on at the time, including my horse being torn asunder by a lightning bolt and nearly being killed by several monstrosities! It did not register until I put the whole armor on that it wasn't there. And if I don't have it, Haili didn't have it, and you don't have it..."

"Then it is the stalkers of the forest that have it," Shesh'ra cut in, her voice cold.

Velorun sighed and let his head droop, holding himself up with both arms on the table. "So that is it. That is how they are still here. There is at least some peace knowing what it is that we're looking for." The elf looked up and around to meet each of the warriors' gazes. "And I am confident in the where."

Farn stepped up to the table and examined the map. Beyond the symbol for where the camp was, and the obvious forest beyond it, Dillen couldn't make heads or tails of what was going on, let alone read the words printed there. Farn pondered over it for a moment before pointing to a spot northeast of where the camp was, in the darkness of the forest.

"You think the helmet is here?"

"Around there. Somewhere very close to where I've marked."

Dillen felt a strange whisper calling to him in the back of his mind, much like how the armor was calling to him in the past.

"How can you tell that?" Farn asked Velorun; Dillen barely heard him, too distracted by the sound he alone heard.

"Here are the areas where the enemy has been heavily on the offense." Velorun pointed to several markers on the map. He then slid his finger over to the area where Farn had pointed. "But here, we found that they act like they are defending something. Aggressive when we got too close, but they aren't pushing from there, like in other areas."

Farn said something else, but the whispers became stronger, causing Dillen to close his eyes. The hushed voice intensified until it mimicked the sound of the wind rushing around him. Within the blackness of shut eyes, Dillen could feel the helmet reaching out to him until he could visualize it in his mind, surrounded by purple shadowed tendrils. When the snaking appendages turned to him, as if to grab him, Dillen pulled his eyes open with an audible gasp, and all around turned to look at him.

"Northeast. It's northeast." The others looked stunned by Dillen's sudden revelation, but he gestured to the map. "Where are we? And where was the area you marked?"

"We're here," Velorun said slowly, pointing on the map. "How do you know it's northeast?"

"The helmet called out to me, it pulled my mind in the northeast direction from where I'm standing. Perhaps it could tell we were looking for it – I'm not sure. But I know what I felt."

Velorun slid his finger on the map, all the while continuing to look at Dillen. He looked down, and the elf was pointing to a marked area.

"That has to be it, then. We have to reclaim the helmet!"

"With all due respect, Sir Dillen, but with what army?" Farn shrugged as he looked at Dillen. "We can't ask to spare any aid if the attacks are fierce as Velorun says, and we can't fight through there with just our current force in the state they're in."

"There yet might be a solution," Velorun said as he stood tall. "I sent a messenger to Druid Haili to request aid. At first, she denied my request – which, after the destruction of Calenemel, I cannot blame her." Even though he was not looking at Dillen, he still felt his heart drop with embarrassment. "But I made sure to tell the messenger to plead our case with the wise druid. Haili knows that we are the last vestige of defense against the darkness deeper within. If we fall here, the scales tip in the favor of darkness. We lose the balance. She saw reason when he explained our situation."

"She does love her balance," Dillen said wryly.

"Then we must defend this location until reinforcements arrive," Lothak said, staring out into the depths of the trees.

"What do we do until then?" Farn asked, hesitantly watching Lothak's gaze.

Velorun looked up, the gravity of the situation reflected in his eyes. "We wait, and we prepare."

*****

Dillen sat with his back against a chest in the small tent. Imariel lay in the bed before him, her chest gently rising and falling, her eyes shut. He stared at the gauntlets he wore, playing with the fingertips gingerly. His heart beat heavily as he thought about the upcoming battle. They were in the depths of darkness, and there was no turning back. Could he do it? Could he get to the helmet and cleanse the forest of these nightmares?

Could he cleanse his own mind of nightmares?

"When do we ready for battle?"

The voice startled Dillen out of his thoughts, and he turned to see Imariel sitting up. Typical of the hunter to get the jump on him, Dillen mused. Despite looking as alert as ever, Dillen detected the slightest bit of exhaustion in the way she held herself up.

"Imariel, I... We're waiting for reinforcements from Haili. Velorun says the fiercer attacks are in other areas." He paused and let the silence hang between them. "How are you feeling?"

"I am fine," she said as she brushed long strands of hair behind her ear. She pushed herself up and out of bed, and she began to ready herself.

"Velorun has found out how they're still here." Silence from the elf. "We left the helmet. I must have dropped it while we were making our escape. We just need to find it and sever their connection."

More silence. Dillen exhaled silently and stood up to leave. He stopped himself and then turned to Imariel. She didn't pay him any attention at first, so he grabbed her by the shoulders and turned her to face him. She did not struggle, because if she did, he knew she could overtake him in a moment. There was hurt in her eyes, confusion, and real, deep pain.

"Imariel, I've laid my soul bare for you. I've told you every secret I hold, secrets I had because it was life and death for me. I can never bring your mother back, I can never mean what she did to you, and I can never make up for what happened to her that day. But through all of this, you've been my constant. I understand that what we had... what we were..." He paused to collect himself. "Every battle that we enter could always be our last. We never know what the Green Lady, the Shining Ones, fate – whatever – has in store for us when we take the field. But these nightmarish creatures, these... stalkers, they're furious. They're vicious. They know we want to rid them from the woods, and they want to claim the land. If we don't make it through this..."

"Dillen." Her voice was low, but she kept her eyes locked on his. She did not speak for a long moment that, to Dillen, lasted an eternity. "I will fight by your side, without question, as I always have. You need not worry about my support. My mother must be avenged, and it's not you who needs to pay that price. I will extract it from these fiends until every tear I've shed for Elissa is satisfied. We will win this fight so that my mother's death will not be in vain."

Dillen let his arms drop to his side, and Imariel's stony expression returned. He was about to say something else, but they both turned to a sound outside the tent.

It was a single, blaring horn.

Imariel only needed another few moments to finish preparing, and the two of them ran out of the tent and followed the rest of the elves preparing at the edge of the encampment. The defenders were spread out across the barricades that had been erected, arrows nocked and ready. Shesh'ra, Lothak, the knights, and the rangers stood apace back, armed and ready to meet the enemy head on if they broke through. Imariel took out her bow and an arrow in one swift motion and joined the other defenders. Dillen armed himself with sword and shield and approached Farn.

"What's going on?"

Farn opened his mouth to speak, but Velorun cut him off. "Word has come down the line that some of the attacks from the other areas have lessened, and the creatures are coming this way."

"Why would they change direction now?" Dillen growled as a scowl crossed his face. "I thought you said they hadn't pressed the attack here?"

"They hadn't." Velorun scowled back, forcing Dillen to soften his own expression. "The only thing I can think of is that they sense their original anchor – either seeing it as a chance to reclaim their strength or prevent us from purging the last piece."

Dillen swore under his breath as he watched the shadows of the trees squirm, as if the roots themselves were lifting up out of the ground and wriggling forward. But he knew better. He could just barely make out the jagged appendages as the creatures surged forward.

Velorun moved forward to stand next to another elf, and they nodded to one another. He held his staff vertically before him with both hands and closed his eyes; it looked to Dillen as if he were channeling his magic.

"Pick your targets!" the other elf shouted, aimed his bow, and loosed an arrow. Dillen watched as one of the creatures dropped and did not get back up. "Make every arrow count!"

The reverberation of bowstrings combined with the growling of the Nightstalkers created a cacophony of death. Dillen waited with baited breath as he clenched the handle of his sword.

"We're holding," Dillen said low, more to himself than anyone around him, "but for how long?"

"We must have faith, Sir Dillen." Farn stood beside him, and despite the brave smile on his face, Dillen could see the fear he was masking. The elves' aim was true and vicious, but with every fallen nightmare, two more took its place. "Do you remember when I asked you about praying?"

Dillen nodded. The conversation felt like a lifetime ago. "Even though a sword has two edges, it cannot cut two ways at once."

"While I feel that the Green Lady will ensure our victory in her woods," Farn lowered his voice and leaned in slightly, a more devious smile spreading on his face, "I believe the Shining Ones are watching over us, yet."

Dillen couldn't help but grin. "One way or another, one of the deities will have their way – whether they watch over us or they come to reclaim our souls. Let's do what we can to make sure it's the prior!"

The small smile that Dillen allowed himself faded just as quick as it sprang to his face. The archers had thinned the hoard of nightmarish creatures, but they were still coming on fierce. Swallowing the last of his nerves and resigning himself to whatever fate was in store, Dillen tore his sword from its scabbard and readied himself.

"To your swords!" the commanding elf shouted, viciously ripping his blade free and raising it into the air. "Stand your ground and defend this spot with your life!"

"For the Green Lady!" the call went down the line as the elves dropped their bows and brought melee weapons to the ready.

Dillen and his companions pushed their way to the front. Farn stood on his right, his expression hidden behind his helmet; the rest of the knights were interspersed with the elves beyond him; Imariel, Sehsh'ra, and Lothak stood to his left, but his eyes lingered on his elven ally. There was rage in her eyes, and he swore she was fighting back tears.

The charging tide of abominations brought him back to the moment. Dillen slammed his shield forward as a scarecrow rushed at him with its scythe raised. The blade raked the top of Dillen's shield, but the creature spiraled aside with the force of the blow. Dillen brought his sword down across the chest of another Nightstalker, its jaw unhinged at a freakish angle, splitting it in two.

He looked down, and the top half was still moving, violently spasming as it crawled toward him. Another scarecrow dove in at him, a blade fixed into its arm where a hand should have been, and Dillen was forced to bring his shield up to block. The distraction caused the scythe-hand to latch onto the top of the shield, and Dillen had to fight to keep control. He thrust his shield forward, trying to knock the malicious entity off, but it held on. It pulled his shield down enough for Dillen to stare into the twisted face, the gleaming eyes of purple, and the maw of pointed and incongruent teeth.

Dillen let out a scream, partly of fear and partly of determination, and stepped to the side as he let the shield hang low. He lopped the scarecrow's head clean off, hoisted his shield back up as his foe slunk off it, and then turned to the crawler. It raised its hand, poised to grab Dillen's leg, but a spear pushed through its body, forcing the last of its energy out with a cry. He looked at the naiad, who twisted the spear in the thing's body to ensure its demise, and then stabbed into the other scarecrow to ensure it remained dead. There was a visceral squishing noise as the blade penetrated the chest; there was nothing straw about these creatures.

"Thank you, Shesh'ra!" Dillen called out as the two warriors regrouped and stood shoulder to shoulder.

"I am to always be watching of your back, it seems!"

Before Dillen could retort, another of the creatures grabbed Shesh'ra's back. She let out a cry, and Dillen's eyes widened as he could see the hook in her shoulder. He whirled on her, watching as the mouth of the Nightstalker grew nightmarishly wide and unhinging. He smacked the head, causing the creature to loll back and Shesh'ra to let out another cry of pain, and then Dillen swung as hard as he could at the shoulder. Armless, the creature hit the ground with a thud, and Dillen stabbed it a few more times.

He turned back to the naiad, and she was on one knee, using her spear horizontally to keep two more of the fiends at bay. Before he could lift his sword, Imariel was on them. Dancing with a fury he had never seen, the elf bent down low to cut into the leg of one offender, then spun back up and drove both blades into the back of the other. She brought her knees up into its back and brought it to the ground, stabbing over and over until it was still. Lothak brought a massive axe down to cleave through the hobbling foe.

Dillen had to rush over to Imariel and pull her off the corpse just before it faded away.

"Imariel!" he shouted at her, staring at the bloodlust in her eyes and the purple drops splashed across her face. "Concentrate! Turn that aggression on those still with will to fight!"

The elf lined up on one side of him, Lothak the salamander on the other. The melee was swirling all around them; knights and elves were hacking away at the scarecrows, but now the shoulder-talon bearing beasts joined the fight. He heard another moan and turned to see Shesh'ra yank the scythe out of her shoulder and make to join them.

"Shesh'ra, I appreciate your resolve, but you're in no shape to fight!"

"I can still be fighting!" the naiad said with a bit of a slur.

"No!" Dillen shouted, swatting back a faceless horror with his shield. "You are injured!"

"And if we are not to be winning this fight, this wound will not matter!"

She punctuated her sentence by smacking another faceless Nightstalker out of the air with her spear as it leapt at them. It was on her in a moment, and she drunkenly tried to stab at it and missed. It knocked the spear away with one of its shoulder tendrils, but Lothak's axe caught it, and the two tussled with the Nightstalker before putting it down together.

They had to win here. If they faltered, even just a little bit...

The Nightstalkers surged upon the warriors with tenacious fury this time. Dillen brought his shield up to block an incoming talon thrust and claw strike. He dug in, putting his weight behind his shield arm, but he heard screams down the line. Dillen clenched his teeth, growled, and pushed back against the foe. A quick glance to his sides showed his allies fared similarly. Lothak was on the defensive, moving slower than the scything talons that weaved in past his axe shaft; Shesh'ra was moving slower than usual, her face a combination of rage and pain; and Farn was a little further away from them – or at least he thought it was Farn – supporting another knight who had taken a serious wounding. Imariel parried and weaved in between heavy slices to deliver slashes and stabs – but it seemed she was having trouble finding a killing blow.

Two claws wrapped around Dillen's shield and pulled it down with more strength than he could manage to support with one hand. The Nighstalker's eyeless face came into view, its mouth slowly opening with every little bit the shield lowered. The creature's tongue lashed out and smacked Dillen in the face. The force behind the lashing caused him to fall, seeing stars. Dillen saw something dark and cloudy in the stars and instinctively raised his shield. There was a great pressure that pinned Dillen down, and then the consistent thumping of the talons stabbing down into the shield, trying to tear apart the very small barrier.

Dillen knew the shield could only take so much more abuse, and he put as much weight into his side as he could muster, forcing the creature off of him. It ripped the shield from his grasp in the roll, but Dillen used that momentum to stab into its chest. He tried to force the blade down, to pin the thrashing monster into the ground, but it drove both of its disjointed legs into his chest. Dillen was pushed back a pace, but luckily the talon-like feet hadn't penetrated his armor.

The creature tossed the remnants of the shield to the ground, and Dillen snarled as he tasted blood in his mouth; something had been injured. He let loose a feral roar and charged the creature. One shoulder-talon soared past his head, and he swung with both hands, tearing the other appendage as it tried to block. The Nightstalker roared and attempted a swipe at Dillen's face, but he managed to lower his head just in time for his pauldron to take the brunt of the attack. He drove his elbow up, silencing the hissing mouth, and then used his spare hand to deliver a violent punch to the face. The thing's head jerked back, and before it could lash out its tongue, Dillen delivered another, and then another, and then another, until the thing fell to its disjointed knees.

With one more savage roar, Dillen tore his sword clean through the body, splashing purple liquid onto the forest floor.

Dillen breathed heavily, but there was no end to them. They kept coming, surging out of the forest. They could sense him. They could sense the armor. They could sense their former anchor.

The line was giving; they couldn't hold out against the endless tide of darkness. Dillen had to buy them time.

"I have a plan! But I need someone to defend me!"

Lothak charged forward and slammed his shoulder into the next fiend making their way to Dillen.

"Make whatever you're planning count!" the salamander roared, smoke pluming from his nostrils. "We might not have another chance!"

Dillen stepped back, sheathed his sword, and felt a moment of panic wash over him. How was he supposed to use the magic of the armor? What was he supposed to do? What did channeling magic even feel like? Scarecrows started filling back in, and Lothak was dealing with three of them as they tried to peel past the haft of the axe. Farn came charging in with the knight he had been helping and engaged two of the enemies.

Concentrate. Calm down and focus. Dillen silenced the thoughts in his mind, took a deep breath, and shut his eyes. Again, nothing came, there was no guide, nothing to show him how to do any magic. He felt his brow wrinkle in agitation, but he took another breath. There was another yelp behind his closed eyelids, close by him, but he forced his mind not to get distracted.

He pleaded with his mind to grasp anything that could help, and then he heard it. Dillen could hear the whispers calling out to him, as quiet and drowned out as they were. As strange as it felt, he reached out to them in his mind, and he could feel the whispers growing. He swam to them in the blackness of his mind, and the words, at first indistinguishable, became a choir of voices chanting.

The chant became so loud that it became all he heard – and then there was nothing. The sounds of battle came back to him, the terrifying cries of the Nighstalkers all around him. He opened his eyes and looked down at his hands. A torrent of water swirled around each fist, moving at such speeds that Dillen nearly mistook the liquid for air. He stared in awe, sputtering for words. He actually managed to do it!

Dillen looked up; the swell of Nightstalkers had nearly overwhelmed them. Lothak was fighting back against three of the fiends again, his axe held diagonal against his body in a protective stance.

"Now! Get back!" Dillen boomed over the sounds of battle.

Lothak roared and pushed the ghastly creatures back, swinging around with his tail to knock them further away. Farn and the other knight aided in pushing back the immediate stalkers, and then all on the front line pushed back to open a path for Dillen.

He took two giant steps and then threw his hands forward with as much force as he could manage. Water – like magic, true and unbelievable magic – rushed from his hands, creating a flowing stream within moments, with waves that rushed up to swallow the front line of enemies. Limbs and talons flailed in the deluge that engulfed them, howls drained by gargling water. Dillen forced the energy out of his hands, straining with the effort, until the swirling began to diminish. Then the spirals span to nothing, and Dillen fell to one knee, straining to breathe.

He heard something being shouted, which his brain couldn't comprehend, but he forced himself to look up once more. Through the spots in his vision, he saw a large break in where the enemy had been. The magic had pushed back more of them than he thought – but they were regrouping. The deluge had killed or mutilated a small handful, but the Nightstalkers lumbered back into battle – and beyond them, there were still monsters crawling out from the shadows of the forest. This fight was not over yet.

"Sir Dillen!" He felt someone come up behind him and grab his arm, forcing him to stand. His gaze fell on Farn, and within his helmet, even Dillen could see the urgency. "We have to pull back! Velorun is calling us all back!"

Dillen nodded through the haze in his brain and let Farn lead him, but he stopped when he saw Imariel. She had a fiend pinned down, stabbing it over and over again; its talons were cut in places but not severed, flailing limply as they desperately tried to reach her. He reached down to pull her away, but she viciously pushed him back.

"Imariel!" he shouted her name as he wrapped his arms around her violently thrashing frame. He forced her around and her arms in the air to avoid being stabbed. "Calm yourself!"

The animalistic rage on her face remained for a minute with a snarl, but then it broke and she started sobbing. Her head dropped against Dillen's chest as she cried.

"It's okay, it's okay," he calmly spoke to her. He eyed the forest with concern as the shadows grew closer. "We have to go, I'm sorry."

Her sobbing stopped and she turned to see the Nightstalkers advancing. She took a deep breath and nodded. Dillen hobbled along with Farn leading and Imariel just in front of him – and he didn't dare look back. He could feel the enemies gaining ground, rushing them with their fresh strength and inhumane fury.

He pushed as much strength into his legs as he could, but he was exhausted from the spell. Every step forward felt like he was going slower and slower. In his mind, he could feel the snake-like whip of a tongue from one of the beasts reach out to wrap itself around his neck, strangling the life essence from him. He forced himself past the bodies of their allies – there were more elves than anything, but there were rangers and a few knights, too.

The ground disappeared from beneath him as Dillen tripped and rolled. He knew this was it. He was too focused on the threat behind him, he didn't consider that the nature he was said to be the 'knight' of could foul him up in such a way.

He rolled onto his back to try and prepare to battle to the end. One of the Nightstalkers leapt toward him, and before he could raise his arm, a bright light enveloped the sky. A magical shield projected in front of him, and the creature was sent flying back with force.

Dillen lay there for another moment, watching as fiend after fiend was repelled. He let out a deep sigh. They had that moment to sigh. He stood up and walked back to the center of camp – where Velorun stood, an aura of energy around him as he channeled the shield to stand against the onslaught.

Chapter XXXVII

D illen sat, slumped over, on a rock. An unbitten apple dangled in his right hand. No matter how much he tried to will himself to eat, to regain some of his strength, his stomach refused to cooperate. Even though they had been spared from the fury of the Nightstalkers, the break was only temporary. After realizing that they were getting struck back by the shield, they bided their time and waited at the edge of the encampment, so silently that it frayed on all of their nerves within the sanctuary.

Dillen's eyes flicked to Velorun. The elf stood in the center of the camp, his staff pressed into the ground, his head resting against the top of it, eyes shut, and he chanted quietly. Another elf sat by him with a waterskin, every once and a while lifting it to Velorun's ever-muttering lips.

They had a few moments to lick their wounds and prepare for how to handle the fiends when Velorun ran out of strength. Lothak, despite his imposing composure and surly attitude, had been wounded more than he let on. Some of the elven healers had been applying salves to his injuries, his body pulsing with dull light as they worked some form of magic on him. Shesh'ra was in a similar state, but the elves were able to draw some sort of bath for her to rest in. The last he had seen of her, she had entered a meditative state as she slid beneath the water, her wounds already starting to look better in a few short moments.

They had lost too many in defending the encampment – in defending the anchor – in defending him. A score of elves that he didn't know the names of, the commander that sounded the attack, and a few of the knights, including Tyred, who had barely recovered from his last set of wounds. Good fighters, and even better men. He ran a hand through his sweat-soaked hair as he let out a sigh. There would be time for mourning later.

Farn and Imariel, while probably suffering the least physically, were dealing with mental turmoil. The two were sitting in opposite directions; Farn was caring for his sword, trying to wipe clean invisible stains, and Imariel stared off into the forest past the barrier. Torn between who to check in on, his mind wandered through the more complex nature of his relationship with Imariel, and he thought it best to check in with the knight.

Dillen stood up, put on the best bravado he could muster, and sauntered over to the knight. Farn looked up and forced a slight smile when he saw who stood before him. Dillen held out his hand with the apple in it. "Apple a day keeps the Nighstalkers at bay?"

"Thank you, but I must decline," Farn said, exhaustion pushing through his voice. "I could barely keep down the berries I was given."

Dillen recoiled his hand and sat down next to Farn. The younger knight put the rag down and exhaled deeply.

"War is war, Dillen. It doesn't change, no matter what side you're on, no matter who you're fighting the battles for. The only things that do are who or what you're fighting, and who stands beside you – who sheds blood alongside you. I've stared down the hordes of the Abyss, unblinkingly, and fought for years to defend my land and my people. When Bhadein and I sided with the Lady's forces, I knew that things would change – everything would change – but here we are, back at war with nightmarish hellions, fighting to defend our home and our people."

Farn looked up at Dillen, and the weight of years at war suddenly made him look much older than ever before.

"War does not change, but my allies have. Bhadein has been laid to rest, the Lady's forces are now among those I call allies, but most importantly is my time getting to know you, the real you, Sir Dillen Genemer. Thank you for that."

Dillen couldn't muster any words to say. His throat went dry as his mind went blank. He simply shut his mouth and nodded. Farn clasped Dillen on the shoulder and gave a weak but reassuring smile.

"I'm fine. Honestly. You and I, we've seen war. We've been in desperate situations, when everything seems bleak. Doesn't make it easier, but I'll... I'll be alright."

Dillen's eyes flicked toward Imariel. She hadn't moved, still staring out into the forest. Alone.

"Right," Dillen nodded and stood up. "Thank you, Farn. And should you need anything..."

"I'll be fine. Seeing as Bhadein isn't here, Shining Ones rest his soul, I should probably check in with the other knights."

Dillen walked over to Imariel and stood beside her. She didn't budge. He cleared his throat, and her eyes flashed to him for a moment, but they didn't linger for more than that. Dillen sat down next to her. Even from where they sat, he could see the Nighstalkers outside the shield waiting tirelessly, some flicking their talons in the air.

"Imariel..."

"I apologize." Imariel's words were short, her tone biting. "I had a moment of weakness."

Dillen's brow furrowed in shock, and he fumbled over his words. "I-... Imariel." His voice took on a bit more of a pleading tone than he'd intended, but he forced calm and seriousness into what he said. "You've been through some very traumatic experiences. I know you still hurt over losing your mother. That rage I've seen, that's not you..."

"You know nothing about me," Imariel spat at him, turning to fix him with an icy stare.

"Be angry with me all you wish," Dillen held his ground, "but do not tell me lies. In our time together, we have talked a multitude of subjects, and even though I don't know you very well, and I don't understand most of what you're thinking, I know some things about you."

Imariel took a deep breath in, and her features softened. The pure anger gave way to show her fighting back tears. Dillen took the chance to continue speaking.

"I know you... or the you that you try to show people. I know the you that you are when you let your guard down." Dillen sighed as he turned away from her to look out at the forest again. After a moment, he turned back to her. "I don't want to bring up anything that will make this situation worse, but for a second, can you please remember the me that you, only you, know? You call what happened a moment of weakness, but you would have never sobbed like that to Shesh'ra, or Farn, or anyone else here."

"You think rather highly of yourself," she murmured dryly.

"Then tell me I'm wrong."

Imariel sat upright, stared into Dillen's eyes, but she did not answer.

"Ah, now there's a bit more of that elven aloofness that I'm used to."

He smiled, trying to further pull her from her dismal state, but she did not respond.

"What is it you're getting at, Dillen?" Her voice sounded utterly tired, drained.

"I don't want you to lose yourself to the feelings in your heart. Your rage, your anger... It will be your undoing if you don't keep them in check. When I said to take your vengeance out on them, I didn't mean to forget who you are – who you're fighting for."

Imariel remained silent for a moment, her eyes flicking away from him and then back again. "I cannot let this blight remain in our forest. My mother fought her whole life to defend the forest from invaders, from those that would cause any harm to the Lady's domain. To her last days, she did not trust you or the other knights, despite Haili's blessing. Whether she was justified in that concern is neither here nor there, but I am determined to follow the path that she led."

"How can you continue her fight if you fall too? I understand what you're saying, but we have to fight to survive, not to exterminate as many of these creatures as we can while giving our lives in the process. Think of the long game, Imariel. If you were to fall here, if we fall here, they will push through us and continue to cause havoc on the forest. We will win this fight, but we have to be smart about it."

"Will we?" Imariel's eyes turned to the edge of the shield once more, and she stared at the creatures that waited to satiate their bloodlust. "They outnumber us. They keep coming with no end in sight. If this is to be the place where we have our final stand, I will make sure my last breaths will come during combat, with my blade claiming another soul in my mother's name."

Dillen grabbed her hands, forcing Imariel to look back at him. "You must have faith. We will triumph, together."

Imariel let her hands fall from his and cast an arm out toward the rest of the encampment. "Look at them all. Velorun can only buy so much time. Everyone is exhausted and has given up hope. What faith do you have?"

Dillen's brow furrowed as he thought on this. He looked at the expression on the knights' faces; determined, ready to fight to their last breath, but there was an utter hopelessness to them as well. All assembled knew that there was no escape. If they ran, they'd surely be cut down by the Nighstalkers as they pushed further into the forest; and if they stayed and fight, it was futile, as they'd be overwhelmed as they nearly had been.

He had to motivate them. He needed to give them hope.

Dillen took a deep breath in and let it out slow, forcing his shaking hands to still. He knew what he had to do.

He got up, giving a puzzled Imariel a wink and soft smile, and walked over to the elf helping Velrorun.

"How much time do we have left?"

The elf stopped what he was doing and studied the softly chanting Velorun. He turned to Dillen, nodded slowly, and spoke softly so the others could not hear. "Five more minutes before Master Velorun collapses. His speech is slowing, he refuses to drink, and I can feel his magic growing dimmer."

"Time enough, then." Dillen nodded to the elf. He turned with his back toward Velorun, facing the rest of the soldiers, and clapped his hands together. "Knights, rangers, elves, and my salamander and naiad friends alike, I'd like to take a moment of your time."

All eyes turned to him. He felt the weight of his fellow knights and the rangers watching him curiously, the disdain or indifference of the elves, and then the comrades he'd fought closest with – Farn, Lothak, Shesh'ra, and Imariel. They were the hardest to look at. Imariel's eyes grew and wavered, as if she knew what he was about to say. He looked at Shesh'ra, and the naiad nodded. She knew too then. Dillen returned the nod and swallowed the last of his nerves.

"We stand at the forefront of a battle that will change the fate of the Forest of Galahir forever more. If we falter here, we risk putting everyone in the forest at great risk of being tormented by these abominations. If they get their hands on this," Dillen pounded an open hand on the center of his armor, "the forest will be forever twisted beyond redemption. Women, children, nature itself will be devoured by darkness. That is the reason why we cannot fail. We must fight them back, and we must turn the favor back into the Lady's hands."

The warriors nodded. Dillen felt his confidence building, and he became more animated as he spoke, pacing back and forth.

"Knights of the former Brotherhood, you stood at the very scar of the Abyss and spat in the faces of the demons that crawled forth from it! You know what it's like to lose your home, and I know that you swore to never let another feel that pain – and you elves, you have defended this very home from every threat that has walked the path of the forest. You will stand shoulder to shoulder with humans, these humans who encompass the very loss you're fighting to prevent! Together, your pain, your hope, your will to protect, will seize the day! We will give it all to fight these Nightstalkers, but we will fight to live – to honor the sacrifices of those that have perished! But no more shall fall. We will give everything to make sure that we left are not only the victors, but the survivors!"

A more confident roar sprang from the fighters as they came to their feet. This was the moment, though, and Dillen exhaled deeply.

"That is why… That is why I need to join you in giving everything. And that means giving you the truth."

Farn's eyes widened, and his fervor subsided as he regarded Dillen with a raised eyebrow.

"The stories that you've heard about me, the stories that the bards sing about my victory here as a paladin of Basilea – they are all false. None of it is true."

He watched the faces of each person react to the statement. Some looked confused, as if waiting for Dillen to announce he was joking; some looked genuinely hurt or shocked; but he continued on.

"My name is Dillen Genemer. I have never been a paladin, I came face to face with an Abyssal Champion but did not slay it, and I am not even a Basilean. I did what I thought was best when I abandoned my post and led you knights to save a village from these very creatures. I did not do so because I was Nature's Knight, but because of who I am and my beliefs. The forest paid a high price that day due to my negligence, and I've been working very hard to try and atone.

"Why am I telling you all this? Because though it may cost me my pride and your respect, I hope that this is one such way to atone. Beyond that, the story of the Hero of Galahir is not who I am. You all know Dillen Genemer, the warrior, the ally, the fighter. I say all this, because I ran from my past once. I am not running right now.

293

"The Armor of Tides chose me, for reasons at first I was unsure of. I found myself unworthy, always searching for my purpose, and then the armor called to me. In his last moments, Bhadein himself gave me his blessing; and thanks to him, I've found my purpose. I am no longer taking the mantle of the Hero of Galahir – I cast it aside to stand alongside you, simply Dillen Genemer, among the ranks of any other knight of the forest." Dillen took his sword out and pointed it into the ground, resting both of his hands clasped atop the pommel. "I stand before you, ready and willing to fight to the last breath alongside you. Ready to defend my allies and your – no, our – home from these Nightstalkers – even if it's the last thing I do!"

"I stand with you, Dillen Genemer!" Farn shouted, raising his sword into the air. There was no resentment on his face, only determination – maybe even pride. Dillen fought hard to keep tears from welling. His sins in the open, Farn still supported him. "You're right, we've all heard the story of the Hero of Galahir, but from the day we entered the forest, we fought alongside and worked with Dillen Genemer. We know your heart and tenacity, and some of us have had the fortunate opportunity to call you a friend. I stand with you, Sir Dillen, to push back these nightmarish creatures and take back our home!"

"Ah, damn," Ragneld spat, standing. "Guess Kevmar would have owed me some money, were he alive. But that doesn't matter. I stand with you. To protect our brothers, our allies, our home."

As he drew his blade and held it high, each knight followed, shouting their allegiance to the bearer of the Armor of Tides.

"We fight with you, Dillen Genemer," one of the elves shouted, causing the others to draw their weapons. "We care not of your past, but you have showed your conviction in wanting to defend our land and fight for the Lady's cause. We will triumph here!"

Lothak snorted and stepped a pace closer to Dillen. "Any man can tell a lie and thrive upon it. It takes a determined man to right his wrongs, no matter how much time has passed. You have the respect of this salamander, human."

Dillen's eyes widened as Lothak drew his axe and raised it with the others. "T-thank you," he muttered under his breath.

Shesh'ra walked forward, no limp evident in her step, but she inclined her head seriously. "Long is the path you have yet to walk, but this is taking of the first step. You must continue this path, and today will not be the end of it."

Dillen nodded confidently as a rallying cry went up around the soldiers. He turned to Imariel, who was about to speak, when Velorun collapsed.

"The barrier!" the elf attending him cried out.

"To arms!" Dillen shouted, giving Imariel one last longing look. "We fight to defend our people! Fight to live and see another day! Fight for all those depending on us!"

The Nightstalkers did not hesitate once the barrier vanished. They rushed forward, snarling, talons swaying viciously through the air.

"Shields up! At the ready!" Dillen called as he took the forefront with one he recovered. Farn and the other knights fell in line, defending against the assault. Arrows came from behind, petering through the rush and taking a few of the fiends out. Dillen hacked with his sword and fought back against the creatures as much as he could, but they pressed hard on his shield arm. Spears were thrust through the gaps from elves trying to force the monsters back as well.

Dillen let out a scream of determination as he pressed his attacker back, swinging down hard with his sword. It was the first time he was able to get a good look at the number of Nightstalkers. They had taken down more in the initial wave than he thought, and it seemed like they didn't have any reinforcements nearby. His heart swelled. They had a chance. If only they could hold on a bit longer...

Other knights and elves around him cried out as they fought the hard-press of the Nightstalkers. They weren't trying to slice through the shields – they were trying to push through them, overwhelm them. What little chance they had to turn the battle was fading with each scarecrow or taloned fiend that pressed in on the shieldwall.

Then Dillen heard something, or someone, else yelling. There was another battle cry that sounded by them, and the press of enemies didn't feel so heavy anymore. Men on horses cut through the flank of the Nightstalkers, tearing down the momentum of monsters on top of the knights. The enemy was distracted; they weren't sure where to put their focus, and Dillen knew they had to press the attack.

He raised his sword high and called out. "Now, men! Strike! Pincer attack, slay them between us!"

Men and elves, and a salamander and a naiad, turned the tide of combat, pressing the attack with spears, swords, and axes catching the confused Nightstalkers in exposed areas. Talons danced in the air as they tried to fend off both attacks at once, but this meant that the fiends were exposed from one side or the other. Scarecrows spun with scythe hands, trying to fend off attacks, but they ended up slicing into their own allies more than they dealt any real wounds to the forces of nature.

The bodies thinned until there was only one of the eyeless fiends left. It roared its gnashing teeth at Dillen, but a knight on horseback rushed in and impaled his sword through the creature's head. Its talons flailed wildly in its death throes, but Dillen was able to sever them before the mounted man could be wounded.

With the last one dead, Dillen sank to his knees, and a shout went up across the defenders. They had won.

The knight dismounted his warhorse and took his helmet off. Dillen was shocked to look up into the face of Benedict. In the heat of combat, so thankful for his saviors, Dillen had not noticed the Brothermark emblems and colors on the warriors.

"Dillen Genemer, is that you?"

"E-Exempler Paladin...!"

The Brothermark knight reached his hand down to help Dillen up, to which he accepted gratefully, stood, and fumbled over his words.

"What... Thank you. You have saved us from dire straits. What are you doing here?"

"I told you that we would see this through to the end. Since we parted, the fiends that infest this forest have been extremely ornery. We've run into our fair share of them, but we've had the Lady's people to help us along the way. They informed us where to find the worst of the fighting, just a bit farther from here."

Dillen turned back to the defenders. The elf that had been helping Velorun made his way forward. "Will Velorun be all right?"

"Yes, Sir Dillen. Our healers are helping him to rest. But if I may be honest, he'd do much better without you here. You are what the Nightstalkers are after."

"Right." Dillen nodded, trying not to let guilt get the best of him. "Then we move onward, with the Brothermark knights! The final push is just ahead! To the heart of corruption!"

Chapter XXXVIII

Sounds of naiads' sea serpents roared through the trees, stomping of forest shamblers and tree herders vibrated the ground, and the belch of salamander flames lit up centaurs as they thundered by to the beating of war drums. The forest was angry, and it was ready to expunge the threat that lurked in the shadows by any means necessary. That much, Dillen could tell as he led the rest of the warriors on foot onward, trailing behind the charging Brothermark steeds. Haili must have rallied every defender that this part of the forest had to offer.

"Follow the drums!" Dillen called out as he raised his sword in the air.

He tried to follow his own advice as he lost sight of the cavalry, but the sounds of nature's defenders were overwhelming. His heart pounded and his mind raced, but where once worry and doubt would have clouded any judgment or action, he felt calm and confident. Dillen was sure that the Armor of Tides was to thank for that, whether the effects were real or just perceived in his mind. The sounds of battle grew ever louder, and he prepared himself to come face to face once more with the nightmarish creatures.

As he ducked past a low-hanging branch and stepped out into a wide clearing, Dillen's breath caught in his lungs. He came to a stop and stared around with awe at the carnage that unfolded. Flames uncontrollably burned all around them, but not the hot red of natural fire, but this was purple and oozed with darkness; it screamed of Nighstalker energy. The large shamblers that he had heard stomping through earlier were locked in combat with scorpion-like entities, similar to Ur-chitak. The Nightstalkers tried to pierce bark with their tail stingers, and some succeeded. Others were fought off with burly limbs, stone heads at the end of their arms bashing down and crushing the fiends. Scarecrows, the shoulder-taloned creatures, and hounds all collided with naiads, salamanders, elves, and centaurs. Elemental creatures were being summoned to cause chaos in the midst of the Nightstalkers' ranks, but they were being quickly snuffed out.

"What are our orders, Sir Dillen?" Farn's voice caught him off guard, but Dillen did his best to keep his composure cool.

"This is it, here! The source of their power must be close!"

"Let us make haste and find it!" Farn cried out.

"No." Dillen shook his head. "This is a task for me alone."

Farn stared incredulously at him. "Sir Dillen, you cannot be serious! I will not let you go out alone into this!"

"I appreciate the thought, Farn, but you see the Nightstalkers before us. I need you all to protect my path. The armor... it calls to me. If you can keep the Nightstalkers here busy, I can find the source quicker by myself." He paused, looking Farn in the eyes. "I need to do this. Trust me."

Farn did not say anything, but Lothak and Shesh'ra stepped forward, brandishing their weapons.

"Then go, and do what you must to cleanse this blight," Lothak growled.

"He is of the right mind, Dillen," Shesh'ra nodded. "We will be joining of the fight, but you must get through and find the source."

Dillen turned and regarded his allies carefully.

"Go." Imariel came up and readied an arrow. She gave him the briefest of looks, but even in that moment, Dillen did not detect the usual chill she'd come to regard him with. It gave him hope. "This is your destiny. Restore the balance in the forest back to the side of light. We will hold them off as long as we can."

Farn gave Dillen one more concerned look before he raised his sword and stood before the knights and elves. "That's right! D'you hear that, everyone? We must buy Sir Dillen time to purge this taint on the forest! We fight to help bring balance to the light! Are you with me?!"

There was a rallying cry as weapons were withdrawn and raised. Dillen met the gaze of his four closest allies, and he saw hope in each of their faces. Despite his years of lying, despite having nightmares every night and unable to cope with the dilemma he had put himself in, they believed in him. He nodded confidently as they took off, screaming into battle, and Dillen ran towards the purple haze of the forest.

He navigated the twists and turns that he hoped would bring him around the back of the Nightstalkers forces. He trusted nature and the Green Lady's will would guide him on the right path, but something about the forest felt... wrong. The trees seemed sick, as the purple fog of darkness hung over every branch, every growth of green, twisting the boughs around him so that Dillen felt unsettled when he glanced into every shadow. As he moved, he could hear the sounds of battle shifting; instead of being directly in front of it, the sounds were drifting behind him.

He heard a voice whispering to him, now that the battle sounds were quieting; but it wasn't the voice he was familiar with. It was there, but hidden within a deeper level of the voice was something darker, more sinister. Dillen began to wonder if this was the Nightstalkers' hold on the helmet, and if so, why was it also calling to him?

A few moments of following the voice brought him to another clearing where the haze seemed to almost cloud his vision entirely. The fog was so deep he could barely see anything around him. He stepped forward, and shapes started materializing – outlines that made Dillen's skin crawl and breath go cold. As if a kraken had risen from the depth of the sea, long winding tendrils rose several feet in the air – and in the center of the mass, they were wrapped around an object, emanating and swelling with purple energy.

There was no time to think. One of the tentacles came down at him, uncoiling like a whip. Dillen had enough sense to sidestep, and then he brought his sword down to sever the limb. The tendril fell to the forest floor and turned to ash almost immediately, fading away. There didn't seem to be a body the tentacles were connected to; they seemed to sprout out of the forest floor, much like the trees around him did.

Gritting his teeth in hopes he could force the growing nausea away, Dillen charged at the mess of tentacles. As they snapped out at him, Dillen raised his shield, blocking most of the thin limbs; and where he could, he swung back with his sword to dispose of them. One managed to flail past him, and he didn't think much of it – until it coiled around his leg and tripped him. He rolled onto his back and kept rolling as more of the tentacles fell down where he once laid.

Finally able to get up and catch his breath, Dillen prepared for the next wave. He yelled as he ran forward, now going on the offensive and swinging his sword like a crazed man. One by one, the tentacles severed from the ground and vanished, no different than if Dillen went into the depths of the forest and cut down the high-growing wild grass.

With the last appendage destroyed, the oppressive feeling around him began to lighten, and the purple began to give way to the light.

"Creatures be damned," Dillen said breathlessly as he looked around.

There it was. He recognized the horse hair topped helmet of gold and topaz, and it called out to him, just like the rest of the armor had. Dillen sighed with relief as he walked over to it.

"And so this is it. It shall be done."

Dillen bent down to grab the helmet, and an unholy cry went up around him. The screech was unnatural, blood-chilling, and he nearly doubled over in pain from it. The purple fog obscured his vision once more, and the evil energy returned even stronger than before. He looked around him, and through the haze, hundreds of eyes gazed at him; bloodthirsty beings lurked from the shadows and tentacles raised all around him, caging him in.

Dillen fumbled for his sword, but he dropped it in his panic. He had no idea what to do; was this all a trap? Was this the end? He begged for the armor to help him, but the water within did not resonate or respond. He cursed loudly as he searched for an escape, but there was none.

Then his eyes settled on the helmet. The duality of that voice called out once more to him; one side pleading while the other welcomed. As sharp claws, twisting tongues, and barking mouths came through the fog and past the tendrils, Dillen did the only thing before him – he put the helmet on.

Instead of seeing the forms of his enemies before him, there was a bright, white light that blinded him. He put his hands up to shield him, instinctively, as if that could help him, and he waited. He wasn't sure what he was waiting for or how long he waited. Was this the end? Was the white light the Shining Ones welcoming him to the great beyond? When he finally was able to see his arms in front of his face, he brought them down and looked around in horror.

This was no paradise of the Shining Ones – he didn't even think this was the Abyss. The fog was gone, everything was clear, but it was also tinged purple. The area looked similar to somewhere in the forest, but no place in particular; this place was damned. Trees rose high, but they were diseased by a sickly purple substance that looked like spider webbing; the water was stagnant, interspersed by a sickly looking fluid, close to what the creatures bled; and jagged rocks, resembling the talon appendages stuck out from the ground.

"Human."

Only a single word was uttered, but Dillen could tell that it was the deeper of the two voices that had called out to him. He looked around, and when he finally found the source, he froze, his teeth chattering.

The speaker resembled a large brain that floated above the ground. At the center of its 'body' was a single green eye that resembled a snake's, with no eyelid; and on both sides were mouths were mangled and distorted teeth. Dangling from below it were tentacles that moved and bobbed passively, but not without threat. The brain inside the creature's casing pulsed rhythmically.

"What… What are you?" Dillen finally made out, his voice raspy, his throat raw. He recognized this type of Nightstalker – when his horse had been electrocuted, it was one of these things that cast the spell. He tried to back away, willed his legs to run, but he was frozen in place. Cold sweat beaded on his forehead and trickled like ice down his back.

The creature did not answer with words. Instead, one of its tentacles stirred beneath it. Dillen felt a searing pain through his head, and he fell to one knee. Images flashed through his mind; it was the creature before him, leading the Nightstalkers onward through the forest. In one of its tentacles was the helmet he now wore, wrapped tightly in its grasp.

Dillen could not stop trembling as he stood and stared at the abomination. There was another throbbing of pain that wracked Dillen's mind, but with it came a word, or maybe it was a phrase. No; it was what the creature was called.

"Mind-screech."

It sent unshakable chills down Dillen's spine as he stared into the one single green eye.

Another sear of pain caused Dillen to fight himself to remain standing. More images came to his mind; he was watching himself, as if he were a bird, but the vision was distorted, elongated. His entire journey, from when he left home to this point, all flashed before his eyes. But the him that he saw was not the brave Sir Dillen that the bards told about. No, his face reflected his inner turmoil; the face he never showed anyone, but the one that he knew lurked behind the surface of every action and thought. There was fear, worry, sadness; he even saw himself crying in moments he knew he had not, but all the same, they were moments that he could have if he had given in to emotions.

"What is this?!" Dillen finally called out, breaking the illusion. "You've been watching me, is that it?!"

The creature extended one tendril, and a blot of purple ink dripped from it, slowly falling to the ground until it spread out and expanded. A human shape rose from it, and Dillen's breath caught as he recognized the shadow of his brother, Kallas, that had haunted him during the hunt for the armor. It sneered at him as it stood next to the hovering brain.

"Yes," the mind-screech's puppet finally spoke. "When you stepped into our domain, all of the secrets in your mind, all of the whispered lies and your haunted past were laid bare to us. Each member of your group had their shadows to be stalked, but yours were the most delectable. Living a lie. Afraid to tell anyone who you really were. Afraid you'd lose it all, again."

"I am afraid of that no more!" Dillen spat out, despite the trembling in his voice, but finally finding the nerve to swing his sword in an aggressive manner. "I have dealt with my demons, I have met my past head-on, and I have told everyone the truth of who I really am!"

"We are aware," Kallas's clone sounded disappointed in its smoky voice, the mind-screech's multiple mouths chattering but the voice not emanating from any of them. "We had such high hopes to use you, manipulate you. Your fear was what we needed to twist you into one of us, but that is gone. The magic you now possess empowers you, but there is still fear and uncertainty in your mind."

Dillen swallowed hard. He knew that the Nightstalker was using Kallas's form as a way to cause Dillen uncertainty, probably hoping he would question if he could really strike at his brother. Even though he knew it was not really him, it never made coming face to face easier.

"The truth is out, but what comes next?" Kallas spat, angrily. "Will you continue living on as Dillen Genemer, the forsaken knight, the failed mercenary, and the protector of the glades and flowers? Your allies will surely strip you of your armor, turn their heads from you, and cast you back out once more."

"That is not true!" Dillen cut in, feeling his pulse raising and his sword hand itching.

"And who is to say that you shall even leave here, alive?" The mind-screech's tentacles flicked with each word. "Our army surrounds you, poised to deliver the armor and its wielder to me once I take over your mind, and our reapers' talons grow sharper with every body they slice apart."

"What do you mean take my mind?" Repeating the words, thinking on what they meant, made Dillen lose every ounce of courage that was building. His knees were shaking again. "And... and where even are we?"

"You and I exist within this plane, mentally. Both are connected with the armor you bare, and through that connection, we can exist in this realm. The magic within this armor has allowed us to exist in the mortal plane as well, acting as an anchor, but its strength was incomplete. The fear that we fed on before you took the armor was enough to let us build our forces' strength. Had you not removed our anchor, this forest would be ours. But since you did... We needed the armor to find a new master and connect with its full strength."

"So then... it was you that called out to me."

"Yes. The ancient magic that is within this armor wanted you to be whole. We wanted you to be whole." The mind-screech hovered forward ever slightly, but Dillen could not pick up his sword. "Here, in this place where our minds are connected, we can fully assimilate, and the power of the armor's magic will be ours to wield. Forever shall we exist in this domain, forever will we sow our shadows across the world. Forever will we feast on your fearsssssss."

The tentacles reached up to either side of Dillen's head before he could react. He screamed as he felt them reaching into the depths of his mind, trying to worm their way in and take control. He fought, but slowly, things started fading from his memory. The naiad, he couldn't remember her name anymore... And there was another companion; someone surly and it... He? She? Who was he thinking about?

The only thing he could remember was a female. Despite her composure and stern expression, there was a kindness, a warmth, and somehow he knew it was meant for only him. This person held themselves in high regard, but they cared for him. He thought. But he couldn't remember her name, and her face began to fade into the darkness.

One last image. A man, about his age. It was as if he was trying to cheer him on, or plead for his success. He felt a great amount of shame and anguish, but the man's smile was determined to fuel him. He was trying to give him hope. His smile faded into the darkness.

What was his name? What was her name?

What was his own name?

He tried to remember as everything around him went black.

Dillen!

That word sounded familiar, but in his mind, it resonated like a dull noise. He couldn't comprehend.

Dillen Genemer! You must not lose faith!

Something snapped within him. That was his name. He could remember that much. Something touched his shoulder, and his eyes opened just barely to see a man standing beside him. He was an older man, and Dillen knew him from somewhere. There was confidence on his face as he stared down into Dillen's.

"You must not give up! You must remember who you are! All of it – the good and the bad!"

Something within Dillen was fighting back. Like waves rushing across his mind, he started to remember images; people, events. He was a mercenary. He had let his family down. He had fought alongside the Basileans. He had watched one die. He had taken credit. He had fought alongside allies – Farn, Imariel, Shesh'ra, Lothak, and even...

"B-Bhadein?"

The older man's features sharpened, and a big grin spread across his face.

Something like lightning shot into his head. Dillen let out a scream and was forced down. He looked at the mind-screech, and there was some sort of magic pulsing along its tendrils.

"Submit!" it painfully echoed into his mind.

"Fight back, Dillen!" This time another hand was placed on his other shoulder. He forced himself to look, and it was another knight that he barely recognized. He was adorned from the neck down in the same armor as Dillen. His name was...

"De... Dernan?"

"You have been chosen by the armor! Fight back, and cleanse this filth from the forest!"

Another course of electricity forced its way through Dillen's thoughts. He felt his mind crumbling, as if his head would explode from the pressure.

"Submit!" the voice cried out once more.

"No!" Dillen screamed back. He forced himself to his feet, and as another blast came across the tentacles, Dillen pulled them with both hands, screaming all the meanwhile, until they detached. The two knights by his side came forward and severed them with a loud whine from the creature.

Dillen took several deep breaths before he stood and stared at the mind-screech.

"My name is Dillen Genemer. I am no one special. Life has not been kind to me, but I have still fought tooth and nail to thrive in this world. I lied about who I was. My time in this forest has been built upon a lie, but I did so, so that I may help others. Yes, part of it was selfish, but I have never stolen from the Lady. I have never intentionally hurt any of her creatures. I follow the rules and edicts of her subjects. All I want to do is to live and help others – and this, this armor has seen my true heart! It has chosen me because of who I am – who I truly am!

"I fear no lies anymore! And I do not fear the shadows in which you treat, Nightstalker! I cast you out, once and for all, from the Lady's forest!"

Kallas's clone laughed, but it was not out of joy. It was low, throaty, as if he was gargling on blood. And then he broke back down into that purple liquid and was reabsorbed by the mind-screech's tentacle.

Dillen turned to look at the two knights on either side of him. "We attack as one!"

"Aye," Bhadein nodded, fire in his eyes. "One last time, Sir Dillen, we fight beside one another."

"For the glory of the former Brotherhood, and all those who stand beside our shattered allies," Dernan said as he readied his sword, "my blade is yours, Sir Dillen."

The knights charged together toward the mind-screech, but the abomination lashed out with three tentacles. One smacked Bhadein in the chest, sending him backward, and one coiled itself around Dillen and pulled him in to the mind-screech. The third one went straight through Dernan's own Armor of Tides, piercing him through the chest.

"No!" Dillen cried as the tentacle brought the knight up and into the air. Dernan tried to hack at the appendage, screaming curses as he fought to muster the strength to swing the blade. With each swing, cuts in the flesh formed with small bouts of purple blood – but these were obviously much stronger and thicker than the ones Dillen had destroyed in the forest.

Dillen struggled and thrashed to get free, but the tentacle held him tight. When he refused to relent, it slammed his body into the ground. Stars dotted his vision as he lost his breath, but he still continued to fight. Again, the creature slammed him into the ground. And again. And again. He finally felt the fight drain from him, growing exhausted and unable to catch his breath.

Even though Dillen was hazy and lost track of Dernan, he saw Bhadein hack away at the tentacle that held Dillen, until finally it started slackening. Dillen used the last of his reserves to break free, and he rolled away. Bhadein was once again batted away, and Dillen rushed to his side. As the burly man stopped rolling, Dillen reached him and kneeled down. He was winded, but he was all right, and Bhadein waved Dillen off. Another moment later, and Dernan was flung off the tentacle toward them as well. The duo tried to help the third knight stand, and he let them after some trouble getting up on his own.

"Seven Circles of the Abyss," Dillen breathed. The mind-screech was coming for them again. It was completely unphased; for all of their efforts, they had managed to skin a bit of its tentacles away, which now thrashed about angrily. Meanwhile, Dernan had been impaled, Bhadein must have had some form of cracked ribs from being struck twice, and Dillen might have had the same on the account of how hard it was to breathe. "How are we supposed to fight this abomination?!"

"Submit," the creature breathed into his mind once more.

"He'll do no such thing!" Bhadein barked. He looked about into the darkness, and when Dillen followed his gaze, he was shocked to see more people marching out of the woods.

"An army?!"

"Not just any army," Dernan said proudly. "They're members of the old Brotherhood. Those that have given their lives fighting against creatures worse than this at the scar of the Abyss."

"And they're here for one last fight, to buy you one last bit of time."

Dillen's eyes widened as he watched Dernan go out to lead them. He called for the attack, and the Brotherhood soldiers rushed head-on at the mind-screech. But it was hopeless. Dillen knew that. They must have known that. Men were getting impaled, men were getting electrocuted, men that were dead were dying again.

"Why, Bhadein? Why are they doing this?"

The old man stood with a sad smile on his face for another moment before he spoke. "That thing, the mind-screech. It said that your minds were connected in this place through the Armor of Tides. It's not just your minds that are connected. Dernan, he wore the armor before you, his mind was connected here as well. As well as so many of the others out there that are giving their lives."

"But you never wore the armor..."

Bhadein finally turned his gaze to Dillen. It was almost hollow, similar to the look of Kallas. Maybe this wasn't the real Bhadein. Maybe it was just an illusion by the armor. But it seemed like the real thing.

"True, I hadn't. And those out there – not all of them had the privilege of wearing the Armor of Tides. But I knew Dernan well, and I began to know you, too. Through the bond you both shared with this armor, and then with me, I was called to aid you as well. Even though I wasn't chosen to wear the armor, I was chosen by the armor to aid you."

"But... what do any of them hope to accomplish?"

Bhadein turned back to the carnage and nodded with his chin. One of the mind-screech's victim's bodies had a pool of swirling water around it. The body raised into the air and became one with the liquid. Then, like an arrow being shot from a bow, the torrent of water shot through the mind-screech. One by one, all of the spirits became one with the water and shot through the mind-screech. Tentacles were severed, chunks of its brain exploded in purple bits, and the mouths on the side of its body became disfigured or destroyed completely.

"What... What is this...?"

"The Armor of Tides is fighting back." Bhadein said. He placed a hand on Dillen's shoulder and gave him a real and honest smile. "Thank you for everything you've done for our people. And for Farn. I might have been his mentor, but you were the friend he needed when I could not be."

Dillen stared, wordlessly, trying to find something to say to tell Bhadein not to go, but it was too late. The knight took off running toward the beast, and he became one with the water, turning into a spear that thrust right through the body of the mind-screech and brought it low.

Even with, Dillen could only guess, around a hundred spears of magic passing through it, the mind-screech still fought to remain. It hovered as best as it could, and it looked right at Dillen.

"For Bhadein," Dillen said to himself as he began to run. "For Imariel. For Elissa. For Farn, for Shesh'ra, for Lothak, for Dernan, Lenel, Ragneld, Tyred, Kevmar, Gordram, and every other person that's been affected by my tale of Sir Dillen! I will right the wrongs my past!"

A rush of water carried him up and into the air, allowing Dillen to dive sword-first at the mind-screech. Its tentacles came up to try and stop him once more. They wrapped around his body, but his arms were already close enough that the tip of his sword pierced the brain and caused a bit of purple to ooze out. Dillen tried to force himself closer, but another tentacle came up to touch the side of Dillen's brain. Lightning shot through his head once more, and he felt his strength slacken.

But he would not relent. Despite the unending pain, both in his head and in his chest, Dillen pressed on. He forced that sword deeper and deeper, and the pain relented as he inched inward, until the pain was gone completely. The tentacles slackened around his body, and he was able to drive the sword up to the hilt.

The Nightstalker crumpled into the ground, and finally, when it stopped moving, Dillen withdrew his sword. He took several deep breaths to calm himself as his vision swam. He wasn't sure if it was his eyes or the purple haze, but everything seemed to be flickering, dotted with stars. Dillen rolled off of the corpse and fell to the ground on his back. He closed his eyes for a moment.

When he opened them, he was back in the forest – the real forest, not a mental projection. Dillen shot up, looking around; but there was nothing there with him. There were no Nightstalkers. No 'reapers' as the screech had called them, no scarecrows, no tentacles, and unfortunately there was no Bhadein and Dernan.

Dillen took a deep breath in. It felt pure. He didn't feel scared. He did not fear what was hidden beyond low boughs. He looked into the shadows of the forest and felt only peace. There was not the slightest hint of purple tinge or dark magic that lingered in the air.

Had they really done it…?

"There he is!" a voice shouted. When he looked toward it, Farn was leading the others to him. They looked no worse than before, maybe a few more injuries between them, but they were all alive as he had left them. Farn came up to Dillen with a big grin. "You did it, Sir Dillen! The foul creatures are gone!"

"Gone? Entirely?"

"It is being true," Shesh'ra said as she stepped forward, leaning gingerly on her spear. "As we were to be fighting the Nightstalkers, they just stopped fighting back. It was as if they were to have lost all life. They faded and they did vanish from the forest entirely. Like dust they did float off in the wind."

"The anchor." Lothak nodded to the helmet on Dillen's head. "You have cleansed it?"

Dillen took the helmet off and looked at it. "Honestly, I'm not sure about cleansed. We'll have to take it back to Velorun and Haili to make sure of that. But we did defeat their leader, that much, I'm certain."

"We?" Imariel asked, looking around.

"It may sound impossible to believe, but I had help. From Bhadein." Farn's eyes bulged at this. "And so many other former Brotherhood knights. The creature and I were linked through… this helmet. And in order to create 'balance,' the Armor of Tides, whatever magic this thing has, conjured the souls of fallen Brotherhood soldiers who were intertwined in the memories of the armor to aid in felling this… mind-screech."

Dillen smiled at them all; Farn, Shesh'ra, Lothak, Imariel, and the rest of the knights.

"We did this. Together." There was a cry of joy that shouted out from them; Dillen even caught the slightest bit of a smirk on Imariel's face. She nodded once to him, and he nodded back. As they started to leave, Dillen looked up to the sky. There was a single beam of light that he could see through the trees.

"Thank you," Dillen mumbled. "I promise I'll do right by the armor, and your memories. You have my word."

Chapter XXXIX

"Thank you again for your help, Sir Dillen." Exemplar Paladin Benedict raised his hand in salute from atop his horse. "Are you sure you do not wish to return with us? Once we return to Basilea, you could arrange transport home, to your family perhaps?"

"I am sure, thank you, Exemplar Paladin," Dillen said and nodded respectfully. "There is nothing left for me back home. This is where I belong now. To be the bearer of the Armor of Tides and defend the forest. I will continue to aid the knights that have allied with the Green Lady. Perhaps there are more suits of armor to find, or perhaps we can find a way to replicate how they were first created."

"Indeed," Benedict said, almost hesitantly. "I do believe there are more suits of armor within the Lady's forest, and with you leading the forces to recover them, I do feel more at ease than if it were... others."

One of the squires approached Dillen with something in his hands. "As you requested, Sir Dillen."

"Ah, yes," Dillen accepted the cuirass gratefully. "Thank you."

He turned to Benedict, who gave the armor a wary eye.

"While I nor the Armor of Tides can return with you, perhaps you would take this in my place."

"Your former cuirass?" Benedict said with a bit of skepticism in his voice.

"No, not mine. This armor belonged to Lord Paladin Tebald Priscon. He believed in me. He gave me a chance to make something of myself and my family name. I watched him be slaughtered by an Abyssal champion, and I took up his armor that day. I told myself that I was wearing his armor to honor his memory, to thank him for giving me yet another chance by pretending to be a Basilean, but that's not the truth of it." Dillen looked at the armor sadly. "It was just another layer to the façade. I'd rather you bring it back to Basilea and tell people the truth of that day. Dillen Genemer was no hero. Lord Paladin Tebald Priscon was the hero who bravely died in combat, and here is his armor to prove it. The Dillen Genemer they sing songs of... He's dead."

Benedict did not say anything for a moment, instead studying the armor Dillen held in his arms. Eventually, he nodded one of the knights forward to retrieve it. Now, with the weight off of his shoulders, both physically and mentally, Dillen beamed a proud smile at the knight, who nodded and smirked back.

"Good luck to you, Nature's Knight. These people will be in good hands."

"And to you, Exemplar Paladin. We will do all we can to balance the tide of combat in favor against those of wicked hearts and intentions."

Dillen made his way past the Eastfort, through the trees, and back toward the familiar paths of Calenemel. The remaining knights, and most of the other non-soldiering staff of the Eastfort were here, helping the elves to rebuild their homes. Man and elf, side by side, worked on repairing wooden walkways and homes. The mood was light; he could see the two sides engaging in conversation, one group above made jokes about a knight's fear of heights and the elves' desire to live above the ground. As he passed, he did not get the looks of hatred and scorn like he once did. Many still regarded him coolly with a nod or a simple hand held in greeting; but there were those who smiled at him and called out his name. He was just 'Dillen' now. One of the knights, and one of the defenders of the forest. There was no weighty title and history to make him seem alien and more prestigious than they were.

He noticed Shesh'ra working on sharpening some blades for their new armory, and she smiled as he approached.

"Well, there is the sight being for the sore eyes, as your people say."

"Shesh'ra, I'm glad to see you!" Dillen beamed at the naiad. "How are you doing today?"

"I am to be doing well. Working hard to be rebuilding Calenemel as all the others do."

"Good, good. Have you seen our friends?"

"Some. Farn works among the other knights, and Lothak is high above building houses. Imariel, I have not been seeing."

"Ah, I see." Dillen still did not know where he stood with Imariel, but he had not seen her since the battle with the Nightstalkers a few days ago. "It's good to see you're still around."

"Yes, for now. I wish to be helping Calenemel rebuild. Then, after, we shall see where the ocean waves take me."

"You're leaving?"

"I mayhap be. I was being brought here by the Green Lady, and I think the druid Haili does have a new journey for me from Her."

"Ah, that's a shame. I have really enjoyed your presence. And your wisdom." Dillen regarded her seriously. "Thank you, for all that you've done to help me. I don't know if I could have come to the truth of this without your help. Without you truly believing in the real me."

"Nonsense!" Shesh'ra waved away. "You are you, Dillen. You have always been you. You would have come to be seeing that with or without me."

"Well, regardless, thank you. And before you go, please make sure to teach me how to make those wraps!"

They both laughed. "Of course, I shall be doing that. Now, go. You must be on your way to see the druid. Do not be for keeping her waiting!"

Dillen nodded and then set off toward Haili's residence once more. The guards nodded and let him through, and he waited in the familiar small room. To his surprise, it was not Haili that emerged from the back, but Velorun. He approached Dillen with a warm smile and head nod.

"It is done, Dillen. The helmet is cleansed, for good. I must be going now, but we shall speak soon. Druid Haili waits for you in the room beyond."

"Thank you, Velorun. It is good to see you well."

"I am still recovering some of my strength, but that would not stop me from banishing these creatures from their anchor for good."

The druid left, and Dillen approached the room where Haili had previously bestowed the armor upon him. She stood at the other side of the table, staring down at the helmet, but her eyes came up to greet him when he entered.

"Welcome, Dillen Genemer. Come, take the last piece of your armor."

Dillen cautiously approached, and he took the helmet in his hands and put it over his head. It felt calm. There was no dark presence; nothing calling out to him. He took it off and held it in the crook of his left arm.

"I knew the armor had chosen you the last time we spoke," Haili said, moving past him. He followed her as they walked the halls out to the front entrance. She stood on the steps and looked out at her people, very similarly to how they had the last time. "I may not be of the Brotherhood knights who take their residence here, but I do speak the tongue of natural magic. The water has been calling for you, and I have heard it as well."

"I still don't understand. I'm just a normal person, with my own severe shortcomings and a history filled with blunder..."

"And you had the most to gain and the least to lose," Haili said as she regarded him very seriously. "No more talk of self-doubt. The armor has chosen you, and you should feel honored."

"I-I do! Trust me, I do. It has given me new purpose. But as much as the armor and I are, uh... bonding... I still can't properly harness the magic. The water only calls out to me when it wants me to, or if I'm in a desperate situation."

"No mere novice can put on a suit of armor and know the ins and outs of magic. The situations in which you have used the suit's magic was, as you have said, of its own choosing. You will find its power lacking now until you can harness it yourself. For that, Velorun will be your teacher."

Dillen's eyes widened. "Velorun?"

"Yes. He has begun to develop a bond with the armor, having cleansed every piece. It speaks to him more than it does I, and he has a better grasp on how the inner workings of the magic of the suit of armor works. He will teach you everything you need to know about harnessing magic. It will take time, possibly years even. Are you prepared for that?"

As she turned to look at him, Dillen stood tall, his chin raised. "Yes, Druid Haili. I will fight for the forces of the Green Lady, and I will bring balance... In my own way."

"Oh?" Haili raised an eyebrow, intrigued. "You will?"

"Yes, Druid. I will bring balance to the forces of good, in whatever way I can. I cannot begin to understand the Lady's intentions, and as we've spoken about in the past, I will not march alongside the forces of the Abyss or the undead, or even these Nightstalkers, should the Lady find strange times where she considers them allies. But I will fight alongside those who wish to see life flourish and grow. I will pledge my sword and shield to saving however many lives I can, even if that means putting my own life on the line to do so."

Haili turned back to the people working and nodded. No more words were needed. Dillen could tell, for the first time in meeting with the druid, that she was finally satisfied with what he had to say.

* * * * *

The sun was beginning to reach the horizon, and the forest was covered in orange. Rays of light shone through the boughs, casting the floor in warmth that Dillen found comforting as he and Farn walked through the paths.

"I do enjoy peaceful patrols," Dillen said with a wide smile. "Sure, the sword can get a bit rusty this way, but it means all the beasts are behaving themselves."

"Well spoken, Dillen," Farn said with a laugh, but he caught himself. "Er, Sir Dillen."

"Dillen." He said with finality. "I'll have no more of this 'sir' when the others aren't around. We're friends, you and I. How much longer until this spot? I'd rather be back before the sun fully sets."

"Just a bit farther... Dillen," Farn said, hesitantly.

"I call you Farn. I've always called you Farn. Is it so much to ask to lose the titles?" Dillen said, playfully, catching a laugh from the other knight. He was about to keep going, but he stopped when they came past the next bend in the path. They had followed a route that wound to the top of a hill, and they were able to look out above many of the other trees, and Dillen could see the sunset in its entirety. He could hear the birds and see them flying with such clarity. He couldn't see Eastower, but he didn't care. The sky was beautiful. "Farn, how in the blazes did you find this breathtaking view?"

"Ah, we all have our secrets, but this is where I used to come and relax."

Farn sat down and exhaled deeply. Dillen sat down next to him, and his eyes danced along the horizon in the cloudless sky of orange.

"Dillen, if I may…"

"Well, you didn't say sir, so go on!"

Farn shook his head and smirked, but whatever was on his mind was obviously something that was bothering him.

"Are we still doing the right thing? Are we still on the right side?"

Dillen sighed and paused a moment before answering.

"I've been debating that same answer in my head since I came here. But I suppose it depends on your definition of right. Did we do the right thing when we disobeyed orders to check that village? Yes, in our hearts we did, and we stopped the Nightstalkers from attacking others; but many here suffered because of it and we found no more survivors. Did we do the right thing in protecting the forest from the Nightstalkers, from the same people who told us not to go help that village? Of course we did, but there might be some who argue that the elves should have been left to fend for themselves as they ordered us away from Talle."

Dillen paused again, staring into the horizon.

"Do I believe we are doing the right thing?" They looked at each other, and Dillen nodded before turning back to the sunset. "Yes. I do. The Green Lady was willing to give us a home, all of us, when we had nowhere else to go. Bhadein seemed to believe we were doing the right thing as well. Even when I saw him that last time, if that was really him, he wanted me to continue protecting the forest."

"He was a good man," Farn said almost in a whisper. "A fantastic mentor."

"I agree. He always meant well, and he was right to doubt me back then."

There was another moment of silence.

"Plus, they know where we stand. They know our convictions. They know what we'll fight for and what we won't. Should the day come where the 'balance' is tipped too far in the favor of evil, we'll tip it right back – regardless if the Lady is allied with that evil or not."

"Right. We'll deal with that problem, should it arrive."

"Exactly."

"Thank you, Dillen. I think that does help to ease my mind, hearing someone else talk about it." Farn stood and stretched. "We should get back before it gets too late."

Dillen waved him off. "Go on ahead of me. I'd like to sit and enjoy the view for a bit longer, if you don't mind me stealing your space of reflection?"

Dillen gave him the wide grin he hadn't used in what felt like forever, and Farn smiled back, shaking his head. "Go on and enjoy it. I don't just share this space with anyone, just so you know!"

He waited until Farn's steps couldn't be heard anymore, and then he let out a heavy sigh. It was the first time in several days he had been able to relax and just think. Between the patrols and helping to rebuild Calenemel, he had spent almost every waking moment busy, only to throw himself down at exhaustion to get a few hours of sleep to begin it all again. He had dreamt about the mind-screech several times and just how terrifying the creature had been.

Thankfully, he had proven the mind-screech and 'Kallas' wrong. The people of the forest had welcomed him back into their ranks. No one had demanded he turn in the Armor of Tides. If he was being honest with himself, he was still let down about the disappearance of one person though…

There was the sound of movement behind him, and Dillen sighed.

"Come now, Farn. I said I'd be right…" When he turned his head, it was not Farn that stood beside him – it was Imariel. Wide-eyed, he jumped to his feet. "Imariel, I…"

She stood with her arms crossed, looking out on the view. She didn't speak.

"Imariel, where have you been? Everyone was worried that you had left… I was worried."

"I have been reflecting on what has happened since meeting you. Once the Nightstalkers were defeated, it was my first time having a true moment to myself since my mother died. While you have been welcome, accepted, I could not feel any more like an outcast."

"That was not my intention," Dillen pleaded. "None of this, starting with your mother's death, was my intention."

"I understand why you were chosen to wear that armor. Your penance for letting the forest down is to now defend it until your last breath." She turned to stare at him, that icy look of daggers had returned. "But I cannot forgive you for my mother's death. Even though you have saved me several times, and you have done all you can to aid me, the hurt is still real and her death is still fresh. The honest truth is that she died because of your actions."

Dillen kept his eyes on her, despite the pain in his chest. He felt tears welling in his eyes, but he forced them away. "I know. I know she did. And I can never make up for that. I can never take that hurt away. I am your scar."

Her face softened, and she brought her left hand up to caress the side of his face. "And I am yours."

He took her other hand in both of his, and they stayed that way for a long moment. Dillen wanted to reach out and kiss her, to tell her that he cared for her like no other, but he knew how very wrong that would be. He had made this mess, and now he must reap the consequences.

"You had said something to me when my bloodlust had gotten the better of me. You said to remember the side of you that no one else knew. The true you. That was the you that didn't rely on the legend of Dillen the Abyssal champion slayer. That was the you that was kind, funny, and honest… with me, at least. That you, I've always known, and you know the true me. You've seen who I am beyond the cold, calculated huntress I try to project to others. And right now, I can see the hurt in your eyes."

"And I can see the same in yours."

She paused again and then pulled away from his head to hold his hands with both of hers.

"I know how hard your path has been to walk one of redemption. I… I am willing to try and walk it by your side, as your ally. To help you when you falter. And maybe… Maybe once this hurt is gone…"

"Maybe we can start over again?"

"Yes." She nodded, and the coldness, the hatred, and the loathing were gone. "Let us try and start over. When that time comes, when the hurting stops, let us try and walk side by side as the real Dillen and the real Imariel, and get to know each other better than we do now. No more masks."

"I'd like that," Dillen said, a tear finally falling down his face.

The two turned and watched the sunset, their hands locked together between them.

Learn more about the world of Pannithor and fun from Mantic games at:

www.manticgames.com

More exciting Fantasy Adventures from ZMOK Books!